"I'm trying to tell you how I feel."

Paige shoved her hands back through her hair, clearly frustrated.

"You're attracted to me," he said, easing around the sofa.

She started to back away, then deliberately held her ground, her chin lifting in deliberate acceptance of his challenge. "Yes."

Alec kept walking toward her, slowly. "But I don't have to worry about it because you're going to keep your distance."

"Yes. It's my problem."

"Is it?" He jerked her against him, swallowing her startled gasp by kissing her mouth. The very air seemed to ignite, the fire racing over his skin, burning through his blood, searing his thoughts so there was only the flavor of her, sweet and intoxicating, the feel of her against him, sleek muscle and soft flesh.

He framed her face, then slipped his hands back to scatter the pins she'd used to pile up her hair so the cool, heavy mass of it rained down her back.

"Alec."

"Don't," he said. *Don't talk, don't shatter the mood*, he thought, and leaned in to take her.

She met him, more than halfway, twined her arms around his neck, laid her long, slim curves against him, and poured herself into the kiss...

ACCLAIM FOR ANNA SULLIVAN'S

WINDFALL ISLAND NOVELS

HIDEAWAY COVE

"A very enjoyable read…The mystery spun around the romance was amazingly written. It's a captivating, thrilling, and sweet love story."
—HarlequinJunkie.com

"An engaging and mysterious adventure full of love."
—Romance.NightOwlReviews.com

"4 stars! Fans of Sullivan's beautiful, remote Windfall Island will thoroughly enjoy this return to the familiar craggy landscape of her Maine setting, and new readers deserve to discover this fascinating place."
—*RT Book Reviews*

TEMPTATION BAY

"Sullivan's contemporary debut deftly combines intrigue, romance, and witty banter…The sizzling passion between Dex and Maggie propels this page-turner forward to its explosive conclusion."
—*Publishers Weekly*

"4 stars! Sullivan brings a sensational sense of place to her first Windfall Island novel, immersing readers in the Maine island and its fascinating population—most notably her heroine, whose fortitude and no-nonsense exterior cover a heart of gold. Sullivan builds the tension between her lead characters and crafts a relationship so compassionate and reciprocal it is simply irresistible."

"Intriguing, sassy, and entertaining...It will keep you anxiously awaiting the next novel."

Secret Harbor

ANNA SULLIVAN

WITHDRAWN

FOREVER

NEW YORK BOSTON

Copyright © 2015 by Penny McCusker
Excerpt from *Temptation Bay* copyright © 2013 by Penny McCusker
All rights reserved. In accordance with the U.S. Copyright Act of 1976, the scanning, uploading, and electronic sharing of any part of this book without the permission of the publisher constitute unlawful piracy and theft of the author's intellectual property. If you would like to use material from the book (other than for review purposes), prior written permission must be obtained by contacting the publisher at permissions@hbgusa.com. Thank you for your support of the author's rights.

Forever
Hachette Book Group
1290 Avenue of the Americas
New York, NY 10104

www.HachetteBookGroup.com

Printed in the United States of America

First Edition: February 2015
10 9 8 7 6 5 4 3 2 1

OPM

Forever is an imprint of Grand Central Publishing.
The Forever name and logo are trademarks of Hachette Book Group, Inc.

The Hachette Speakers Bureau provides a wide range of authors for speaking events. To find out more, go to www.hachettespeakersbureau.com or call (866) 376-6591.

The publisher is not responsible for websites (or their content) that are not owned by the publisher.

For Ian
with love

Secret Harbor

Prologue

Jamie Finley stood in the small front room of a little frame house, on Windfall Island, off the coast of Maine. In one arm he held a baby swaddled in serviceable cotton and plain wool. She'd come to him wrapped in silks and satins, a king's ransom in jewels around her neck. It seemed all the same to her, though, wool or satin, as long as she was dry and warm and boasted a full belly.

The jewel that had adorned her now weighed heavy in his pocket, as heavy as it lay on his conscience, a necklace of diamonds and rubies the color of blood— No, the color of her blood was blue, he reminded himself, no matter the plainness of the clothing on her little body.

By rights the necklace should go back to the Stanhope family. Yes, he knew where the babe had come from now, how she'd found a place in the little boat they'd rowed back from the rumrunner called *Perdition*, just before it exploded and was swallowed up by the hungry and unforgiving depths of the Atlantic Ocean.

He'd heard of the maid who'd taken her from her rich crib in the palatial house. Selfishness she'd claimed, just a young girl wanting a night of fun. The bauble in his pocket told a different story altogether. The bauble spoke of greed.

There'd been a search, of course; those with such great piles of money could not only afford it, but they'd demanded it. The cops and the Feds had come to Windfall Island, but their questions and their nosing about had been halfhearted at best. They all thought the poor lass dead, and their efforts were made only to placate and humor a mother who must be grieving terribly.

. That weighed on Jamie, too, another stone added to the boulders already sitting on his shoulders. But there were other mothers grieving, so many on this tiny island plagued with a measles epidemic that plucked the very old and the very young like apples from a tree, with no rhyme or reason. He'd always believed things happened in God's time and for God's reasons, but sometimes it made little sense to a simple man.

Jamie sighed, his hand dipping into his pocket to feel the cool, smooth stones, the corners on the diamonds and rubies nestled in their points of gold. No, he couldn't send the necklace back without causing a furor. He couldn't sell it, either, wasn't clever enough to know how to go about such a thing without bringing wrath and ruin down on his little community.

As for the child, well, there'd be no sending her back, either.

When he'd left the Duncan house, he'd walked the village with her, warm and asleep, propped on his shoulder. The babe's fine blanket remained with the Duncans, fair exchange for the dry clothing she now wore, and the hardy wool that had kept her bundled so warmly against the chill, damp night air. He'd searched his mind, and his heart, hoping to find the right course of action. Now the choice had been taken out of his hands.

He looked across the room to the woman rocking by the fire, rocking with her arms empty, her heart broken, and her mind...God forgive me, he thought as he crossed to her and put the child into those empty arms, as he listened to her call the babe by the name of her own daughter, nearly the same age, that she'd lost only hours before.

When her rocking evened out, when the lines sorrow had dug into her face smoothed, when she looked up at him and the shadow of loss was softened in her eyes, he knew he'd do it again, a thousand times over, to spare her one more minute of the kind of sorrow only a mother could feel. He made himself forget she wasn't the only mother suffering.

As for the necklace, well, he'd rest on his faith there, too, faith and tradition, for what else could a man trust to but God and the law?

Since the salvaging days, Windfall Island had always been led by one man, chosen by the others because he was the smartest, the fairest, and the hardest. A man who could look past friendship when he arbitrated disputes, who'd consider what was best for the island when it came to dealing with the outside world, and do what it took to get all the islanders on board. And at times, he'd have to hurt some to do right for all.

John Appelman was that man. Jamie took the necklace out of his pocket—minus the egg-sized ruby pendant surrounded by diamonds that he'd already removed. He couldn't quite bring himself to rob the child of her heritage altogether. She'd learn of it someday, he thought, and there providence would guide her as it had guided him.

John took the circlet of smaller diamonds and rubies and slipped it into his own pocket. They walked to the door, both of them pausing at the threshold to look back.

"You did right by her and the babe, Jamie," John said, clasping his shoulder. "Now I'll do what's right for the rest of Windfall with this." He patted his pocket as he pulled open the door. "It'll get us all through the winter and then some."

John had never let the island down before; he wouldn't fail them now. The necklace would be disposed of carefully, and the proceeds used to provide what Windfall needed. And John would talk to the others, Giff, Norris, Meeker, make sure their tongues stayed behind their teeth, though they'd never know what really happened to the child.

And he, Jamie thought as he took one more look across the room, would have to find a way to live with his conscience.

Chapter One

Paige Walker, Oscar winner, Tony nominee, Hollywood's Darling and America's Sweetheart, surveyed her gurgling toilet and thought about just how far she'd fallen. One minute she'd been on top of the world—hell, she'd owned the world, or at least the part of it that either made movies or saw them. And those were the people who'd mattered to her.

It gave her no pleasure to admit that now. In fact, it made her feel even smaller—if that were possible—after the very people, those moviemakers and moviegoers she'd once treasured, had dropped her flat on her religiously exercised and very well-shaped ass.

And then she smiled, because instead of the inevitable rocky landing, the people of Windfall Island had caught her. Or maybe they'd let her catch herself. It had been her idea to come home, but after ten years without a single visit, they could have shunned her. Or worse.

One call to the press would have brought reporters

circling like vultures to peck at her already-bruised feelings and photographers to snap up whatever scraps of her privacy remained, so they could perpetuate and feast off the scandal that had rocked her world and sent her running to the only place she could find shelter, welcome, acceptance.

Whether or not the Windfallers believed she'd made the sex tape currently burning up the World Wide Web, not one of them had ratted her out. Once a Windfaller, she thought fondly, always a Windfaller. There'd been a time that would have embarrassed her.

But she'd learned the value of friendship.

She'd learned the value of home, too, something else she'd discovered too late.

Her mother had died when she'd been a little girl just shy of ten. Suzie Walker Morris had been beautiful, almost ethereal, slim as a wish, hair like sunshine, the face of an angel. Her head had certainly been in the clouds, Paige remembered, even if she'd married a man so earthbound he made his living digging in the dirt. Good, clean dirt and good, clean work, Matt Morris had always called the small fields he'd tilled and the odd jobs he'd done in order to make ends meet.

Her father hadn't been what anyone would call demonstrative, but he'd been even-tempered, fair, and in his way loving. He'd fed her, housed her, and seen to her needs as best he could, even after Suzie died, and caring for a moody, emotional girl growing into her teens couldn't have been easy for him.

And he'd kept the truth from her because he'd known the truth would hurt.

She'd never let him know he'd failed.

Paige had learned the details of her mother's death anyway; she could hardly have avoided it on an island like Windfall, where everyone knew everyone else and gossip was the first order of business. Her mother had been in a fatal accident on the mainland. Wrong car, wrong man— or maybe wrong drunk would be more appropriate. It hadn't been the first time Suzie had broken her vows, though it had been the first time Paige had heard of her mother's inconstancy, and her father's tolerance and forgiveness.

It had been the first time she'd understood that old saying about books and covers. The first time she understood that she could be whoever she chose to be. And that image was everything—whether or not it was the truth.

She'd taken her mother's name, if only to remind herself that the life she'd chosen very rarely resembled reality. And to thumb her nose at those who'd found joy in dragging a dead woman's reputation through the mud.

But it was her father she missed, desperately. Matt Morris had passed away suddenly while Paige was off making her mother's name into something she could be proud of. She'd gotten the news of his death on a movie location in a patch of eastern European countryside so remote she wasn't sure the locals even knew about television, let alone movies.

By the time her publicist managed to contact her, it had been too late for her to make it back to Windfall Island for the funeral. Of course, she'd been judged for that, and for not coming back to at least visit his grave, because that would have meant accepting. It had been too devastating to lose her only pillar, the man who'd been so quietly proud of her, though the one time she'd brought him to Hollywood he'd been unhappy and out of sorts. And she'd always been too busy to come back to Windfall. Or so she'd told herself.

Silly now, she thought as she looked back, silly and stupid to believe the world wouldn't have accepted her humble beginnings. But she'd been silly and stupid in the early days, and then it had become a habit to keep her private life private, not to mention good sense in a place where reality and truth were just concepts to be interpreted and presented to the world. She'd become a commodity; Paige had accepted that. She refused to become a cash cow for greedy, deceitful scum who considered it a satisfying day's work to trash reputations and peddle lies in pursuit of that almighty dollar. Her father, she knew, had understood.

Her doorbell chimed the first four notes of "Somewhere My Love," and the corners of her mouth curved up as she made her way downstairs. "Somewhere My Love" was the theme song of *December Sunshine*; Laura Galloway had been her breakout role, the one that had made her famous at the ripe old age of eighteen. It felt like just yesterday, she recalled, and oh so long ago.

She opened the door, then stepped back, feeling the smile bloom slowly on her face and heat rush through her—the kind of sudden, breath-stealing desire she hadn't felt for a man in a long time. She let her gaze skim down from his dark hair, barely registering handsome features before moving down a coat-covered body to strong legs clad in jeans, worn white at the stress points. And then she noticed the toolbox in his hand.

Her eyes lifted to his. "Are you the plumber?"

"No," he said shortly, shaking the rain out of his hair. " 'Somewhere My Love'?"

The mocking tone in his voice snapped her back.

She drew Paige Walker—the slightly raised brow, the purposely sarcastic smile, the overtly sexual body language—around her like armor. "I had the house renovated after my father died," she said with deliberate calmness, and felt the instant, familiar pang.

Even knowing her father was gone, she'd hadn't had the heart to sell the house. Instead, she'd had it remade to her exacting specifications, then rented it out to summer vacationers who preferred the semblance of home to the convenience of a hotel. When she'd first walked in, she'd been pleased and surprised to discover it still had the feel of a cottage, even with the modern improvements.

She'd had the back windows widened to bring Secret Harbor and the Atlantic beyond, with all her moods, right into the house. Otherwise, she'd gone for utility, comfort, and peace. The kitchen was granite, glass, and stone, with appliances paneled to match the cabinets. The rest of the house boasted dark wood floors, furniture chosen for comfort, and walls in a pale cream color that seemed to glow warmly in even the tiniest amount of light.

"I'm not sure what the contractor was thinking when he chose those particular chimes for the doorbell," she continued, "but since he's a Windfaller, I'm leaning toward humor rather than flattery."

"There was nothing funny about *December Sunshine*."

"Ah, you're a moviegoer."

He shrugged. "I was dating a woman who liked that kind of sappy melodramatic romance."

"Oh, well, I'm sorry she made you suffer so horribly. But you probably deserved it."

"No man deserves that kind of punishment," he said, a touch of humor diluting the disdain in his voice.

Paige leaned against the edge of the door, truly amused now, instead of only acting like it. "Millions of people around the world would disagree with you, including the critics. *December Sunshine* won several awards." And so had she.

"No accounting for taste, I guess."

"True, but it's not too late for you to cultivate some," she said, nearly laughing out loud when he only sent her a blank stare. "I don't remember you." And there was no way she'd have forgotten this man. And it wasn't just his looks. He had charisma, that undefinable something that just naturally made a person look at him twice, then look again. "What's your name?"

"Alec Barclay."

She straightened, feeling a split second of shock before she retreated back into her role. Alec Barclay, friend to Dex Keegan and Hold Abbot, scion of one of the wealthiest Boston families, lawyer to the Stanhopes, and arguably the most eligible bachelor in America. A man who didn't think twice about saying what was on his mind, even when he had no idea what he was talking about. Or to whom.

She'd managed to avoid him completely when they'd all been in Boston a couple of weeks before, trying to unravel the mystery of who Eugenia Stanhope's long lost heir was. Or maybe he'd missed her. But clearly he hadn't missed her sex tape.

"Alec Barclay," she said, careful to keep her voice even and her tone lightly amused. "What was it you were quoted as saying about me and my...situation? 'I wouldn't have expected an actress of Paige Walker's caliber to stoop to that kind of publicity stunt, but it's been a few years since she's won a major award.'"

He held up a hand to cut her off. "I remember."

So did she, Paige thought. He'd finished the quote with a tongue-in-cheek reference to her "going the extra distance" to get a role, which might have been amusing if it hadn't referred to a particularly embarrassing portion of the tape that had the woman everyone thought was her on her knees.

"I don't suppose you'd believe me if I said I was misquoted."

"Were you?"

"No."

When Paige found it difficult to hold his gaze, she reminded herself that she'd done nothing wrong, even if Alec Barclay and the rest of the world thought they knew differently. But she had to swallow a couple of times before she was confident she could get words out. "Why are you here?"

He held up the toolbox.

"You're here to fix my toilet?"

"I can fix a toilet," he said with the snap of defensiveness in his voice.

"Who said you couldn't?"

"You did, by the way you looked at me."

"Well, Counselor," she said, "it's not every day one of

the Boston Barclays shows up at my front door to play plumber."

"There's more to me than a suit and a family name."

She smiled in satisfaction. "Don't like it when some-one makes assumptions about you?"

His eyes went frosty gray. "Can we just get this over with so I can get Jessi and Maggie off my back?"

At the mention of her two closest friends, her smile widened. She'd missed them more than she'd realized in the ten years since she'd left Windfall. And okay, she was the one who'd neglected to maintain the connection. But now they'd come back together and proved there was a silver lining in every cloud.

Those who'd sought to bring her down had instead re-minded her of what was important in life and given her a precious gift, one she wouldn't take for granted again.

He stared at her and she realized she'd let her guard down. She wiped the smile off her face. "I'll wait for Yancy," she said curtly, referring to the island's one and only plumber.

"Now you're just being stupid."

"Well, put another black mark in my character col-umn, Counselor."

"This is ridiculous." Alec shoved by her to stand, dripping, in her foyer. "Where's the bathroom?" He stripped off his coat and handed it to her, retrieved the toolbox from where he'd set it, then turned a slow circle before heading off toward the kitchen.

Paige dropped his coat on the floor and followed him, collecting the throwaway, untraceable cell phone she'd bought before she left Los Angeles.

Alec strode into the little hallway leading to her back

door, with her laundry room on one side. He took one look into the powder room opposite, with its pale blue walls and crisp white and chrome fixtures, and turned on his heel. "That one's fine," he said abruptly, brushing by her again to retrace his steps to the staircase opposite the front door.

She whisked up the stairs behind him and into the master bedroom, and found him staring at her bed, an old iron frame she'd found online and hired Maisie Cutshaw to paint white and dress with a quilt of her mother's.

He glanced over his shoulder, their eyes locked, and heat slammed into her, a wall of heat and hunger that arrowed straight to her belly, then spread through her. And when his eyes dropped, she felt his gaze slide over her like a caress, a not particularly gentle one, considering the set of his jaw. But then suddenly she wasn't craving gentleness.

"Calling the sheriff?" he said. "Going to report a breaking and plumbing?"

She looked down, remembering the cell phone in her hand. And felt foolish for thinking he'd spent even a split second admiring her body. Alec Barclay obviously wanted nothing to do with her, lust notwithstanding.

This time when she met his eyes, she had no trouble recalling that. "I'd tell you to stop being an ass, but it's too late."

"I'd tell you a thing or two," he said with a faint smile, a quick glance at the bed, "but my mother would know somehow."

"Afraid of your mother?"

"I'd call it healthy respect."

"Nice to know you respect someone."

"I respect a lot of people."

"Just not me."

He shrugged. "You said it. I didn't."

"Right." She crossed her arms. "Because nothing you've said or done could possibly lead me to believe your opinion of me is subterranean?"

"Well, it gives you plenty of room for improvement."

"If only I cared what you think…" His grin brought a reluctant smile to her face. They both liked a little conflict, it seemed. "Now, if you don't mind, I think I'll watch one of my movies and bask in my own greatness. I'd say it's been nice, but—"

"But you don't like me. Since I'm only here to provide menial labor, you can think of me as one of the little people who are easily overlooked."

That did it. Maybe because he was right—not that she'd overlooked the "little people," but because she'd thought of them like children, whose love she never had to question. Until they bought into a lie—just like Alec Barclay had.

She stepped in front of the bathroom door. "Get out."

He simply shifted her aside. He didn't touch her any longer than necessary, she noticed.

"I'll go," he said, "just as soon as I'm done." He walked into the bathroom and set down his toolbox. His eyes went from the still-gurgling toilet to the bathtub, a bottle of cleaner and rubber gloves on the edge of it. He looked over his shoulder, both eyebrows raised.

"I know how to clean a bathtub."

He snorted softly. "I'd take some photos, if I thought anyone would believe it."

No, but they'd believe she would prostitute herself with a director so he'd cast her, when all it would take was a phone call from her agent to have him begging her to be in his little movie.

But while she didn't blame the public for being taken in, Alec Barclay should have given her the benefit of the doubt. There were two sides to every story, right? A lawyer should know that. A lawyer should at least ask her if the rumors were true. Alec Barclay, well, she didn't know why he wanted to believe the worst of her.

And she didn't care. "Small minds always believe what's easiest."

"All minds believe what they see."

"Oh, so you've watched that tape?"

"No." And she could see he realized how neatly he'd trapped himself. "But you haven't denied it."

"I don't owe you any explanations, Counselor."

"You're right," he said equably, "but no matter how far you run, you still have to live with yourself."

"Get. Out." She bit off the words, let anger take her toe-to-toe with him.

He loomed over her; she glared up at him. Her heaving chest brushed his and with their mouths only inches apart, the sear of fury turned to a fire in her blood. Her eyes dropped to his mouth. If she lifted to her toes, or he leaned down...

She raised her eyes, saw the heat in his, the edge of temper turning to desire. But as he started to close the distance between them, she took a step back.

She had no idea what to do with the need burning through her like molten gold, but she knew if he saw it they were both lost. So she turned away. If he kept pushing, she'd let him think whatever he wanted, as long as he touched her. Took her.

It made no sense; they'd just met, and he harbored such a low opinion of her. Still, Paige told herself, she was having a physical reaction to a handsome man, nothing more.

"I'm sorry," he said, his deep voice still so close beside her it made her shiver.

"Suppose we call a truce?" she suggested as she eased away from him. "I don't like the idea of pulling our friends into"—she spread her hands, risked a glance at him—"whatever this is."

"Yeah," he said after a moment. "I'll be at the Horizon later. Why don't you let me buy you a drink? Maybe we can be friends."

"No, I really don't think so. I've had too much experience with people like you—"

"People like me?" He stepped around to face her. "Care to elaborate?"

She really shouldn't have. There was enough animosity between them already. But, hell, he'd made no secret of how little he thought of her. "You're a judgmental hypocrite," she said. "Before you even met me you decided what kind of woman I was. You think I made that sex tape, that I made it and released it for publicity."

"Tell me you didn't."

"What's the point?" And hell would freeze over before she defended herself to him. "You've already decided what kind of woman I am. But you'd go to bed with me anyway."

"Aren't you taking a lot for granted?"

"No."

"Now there's a word you weren't saying a minute ago."

But she was the one who'd backed off first, and they both knew it. "You should go."

He held her eyes, then nodded. "Just one thing. We're going to be seeing a lot of each other until we can all unravel who the Stanhope descendant is and keep everyone safe."

"And?"

"I won't have any trouble keeping my hands to myself. Until you ask me to put them on you."

"Aren't you taking a lot for granted?" she parroted back at him.

"No."

She shook her head, smiled a little. "There's heat between us, Counselor, I won't deny that. But there's no warmth, and I find these days that I value warmth much more."

"So you're looking for love and devotion?"

"No." Not from him, at any rate. "Some level of respect would be nice, but you don't strike me as a man who changes his mind or his opinions."

"Not without a good reason."

She spread her hands. "I can't give you one."

"Can't or won't?" He stepped forward, but the hand he reached toward her curled into a fist before he dropped it back to his side. "Give me a reason, Paige."

She shook her head. "As you said, we're going to be seeing a lot of each other. Best you hold on to that low opinion of me. It'll save you from doing anything you'll regret."

He stared at her for a long, humming moment, his

eyes as unreadable as his expression. As he turned on his heel and stalked off, she breathed a sigh of relief. She'd lied to him, after all, Paige thought.

Alec Barclay desired her; it was straight and honest lust. But she didn't feel heat unless there was warmth, too, at least on her side. Heaven only knew why she should be drawn to Alec—his strength maybe, his intelligence, his humor.

But even if he knew the truth, sooner or later she'd do something to disappoint him.

She always did.

Chapter Two

The streets in Windfall Village were unnamed, as were the businesses, except for the pictograph signs that harkened back to a time when few of the island's inhabitants boasted the skill to read. The tourists found it quaint. The Windfallers just shrugged it off; they knew where they were going.

The Horizon Inn had occupied the same spot on the main street in Windfall Village for nearly three centuries, just across from the docks. It had started life as a rough place that catered to the rough men who did what needed to be done to survive. With Prohibition, a kitchen was added and food was served—along with illegal booze— and when the island began to attract attention for its history, rooms were added for the tourists who flocked there in the summer, bringing prosperity at long last.

The Horizon's clientele might run toward law-abiding citizens now, but its big main room had changed little.

The bar was made out of the curved side of a ship,

salvaged when taking what they needed from the un-lucky had been the island's main business. The walls were blackened by decades of smoke from the huge fire-place, from the pipes and cigarettes of its patrons, and from a grill that had never vented properly. The wood floor was scarred, as were the tables and chairs, and the leather of the booth seats wanted replacing.

The people, though, hadn't changed much, at least not in temperament. Windfall Village was still inhabited by the quirky, the eccentric, those who felt like outcasts from society. The Horizon was the place they went to find the like-minded, to have a meal and a beer, and to nurse their discontent.

Alec Barclay could sympathize. He might be the sym-bol of everything the Windfallers disparaged, but he knew how it felt to be the Outsider, with a capital *O*. Paige had shown him. Not that he didn't deserve it—and it was that truth that had him sitting at the Horizon's long curved bar, nursing a beer and pretending to listen to Dex Keegan and Maggie Solomon, Hold Abbot and Jessi Randal, engage in a spirited debate.

Not surprisingly the men had squared off against the women, both sides actively soliciting his support. As he was a man of firm opinions, he'd have had no qualms about taking sides. Trouble was, he had no idea what they were arguing about.

He couldn't get Paige out of his mind, the way she'd looked that morning, her fabulous figure covered in yoga pants and a long, curve-skimming knit tunic that bared only her face, hands, and feet, but left not a single inch of her stunning body to the imagination. The tunic had been pink as bubblegum, so had the polish on her bare toes.

Her eyes were a shade of blue that made him think of the deepest ocean under a sun as bright as her honey-blond hair, and her face, well, if she was beautiful on-screen, she was impossibly lovely in person.

He'd wanted his hands on her, his mouth on hers, he'd wanted to watch her peaches-and-cream skin bloom with heat, and to have every luscious inch of her pressed against every desperate foot of him.

The strength of the desire, the immediacy of it, stunned him. Even hours later he could still smell the musk of her skin, still feel the strength and suppleness and heat of her body when he'd moved her away from the bathroom door. He remembered the way her breath had caught, telling him that she felt that fast and unreasoning need, too. And he remembered the way she'd stepped away from him, very deliberately.

It still galled him. Alec prided himself on his ability to be in control at all times, but Paige had established the distance they'd both needed. Because of that tape. Or rather, his opinion of that tape. And to have made a public statement like that? Not his usual style, either.

He'd meant it to be offhand, flippant, a joke to make the reporter laugh, not something that would actually make it into print, even though he happened to be a local personage of sorts. He'd never given a second thought to how his opinion would affect Paige Walker, and he'd certainly never expected to meet her, with those words hanging over his head like an accusatory spotlight.

And when he did meet her? He'd handled it badly, no doubt about that. He'd been embarrassed—and angry about being embarrassed. He'd been attracted to Paige— so incredibly attracted that he'd done all he could to push her away. For his own comfort and peace of mind. And when she'd gotten the message, that had pissed him off, too.

"Ridiculous," he muttered under his breath.

"You better not be talking about me," Maggie threatened him good-naturedly.

Alec mustered up a smile. "You're Keegan's problem, not mine."

"And by problem you mean..."

"I mean he's the luckiest bastard on the East Coast—next to Hold Abbot," he added when Jessi sent him a look.

"That's what I thought," Maggie said.

"How's Paige's toilet?" Jessi put in. "All right and tight?"

Alec took a deep breath, forcing himself to rein in his temper. "We both know that was just a ploy," he said evenly.

"Excuse me?"

"Be careful," Dex warned him, grinning.

Alec shrugged. "You let them send me over there to—"

"To what?"

Knowing he'd given away more than he wanted to, Alec picked up his beer. The swig he took was neither cooling nor soothing.

"What, exactly, happened when you were at Paige's house?" Maggie asked him.

"As if you didn't know."

"I don't, but I think we're about to find out."

Alec heard a clang, looked down, and there, beside his stool, sat the toolbox Maggie had loaned him. The toolbox he suddenly remembered he'd left at Paige's house. He jerked around and found her standing behind him, movie star perfect and glorious in a full temper, with her blue eyes shooting sparks and her hands fisted on hips wrapped in hot, clingy red that matched the color slicked over her full lips.

She smiled at AJ, owner and proprietor of the Horizon, then lifted a hand in greeting to whoever called out her name—and took her time getting back to him, Alec noted. He knew it was meant to annoy him. It worked.

"You left your tools at my house," she said.

"Yeah, right, tools!" someone crowed.

"He can bring his tools to my house anytime," another voice, a female voice, shouted out. "I can think of a thing or two he can, uh, fix."

The place erupted in hysterical laugher, additional suggestive commentary from the women, and more than one black look from the men present.

And then they moved on to more weighty matters.

"What are you doing here" a man called out, "besides fixing Paige Walker's...equipment?"

Alec lifted his beer and kept a pleasant smile on his face despite the burn inside him. "Having a drink with friends."

"Long way to come for drink," Josiah Meeker said from a table right behind them.

"I'm on vacation," Alec observed blandly.

"Interesting choice of destinations, with the mercury below the freezing point. I'd think a man of your resources would go somewhere"—his gaze shifted to Paige, then back to Alec—"warmer."

Everyone else in the room was thinking the same,

Alec mused, so why did it bother him coming from this guy? He tried to put a finger on what troubled him about Meeker, shrugging it off when nothing specific came to mind. Meeker seemed to look down his nose at everyone, but hell, Alec thought, most of the people he knew in Boston, including many of his own relatives, thought they were better than the rest of the world.

"I came to see why my friends find this place so fascinating"—he tipped his beer to Maggie and Jessi— "besides the women." He hadn't realized how closely everyone had been listening until his answer set off another round of hooting, catcalls, and male-female sniping—which cut off as abruptly as a remote muting a television.

Alec turned, along with everyone else, and saw a woman at the door, her face lined but her eyes bright and intelligent. Though she leaned heavily on a cane, her back was straight, her shoulders square, even with the weight of all eyes on her, and the invisible mantle of authority she wore.

"Ma Appelman," Maggie said quietly.

"So I gathered." George Boatwright was the law on Windfall Island, Alec knew, but Mother Appelman ran everything else. She was judge and jury in civil matters, and no Windfaller even contemplated taking a complaint to what they considered the vagaries of mainlander justice. It had always been that way. Ma was only the latest in a long line.

Conversation picked up as she made her way slowly across the room. She never sat, although someone stood at every table to offer her a chair. Even Josiah Meeker got to his feet when she came near, pulling out a chair at his otherwise unoccupied table and inviting her to join him.

"Sucking up, Josiah?"

Meeker went red, then white.

"Careful," Ma said when he ended with what passed for a smile. "There are kids in here."

Meeker's smile, even when he meant it, was frightening. But no one laughed.

"You know I'm the best choice to succeed you," he said, looking around the room.

"Still waiting for me to die, I see." Ma waved off his attempt to backpedal. "There's more to what I do than being feared, Josiah. You have to be fair, too, you have to think about what's best for Windfall, and it helps to be liked, takes the sting out of a hard decision that doesn't go someone's way."

"And you've already decided I don't measure up."

"Already?" Ma snorted. "You're a middle-aged man, Josiah."

"And you can't teach old dogs new tricks."

"Old dogs are every bit as adaptable as young ones. If they're open to change. Not tonight, Josiah," she added wearily when he opened his mouth to speak. "We've had this conversation before. It's going to end the same way it always does, so unless your memory is failing—"

"My memory is fine."

"Well, then." Ma turned to Hold and Alec, who both got to their feet. She let Alec help her onto his stool, then looked him up and down with a measuring eye. "You'd be that Boston lawyer I've been hearing about."

"You'd be the don of Windfall Island. I've been hearing about you as well."

Ma laughed. "I'm not one of them eye-talian crooks."

"But you run this place."

"Me? I'm just a little old lady."

Now it was Alec's turn to laugh. "From what I hear, you should be in charge of the justice system in America."

She shook her head. "Old John used to say—that was my father-in-law's name," she added for the benefit of those who didn't know, "the John Appelman who passed the responsibility on to me, not the John I married—"

"Hey," Maggie cut in.

"Don't point your finger at me, girl," Ma said to her, the stern note in her voice belied by the fond twinkle in her eye. Maggie had always been one of her favorites, so Alec had heard. And Maggie loved Ma like a grandmother.

You couldn't have seen it in the look Maggie shot Ma before she swiveled to AJ, finger still pointing. "John. That's your middle name, right? John."

AJ smiled, the kind of smile that said while he liked the running contest with Maggie to discover what his initials stood for, lying to perpetuate it wouldn't be fair. "You got me. Thanks, Ma."

"Girl guessed fair and square," Ma grumbled, but she eyed Maggie. "Could've waited a bit so he didn't blame me for it."

"But I figured it out because of you." Maggie's grin had a sarcastic edge to it. "You deserve the credit."

"Shouldn't've needed any hints from me, smart girl like you. Been staring you right in the face for years."

"So it has." Maggie kissed Ma on the cheek, then turned to AJ. "And since I'm halfway through the *A*'s already, it won't be long before I get the rest of it." But she didn't make any guesses. She enjoyed the contest, too.

"And here's the prodigal," Ma said, turning to give Paige a critical once-over. "You're all polished up, but I still see my girl in there."

Paige smiled, a little wobbly. "Ma."

"Well," Alec said, "now that I know you're related, I see the resemblance."

"We're not—"

Ma held up a hand, cutting Paige off. "Either you're insulting her or complimenting me," she said.

"It's not your features, it's your attitude."

"You haven't said whether it's an insult or a compliment," Ma observed in the bland tone that had lulled many an unsuspecting islander into a false sense of security.

"No, I haven't," Alec said, just as blandly.

Ma hooted with laughter. "We're not related, but I'd be proud to say otherwise." She turned to Paige, sobering. "So, you're home, are you?"

"For now," Paige said, and yeah, Alec could see the resemblance—not in looks, though he'd have bet Ma's father had had to beat the boys off with a stick. It was more the tilt of the head, the challenge in the eyes, the tone of their voices. Paige's was just as cool and decided as Ma's. They both enjoyed the byplay, though neither would admit it to the other.

But Paige, as was right, relented first. She bent to kiss Ma's cheek. "It's good to see you."

"Then where have you been?"

"Getting settled," Paige said.

Ma reached over, took her hand. "You never have to question your welcome, child, on this island or with me."

"You'd have read me the riot act."

"Well, you deserve it, and I always believe it's best to take your medicine in one fast gulp. May sting like the devil and taste worse, but it shortens the suffering."

"Not always." Paige's gaze slipped to the television at the end of the bar, tuned to the evening news. Sorrow clouded her expression, just for a second or two, but long enough for Alec to see it before she turned back to Ma, her pain safely hidden behind the mask of the actress. "Sometimes retreat is the best course of action."

"It's hardly life-or-death, child. Now, help me find a nice soft chair to rest my old bones."

Paige took Ma's arm on one side, Alec the other. They helped her down from the stool to a table not far away.

"Bring me some dinner," she called out to her son, "and none of that experimental cue-zeen you like to pass off on the rest of these yahoos."

"She's right," Alec said to Paige, "your thing isn't life-and-death."

Paige swung around, one delicately arched eyebrow inching up as she gave him a long, cool study. "Telling me how to live my life, Counselor?"

"Maybe."

"I'll take it from her. She may not be family, but I respect her."

"Ouch."

Paige lowered her bluebell eyes, sighed. "I'm sorry," she said. "We seem to bring out the worst in each other."

"Why is that, do you think?"

She only shrugged.

"I'm not important enough for you to figure it out?"

Her gaze cut to his, narrowed a little, and sparkled with the same amusement that quirked up the corners of her mouth. "Oh, I have you figured out." She dropped her eyes to his mouth and leaned in until she was close enough for him to feel the whisper of the breath she let out on a little back-of-the-throat purr.

A sudden storm raged through Alec's body and shorted out his mind. He leaned in to close the distance, confused when he felt a pressure on his chest. It took him a minute to understand that the pressure didn't come from inside him, from heat and hunger and blind, raging need. The pressure was her hand on his chest, preventing him from taking what he craved because this time she *was* teasing him. She straightened, smiling like a cat with canary feathers sticking out of its mouth. "Tell me again how you're such a mystery?"

"You're playing with fire," Alec said softly, enjoying the flare of fear he saw in her eyes.

He had to give her credit, though, she recovered fast. "If you have to point that out, Counselor," she said, smiling in pure female satisfaction, "it's probably just your ego talking."

Maggie took her by the arm and said, "Why don't we have a drink, just us girls?"

Paige took a couple of steps before she looked back. "Should we send you something with ice?"

Alec looked down at his scotch, neat, and said, "Why don't you just come back here and stick your finger in this? I've never seen alcohol freeze before."

Paige kept her smile in place, but behind it he could

see her fuming. "I intend to keep my finger, and the rest of me, as far away from you as possible."

"You need some better tools, son," one of the men called out. "I'd say bigger, but a man'd have to have a good-sized pair to take on a woman like that."

The whole bar erupted as he watched her saunter away, laughing.

Let her laugh, Alec thought. They weren't done with each other, not nearly. And he was going to enjoy the contest.

Chapter Three

What the hell's wrong with you?" Maggie hissed.

Paige shook Maggie off, but she followed her to a booth in the back. "He's an ass," she said as she slipped her coat off and dropped onto the cracked, duct-taped seat. "A hypocritical ass."

"So he deserves to be embarrassed in front of half the population of Windfall Island? Do you think he'll just let it go?"

"Yes." Paige slid over so Jessi could sit next to her. "He considers me beneath him."

Jessi snorted. "Wants you beneath him would be a better way to put it. You really shouldn't have teased him that way, Paige."

"He earned it." She sat back, feeling ashamed and sulky, and uncomfortable with the way Maggie was studying her.

"What the hell happened when Alec came to your place? He'd never met you before."

Paige sat back with a little huff. "It might have been the first time he met me, but he'd already made up his mind, courtesy of the Internet. It's bad enough being labeled by the whole world. I'm not going to put up with it in my own home."

"And I repeat, what the hell happened today?"

"Typical Maggie," Paige sniped, "I've always hated the way you could suck the drama out of any situation."

"I think we've had enough drama tonight. Stop playing the victim and spill."

"I don't want to talk about it."

"It must have been personal, considering the way you went about paying him back."

"Not to mention how reluctant you are to talk about it," Jessi said archly. Jessi, despite her innate sweetness, was a hell of a natural judge of people. She could get anything out of anyone, and she was unapologetically shameless and absolutely ruthless about the weapons she chose. "It's not like he's pining for you, Paige, with all those women sniffing around him."

Paige couldn't help glancing around the end of the booth. Three—no four—women hovered around Alec, with Trudi Bingham, barely twenty years old, all but in his lap.

"He certainly is pretty," Jessi finished. "Maybe you should give him a whirl before one of those lipstick-wearing barracudas gets their teeth into him."

"He's welcome to them. I hope his philandering comes around to bite him on the ass."

"I imagine they intend to."

"You know what I meant," Paige shot back at Maggie, who only grinned hugely.

"It sure would be nice if you and Alec didn't snipe at each other every time you get in a room together," Jessi put in.

"Well, why don't we just become a couple," Paige said sarcastically, "then it'll be all nice and tidy."

"There's nothing wrong with tidy," Jessi said.

"It's hardly a recommendation when you're talking about sex, and you are talking about sex, right?" Maggie said to Paige. "Unless you're ready to settle down, then I'd tell you to steer clear, because Alec isn't. And even if he was, he's from wealth, the old kind. His family has him slated to marry a *Mayflower* princess."

"Well, that just gives me another reason to...never mind."

"Give," Jessi said, wiggling her little body over until Paige was crammed into the corner. "You're not leaving until you do."

"Fine." Paige pushed back until Jessi moved over again. "The two of you coerced him into coming to my house—don't deny it," she said to Maggie when she started to do just that. "You're both in that rose-colored haze of new love, and you can't stand to see anyone single and happy, so you sent him over there to fix my toilet."

"Clean your pipes, more like."

"Use whatever metaphor you want, Maggie, it all amounts to the same thing. And let me tell you, Alec Barclay didn't want to be there any more than I wanted him there, so thanks for that."

"We really didn't mean anything in sending him," Jessi said. "Hold is helpless with a tool in his hand. Dex went with Maggie on her errand run, and I know how long it takes Yancy to get anywhere. Besides, Alec actually kind of volunteered."

"Really? Enlighten me."

"Well, he said he could probably fix something simple."

Paige snorted. "Tell that to my toilet, which is still bubbling like Old Faithful ready to erupt."

"So, it wasn't something simple?" Jessi wondered.

"How would I know, he never even looked at it. First, he shoved his way into my house, when I specifically told him I preferred to wait for Yancy."

"So you slapped him in the ego," Maggie interjected.

Paige ignored her. "And when I wouldn't tell him which toilet it was he dripped water all over my house looking for it."

"So you put obstacles in his way."

"Well, the bed wasn't one of them," Paige ground out, "but he stopped and stared at it a good long while." And she pressed a hand to her stomach under cover of the table, feeling the flutter and ache low inside, the same flutter and ache she'd felt watching him stare, slack-jawed, at her bed. She hadn't wondered then, she didn't wonder now, what had been going through his mind, and it stole her breath again, made her heart pound in her chest.

She shoved it all away, just as she'd done earlier that day, refused to acknowledge the need and whatever might be behind it.

"So then you dangled sex—"

"I did no such thing. I didn't break the toilet to get him up there."

"Are you sure?" Maggie said, laughing. "Although

that would be quite a risk, especially if you had only one bathroom."

"I have more than one bathroom, by the way. And for the record, I don't need to trick men to get them in my bedroom."

"Aw, of course not," Jessi said patronizingly. "I imagine most men would weep tears of joy to be in your bedroom."

Paige just rolled her eyes at them, still riding her temper. Anger was so much stronger and cleaner an emotion than the hurt and humiliation of facing a man who knew nothing about the real Paige Walker, but who was willing to judge her by rumor and innuendo. A man she'd been instantly attracted to, but who'd made her feel ashamed when she had absolutely nothing to be ashamed of.

"Then do you know what he did?" she demanded, swallowing back the urge to cry. "He smirked at me. He saw I was cleaning, and he had the nerve to actually smirk, like I'm incapable of cleaning a damn bathtub. Look, he's doing it again."

They all looked and sure enough, Alec sat at the bar, ignoring the women still gathered around him to stare at Paige, his mouth tipped up at one corner. He lifted his glass, tipped it in their direction, and sent Paige's temper soaring another dangerous notch.

"And then," she said, biting off the words with her eyes still on his infuriating grin, "he had the nerve to come on to me."

"Now it's getting good." Jessi wiggled in her seat.

"He doesn't even like me," Paige said, a little bafflement sneaking in around the edges of her anger. "He certainly doesn't respect me."

Jessi squeezed her hand.

Paige looked over at her, smiled a little. "He doesn't know me, but he thinks I released that tape for publicity. He thinks I would do that, but he's willing to put aside his disgust for my character so he can indulge his libido."

Paige caught the frown on Maggie's face. "What?"

"Alec doesn't strike me as that kind of man."

"That's because he respects you, both of you."

"Maybe you should tell him the truth, Paige."

"No."

"But—" Maggie began before Jessi cut her off.

"Paige is right. I went through that with Hold. Either he believes in her or he doesn't."

"But Hold didn't really believe you were after his money," Maggie pointed out.

"No, he had trust issues."

"Alec doesn't have that problem," Paige put in. "He's an opinionated hypocrite who makes snap judgments about people without all the facts. I don't think he can even consider a scenario where he's wrong."

"Maybe you should give him the benefit of the doubt," Jessi suggested.

"When he doesn't give me that same courtesy?" Paige shook her head. "Better I keep my distance."

"That's going to be difficult if you plan to help us with the . . . thing," Maggie said.

"There are all kinds of distance," Paige said.

"Sure, but you might want to choose a different one than you did a minute ago. You keep teasing him that way, it's bound to get you in trouble."

"You're right, Maggie." But Paige looked at Alec again.

He sure was pretty, just like Jessi said, and he appealed to her on so many levels. Truth be told, he'd gotten through her defenses and under her skin too quickly for her not to see that he could be a real danger. She'd never been a woman who threw herself into relationships, and not just because her actions would be held up to public scrutiny.

So she'd take what Maggie said to heart and stay clear of Alec Barclay. And she'd remember her mother; Suzie Walker had chased happiness into the arms of a man, and it had brought her, and everyone in her life, nothing but heartache.

* * *

Josiah Meeker sat a table behind the long bar in the Horizon, silent and solitary in a sea of conversation, laughter, and human interaction. It had no doubt bothered those around him at first; he wasn't one to join the social whirl, they'd be thinking, not because he preferred to keep to himself, but because he thought himself above the other Windfallers.

They were right; he was better than all of them put together. He was smarter, cannier when it came right down to it, and he understood his fellow islanders more thoroughly than they could even begin to know. They'd soon gone back to ignoring him, beer and liquor fuddling their already simple minds. They dismissed him—*she* dismissed him, he thought, hearing Ma Appelman cackle from her table behind him. Let her hold court, let her lord it over the rest of the peasants. They'd not discount him much longer.

Because he held the proof—at least more of it than anyone else had—to solving the crime of the previous century.

In October 1931, Eugenia Stanhope, eight months of age, had been taken from her crib in the mansion of her wealthy parents by a nursemaid angry at being stuck on duty when she wanted to party.

Prohibition had been in full swing, almost twelve years after the passing of the Eighteenth Amendment. The maid had brought Eugenia with her to the *Perdition*, one of the rum-running ships that had anchored off the shores of Maine, out of Coast Guard reach. Somehow, during the nightly party that raged from one deck to the other, the *Perdition* had exploded into an alcohol-fueled inferno and had sunk beneath the waves of the Atlantic Ocean. Eugenia was believed to have died in the wreck.

Or had she?

When Keegan showed up and sent Maggie Solomon after the Windfall journals Josiah had meticulously collected, Josiah suspected Eugenia had lived.

When Holden Abbot arrived and Jessi Randal began asking discreet questions about the origins of the other Windfallers, Josiah had sat back and waited.

Now, with Alec Barclay, former lawyer to the present-day Stanhopes, joining the party at Windfall Island Airport, Josiah knew the time was near for him to act.

Clayton Stanhope thought he controlled matters on the island; Josiah meant to see he paid dearly for that delusion. Clayton didn't understand—none of them were aware of just how much Josiah knew about Eugenia's fate.

Oh, they'd talked to Deke Gifford, Sam Norris, and

Emmett Finley, descendants of the usual crew who'd made the trip out to the *Perdition*, and who'd stood on the beach when the ship had exploded that frigid October night. But Keegan and the others hadn't talked to him. Josiah thought they probably weren't even aware his grandfather had been there as well; Floyd Meeker hadn't worked the bootleg crews often. Only when it counted, it seemed.

Still, for Floyd Meeker there'd been no way to capitalize on the situation without putting every man on the island in jail, including himself. He'd put the story down on paper instead, about the child, how she'd been wrapped, the necklace Jamie Finley had believed he'd hidden. Rubies and diamonds.

Josiah had read the frustration in every word of the old man's account, had seen how fear and impotence had further twisted a temperament already tending toward resentment and bitterness.

From the moment his grandfather had told him about Eugenia, Floyd had begun collecting island journals, buying them when he could, stealing them when there was no other option. Not that he had anything against theft, when it suited his purposes. But getting caught would have been unacceptable.

He'd spent years poring over the dry-as-dust accountings of long-dead salvagers, the whining wishes of unfulfilled housewives, even the insipid dreams of teenage girls, looking for clues to Eugenia's fate. If the Stanhope girl had replaced a Windfaller baby who'd succumbed to the measles epidemic, Josiah reasoned, she should be easy to track down. Easier still to let others do the heavy lifting.

Keegan and Abbot had done a fine job of revealing the likely candidates. First that bitch Maggie Solomon—and didn't it burn his behind that she was still alive? She was going to pay for what she'd done to him, pay like she'd made him pay all these years for one moment of weakness, for tempting him, luring him, teasing him. Refusing him.

Maggie would be dead already, if only Josiah had hired someone more effective than her handyman, Mort. But you worked with the tools available, Josiah reminded himself. And once he had all that lovely Stanhope money, he'd ruin Maggie instead. Better she live to see her life's work destroyed, to suffer and hate and endure as he'd done.

Jessi Randal would be married to Hold Abbot soon, and out of his reach, but she was a sweet, inconsequential girl. Using her, maybe killing her, had been nothing more than necessity. Again, he'd chosen poorly by bringing her ex-boyfriend back. But Josiah had learned something from Lance Proctor: he was thinking too small.

Being Clayton Stanhope's lackey was all well and good; the man paid handsomely. But Josiah wanted more. He deserved more. So he wouldn't rest until he found a way to get it. He needed to be careful though, so he'd have to see to the job himself this time. Bide his time, keep his ear to the ground, and watch the key players—his eyes drifted to the back booth, to Paige Walker—and strike when the moment was right.

Chapter Four

The wind was fresh in her face when Paige set off the next morning. The weather had turned soft—for Windfall Island in November. Though it was a short walk into the village, she'd dressed for the cold, jeans and a heavy sweater under her knee-length coat, boots that were fashionable yet serviceable, and a smile a mile wide as she arrived at the beginning of the main street.

It felt wonderful to go outside whenever she wanted, to walk the crooked, picturesque streets of her hometown and raise a hand in greeting to someone who still thought of her as Matt Morris's little girl.

She stopped into Carelli's, laughing out loud when Peter Carelli and his wife, Lisa, threw their hands up and pretended to bow down before her greatness. She curtsied flamboyantly, letting the warm air and the rich scents of pizza sauce and fresh dough fill her lungs—although habit kept her from indulging.

Many of the businesses were closed for the winter

season, including Maisie Cutshaw's gift shop and the ice cream parlor next door. After that she came to the island's one and only market. She swung through the front door with its jangling bell, and found Mr. McDonald, owner, cashier, stock boy, and deliveryman in the winter when only the island's inhabitants patronized his store. Mr. McDonald had one expression: dour.

When he saw her, she could have sworn he cracked a smile. "I'm happy to see you, too," she said.

"Hmph," he said.

But Paige saw his eyes sparkle. "I have a list—"

He snatched it out of her hand, frowning and scratching his head. "Come back in a couple days," he said as he shuffled away, muttering to himself.

She could have asked Maggie to do her shopping on the mainland, Paige thought as she slipped out into the cold, but Maggie was so busy, and this way she'd only have to pick up the order Mr. McDonald called in. Besides, Paige liked to give a boost to the local businesses when she could.

Once her errands were done, she walked into the Horizon, warm and homey with its big, roaring fireplace and comfort food. She'd intended to take a seat at the bar and see who happened by. Instead, she spied Alec Barclay sitting alone in a booth. And he spied her.

Much as she wanted to, she couldn't ignore the hand he raised. Even when he beckoned with it.

Polite smile firmly in place over her gritted teeth, she shifted course. "Counselor," she said when she stopped next to his table.

"I just got here. Why don't you join me?" He stood and called out to AJ, "Double my order, would you?"

"Sure thing," AJ yelled back.

"What makes you think I want whatever you're having?" Paige said, irritated by his high-handedness.

"Because I ordered the special, which is what anyone who knows AJ orders."

Yeah, and didn't it burn her that he already knew that, and left her with no way out that didn't make her look foolish. "And I'm having lunch with you because...?"

"It would be rude not to."

"Well, you are the authority on rude."

"Then I should know."

She opened her mouth to fire back, but he took her by the arm and incinerated every word in her vocabulary.

She couldn't feel the heat of his hand through her coat and sweater, but he was only inches away from her, and he was tall, and attractive, and he smelled so good. She caught herself sniffing and exhaled sharply instead. Then his hands settled firmly on her shoulders. He slipped her coat off and gestured to the bench seat across from where he'd been sitting, turning away to hang her coat on the hook nearby. She collapsed onto the seat, mostly because her trembling knees gave way. She wasn't sure how she managed to tear her eyes off his backside, so nicely packaged in jeans, but somehow she did it. And by the time he'd slid into the opposite seat, she'd composed herself, but only because she'd had a lot of practice at putting on the appropriate face for any situation.

She even managed to string some words together, pleased that they actually made sense. "Where are the others?"

"Maggie's in the air, Jessi is at her desk, Hold is in the

small office, pretending to work so he can keep an eye on her. I don't know where Dex is, but he took off early this morning. What brings you into town?"

Settling back into island life, she thought, the slower pace, the steady rhythms, the ability to go outside whenever she wanted without being followed. It all contributed to a state of peace she hadn't felt in too long.

That was much too personal to share with Alec Barclay, so she simply shrugged. "I had some errands, so I walked—"

"What? It's freezing out there."

"And? I don't have a car, and my house is just outside the village."

"You could have called the airport. One of us would have picked you up."

"I'm capable of walking less than a mile, Counselor."

"That isn't the point."

"Then what is the point?" she said, then immediately softened her voice. She could be as annoyed as she wanted; she wasn't allowed to show it. "I'm an adult, and while I enjoy being pampered as much as any other helpless, ornamental actress, I grew up here, and I know how to dress for this weather. Or, if you prefer, it takes exercise to maintain my figure, and there's no fancy gym on the island. Is that more in line with your opinion of me?"

"Are you done putting words into my mouth?" Alec countered, looking as cranky as she felt.

Which, oddly enough, made her smile—and apparently caught Alec off guard.

"How about we start over?" he said. "Would you like to have lunch with me?"

"It seems I already am," she said, sitting back so AJ could slide a bowl of minestrone soup in front of her. He set a steaming breadbasket on the table between them, and added a bottled water and a glass of ice with lemon for her before he served Alec. "And look, I ordered the special, like any true Windfaller would have done."

She met his eyes, but she looked away quickly, before she was caught up in the moment and let herself think Alec Barclay wasn't opinionated, high-handed, and overbearing. She was a woman who took her time where men were concerned, Paige reminded herself. She'd learned that from her mother.

It didn't mean she couldn't have lunch with him, and polite conversation. She took a spoonful of soup, closing her eyes in appreciation as the tangy tomato broth burst on her taste buds.

"AJ is a genius," Alec agreed, breaking open a flaky roll and buttering it. He started to hand it across the table, then thought better of it. "Manners," he said with a bump of one shoulder.

Paige simply let it go. "So, tell me about yourself," she said, choosing a roll very carefully and setting in on the plate beside her soup bowl. "Why aren't you married to a debutante and raising two-point-four private-school-educated children?"

"Who says I'm not?"

This time when she met his eyes, she held his gaze, let him see the astonishment. "A man of such high morals would hardly be..."

"Coming on to you if I was involved with someone else?" he finished. "Maybe I was overcome by your charms."

Paige laughed, which was all the response that comment required.

"What about you," Alec said. "Who was it you were linked with recently?"

"Jackson Howard," Paige said flatly. She hardly needed a reminder of the director she'd supposedly made that tape with.

"No," Alec said hastily, "there was another name."

"There's always another name, Counselor. If I so much as stand next to a man and a photo is taken, the press suggests I'm madly in love, secretly engaged, you know the drill. You probably shouldn't be seen with me," she added. "You could find yourself in the tabloids."

"Not on Windfall Island, I hear."

"No, not on Windfall," she said, a bit of the warmth creeping back into her. She met his gaze, not surprised to find him watching her closely. When she wanted to fidget and look away, she raised a brow and lifted her chin instead. "The only person who has the right to talk about a Windfaller is another Windfaller. We don't share Island business with outsiders. It's a tradition that goes all the way back to the salvaging times."

"I can understand why you came back here to—"

"Hide?" she asked pointedly.

His eyes shuttered. "It's probably the only place in the world you can have complete privacy."

"But not freedom from judgment. Relax, Counselor," she added. "You aren't the only one with strong opinions. Just about every Windfaller will be happy to tell you what they think."

But they both knew the tenuous peace between them had been strained to the breaking point.

AJ brought the check, and they both reached for it but Alec got there first. Paige tried to object, but he only said, "You didn't eat much of anything. I suspect that's my fault."

Paige slid to the end of the booth. "Flatter yourself if you want, Counselor."

"I don't make you nervous?"

"You don't make me anything," she said with an edge in her voice.

He reached across and took her hand before she knew what he intended. "Why are you trembling?"

She snatched her hand back and shot to her feet, barely taking the time to grab her coat on the way by. She didn't run, but she would have said she bolted.

There was no other word for it.

* * *

Alec was nervous, and a woman had never made him nervous. Before Paige Walker.

He forced his feet to walk up her front walk, his hand to knock on the door, and hoped like hell his expression looked normal. Not that it mattered. The only thing Paige saw when she opened her front door was the toolbox in his hand.

"I came to fix your toilet for real this time," he said, then rolled his eyes at himself. He sounded like an undertaker who was scared of dead bodies.

"Yancy is coming tomorrow," Paige said, and oddly enough her objection shoved him back to himself.

"I'm here now. And I heard Yancy is far from reliable."

"And you're the expert on home repairs?" But with a resigned sigh she stepped back and let him in.

"I wouldn't call myself an expert, but I have a house in Boston I'm renovating."

That coaxed a smile out of her. "Writing a lot of checks, are you?"

"Yes," he said, determined not to let her wind up his temper. Part of the reason he'd decided to come was to prove to himself that he could spend more than five minutes in Paige's company without somehow insulting her. "But the repairmen let me watch and help with simple tasks."

She made a game-show model gesture toward the staircase. "By all means, practice on my toilet. But if you make a mess, you're cleaning it up."

"And deprive you of the simple pleasure of house-work?"

"Just because I can clean doesn't mean I want to." She took his coat and hung it on the coat rack in her entry-way, frowning when she turned back and found him still standing there. "You know where it is, so I'll just..." She eased toward the kitchen.

Since Alec didn't want her to find him speechless and staring again, he headed for the stairs, then had to come back and pick up the toolbox he'd left by the door. He couldn't resist another glance at her.

She stood at the end of the kitchen island, wearing jeans that looked like they'd been painted on, and a top the color of spring leaves, long-sleeved and long-hemmed, and just as form fitting as the jeans. Her hair was piled into a messy knot on top of her head, leaving her neck bare.

He hurried in the other direction, before he nipped into her nape so he could feel her shiver. He wanted his mouth on her, his hands, before he put her up against the island, or on top of it so he could have her body against his. Seeing her bed again didn't help curb his imagination. He could all but see her hands fisted around the iron rungs, her body bowed back.

Alec shook himself a little, very deliberately removing the lid of the toilet's tank. There was nothing in the least attractive about the insides of a toilet, so not only did it enable him to get himself back under control, but he immediately saw the problem, which made him feel pretty good about himself. Until he disconnected the float thingamabob and water started spraying everywhere.

"Paige," he yelled, holding parts together, which meant he couldn't reach the shutoff valve behind the toilet.

Paige raced in, skidding on the water slick. "What the hell?"

"I, uh, forgot to turn the water off," Alec said, completely failing to keep the sheepishness out of his voice.

Paige sent him a scowl before she contorted herself around the toilet bowl, having to slide between him and the toilet seat to get there. Although he knew she was wrestling with the ancient valve, the way she was moving...he couldn't take it any longer.

He pulled her up, grabbed her hand, and said, "Keep your finger right there." Then he took her place, applying all his frustration to the old valve until it turned and the water stopped sputtering around Paige's finger.

She let go and stepped back, all the way out the door,

her eyes wary on his until she got what she thought must be a safe distance. Alec could have told her there was no safe distance, not when he could tell she was every bit as aroused as he was.

"So," she said with a crooked smile, "you forgot to shut off the water. Kind of a rookie mistake, huh?"

"Yeah," Alec said, but it had nothing to do with experience. It was her, distracting him—even when she wasn't in the room.

"No matter," she said. "It's not like you don't have a career to fall back on."

He sent her a look, which only made her smile widen.

"I'm not laughing at you, Counselor, I'm laughing with you."

"But I'm not laughing."

"That's too bad. The ability to laugh at yourself is vastly underrated." Alec bent back to the toilet. He couldn't continue to look at her, so open and happy for once, and keep his hands off her.

"Maybe we should just agree to keep our distance," she suggested into the silence.

"How do you think that'll work, exactly?" Alec said, keeping his attention on the repair and not her.

"Just because we have to see each other when the group is together, doesn't mean we have to share meaningful conversation," Paige said.

Alec nodded, but he didn't want to avoid her—that was the problem. Whenever he was around Paige, all he could think about was how much he wanted her. He said the wrong thing, he made a fool of himself, and he hurt her because he wanted, *needed*, to establish some distance for his own comfort.

"At least your toilet is fixed," he said.

"Thanks for that, anyway."

"Anyway?"

She sighed.

Alec washed his hands, gathered his tools, and eased past her.

"You're just going to leave this mess for me to clean up?"

"It's just a little water," he said on the way through her bedroom, keeping his eyes firmly off her bed. And he wasn't running away, he assured himself. It was best for them to steer clear of each other.

He wanted her, sure, but it wasn't just physical. He'd never been tongue-tied and absentminded around a woman before. He didn't like it, and he refused to think about why. But he was getting the hell out of there before he did anything really stupid.

Like kiss her.

Chapter Five

Two days later, Paige set off for her morning walk under lowering skies. Her house sat at the extreme edge of the village, and the road beyond skirted along a cliff rising high above the Atlantic Ocean. Trees lined the curving, rocky cliff, those on the outer ridge gnarled and twisted like wounded soldiers guarding the tall sentinels behind.

Below the cliff sat a wide, deep pool of water. A shoal of rocks and sand curled like a comma across the seaward edge, creating a hidden, sheltered natural harbor that had been used by pirates, pleasure boaters, rum-runners, tourists, and the family who lived in the pale blue house perched high on the cliff above.

Suzie Walker Morris, Paige's mother, had called it Secret Harbor.

When Paige had been a little girl, that had seemed like a fairy-tale name. Before she understood the damage secrets could do.

Ten years had passed since she'd walked this coast, with its sturdy forests and soaring gulls. Ten years since she'd seen the ocean foam upon the stingy curve of beach, spraying and spuming against the rocks and boulders crowding the coastline. The simple pleasure of it surprised her, the way her heart soared, then settled. She'd never understood how important Windfall Island was to her until she came back. This was her place; she didn't have to be perfect here.

Some habits, however, were hard to break. She'd learned the value of appearances, learned to guard her privacy jealously, to let the world see what she wanted them to see. And what they saw was calm, cool perfection.

These days, Paige Walker put her emotions only into her work.

She knew exactly who she was, but she didn't believe it helped for the public to know too much about her private life. Perhaps that was why it was no sacrifice to let the world see her as a blank slate upon which she could sketch out whatever character she'd chosen to become.

The trouble was, anyone could write on a blank slate. And she had no way to control the message.

Still, she thought as she stopped next to an antique, yet lovingly preserved, wrought iron gate, there were things that were more important than the smear job done on her reputation.

A half dozen huge old oaks, twice as big around as a grown man's arms could encompass, stood beyond the gate. Even bare, the branches seemed to shelter the stones beneath, from the tall granite monuments popular in the eighteenth century to the more common stone markers, some mottled with lichen and nearly illegible, some as new as her grief.

The gates of the Windfall Island cemetery were never locked, but Paige simply closed herself away from her feelings with the ease of long practice and continued walking. She wasn't ready to go in yet. This reality, she'd decided, would be faced in her own time. When she'd set off from her house after breakfast, there'd been a slight drizzle, and if the wind had had a bit of a nip to it, a light slap, it was nothing a slicker and an umbrella couldn't handle. Lady Atlantic, so Paige had always thought of her, was in a mood today. A rapidly deteriorating one.

The nip had now snarled its way to a bite, the slap to a punch that nearly took her off her feet and turned the drizzle into icy needles that rattled against her coat and stung exposed skin. The umbrella she'd brought out with her was torn away to dance on the wind raging between the purpling clouds and the roaring whitecaps.

She turned her back to the driving wind and headed home, stopping at the back door to load her arms with wood from the pile stacked under the eaves. The day just demanded a fire, she decided, a fire and a glass of wine, and the wood box on her hearth had run pretty low.

So, her arms loaded with split logs, she wrestled the back door of her house open. A blast of wind and sleet shoved her through, her wet boots skidding on the polished floor. Alec Barclay caught her before she fell over and planted her face in the ceramic tile.

She dropped the wood to catch her balance, and they ended up with their arms and legs tangled, all but mouth to mouth before they sprang apart again. Paige was glad she had the storm to blame for stealing her breath.

Alec didn't give her time to get it back. "What the hell were you doing outside in this? Are you crazy?"

"What the hell are you doing in my house?" she shot back, stooping to gather up the wood.

"You weren't answering your phone."

Because she hadn't taken it with her, Paige thought. "I wanted a fire," she said, though it took every bit of her acting chops to say it evenly.

He took the firewood from her. "You've been gone longer than it takes to gather a few sticks."

"I went for a walk." She held up a hand before he could snarl at her again. "And if you recall, it wasn't storming like this an hour ago."

"Ever heard of checking the weather service warnings?"

"The bad weather wasn't expected until later today."

"And the weather forecasters are never wrong."

"So I should check the forecast, but not believe it?"

"You should use good sense."

"Alec."

Paige looked past him and saw Jessi Randal standing in the doorway leading to the kitchen.

"I know you were worried about Paige," Jessi continued, "so stop badgering her and let her get out of her wet things."

Alec's expression remained as sullen as his voice. "I wasn't worried."

"So you weren't on your way to find her?"

"She clearly doesn't have enough sense to stay indoors in weather like this. Somebody had to go after her."

"Paige grew up on Windfall, Alec. We all tried to tell you she knows how to gauge the weather. You wouldn't listen." Jessi turned to Paige. "He wouldn't listen."

"Of course not. You see, he knows me so well." But it gave her no joy to see him flush over the reminder of the quote he'd given the Boston papers about her. "As I recall, I came back on my own, and in one piece. And I had the forethought to bring in provisions." Paige dropped her eyes to the wood in his arms and put as much lady-of-the-manor in her voice as she could, if only to put them back on familiar footing. "You can put that in the woodbox on the hearth."

"Wow, you guys are good at fighting," Jessi said with a laugh. "I wonder if that'll make it better when you sleep together."

"I doubt it," Paige said, lightly enough, she thought, to hide the way her nerves jumped and her pulse spiked at the thought of sex with Alec. "The package is tempting enough, but the conversation afterward would only ruin the mood."

"We don't have to talk afterward," Alec said.

"Oh, you're one of those men who are in a hurry to get out the door."

She watched him search for a retort, and smiled.

"Oh, come on," Jessi said to him, "you're not going to let her get the last word, are you?"

"Apparently she's very fond of words," Alec said. "It seems only polite to let her have the last one."

"I'm fond of words?" Paige sent him a sidelong glance, then added a shake of her head. "I can think of a couple dozen I took an instant dislike to."

He grinned, the brow he lifted giving it an edge of

snark that, God help her, she found invigorating. There was nothing like a man who could keep up. "Going to hold a couple dozen words against me forever?"

"Words are never just words."

"No, but sometimes they're a mistake."

Paige went still, except for the tiny spark of hope inside her. "Is that an apology?"

"Do I have something to apologize for?"

Yes. The word trembled on her lips, but she couldn't force it out. "You want me to defend myself, but all I can give you is words. You're the kind of man who needs to see the truth to believe it."

He didn't bother to give her any words. She wouldn't have believed them anyway.

"I'll save my breath, too," she said, and headed for the kitchen.

"Running away again?"

"Alec," Jessi began.

He only brushed past them to take his armful of wood into the family room.

"Are you going to let him get away with that?" Jessi demanded.

Paige looked in the direction he'd disappeared. "I know a lost cause when I see one."

"If he knew the truth about that sex tape—"

"He won't hear it from me."

"Or me," Jessi said, "but is your pride worth it, Paige?"

"In his case? Yes. But it's not just my pride, Jess. He won't believe any explanation I give him—not completely, anyway."

"And you want him to believe in you? Blind faith?"

Jessi helped her off with her coat and hung it on one of the pegs by the back door.

"I want everyone to believe in me."

"I get that," Jessi said. "I can't speak for everyone, but Alec was pretty concerned about you, if that counts for anything."

Since that seemed ridiculous to her, Paige waved it off, starting down the short hallway that led to the kitchen. "He's no different from a thousand other men who watch my movies and think they know me, Jess."

"Have you dated a thousand others?"

"Let's just say I've done a statistically meaningful survey."

"Paige, Paige, Paige." Jessi shook her head. "You know you've never been good at math."

"This kind of math is a snap." She stopped at the doorway to the kitchen. "How's my makeup?"

"Perfect. Now *that* you're good at."

She stepped into the kitchen, stopping short when she saw Maggie, Dex, and Hold. She'd assumed Jessi had brought Alec to her house because she was worried, too. She hadn't expected everyone else. And she was instantly suspicious. "Why are you all here?"

"No, the question is where were you?" Maggie wanted to know.

"Out walking," Alec said as he joined them.

"Well, that was stupid," Maggie observed with a grin.

"I wanted the outdoors," Paige said. "And I'll point out—again—that it was barely raining when I started out, let alone snowing. And I don't believe for one second you're all here because I didn't answer my phone for a half hour. This is about Eugenia. And me."

None of them bothered to deny it—including Alec, who dropped his load of wood off at the family room hearth and came to stand next to her.

With six people and an island crammed into it, the kitchen seemed tiny, and she was left with little choice but to stay beside him. It was that or leave, and she'd fought hard to be included. After all, Windfall Island was her home, too, and that made Eugenia Stanhope's fate as much her business as that of the rest of them—more when it came to the men, even if they were working just as hard to solve the mystery.

"We know Eugenia Stanhope survived the sinking of the *Perdition*," Dex began, "and that she came to Windfall Island after she was kidnapped." A PI masquerading as a lawyer, Dex had started the search for Eugenia, at the direction of the Stanhope family. "We know she was probably substituted for a child lost in the measles epidemic that decimated the island's population of children eighty-plus years ago."

"The genealogy eliminated Maggie and Jessi as possible descendants of Eugenia Stanhope," Hold said, picking up the story. He'd been brought to Windfall by Dex to research the inhabitants of the island, in hopes of tracing one of the current residents back to Eugenia. So far he'd done a great job of ruling people out. "Negative DNA tests confirmed that. I've also eliminated the rest of that generation, with one exception."

Paige didn't need to see them all turn to her to know who that exception must be. "I'm the same general age as Maggie and Jessi, the right age to be Eugenia's granddaughter."

"A DNA test is the only way to be sure."

"You're right, Alec," Dex said, "but the minute we send anyone's DNA to the lab, that person becomes a target."

"So send it anonymously."

"Can't." Hold crossed his arms and leaned a shoulder against the wall. "The lab requires a Social Security number."

"There's no reason to send it at all," Paige insisted. "No one knows I'm here, or even that I'm from here, except Windfallers."

"Which is the only reason we've let it go this long," Dex said. "But word is bound to get out sooner or later."

"Clayton may already know," Alec said flatly. "He may own one of your friends or neighbors."

"Then why hasn't he made an attempt on me? He didn't wait for DNA results when he tried to have Maggie killed."

"There's a point," Maggie said. "As soon as he knew about me, he tried to take me out, even before the DNA results came back. Same with Jessi."

"Clayton Stanhope tends to hedge his bets," Alec said. "An ounce of prevention, he figures, is worth a third of the family fortune. Sooner or later he'll find out you're here, Paige, and he'll send someone after you."

"It'll only be sooner if I send my DNA in now. The minute it hits the lab, he'll know."

"And we'll control the situation."

"Like it was controlled with Maggie?" Paige rounded on Alec Barclay. "Or Jessi? I don't see how anything was under control—no offense, gentlemen."

"None taken. But Clayton Stanhope caught us off guard the first time," Dex said. "There was no reason to believe anyone was in danger, so we certainly didn't expect an attempt would be made before there was definitive proof that Maggie was related."

"And Lance was my fault," Jessi put in. "I wasn't supposed to go off on my own."

"Lance was my fault," Hold corrected Jessi.

She smiled up at him. "Okay, Lance was your fault. But you saved Benji," she said, referring to her seven-year-old son. "And me, in the end."

"You saved yourself."

"I don't need to be saved." Paige squeezed Jessi's hand to take the sting out of her cool observation. She was happy for Jessi and Hold, but seeing them bill and coo only seemed to make her more melancholy. And more determined to stand her ground. She'd been alone a long time; much as she appreciated their good intentions, she was perfectly capable of looking after herself. "But I'll be careful."

"'*She was careful*,'" Alec said starkly. "That'll make a nice epitaph."

"That's a little harsh," Jessi said.

"Oh, don't sugarcoat it for her," Maggie put in, but before she could say anything else they heard a knock at the front door. Alec was already on his way to answer it by the time Paige had even begun to wrestle with how to get past him.

When he opened the door, she heard the deep, distinctive voice of George Boatwright, sheriff of Windfall Island. She glared at each of the others in turn. Dex and Hold looked away, Maggie and Jessi just returned her stare, Maggie with an eyebrow raised, Jess with all the patience in the world. And then George walked into the kitchen; she took one look at his face and knew whose side he was on. George was a quiet man, who could act fast if danger presented itself. Otherwise, he took his own sweet time coming to a decision. But once he'd arrived at one, moving him was like stopping the waves that washed up on the island's shores.

"Come to tell me I need to have my DNA tested?" she said to him.

"I came to fill you all in on what's going on in Boston," he said.

"Not everything's about you," Alec added, his voice staying mild, and making the comment all the more cutting for it.

She wasn't the only one who noticed, judging by the humming silence, and the five pairs of eyes that shifted from Alec to her.

"I like to give Paige grief as much as anyone," Maggie said, referring to the teenage grudge they'd settled not long before, "but even I think that was uncalled for, Alec."

"Egotistical is at least a nice change from being called idiotic," Paige observed.

Jessi rubbed Alec's shoulder. "He didn't mean—"

"Of course he did," Paige said evenly, then turned to the others when she knew she couldn't continue to look at Alec and hide the hurt. "If this isn't about me, why did you all invade my peace and quiet?"

"She's got us there," Maggie said.

Paige turned to George. "Does Clayton know I'm here? What did Rose tell you?"

Rose Stanhope, Clayton's niece, truly wanted to welcome any long lost relations back into the family. After hiring Dex to search for Eugenia, Rose had contacted George to make sure Windfall Island's law enforcement knew of the search and could keep an eye on the citizenry. Since George constituted the entire police force of the island, she'd kept in touch with him, and along the way, she and George had...become attached.

"Rose doesn't know exactly what Clayton is up to, but she says he's aware of where her loyalties lie. She's walked in on Clayton and his son a couple of times, and they stop talking immediately. There's no way to know if he has eyes and ears on the island, Paige. And Hold tells me you're the only Windfaller in the same generation as Maggie and Jessi that he hasn't ruled out."

"If she had some living relatives—"

Paige rounded on Alec. "Sorry to disappoint you again, Counselor, but I won't apologize that my parents had the nerve to die before you could question them."

Alec snapped his mouth closed, sparing George a burning glance. And made her feel ashamed. She'd promised herself she wouldn't let him get to her, and here she was, jumping on him the minute he opened his mouth because she assumed he'd say something insulting or hurtful.

"Maybe there are some family papers we could go through," Jessi, always the optimist, said. "Your father's things are still here, right?"

"Yes." Paige lifted a hand, then let it fall again without rubbing at the pain in her chest. "Maisie put everything in storage for me, when..." When her father had died, suddenly and alone. "I doubt we'll find anything. My dad wasn't one for sentimental keepsakes."

"He was a simple man."

Paige met Jessi's eyes, saw the sympathy there, and it steadied her.

"Your dad was the best," Maggie said into the silence. "But it doesn't change reality, Paige. You're in danger."

"George will watch out for me. And don't forget Rose is on our side now," Paige added. "She's keeping tabs on Clayton."

"And Clayton knows it," Alec said. "Even if Rose could look over his shoulder every hour of the day and night, he's not going to tip his hand. And he's not going to come after you himself. All it takes is a phone call and you'll have a target on your back."

"You're all alone here," Jessi added, and though the look she sent Paige was apologetic, her voice held no hesitation. "You're not even in town, where you could run to a neighbor."

"So if Clayton knows we're on to him," Paige countered, "maybe he's given up."

"Alec is right," Dex chimed in for the first time. "As soon as Clayton finds someone to do his dirty work, Paige, you'll be in danger."

Paige hissed out a breath. She spent so much of her life on movie sets, surrounded by cast and crew, or on press tours, being asked intrusive questions in the interest of promotion. In Los Angeles she couldn't step out of her own house without being hounded by fans, which she didn't really mind, and press, which she did.

She might be alone on Windfall, she might be lonely, but at least she could go out in public without worrying about anything more than having her outfit critiqued at the Clipper Snip. She could open her curtains, go for a walk on the beach, and not think about who might be hiding in the rocks with a telephoto lens, hoping to catch her in an embarrassing moment.

And here she was, being steamrolled out of having one second to herself.

"As soon as Rose convinces the lab to do the test anonymously," Maggie said, "I'll deliver your sample personally. Until then, we'll have to make sure you're never alone." She turned to the others. "We can all take turns during the day, and Alec will spend his nights at your house."

"Now, you just hold on," Paige began.

"Maggie is right," Dex said.

"But—"

"She could stay with me," Jessi offered.

And although Paige wanted to kiss her for being so kind, she only said, "And put Benji in danger? No."

"I have room," Maggie said.

"I'm not intruding on your privacy, either."

"All my bedrooms have doors. The bathrooms, too."

"And the whole island will wonder why I'm staying with you when I have a perfectly good house of my own."

"Paige—and it pains me to say this—is right," Alec said.

"How much pain?" Paige asked him sweetly.

"Enough," Alec said equably, "but I imagine anyone who has to be around you for long learns to suffer in silence."

"Then I take it you're a masochist."

"I'm a realist. You may prefer to put your head in the sand when anything unpleasant happens—"

"I'm fresh out of sand. I'll have to order some up, since you're going to be imposing yourself on me."

"What's wrong, can't ignore me without help?"

"Your ego is so big it can't be overlooked."

"It takes one to recognize one."

"Jerk," Paige hissed at Alec.

"Diva."

"Hypocrite."

"Were Dex and I this obnoxious when we had the hots for each other and couldn't admit it?" Maggie asked Jessi.

"Well, you and Paige have some of the same qualities. The sarcasm, the pride, the hostility. But you don't use your sex appeal as a defense, and Dex didn't let you send him running."

"Defense against him?" Paige snapped at the same time as Alec said, "Who's running?"

There was a beat of silence, then Maggie said, "Bull's-eye, Jess," and they burst out laughing, along with Dex, Hold, and George.

Paige flounced to the window to look out, but not before she saw the tight expression on Alec's face. Nor could she miss the even tone of his voice, the brittleness she'd already come to recognize as brutal control, when he said, "What else?"

"There's nothing left to talk about," Dex said. "Hold will finish the genealogy, I'll work with George and Rose to see if we can find out what Clayton is up to, and you will stay here, with Paige."

"What about us?" Maggie asked, meaning her and Jessi, Paige figured. God forbid any of them actually imagined her capable of seeing to her own safety.

"Keep your eyes and ears open," Dex said. "Try to find out if anyone on the island is acting funny, asking a lot of questions, or has come into a sudden windfall."

"Be nosy, you mean." Maggie bumped Dex with her hip. "You wouldn't be trying to keep us womenfolk out of the way, would you?"

Dex smiled, though a blind man could have seen the worry in his eyes. "Maybe a little." He ran his hand from her shoulder down her arm, linking his fingers with hers. "The truth is, there's nothing much any of us can do at the moment, and with the new charter business, you're going to be in the air a lot of the time anyway."

"I, for one, am glad to stay out of the way," Jessi said.

Hold slipped his arm around her waist, snugging her against him.

None of them wondered at his need to keep her close. Only a couple of weeks had passed since she'd been abducted and nearly killed. Hold had been forced to choose between saving her or her son, Benji. He'd chosen the child, partly because she'd begged him to, and because he'd trusted her to save herself.

Jessi had justified Hold's trust, but she'd been injured. She'd healed almost completely, but it was clear they were both still dealing with the aftermath of those moments of terror.

"I have to go check on Benji," Jessi said. "I left him alone at Maggie's."

"The doors are locked," Maggie said. "We haven't been gone more than an hour. I'm sure everything is fine."

"Chewie, the one-puppy demolition crew, is there, too."

Maggie jerked to her feet. "If that dog has put a tooth mark on anything, you're replacing it."

Jessi only grinned. "Just wait till you have kids."

"My kids will behave perfectly."

"Right. I bet they'll sleep through the night from day one, eat their vegetables, and never give you a moment's worry."

"They'll be good fliers, too," Maggie said with a laugh.

"No child of ours would dare be anything less," Dex said.

Maggie smiled softly. "Any child of ours can be whatever they want to be."

The look they shared, so intimate, so loving, made Paige's heart ache. She'd gladly give away every bit of the fame she'd attained to have one moment of that kind of soul-deep love, and the absolute faith that her love was returned.

Her eyes shifted, drawn to Alec, and when she found him staring her, she couldn't stop the warmth that stole through her, spreading temptingly in a way that wanted to bring her to life, to waken parts of her she'd closed off.

She looked away and automatically pulled Paige Walker, movie star, around herself. The armor might have developed a hole or two recently, but it was still her best defense. It helped when she reminded herself that Alec Barclay was the last place she could expect to find either love or faith. He wasn't even nice to her, and that, she decided, was for the best. "Come on, Paige," Maggie said.

Alec turned in time to see the other two women each snag one of Paige's arms and pull her out of the kitchen. He followed.

Paige seemed to shake herself a little, sloughing off the shadows their confrontation had put in her eyes. Even as he knew she was only acting, as he acknowledged it presented a challenge to him, that he needed to poke and prod until he could see the real Paige, Alec envied her that ability.

"Jessi and I will stay here while you and Dex and Hold go get your things," Maggie said to him. "There are some packages for Paige at my house. Bring those, too. It will save me a trip."

"Isn't that tampering with the mail?" Paige asked her.

"I'm responsible for picking up the mail and delivering it to the island," Maggie said with a bump of one shoulder. "This is just cutting out the middleman."

"I'll get them later," Paige said. "They're probably scripts."

Alec caught her wrist, hating the chill that dropped over her features when she looked in his eyes, the way she drew herself up to stare haughtily at his hand.

He removed it. "Who knows you're here?"

"My agent."

"Do you think that's smart?"

"It's a bit late to untell him, since he brought me here—and I'll point out if he was going to let the press know, he'd have leaked it already. And before you make any unflattering accusations, he won't breathe a word."

"Because you'll fire him?"

"Because I asked him not to, and I trust him."

She turned away, and Alec fielded a long, cool look from Maggie before she turned as well, following Paige down two steps into the living room.

Alec joined Dex and Hold in the entryway to pull on

twenty pounds of outwear against the frigid cold and pounding sleet.

"Can I read one of your scripts?" he heard Jessi ask.

"Sure, knock yourself out," Paige replied, and then the outside door closed behind them.

"What the hell is wrong with you?"

Alec swung around to stare at Dex, buried his hands in his pockets, and said nothing.

"You keep picking fights with Paige..." Hold began, then he grinned. "Aha."

"One of you needs to keep an eye on her," Alec said, half demand, half plea.

"Don't worry," Hold said, his breath clouding on the air before the wind tore it to shreds, "there's no chance she'll have anything to do with you now."

"Exactly." But he knew he could change that, if he wanted. *When* he wanted. "She doesn't trust me," he pointed out. "What are the chances she'll ditch me and go off on her own?"

"That's your problem," Dex said with a shrug. "You alienated her, you fix it."

"How?"

"Apologize," Hold said with a huge grin. "After a whole lot of groveling, she might just let you off the hook."

"Groveling? No, I don't think so." An apology he could manage, Alec thought, but she could either accept it or not. He wouldn't be doing any begging.

Hold shook his head sadly and looked at Dex. "Some people just have to learn the hard way."

Chapter Six

The men returned an hour later with Alec's things, Benji, and enough food to feed half the island. They built cold-cut sandwiches, grabbed chips and soda or water, and found places to sit in Paige's small kitchen and living room. Benji perched on the steps between the two rooms. His puppy, Chewie, cadged tidbits from everyone, scrabbling his little paws up shins when offerings didn't come fast enough to suit him.

Conversation flowed, Maggie and Dex sniped at each other, and Jessi all but sat in Hold's lap, both interactions equally loving. And Alec watched Paige while she pretended not to notice. Why let him ruin her enjoyment?

It seemed every time she turned around, since she'd been back on Windfall, she had the kind of moment she hadn't realized she'd missed, a moment that filled some empty space inside her. She could almost be thankful for what had pushed her into coming home. Only almost, she thought, her gaze shifting enough so she could see Alec frowning at her from across the coffee table.

It would be useless to wonder what might have happened if they'd met under other circumstances. No point in imagining what it would be like to share a quiet meal with him in the dark corner of some lovely restaurant, being driven home by him, her mind just a little hazy, pleasantly drifting from wine or champagne, of inviting him in. Of taking him to bed.

She shivered a little at the thought of his hands on her, his mouth on hers, his body . . .

But not his mind.

Sex, really great sex, meant losing the ability to think, surrendering to glorious, primal sensation. But there was always after. In the past decade, she'd been very careful to make sure she liked the man she spent that kind of time with. And to know he liked her.

She'd begun to discover, now that she'd come back to Windfall Island with its tight-knit family-based community, that she wanted a future with someone. She wanted it desperately. But only with someone who respected her.

The puppy nudged her leg, scratching politely with a paw. She took a bit of ham from her untouched sandwich and slipped it to him, letting her lips curve at the feel of his sharp little teeth nipping it away, his warm, wet tongue licking the salt from her fingers. Maybe she'd get a dog, she mused, one of those little ones she could carry around in a purse and take with her wherever she went. The tabloids would have a field day with it, but what did she care?

"So, you do know how to smile," Alec observed.

Paige glanced up and saw that everyone else had left

the family room while she'd been lost in her own little world. She stood, gathering her plate and glass.

"But not for me, it seems. You're supposed to eat that," he added, indicating the sandwich she'd barely touched, "not feed it to the puppy."

"I only gave him a little."

"You'll make him sick."

Paige sighed and headed for the kitchen.

"You didn't eat very much," Jessi said.

"So I've been told."

Maggie wandered over to take the plate and frown at it. "My food isn't good enough?"

"Nitrates," Paige said, smiling for what felt like the first time that day, because she knew Maggie was only teasing, trying to lighten her mood. "Preservatives, white flour, high-fructose corn syrup, and enough salt to brine every fish in the Atlantic Ocean."

"Stop, you're making me hungry again."

"You're making me feel guilty," Jessi said. "I shouldn't be feeding Benji any of that stuff. In fact, I won't. I'm turning over a new leaf right now. No more junk food."

"No pizza, no hot dogs? He'll run away from home."

"Okay, mostly healthy."

"Which you already do," Maggie pointed out.

"Except when we're at your house and there's nothing green to be found."

"I have pistachios. I think."

Jessi huffed out a laugh. "The only green thing is that year-old hunk of cheese in your fridge."

Paige left them squabbling good-naturedly in the kitchen, slipping out to the cool gloom of her back hallway. The storm had eased off, no one was paying attention to her, and while she loved the warmth and the noise, she was feeling just melancholy enough to want to be alone for a while. She pulled her coat on, not bothering with a hat and gloves. She just wanted a breath of fresh air—

"Going somewhere?"

She jumped, slapping a hand to her chest, although she didn't know why when her heart had jumped into her throat. "Do you have to sneak up on people like that?"

"I wasn't the one sneaking."

"Neither was I. I just didn't want to break up the party."

"It occurs to me that I'm doing just that while I'm crashing with Maggie and Dex. They insisted I stay with them, but my being there is a loss of privacy for them."

And her privacy wasn't important, she got that. It didn't mean she had to like it. "There's no need for you to play babysitter yet. Maggie isn't dropping off my DNA sample until she can get down to Boston in a few days."

"We discussed this. You're in danger now."

She only smiled slightly. "Maybe I think my solitude is worth it."

And bingo! she thought as his eyes narrowed and his mouth went flat. She'd irritated him. She'd meant to, and more, she'd wanted to put him off guard. She'd grown tired of the self-assurance that made him think he could treat her however he chose to treat her, tell her what to do anytime he wanted.

As if to prove her wrong, he clamped a hand around her wrist and towed her back to the kitchen. She went, refusing to give him the satisfaction of resisting. For now.

"Keep an eye on this one," he announced to the room at large, and hardened her resolve into a cold, hard ball of vengeance.

Oh yeah, he'd pay.

"She tried to leave the house without me."

"Really?" Maggie said with her eyes on the hand he still had clamped around Paige's wrist. "I wonder why."

"She doesn't like me."

"Maybe it has something to do with the caveman routine," Jessi offered.

Dex and Hold, wisely, kept their thoughts to themselves. But Paige wondered if Alec could see the *poor bastard* sympathy in their eyes. Maybe he was smart enough, she decided when he unfurled his fingers gingerly and gave her a wary sideways glance.

"I only wanted a breath of air that isn't tainted with good intentions." She looked around, satisfied that they all got her meaning, even if they weren't willing to back down. "Since I already have my coat on, I'll get those packages out of the car, Maggie," Paige said evenly, "if it's all right with the Neanderthal you all sicced on me."

"I'll help," Maggie said. She rounded the kitchen's center island, stopping to study the red marks on Paige's wrist.

Paige simply pulled the sleeve of her coat down to cover them.

"Paige, I..." Alec began.

She shifted around, gave him a long, steady stare, them simply turned her back and sailed out of the room.

"You're in trouble," Maggie sang under her breath to Alec as she passed him on her way out of the kitchen—only to stop dead just beyond the doorway.

Paige grabbed Maggie's hand and pulled her into the gloom. "I'd watch my back if I were you," she heard Hold say in his slow drawl, and eased around the jamb just far enough to see Dex shake his head in disgust and disappointed male pride before she towed Maggie toward the front door. Immediate satisfaction wasn't worth getting caught eavesdropping.

"You're going to have to teach me that," Maggie said.

"Teach you what?" Paige asked innocently.

"How to inflict guilt and fear without saying a word."

"No. You have a man who's madly in love with you. Words are what's called for between you and Dex, Maggie, not games."

"I want to punch him half the time."

"You probably do, and unless I've lost my ability to understand human nature, it ends with a mutually satisfying wrestling match." And the kind of sex she dreamed about, Paige added silently. The kind of sex built on respect, genuine caring, and a love that stirred the emotions, lifted the heart, and filled the soul.

The kind of love she couldn't quite give up on finding for herself, even though she knew it might very well be impossible for any man to love Paige Walker the woman without confusing her with Paige Walker the movie star. If she'd known that ten years ago...

She wouldn't have altered her path by a single step, she admitted. Like most girls her age, she'd needed to learn by experience. And she'd had some amazing experiences, ones she wouldn't trade—or regret—for anything. It didn't stop her from wanting more. Love, after all, was the experience of a lifetime, and if you were very, very lucky, lasted that long.

Paige didn't realize she was staring toward the brightly lit kitchen until Maggie slung an arm over her shoulder.

"Alec will come around."

"He's not the one for me," Paige said, thankful her voice came out evenly enough. "But I envy you Dex, and Jessi Hold."

Instead of tossing her some empty platitude, Maggie only squeezed her shoulder. When they got to the old Range Rover Maggie had rehabbed to drive in the winter, she popped the back open, handed Paige a couple of boxes, and picked up the rest herself.

"I know it won't be easy on you," Maggie said as they schlepped their armloads back to the house, "but we'll all sleep better at night if we know you're safe."

"I get it, but...he's just so irritating. And he does it on purpose. It's like he wants to get a rise out of me. And don't smirk at me like that."

"Dex and I were at each other's throats from the minute we met."

"There's a difference, Maggie." Dex had respected her. But then, Maggie had always deserved respect. "I guess I'm paying for past sins."

"And don't think I'm not enjoying it," Maggie said with a smile, but there was sympathy in her eyes. "Maybe it's time you forgave yourself, Paige. Stop worrying about the past and live today."

"Oh, I've always kept my eyes firmly focused on the present, Maggie, and the future." Still, she believed she needed to do the past some justice before she put it away for good.

"Just don't beat yourself up too much." Maggie dumped her armload in Paige's entryway, then took Paige's and piled them on top of the others. "It seems to me there are enough people willing to do that as it is."

Paige smiled a little, careful to keep Maggie from seeing the tears in her eyes. Neither of them would be comfortable with that kind of emotion between them.

Seeing Alec at the kitchen doorway was enough to snap the steel back into her spine.

"My money's on you." With that quiet parting comment, Maggie went back into the kitchen, pausing to speak a few words to Alec as she passed him by.

He grinned. And never shifted his gaze from Paige.

"What was that about?" she asked him when he joined her by the open front door.

"She told me to behave or she'll kick my ass."

"She wasn't joking. She kicked mine a time or two."

"Really?" His eyes lit, his grin widened. "Was there mud? Jell-O?"

Paige rolled her eyes. "Men are so easily amused." And she could tell he was only trying to lighten the mood. Unfortunately it would take an industrial-sized crane to raise her spirits.

He picked up the expensive case he'd brought in earlier, not big enough for more than a change of clothes and some personal items. "I'll get the rest tomorrow."

"You're not moving in."

"I'll be sleeping at your place for the foreseeable future."

"I'm not giving you a key."

"I'll be changing the locks, so maybe I won't give you a key."

"My locks are fine."

"You've rented your house out for several years. There's no telling who has a key besides the rental agent."

She laughed a little. "The rental agent is Maisie Cutshaw. Trust me, no one has a key except her." Maisie took her duties seriously, better than any guard dog. Not to mention the prestige she got from being in charge of the home of a movie star.

"No point in making it easier for someone to get in than we have to," Alec pointed out, in such a reasonable voice she could only hiss out a breath in frustration.

"You sound like a leaky tire when you do that. The decision's been made, no use in arguing."

"The decision's been made, my ass." Paige swung around, saw the others packing up the leftovers and getting ready to leave.

"You can argue with them about it, if you like. I'll wait here for you."

And what good would it do with everyone aligned against her already? She sucked in the breath she'd been about to hiss out and started to peel off her coat, only to have Alec take her arm.

This time she jerked away from him, not just because she was furious, but because his nearness shot through her and took the already towering heat of her anger and turned it into something deeper, darker, something that burned.

"I have to pick up the lock sets," he said before she could ask. "You're going with me."

She saw the others off, not capitulating to Alec's high-handedness but rather accepting the inevitable. She wasn't about to pretend she liked it. When he reached for the door handle of the car Maggie had loaned them, she body blocked him and opened it herself. They weren't on a date, for heaven's sake.

The drive into the village was mercifully short and absolutely silent. "If you mention those lock sets are for me, everyone in the village will know about it by nightfall."

He shrugged. "I'll tell them Maggie asked me to pick them up. And for now, we'll keep Maisie in the dark, too."

"But—"

"No key for Maisie. I'll give one to Dex and we'll keep the other."

She flopped back against the seat.

"Good, you're already learning not to argue."

She twisted around, stared out the window, and ignored his chuckle. The village was only a couple of miles past her house, so she didn't have to bear his arrogant company for long.

"Are you coming in?" he asked after he'd pulled up in front of the little hardware store in the village and turned off the Jeep.

"No, thank you. I'll leave you to demonstrate your manhood all by yourself. You know, overbearing men are generally compensating for some...personal shortcoming."

"Overbearing men are generally saddled with stubborn, self-indulgent women."

"No"—her eyes drifted down to his lap—"I don't think that's it."

He lifted his brows, but he got out of the car without saying anything, reaching in as an afterthought to take the keys from the ignition.

As soon as he disappeared through the door of the hardware store, she scooted out and walked a block down to the market. Mr. McDonald, proprietor and sole employee in the winter when there wasn't enough business to keep even a part-time stock boy or cashier, was leaning against the front checkout counter when she came in.

"Hello," she said around the cheerful jangle of the bell that had hung over the door for as long as she could remember. "Is my order in?"

Neither the brightness of her greeting nor the smile she sent him could gain her more than a "hmph" from him, but it made her feel right at home. Nice to know some things never changed, and that there were people who didn't give a damn about her fame.

She set off after him, down the center aisle to the back of the little store, waiting while he scooted through a swinging door with an EMPLOYEES ONLY sign tacked to it. He swung back out in no time, muttering about free-range this and organic that, dumping several packages wrapped in butcher paper into her basket.

She followed him as he ambled down the aisles, plucking things off shelves—including ones she hadn't ordered. She didn't trouble to point it out, though most of the extra items were loaded with fat, sugar, and preservatives. Alec could have those; what did she care about his health?

She heard the doorbell jangle again; she knew it was Alec even before they came to the end of the aisle and she saw him standing at the front of the store, his expression as dark and threatening as the lowering sky outside.

Mr. McDonald shuffled ahead, muttering "outsider" as he rounded the end of the next aisle. She followed along behind him, up and down each and every aisle, ignoring Alec until they arrived at the checkout counter.

"Good, you're learning to be patient while I shop," she said to Alec when he joined them.

He wasn't one to seethe in silence. "I could leave you to walk home, you like to walk so much."

"Now what kind of guard dog would that make you?"

"Careful, dogs tend to bite." His eyes dropped to her mouth, darkened.

Mr. McDonald cleared his throat.

Alec's gaze shifted, then shifted again, the muscle in his jaw bunching.

Paige jerked around and saw the tabloid in the magazine rack behind the counter. Her picture wasn't front and center anymore, but she still rated a corner, an atrocious shot of her in her early days before she'd learned not to leave the house without being perfectly turned out. Below it was a grainy still of the tape, not X-rated but clearly showing a naked woman and a naked man in a suggestive pose. She didn't bother to read the lurid caption. Next to the disgust on Alec's face, mere words were meaningless.

Chapter Seven

Alec followed Paige into the house, depositing the bags he'd carried on the kitchen counter. By the time he'd brought in the rest of the market bags and ferried her scripts from the entryway to the living room, Paige had her coat off and had begun to put groceries away.

She didn't hurry, didn't slam cupboard doors, and her features were perfectly placid. Anyone looking at her would conclude that the tabloid hadn't fazed her at all.

Anyone looking at her would think she'd made that damn tape on purpose and was standing back to let the publicity roll. Only a few days ago there'd been no question in Alec's mind that she'd done just that. So why was it that he didn't want to believe it now?

If she hadn't made that tape, shouldn't she be outraged? And if she had, there should be some sign of embarrassment. Paige showed neither. Her face could have been carved out of marble, for all the emotion she showed.

Alec stepped into the kitchen, and she flashed him a look so calm he wanted to put his hands on her, to shake her until she told him the truth. He settled for pulling a bag over, dumping its contents on the counter, and stowing things wherever.

The fact that Paige followed behind him, moving them to other places, only inflamed his already raging temper. He tore open the front of the old-fashioned metal box on the counter, grabbed the loaf of bread inside, and shoved it back into the refrigerator where he'd first put it.

"I don't often eat bread," she said, "but I'd rather you didn't mangle it."

Alec could only stare at her.

"Why don't you just say what's on your mind, Counselor."

"I don't think so."

"Doesn't matter." Her smile, already thin, wobbled even more. "I know what you think. I know what the whole world thinks."

"Maybe you should face up to it, stop running away."

You made your bed. It was one of his grandfather's favorite sayings, always delivered in that chewing-gravel voice that could cut so bloodlessly, but always with deadly accuracy. Garrett Barclay's opinion not only mattered, his opinion built worlds. Or destroyed them.

Learning to live up to his strict standards had certainly been no picnic. Now it was second nature. Automatic.

"Why would I be running away?" Paige asked him with a slight shrug. "According to you I wanted all this publicity."

"Then why are you hiding out here?"

"Who says I'm hiding out?"

"The press doesn't know where you are."

"Until I choose to tell them? Or my agent does. That's what you think, right?"

It was what Garrett Barclay would have thought. Alec didn't say it, didn't voice any of the other comments that came to mind, comments meant to push her into just admitting she'd slept with that director.

He shoved his hands into his pockets. Whatever—whoever—she spent time with was her business. What bothered him was having it out there for everyone to see, to drool over or to make jokes about. What did that make him?

A hypocrite at the very least.

Maybe he'd been raised to keep his private business private, but that didn't give him the right to judge Paige based on that tape.

And maybe that felt a little self-serving now, because he wanted her. He'd wanted her since the first second they'd met, and sure, that had been clean, pure desire. But it wasn't just about sex anymore. The more he got to know Paige, the harder it was to believe she'd made that tape—at least on purpose. He kept pushing her away, because he was afraid of what could grow between them if he didn't.

"Cat got your tongue, Counselor?"

He picked up his glass but didn't drink. It seemed too telling a reaction. "I plead the fifth."

"No matter." She eased past him, her body just brushing his in the narrow passage between the island and the counter. "Your face says it all."

As she continued by, her scent drifted to him, heady, insidious, slipping through his defenses to steal his thoughts when logic was what the situation called for.

But logic stood no chance against the need and yes, anger, he felt when just a whiff of her perfume grabbed him by the gut and dug in with hooks he wasn't sure he could ever slip free.

He watched her walk away, couldn't take his eyes off the languid roll of her hips, though he knew it was exactly what she intended.

He heard her footsteps overhead. In her bedroom. And found himself at the foot of the stairs before he knew what he was doing. He reached for the rail. The glass still in his hand clinked against the wood, and the sound shocked him back to himself, enough at least to send him back to the kitchen. It took a few minutes, but he was able to laugh at himself, for having such a . . . a teenage reaction to Paige.

The next time his feet moved, he made sure they carried him to the front door and out of the house. He wasn't a handyman by any means, but he could muddle through most minor household tasks given enough time. Still, he was frozen through by the time he tested the back door and decided the new lock he'd installed worked to his satisfaction, as had the front.

He went in, stripped off his outer gear, and hung it in the small mud room just inside the back door, then headed for the kitchen.

It was there he found Paige, leaning in the open doorway with her back to the kitchen, while something that smelled like heaven simmered on the stove behind her.

She'd piled her honey-blond hair into a loose knot that left her face unframed, and draped some kind of loose throw around her shoulders that trailed to the floor and left her a shapeless lump. It didn't matter.

Thoughts of hot coffee disappeared as heat spread through him, almost painful to muscles frozen through from a couple hours in the Atlantic winter breeze.

Although she had to have heard him come in, she stayed in profile, staring through the gloom of the living room and out the wide window that brought the Atlantic right into the house. The sky, though not as angry as before, was still low and heavy with clouds. The light snow that had begun while he'd finished up outside had thickened into big, fat flakes that quickly curtained them from the world outside.

"If this keeps up," Alec said, "we'll have serious accumulation by morning."

"Probably."

She was so closed off he wondered if he'd actually heard her speak, or just imagined it. The very air around her felt like a barrier. The accessibility she was famous for, her ability to lay her emotions bare and draw people in to live them with her, was gone. No, not gone, just carefully guarded. She turned, Paige Walker firmly in place, from the slightly amused expression on her face to the subtly sexual body language. She'd slipped off the throw and put on the real disguise, Alec decided.

He let her have her pretense, kept his voice brisk and nonpersonal. "I replaced the locks on both doors. The keys are on the counter."

"Thank you," she murmured.

"Something smells good. Is there enough for two?"

Finally she glanced over at him, then moved into the kitchen, into the light. "I put your things in there."

He peered through the door she indicated, saw a room so small the double bed took up most of the floor space. A dresser occupied one corner, and a matching—and equally old—nightstand sat by the bed with a pearl-glass lamp centered on a crocheted doily. "The maid's room?"

"We were never rich or pretentious enough to have a maid. My grandmother stayed there, before she died."

"Um…did she die in there?"

She sent him a look, part amusement, part scorn. "Afraid of ghosts?"

If she'd been anything like Paige? Yeah. "Maybe I should sleep closer to your room. It'll be easier to protect you if I'm nearby."

"All the doors are down here," she pointed out.

"And the stairs are at the other end of the house. By the time I got to you it would probably be too late."

She shrugged. "Suit yourself, but the only other bedroom upstairs is more of a nursery than anything else. There's a small twin bed in there, a nightstand, and a dresser. I'm sure it's a far cry from what you're used to. And you've seen the bathroom. You have to go through my room to get to it."

He grinned. "I can control myself if you can."

"What's to control?" She turned away, but not before he saw that he'd gotten under her skin.

Her color was back, though, and she'd lost that air of fragility that made him want to wrap her in his arms, to don his armor and…what? Slay the dragon for her? As long as she hid from reality, she was her own dragon.

He came back, lifting pot lids to find brown rice in one, and vegetables and a little sautéed chicken in the other. "Have you eaten?"

"No." She opened a cupboard and took out a bowl then, after a slight hesitation, handed it to him and took out another. "Help yourself. I always make enough to feed an army, then eat the leftovers for a week so I don't have to cook as often. What?" she said, one well-shaped eyebrow lifting at the look that must have been on his face. "It surprises you that I cook?"

"Why would you?" he said and, taking her lead, schooled his features to reveal nothing.

"I learned out of self-defense" was all she said. "I could hire a chef, but having live-in help means no privacy. And I like my privacy."

As soon as the words left her mouth her gaze flew to his. And instantly put him on the defensive.

"I didn't say anything."

But they both knew he'd been thinking it.

"You know where the glasses are," she said, then pointed to a drawer. "Flatware there. And there are no maids here, rich boy. You'll be cleaning up after yourself."

"I know how to load a dishwasher."

"Good for you." Shoulders stiff, she dished out a stingy spoonful of rice, added some of the chicken-vegetable concoction simmering in a wide, deep cast-iron skillet, and sat at the island bar. She picked up a magazine and flipped it open, but she never turned a page or ate a bite.

Alec filled the bowl she'd given him and took a seat at the second barstool. Paige angled her body away from him, which only added to his temper. But he was angry with himself as much as with her, anger fueled by guilt and embarrassment.

He'd judged her from the moment they'd met. Instead

of an open mind, he'd allowed preconceived notions to color his opinion of her. Now, no matter what he said or did, he was fighting her first impression of him as a judgmental jerk.

"Paige"—he took a deep breath—"I want to apologize."

She eased around a little, flashed him a quick glance. "I'd rather you didn't. It's actually refreshing to come across someone who doesn't feel a need to pull their punches."

"Punches? I definitely need to apologize."

"Not necessary, but it would be nice if you could try not to insult me anymore."

"You haven't exactly worried about my feelings."

She sighed. "I know, so now I'll apologize and say I'm feeling a bit raw just now. I'm usually pretty forgiving about this sort of thing."

"But the sharks are circling and you're feeling defensive. So not only did I kick you, but you were already down." He wouldn't have thought he could feel any worse, but he did. "I actually have a pretty good track record at offering my shoulder."

"Sympathy won't help."

"Meeting it head-on might."

She shifted around, meeting his eyes for the first time. "I have my reasons for leaving it alone."

And so should he, Alec decided, and closed his mouth over yet another attempt to get her to deal with that damned tape.

Instead, he picked up his fork and dug in, closing his eyes for a moment to simply enjoy. "This is really good," he said, "but there's one thing missing."

"Now you're a food critic as well?"

Alec got to his feet and, after a moment of searching, found a package of rolls. He took one for himself and offered her the package.

"I don't eat white flour."

"So you bought these for me?"

She flashed him another one of those looks. "Mr. McDonald thought my shopping list lacked a few things."

"Remind me to thank him next time we're in town. White flour and actual meat."

"It's organic."

"Hey, I'm not complaining," he said as he shoveled in another flavorful bite.

"I can't quite bring myself to go vegetarian all the way."

"Why would anyone?"

She smiled, this time letting it spread to her eyes. It signaled a détente.

And dazzled him.

"You'd be surprised at what people will do in the name of health," she said.

Alec barely heard her talking about the crazy eating habits of the rich and famous. He tried to concentrate on his food and to make polite noncommittal comments so she'd believe he was listening, instead of trying desperately not to clear the counter and take her.

He wanted her with a need that was unreasonable, nearly uncontrollable, and, in the end, impossible.

* * *

The rest of dinner passed uncomfortably, the result of Paige's assumption that he'd stopped talking because he disapproved of her Hollywood chatter. Nothing could be further from the truth, but Alec could hardly tell her the real reason he'd gone quiet.

It might be for the best if she kept giving him the cold shoulder, but it would make living together—even in their limited way—impossible.

"We have to at least coexist," he said into the heavy silence.

"We are."

Alec blew out a breath as she skirted carefully around him to scrape her untouched dinner into the trash and put her plate in the dishwasher, then gave him equally wide berth as she went to the stove to put away the leftovers. All in complete silence.

She disappeared after that, leaving him to rattle around on his own. There wasn't a whole lot of territory to cover, and he wasn't snooping, exactly, but he found more of Paige—the real Paige—there than he'd expected.

A set of built-in bookshelves in the living room stretched wall to wall at one end, with interesting cubbyholes built in at random. Books filled the shelves, of course, biographies and histories and fiction—classics and popular. There was a small flat-screen television, a DVD player, and a compact stereo. Drawers below held DVDs and CDs, board games for all age groups, crayons and paper, and art supplies in the event those who rented the house had children.

A large ceramic bowl glazed in swirls of greens and blues filled one cubby, propped on its side with seashells combed from the beach below spilling out of it. Another cubby held an interesting twist of driftwood. There were photos: of the island taken from the air, probably by Maggie, of the village waterfront taken from offshore, again likely from one of Maggie's ferries. There was a beautiful sunrise that had to have been shot from the bluff behind the house, and there were photos of Paige.

Paige at about ten with a man Alec decided was her father. Paige posing in cap and gown with the same man, older-looking now, at what had to be her high school graduation. The two of them again, cheek against cheek, both grinning in the bright sunshine with the Hollywood sign in the background. And in all of the pictures she shone with a kind of inner light that made Alec wonder how anyone could resist her.

There was just something about Paige, something that drew the eye and engaged the emotions. Fame, for her, had been inevitable. But beauty and irresistibility and fame didn't always invite adoration. There would have been jealousy, too, people who'd wanted to take her down—

"My dad built that bookcase."

Her voice, though low and soft, startled Alec, as did seeing her leaning against the door frame, watching him. Wary, guarded, carefully contained, and giving away nothing. And still he felt drawn to her, and a little resentful that she could pull him in so effortlessly, make him crave her with a greed that shook him to the core. He'd have her, he knew—they'd have each other—sooner or later. And it would never be enough.

And that, he decided, was why he'd judged her so harshly. Self-defense. Which made him a complete coward, if not worse.

He looked up, met her eyes, and for the first time in

his life couldn't find the right words. How did he apologize without explaining that he'd made her feel...less so he could feel safe?

"I don't see any pictures of your mom," he said instead, the first thing that sprang to mind.

"Oh, they're around somewhere." But she wasn't meeting his eyes anymore. "I put those out only because I could get to them easily. The rest of my personal things are buried in the storage shed under the house. Better nobody knows this place is mine."

"It's a shame," Alec corrected.

Paige shrugged, a languid, careless bump of one shoulder. "It's the price I pay. I just came in to tell you I'm going to...I'm going up for the night."

"Okay. Paige?"

She turned back.

"I'm sorry. For earlier."

She smiled a little, that slightly mocking smile. "I deal with other people's opinions on a daily basis. I try not to let it bother me."

But he could see it did. "I..."—he spread his hands—"I'm usually not this big a jerk."

"Nice to know you're going above and beyond on my account." Her lips curved higher, the smile more genuine now, and Alec found himself grinning back.

"Maybe we could call a truce while I'm here."

"Okay," she said dubiously.

"What's wrong? Can't control yourself around me?"

She huffed out a slight laugh. "So much for the truce."

Alec stuffed his hands in his pockets, ashamed for the first time in as long as he could recall. He just couldn't seem to stop poking at her.

"You want to coexist," she continued, "but how are we going to do that peacefully until you figure out why you're such a jerk—your word—to me. And before you say anything, I'll admit that I overstepped the other night in the Horizon."

And just like that Alec flashed back to that moment, to the heat of her, the scent of her. Her mouth had been all but pressed to his, so close he'd sworn he could taste her, dark and sweet as brandy on his tongue. He'd almost closed that breath of distance, and to hell with everything else.

"It won't happen again."

"Huh?" Alec said as he checked back into the conversation. "What?"

"I said it won't happen again. I won't tease you anymore."

And that should have relieved him. Less temptation meant more control for him. So why did he feel a little panicky, all of a sudden?

"I'm attracted to you, which is why I let you get to me," Paige continued, sending his pulse galloping. "But you're right, we need to keep our distance."

"When did I say that?"

"You say it every time you snipe at me. You're pushing me away because you're attracted to me and you don't want to be."

"Now you're a psychologist?" he grumbled.

"No, but I've made a study of people, why they do what they do. It helps me in my work."

"So you get to tell me how I feel?"

"No." Paige shoved her hands back through her hair, clearly frustrated. "I'm trying to tell you how *I* feel."

"You're attracted to me," he said, easing around the sofa.

She started to back away, then deliberately held her ground, her chin lifting in deliberate acceptance of his challenge. "Yes."

Alec kept walking toward her, slowly. "But I don't have to worry about it because you're going to keep your distance."

"Yes. It's my problem."

"Is it?" He jerked her against him, swallowed her startled gasp by taking her mouth. The very air seemed to ignite, the fire racing over his skin, burning through his blood, searing his thoughts so there was only the flavor of her, sweet and intoxicating, the feel of her against him, sleek muscle and soft flesh.

He framed her face, slipped his hands back to scatter the pins she'd used to pile up her hair so the cool, heavy mass of it rained down her back.

"Alec."

"Don't," he said. *Don't talk, don't shatter the mood,* he thought, and dived back in.

She met him, more than halfway, twined her arms around his neck, laid her long, slim curves against him, and poured herself into the kiss with a sexy little purr.

And he could still hear the hesitation, the uncertainty, in her voice when she said his name. Just his name, like a plea.

He could convince her, he told himself as his hands raced over her and he felt her shiver against him. He could have her, he knew, as he feathered his hands across the sides of her breasts and heard her moan. He'd already gotten through her defenses. Her arms were banded around him, her legs tangled with his, and her pulse hammered like a piston. But he already understood that she wasn't ready.

She simply stared at him when he let her go, swayed a bit, enough so he had to squash the urge to reach out and steady her. He wouldn't be able to let her go a second time.

It didn't take her long to steady herself. "Don't do that again," she said.

"You weren't exactly fighting me off."

"Well, another black mark for me."

"Stop putting words in my mouth."

"I think you should go."

"Worried your charms will be too much for me to resist?"

She let out a half laugh. "My charms are no match for a paragon's sense of right and wrong." She sighed, held up a hand. "You see? We can't coexist peacefully, and I came here to find peace."

"Death is peaceful." He regretted the words instantly, and not just because she went pale. "Paige—"

"You made your point."

And sent her running again, which was exactly what he'd aimed to do. He heard her footsteps on the stairs, then overhead, as he settled in to wait. Water shushed through pipes, he heard her moving around, then nothing but the wind outside the windows, the slight creaks and groans of the house settling.

After ninety minutes of silence, Alec made his way up the stairs. He hesitated when he saw her light, but he wouldn't allow himself to avoid her. What kind of protector would that make him? Especially when he'd already seen to it that she wouldn't trust him.

He knocked lightly on her door frame, said, "Okay if I come through?"

It took a minute, but she gave him a clipped, "Yes."

He stepped in, and though he'd braced himself, need slammed into his chest and stole his breath.

Paige sat, propped by several pillows against that amazing iron bed frame. What must be scripts were scattered around her, but she was reading an actual book. Her hair was bundled messily back, she wore no makeup, and looked impossibly young and fresh—and appealing, with a pair of dark-rimmed square reading glasses perched on her nose.

As if to offset her beauty, she wore an old, baggy sweater, buttoned down the center but veed, just a bit of lace peeking through to make him wonder what was going on beneath. If she'd hoped to repel him, she'd failed miserably.

She peered over the tops of those black frames, her eyes met his, and the need already bubbling under his skin would have roared to life again if he hadn't seen the wariness there, in the way she plucked at her sweater so self-consciously.

"It was my dad's," she said.

And turned whatever he felt for her into tenderness, which neither of them were comfortable with.

"Maybe you should make it a cold shower," she said, and reminded him how easily she could read him.

"I only want to brush my teeth."

"There's a bathroom downstairs."

He grinned. Her hostility was so much easier on them both. "I must have a masochistic nature. I couldn't talk myself out of seeing you before I went to bed."

One eyebrow inched up. "And?"

"Every straight male in America would hate me right now."

"So you've switched from insults to empty flattery."

"I'm a paragon, remember? Paragons always tell the truth. Besides, if I can't insult you and can't flatter you, then we won't have a whole lot to say to each other."

She relaxed enough to smile, to let it be full and teasing. He wanted, desperately, to bite into that unpainted lower lip and feast, to feel that long, luscious body moving against his.

"You can flatter me," she said, her voice low and husky, "just do a better job of it."

"I'll try." And although he had an urge to tell her right that minute just how appealing he found her, he couldn't give her any more weapons.

They might have called a truce, but he still felt like he was fighting a war.

Chapter Eight

At the edge of the cliffs behind Paige's house was a natural fissure where weather and time had carved a jagged pathway from top to bottom. Working with what nature had already provided, Paige's father had carved rough steps into the rock.

Paige picked her way carefully down those steps, mindful of the treacherous footing and her own exhaustion. She'd hoped the fresh, freezing cold air would perk her up, but fatigue still weighed her muscles and dragged down her spirits.

She settled on the big rock at the foot of the steps, pulled her knees up, and rested her chin on them, barely noting the bleeding colors of the sunrise but for an automatic and absentminded acknowledgment of what it portended.

Red sky at night, sailor's delight, red sky at morning, sailors take warning.

The old adage circled her head as she listened to gulls

screaming, felt the emotions fluttering inside her as if they had wings that beat at her, desperate to get out.

Was this what had driven her mother? Paige wondered. Had she met a man who'd kissed her the way Alec had kissed Paige the night before? A man she'd wanted with such unreasoning hunger that she'd left her husband and child and gone off to the mainland in search of...what? Freedom? Happiness? Everlasting love?

Did those things even truly exist? Her mother had chased them to her death. Paige had chased them to Hollywood, and what had it brought her but trouble and sorrow? She'd wanted, just as desperately as her mother had, to get away from Windfall Island, with its confining shores and small-town ways.

She'd craved attention, and the adoration of millions. She'd achieved those goals and discovered the dark cloud around the silver lining. Still, long after the attention palled, Paige had continued acting because she'd fallen in love with her craft.

She still loved acting, but after a decade of constant work, one role had begun to bleed into another. She was too much the perfectionist, too aware of her reputation, as carefully crafted as her image, to give less than her best to whatever character she slipped into.

So she'd opted not to fill the handful of months before she started her next big project, ignored the piles of scripts her agent sent her. Harvey Astor hadn't been pleased about it, but he was her friend as well as her representative. He was also canny enough to know her performances would only benefit from a hiatus, and gifted enough in his powers of persuasion to believe he could talk her back to work when *he* decided it was time.

Then the scandal hit, and they'd both been grateful for the break that took her out of the public eye.

The Paige Walker who'd roared into Tinseltown with a hundred dollars in her pocket and the absolute conviction that she'd have them all kneeling at her feet would never have hidden her face. That young, brash girl would have lifted her chin and dared anyone to comment.

The woman she was now, well, she understood that work could sustain for only so long before you noticed, even through exhaustion, that you were alone. She'd come to realize that the fickle adulation of millions meant nothing compared to the adoration of one person who loved you enough to stick by you in the bad times, who believed in you, even when the lies were easier.

Like the mother she so closely resembled—both physically and emotionally—Paige had come to suspect that she would never find true love. She rubbed the heel of her hand over her breastbone, though it did little to ease the ache there. Nothing, she feared, would. In achieving the fame and fortune she'd craved, she'd created a reality for herself that made it impossible to find happiness. Those men who sought her company were really interested in the things she could buy or the boost she could give a career. And those men who might have loved her for herself hated the fame that stole their normalcy.

And there was nothing she could do about it, but continue to place one foot in front of the other and see what life brought her.

She stood, stretched, then ran, heedless of the danger. This was no tropical beach deep with beautiful sand. What sand there was was hard-packed. The rocks, smoothed by millions of years of pounding surf, were wet and slippery. She skipped over them, years of dance classes keeping her light enough that even when she felt a foot slip, she was already gone.

When she got to the end of the curving shoal, she bent at the waist, her throat and lungs burning with each breath of damp, frigid air she gasped in. And no wonder, she thought as she trotted in circles, shaking her legs and feet as her muscles, heated too quickly, were now cooling too fast and wanted to cramp. She'd run a good mile at an all-out sprint, and still she felt jumpy, unsettled.

She set out to walk back, deliberately taking her time and still reaching the cliff steps too quickly to suit herself. She climbed them before she could talk herself out of it, so relieved to see the Jeep gone when she crested the cliff it was ridiculous. She was chilled to the bone, but she'd already been finding reasons not to go inside. To avoid Alec.

She'd wanted to give in last night, to be held, to pretend, she admitted, for it surely would have been a pretense to believe Alec Barclay cared for her beyond the physical.

But he was gone, and the feeling of freedom lifted her up the stairs two at a time. She wanted a bath, to relax in a tub full of scented bubbles. She couldn't risk it, not knowing when Alec would be back.

So she'd settle for a shower, let the water beat hot over her skin like the kneading hands of a masseur. Not a lover.

She was already shedding clothing as she crossed the room, was down to her jogging pants and bra, unhooking the clasp as she stepped into her bathroom.

And, with a gasp, managed to clasp her bra to her breasts with both hands before it fell off and left her half-naked. "What the hell are you doing in here?" she demanded.

Alec jumped to his feet, a bag in one hand, a screwdriver in the other. "I, uh"—he lifted the bag, filled, Paige saw now, with parts—"the shower was leaking."

She backed out of the doorway, her hands still pressed over her breasts. "I didn't see the car."

He followed, never took his gaze from her. And forced her to duck into the closet.

"I thought you were gone," she blurted out, fumbling in her haste to pull on whatever came to hand, in a panic now that she'd shut herself off from temptation.

"I know you didn't plan this," Alec said, and gave her the courage to open the closet door.

He grinned when he saw her, shook his head. "Your father's sweater again?"

Paige looked down at herself and laughed. "It wasn't intentional."

"It worked anyway."

"He'd laugh over that." But she sobered. Her father hadn't been one to intimidate the boys she'd gone out with. He'd trusted her to respect herself, and to make sure those around her respected her as well.

"You miss him."

She dropped her eyes from Alec's, turned away.

"Another subject that's off-limits?"

Then back to face him. "Actually, yes."

Alec shook his head, seemed to think twice, then spoke anyway. "I know you'll take this as me telling you how to live, Paige, but life's little pains only get bigger if you try to ignore them."

"Losing my father wasn't one of life's little pains."

"No, I don't imagine it would be, and I'm sorry if it seemed I was trivializing a loss that major. I just...I wonder if your father would want you to grieve forever, or if he'd rather you work through the pain so you can remember the good times."

"I do remember the good times." It was that she wanted to hold on to, the good memories rather than a cold grave watched over by even colder words carved into stone.

Still, Matt Morris had been a get-over-it-and-live-your-life kind of man. He'd sigh and shake his head if he knew she was memorializing him rather than facing reality so she could think of him without the specter of his loss shadowing every memory.

The fact that Alec understood that only made it worse. And maybe if he hadn't pointed it out to her in all his judgmental splendor she might have openly agreed, instead of stewing over it.

"This isn't a big house, Counselor, we're all but in each other's pockets."

"And I should keep my opinions to myself. Since we're stuck with each other."

"Yes, we're stuck with each other," she said to Alec. "Until we get this thing settled."

"Paige..." Alec stepped forward, brushed his fingertips over her cheek.

She closed her eyes, loving the warmth of his touch even if she couldn't bear to see the question in his eyes, not while the answer to it was rising inside her.

He brushed a kiss where his fingers were, then, to her surprise, moved away. "I wish I could go back to the moment I made that comment."

Her eyes fluttered open, saw the regret in his. "Don't apologize for being honest, Alec. You feel what you feel."

"Yeah, but sometimes even I'm wrong."

Now she let her lips curve. "This'll be easier if you keep being a jerk."

"I don't think anything will make this easier." He stuffed his hands in his pockets, looked away, then back. "We could try to be friends."

"I'm not sure it's a good idea." But she took the hand he offered, and though she was already braced, she jolted nonetheless. And craved. Here was heat, and in it the oblivion she wanted so desperately.

She let his hand go and told herself the wise course was to keep her distance in every possible way. Alec already appealed to her physically, but involving her emotions, even a little, would only make it more difficult when he was gone, and she found herself alone again.

* * *

The storm came with the dawn, fast and hard, another blow to an island already battered. Winter, barely begun, promised to be brutal.

The last thing Paige expected with the wind and rain gusting hard enough to knock an elephant off its feet was a visitor, but when Jessi showed up on her doorstep, Paige was so happy to see her she could have kissed her square on the mouth.

"What are you doing out in this?" she asked as she dragged Jessi through the door, then went to fetch some towels from the downstairs bath while Jessi unwrapped herself.

"Mother Nature has grounded Maggie," Jessi called back to her. "I left her to man the phones—"

"And bitch about it, if I know her."

"Every second." Laughing, Jessi took the hand towel Paige offered and mopped at her face. "She can't fly in this, and I was stir-crazy enough to want out of the office. Add in that you need to go through your dad's papers, and here I am."

"You're just plain crazy, but I'm glad to see you," Paige said, desperately grateful for company that wasn't Alec Barclay. She helped Jessi out of a mackintosh, then the big yellow puffy coat and a quilted vest, finally getting down to the petite curvy body decked out in jeans and a bright red sweater.

"I like the snowman," Alec said.

Both women swung around, both pairs of eyes shifting from him to the front of Jessi's sweater.

"Thanks," Jessi said.

"Paige," Alec said by way of greeting.

"Alec," she said with just the same slightly mocking smile. "Sleep well?"

"Actually, no."

"Maybe you should try the bed down here."

"Not the one I was considering."

"It's your only other option."

He shoved his hands in his pockets and rocked back on his heels, giving her a wide grin that said, *For now*.

After all his big talk last night about being friends, he was already pushing for more.

"I came over to help Paige go through her dad's things," Jessi said when the silence drew out.

"I could..." Alec began, before his gaze lifted,

clashed with Paige's, "use some coffee." He walked past them and into the kitchen, coming back out in under ten seconds with a cup of coffee in his hand. He walked by them again, giving Paige a wide berth, and disappeared up the stairs.

"Well," Jessi said, "that was awkward."

Paige turned on her heel and led the way into the kitchen.

"The temperature went up fifty degrees when he walked in, then dropped to subzero the next minute. I was dying to know how it's been going, but I think I just got my answer."

Paige took down a couple of mugs, and since she couldn't imagine putting coffee into a stomach already churning, she put the kettle on for tea. Which Jessi, blast her, interpreted better than anything Paige could have said.

"It's going to be difficult to live together if you keep giving him the cold shoulder."

"I'm not going to sleep with him."

"It doesn't look like you're sleeping without him."

"Well, so much for my skill with makeup."

Jessi only smiled. "I'm more observant that most people."

"Yes, you are." Paige took the sputtering, whistling pot off the stove, feeling the same, like so much pressure had built up inside her it was about to spew out on a cloud of steam. "I just don't know how to handle him," she blurted out.

"And you're used to handling men."

That brought a reluctant smile to her lips. "I suppose I am."

old lawnmower and a wheelbarrow with a flat tire. Paige's heart ached when she caught sight of her father's table saw and got a flash of him using it to build the bookshelves in the family room. She could still feel his calm, steady presence, the essence of him that had brought her comfort, even when they'd been continents away from each other.

"God, I miss him, Jess," she said, resting her hand on the table saw, gone dusty and rusted with idleness. "I should have been here."

"You were where you needed to be, Paige. He understood that."

Yes, she thought, just as he'd seemed to understand what took his wife to the mainland. She'd asked him once, when she was older, and all he'd said was, "Suzie always came home to me."

"Maisie sure wrapped these boxes up tight," Jessi observed, dragging Paige back to the present.

She sniffed, swallowed back her tears, and went to join Jessi by the shelves. Boxes were stored neatly on the middle two shelves, which put them out of the way of any flooding and handily in reach. They started at opposite ends, carefully pulling away the heavy plastic until they could open the lids.

"Bless Maisie," Paige said after they'd opened and reclosed the fourth box filled with odds and ends from the house. "She didn't throw out anything."

"Paige," Jessi said quietly.

Paige turned, memories battering her again, memories of sitting on her mother's lap while she put on her makeup, of being spritzed with her perfume, heavy with the scent of roses.

Paige took the small wooden box Jessi held, ran her fingers over the whorls of the roses carved into the lid before she lifted it. Inside was a tray lined in red velvet, one end sectioned off into small compartments, the other in the tight rows designed to hold rings.

"Their wedding bands," she said, lifting her father's. He'd worn it until the day he died.

"What was Maisie thinking, to put that out here?"

"I told her to box everything up," Paige said faintly. She turned to lean against the shelves. "*I* wasn't thinking."

"Of course you weren't," Jessi said. "You'd just lost your father, and by the time you were notified, it was too late to even come back for the funeral."

"I should have come anyway but, well, I couldn't face it, Jess. I just couldn't imagine…It was like, if I didn't come back he wasn't gone."

But it hit her now, surrounded by his everyday tools. Holding his wedding ring in her hand, she felt his loss so keenly it tore a sob from her throat.

Jessi's arms came around her instantly, or she tried at least, and made Paige laugh through her tears because they both wore so many layers Jessi's short arms simply slid off.

"Delayed reaction, Jess, I'm sorry," Paige said, already past that first heavy rush of grief. "The house looks so different, now. The furniture I grew up with is gone, and with my dad's things already in storage"—she shrugged, looked around through the fresh tears welling in her eyes—"it was easy to remember him without missing him so much. In here with all his things, well, he never took this off." She held up the ring, then slipped it back into the slot time and cold had imprinted into the velvet holders. "He never would have taken this off. He should have been buried with it, but I wasn't thinking of anything but myself." And selfishness was just another character trait she had in common with her mother.

"Stop it," Jessi ordered. "The last thing he'd want is to know you're…"

"Feeling sorry for myself?" Paige finished for her with a wry smile. "It's always about me."

"Paige."

"Don't give it another thought," Paige said, pretending she didn't see the concern still on Jessi's face. She poked around the little box, avoiding the wide gold band with its smaller, slimmer mate. There wasn't much there but a few pieces of costume jewelry.

Still, it had been her mother's, and until now she'd had nothing of Suzie Walker Morris but her photographs and a few blurry memories.

"That's pretty." Jessi pointed to a brooch with a red stone the size of a robin's egg, surrounded by paste diamonds.

Paige worked it free of knotted, tarnished chains and a pair of opal earrings. "I don't remember my mother ever wearing this." She held it up so the meager light shone through the red glass.

"It looks so real."

"I'm sure it's not." Paige rubbed it on her sleeve to shine it up, then pinned it to the lapel of her coat. "I'm glad you found this, Jess." It reminded her she'd had a family once. She hadn't always been alone.

Jessi, of course, read the wistfulness on her face. "Thanksgiving is only a few days away," she said. "What are your plans?"

Paige set the jewelry box aside and went back to peeking in boxes. "I'm just staying in, cooking something simple."

"Cooking," Jessi said with a sigh as she unwrapped yet another box. "I can't remember the last time I did more than open a can of soup. I've barely been home for dinner since Maggie picked up that charter contract. And when I am home I'm too exhausted to cook.

"Hold has been getting takeout almost every night, which is pretty limited on Windfall in the winter. He and Benji have even been cleaning."

"He's one of the good ones, and I'm sure you're not neglecting him completely. And anyway, you won't have to cook for Thanksgiving," Paige continued, shoving down the spurt of envy Jessi's smile brought on. "You're going home with Hold, right? You and Benji."

"He doesn't want to leave right now with the search up in the air, and the results of your DNA test due in."

"Really?" She'd forgotten about that. Rose had convinced the lab to run the results anonymously, but it had been only a few days since Maggie had taken her sample in.

"Hold called, they said they haven't gotten to it yet. They're really busy with people trying to trace their ancestry."

"What?" Paige straightened and looked over at Jessi, working her way down the shelf of boxes.

"It's something new. People have their DNA tested to find out their origin, back to the cavemen or something. Hold says they'd be slower over the holidays anyway, with people taking vacations, going home to visit relatives..." Jessi trailed off, looking guilty.

"His family can't be happy, but it's not your fault."

"His mother has tried everything from threats to bribery, but he won't budge."

"Well, you're welcome to come here, but like I said—"

"That's perfect." Jessi swung around, clapping her gloved hands. "Dex and Maggie will come, too."

"I was only going to cook something simple," Paige finished, already feeling the trap spring closed.

"There's nothing to cooking a turkey."

"Of course there is." She'd taught herself to cook, but nothing as elaborate as a full Thanksgiving dinner. "Besides, I don't have a turkey."

Jessi waved that off. "I'll have Maggie pick one up. She'll be doing a last-minute grocery run for Mr. McDonald anyway."

An hour later, Paige found herself alone in her kitchen with a half dozen boxes, several lists, a spinning head, and a warm feeling in her chest. Had she felt alone just that morning? she wondered with a smile. She might not have true love, but she had people in her life who truly loved her. She'd never feel completely alone again.

Absentmindedly, she answered her ringing phone, and her smile widened.

"Paige," AJ's big voice boomed out, so loud she had to hold the receiver away from her ear. "Ma wants me to invite you to Thanksgiving dinner with us. That'd be me and Helen and her. Says she wants to hear all the Hollywood gossip firsthand."

"I'd love to, AJ, but I just got roped into having Dex, Maggie, Hold, Jessi, and Benji. And Alec Barclay." And what was three more people? she asked herself. "Why don't you all come over here?"

AJ's heavy sigh told her he'd have liked nothing better than to take her up on the offer. "Ma doesn't like to leave her house much anymore," he said instead, "and her place is so small, not room enough for ten people. She's been asking after you, though."

"Tell Ma I'll come visit her soon," Paige said into the receiver, and by the time she'd hung up the phone, she felt a cold rush of air and heard Alec come through the front door.

He helped himself to a bottle of water from the fridge. "How did the search go?"

"We made it through all the boxes. The ones we brought in seemed to contain the older records." Along with her mother's jewelry box, which was already safely in her bedroom. She didn't want Alec asking any questions while she was still hurting. "I'll go through them in the next few days."

Though she'd expected him to offer his help, had, in fact, already formulated a polite but firm refusal, he only rolled his shoulders a little. "What are the lists for?"

"Oh, Jessi finagled me into having Thanksgiving dinner."

"Really?" Grinning, he leaned back against the counter. "It's only a few days away."

"Yeah, I'm not sure how I'm going to get it all done in time."

"You mean *we*."

She studied him for a minute, but she'd already made her decision. He was trying to make their temporary living arrangement less stressful. The least she could do was meet him halfway. As long as she didn't let him push her over that line.

"Okay, let's get started. First I—we," she amended, careful to keep it friendly and nothing more, "have to find a way to seat seven people."

Chapter Nine

Paige took her time changing into slim black jeans topped with a hot pink turtleneck under a fitted black-and-gray-checked jacket. She'd stolen a few minutes to repair her makeup before she slipped her feet into fur-lined waterproof boots and made her way downstairs.

Alec waited in the entryway, body language set to impatient, expression carefully blank. "We're only going into town."

She lifted one brow. "There's no excuse to let myself go, just because there are no photographers around."

"I suppose it was worth the wait."

She shrugged. "A woman dresses for herself first, then for other women. But what she wears beneath her clothes, that's so she feels confident. Sexy," she said with a smile. "It's for herself first and sometimes for a man."

He grinned. "Now we're talking."

"Not just any man, cowboy," Paige qualified, smiling to take the sting out of the rejection.

"I'm not just any man, though."

"No, you're not." But he wasn't *the* man, and they both knew it. Still, she'd taken some care with her lingerie. Sexy was confident, like she'd said, and confident was strong. She'd let Alec put her on the run long enough; time to remember who she was, who she'd worked so hard to become.

She slipped into the coat he held up, pulled the hood over her hair, and let him open the door for her. And kept it all friendly. It was a fine line, but the consequences were more than she wanted to suffer.

"A couple of card tables and chairs are all we need," Paige said as Alec pulled out onto the road for the short drive into the village. "There's no room in the kitchen for a big table, but we can move the living room furniture out of the way temporarily. Meeker's," she added in response to his baffled frown.

"Is he open?"

"He's always open. I don't know who'd be shopping in this weather—except us, but Meeker never closes."

"His wife probably encourages it," Alec said dryly.

"She left him a long time ago," Paige said. "His daughter, Shelley, still lives at home, though."

Alec made the last turn into the village. "I don't think I've met her yet."

"Trust me," Paige murmured, "you'd remember Shelley Meeker," and let it go at that, since Alec had pulled up in front of Meeker's Antiques.

She'd never felt comfortable with Josiah Meeker, but the wind cut through her as soon as she climbed out of the car. So she fought the front door open, stepped inside—and found herself shivering for entirely different reasons.

The place must have been an old warehouse at one time; the rafters were high, nearly lost in the darkness overhead. Goods were piled haphazardly, sometimes twenty feet high, stretching off into the gloom in every direction, like giant misshapen skeletons.

Meeker could have put in some ceiling lights, if he hadn't been so cheap, could have organized the place better instead of adding things like some sort of nesting troll. But it was just furniture, Paige reminded herself.

Lamps sat atop chairs, which rested on tables or chests of drawers. Antiques were crowded against flea market–quality and outright reproductions, in a mix of styles and eras that defied any sense of logic or order. Glass-fronted cabinets held costume jewelry jumbled together with smalls, little collectible items that ranged from the worthless to the priceless.

Pathways led off at random angles, meandering between the merchandise like trails in some twisted nightmare forest. She'd intended to stay by the door until Alec joined her, but through the open spaces in the nearest stacks, her eyes landed on a pair of folding tables leaning against a sideboard that looked to be seventeenth or eighteenth century.

Already thinking about where she could get a cloth long enough to cover both tables, she set off into the maze. And found herself wishing for bread crumbs to leave a trail. What had seemed to be a straight line twisted her around so quickly that when she tried to backtrack she only became more lost. And a little panicky.

Eyes wide, heart pounding, she stopped and looked around, but the stormy gray sky outside meant there was no telltale lightening of the gloom to lead her back to the doorway. She could hear the wind, though, battering at the front windows and whistling around the eaves. The building shuddered and groaned. Even the piles of furniture seemed to creak, and she could have sworn, when she looked up, that the aisles were closing in on her.

When she caught movement out of the corner of her eye she didn't think, just moved, jumping in the opposite direction, then running as fast as she could along the cramped aisle, half-bent with her hands over her head, as a horrendous crash sounded behind her, then another and another. She kept going, blindly following the pathways to the sound of breaking glass and splintering wood, until she turned a corner and screamed at the top of her lungs.

Josiah Meeker, arms waving like a spider whose web had been disturbed, scurried out in front of her. His undertaker's face was mottled red and stretched into a mask of rage. "My place, my things. What are you doing?"

"Nothing. I—"

"You'll pay for this," he spat into her face. "I'll take that pin you're wearing." His bony fingers reached for the gaudy brooch she'd found among her mother's jewelry and pinned to her coat. She'd forgotten it was still there.

Paige took a step back, covering the brooch with her hand. "This belonged to my mother."

His eyes sharpened. "I'll buy it, give you a good price."

"It's not for sale at any price."

"We'll see about that." He grabbed her, bony fingers curling around her wrist.

Paige pulled at her arm, jerked, twisted, and when she couldn't get free, kicked him in the shin instead. Meeker lifted his other arm—

Alec stepped between them. "No." It was all he said, just "no," but Meeker paled, all the color leaching out of him as he dropped his arm.

"Let her go."

Meeker stared at his hand for a second, as if he was surprised to see it still wrapped around her wrist. "Look what she did to my things," he whined, but he threw her arm with enough force to let her know he was still angry. "She has to pay."

"I had nothing to do with that," Paige said, and while she was grateful to Alec, she wasn't going to hide behind him. "It's your own fault for piling things up like some sort of demented pack rat."

"It doesn't mean you can just come in here and destroy half my merchandise."

"Actually, it does." Alec stepped in front of her again, and had Meeker backing off. "You should know you can't charge for incidental breakage on items you voluntarily put on display and made accessible to the public. It's your risk."

"Lawyers," Meeker sneered. "We were fine here before you came along spouting your legal nonsense."

"Well," Paige drawled, stepping up beside Alec. Again. "Since you don't want to bring in mainlander courts, we could ask Ma." She smiled slightly. "In keeping with island tradition."

"You're rich."

"Not the point," Alec said. "The damage is your responsibility, and I imagine you have insurance to cover it."

"I hope there's a liability clause in that policy," Paige said. "I could have been seriously hurt. Or killed. And it would be your fault."

"You're a fine one to be making accusations like that," he snapped. "You shouldn't act so high-and-mighty, now that everyone knows you're just a—"

"Careful," Alec growled. "You don't want to slander my client and open yourself up to a lawsuit."

But it wasn't a legal remedy Alec wanted, Paige realized. There was violence in his eyes, in the fists curled at his sides. Meeker saw it, too.

"I didn't mean anything," he said sullenly. "I'm just upset, that's all. The loss of merchandise, the cleanup..."

Alec took her arm and turned her toward the door— or at least she hoped so. It was away from Meeker, and that was all she wanted.

"Wait." Meeker scurried around in front of them. "What did you come in for? Aren't you going to buy anything?"

Alec started to turn back, but she put her hand over his. "Don't give him anything to sell to the press."

He met her eyes, and she saw such fury in his. "You pointed it out, Paige. You could have been seriously hurt."

"I wasn't, and if it comes down to it, I can certainly afford to pay for the breakage."

He glanced back, took in the destruction, the tangled, broken mess that could have crushed her, Paige realized with a shiver. Meeker was nowhere to be seen now.

"Alec?"

He looked down at her.

"Aren't you overreacting a little?"

It took a second, but she could see when the rage started to ease out of him. "I've been told I'm a little overprotective of my friends."

She smiled a little. "So you'd be on the verge of beating up Meeker if it had been Dex or Hold facing death by Chippendale?"

"They could hardly beat him up themselves if they were trapped under a pile of antiques."

"That's a point." One she didn't have to mull over when he took her hand and simply held on, even when they found the door and went outside.

"I'd bring the car around, but you'll probably get into trouble if I leave you alone again."

She laughed, let her head fall back and just laughed, the rest of the tension easing out of her. "I'd like to visit Ma, and then we'll go by the Horizon. AJ will loan us some tables and chairs."

"Why didn't we go there first?"

"His tables don't fold down. We can't haul them in the Jeep. But I'm sure Maggie can find a way. She's just going to fat-ass and watch football while Jessi and I do all the work to get dinner on the table, so we'll call it her donation to the day."

* * *

Ma lived on the landward end of Windfall Island, in a stone and wood house built two centuries before. Though the house had a small footprint, it rose two stories, topped by a widow's walk used not so much to watch for ships at sea, but to keep an eye on the mainland.

There'd been a time when mainlanders brought only trouble.

That time had passed early in the previous century, so the widow's walk served only as a reminder. Not that the Windfallers needed one. Caution, like old habits, died hard.

Ma took her sweet time opening the door, but then she was arthritic and cane-bound.

"'Bout time, girl," she said by way of greeting.

"I know, I practically froze solid waiting for you."

"Ha. Where's that lawyer you're shacked up with?"

"His name is Alec Barclay," Paige said equably as she stepped through the door Ma held open, "and we're not shacked up."

Ma gave the door a shove; it closed with a solid, air-tight thunk. "Is he sleeping at your place?"

"Yes, but not in my bed."

"'Course not—if he's sleeping, you're doing something wrong."

Paige had to laugh at that. "He's not visiting my bed, either. He needed a place to stay, I have extra rooms."

"Hmph." Ma stumped her way into the living room, dropping heavily in her easy chair. "Why isn't he here with you, paying his respects?"

"He had some errands to run." That was how he'd phrased it: errands. Paige hadn't pushed, in part because she didn't want to disrupt the tenuous peace they'd achieved. And she hadn't wanted to explain him to Ma. She should have known the gossip train had already made a stop. "Speculation running rampant?"

"Tongues will wag."

"True, but it's not what everyone thinks."

"I don't give a damn what everyone thinks, and I couldn't care less if you set the rest of the local yokels straight. I want an explanation."

"I can't," Paige said, "I'm sorry."

Ma set her jaw and narrowed her eyes. It would have worked—had worked—on her when she'd been a little girl, Paige allowed. God knew it still worked on most of the islanders, Ma's look of anger and unspoken retribution should she be lied to or thwarted. Now? Paige couldn't allow herself to be bullied into revealing secrets that would only put people, Ma included, in danger.

"It's nothing for you to worry about."

"Ha. I've been worrying about this island for near to sixty years. I know when something is afoot."

"Ma," she began. But what was she going to say to a woman who'd stepped in, offered her a shoulder, an ear, or a kick in the ass when she'd needed any of the above after her mother died?

"Exactly," Ma said, pointing a gnarled finger at her. "I taught you not to lie."

"At least not to you," Paige said with a smile. "I kind of lie for a living."

"Hmph. Seen your movies. Proud of them." Ma sent Paige another look, this one just as stern, but tempered with the kind of faith and fondness that brought tears to Paige's eyes.

"Wish you'd deal with this scandal head-on, but that's your business, and you'll set the record straight when you're ready. And don't sniffle, child. You got too much pride to trespass on a man who's said vows to another woman, and too much spine not to hold your head up when the ignorant and jealous are throwing barbs."

Paige plucked a tissue from a nearby holder and carefully dabbed her eyes before her makeup was ruined. "You and Jessi and Maggie," she said, "you're the only ones who believe me with no proof."

"True friends don't need proof."

"My mother—"

"Was a flighty, unhappy woman who always wanted more than she had," Ma said with more pity than unkindness. "She searched for happiness in all the wrong places."

Paige lifted her gaze, met Ma's. "Am I doing the same thing?"

"You don't need me to answer that question, girl."

Maybe not, but it would be so nice to have someone tell her she was on the right path, that she would find her own happiness, in time.

Instead, she had to live with the voices of doubt and judgment—those in her own head, and the one that currently lived in her spare room. Alec Barclay was making nice now. It didn't mean anything had really changed.

But, as Ma had pointed out, how she dealt with Alec and his opinion was up to her.

She rose, kissed Ma's wrinkled cheek. "Thanks, Ma. It's nice to know someone has that kind of faith in me."

"Well." Ma sniffled a little herself. Her sentimentality didn't last long. The woman was nothing if not persistent, just one of the qualities that made her so good at helming Windfall Island. "You ought to reciprocate."

"I wish I could."

"Hmph. I'm no idiot, child. If Dex Keegan is a lawyer, I'll get up and turn handsprings across this room." Which would be quite some feat, and not just because of Ma's age and arthritis. There was barely a square inch of floor space in the small living room that wasn't crammed with something, chairs, tables, bookstands, sofas, all neat as a pin. "And Hold Abbot," Ma continued, "what's he doing here?"

"Marrying Jessi."

"He wasn't marrying her when he snuck onto my island and holed up out at the airport for weeks at a time. Now, Alec Barclay..." She held up a hand; Paige was shocked to see the slight palsy. But then Ma was eighty years old, and Windfall wasn't an easy place to live, even without the stress of worrying about everyone and everything on the island. "There isn't a soul in the world who hasn't heard of the Barclays," Ma said. "I even met his grandfather once. Garrett Barclay'd be an old bastard now."

"Ma."

"Bastard is a compliment in his case, and don't you think otherwise. A man doesn't get his kind of power without stepping on more than toes along the way. And his grandson used to work for the Stanhopes. Two powerful families. There's speculation about why he up and quit, folks saying he was involved with the youngest girl, Rose, though there's no proof. It's being said they broke up and that's why he quit. Close your mouth, girl, I know how to Google. Could have seen that tape if I'd a mind to."

Paige sat back with a thump, but not because she'd given that tape even a passing thought. The shock she felt was all about Alec. Involved with Rose Stanhope? Rose would be perfect for him, same social standing, same blue blood, same healthy bank balance.

Yes, the two families would no doubt be ecstatic to see Alec and Rose marry.

And she certainly didn't care, Paige told herself. So why the surprise, and why the spike of...what? Jealousy? Now wouldn't that be foolish. Whatever was between her and Alec, today, tomorrow, next week, it certainly wouldn't last into forever.

"Paige."

Ma's impatient voice and cane-thumping snapped her back to the conversation, even if she couldn't quite get her stomach to settle again.

"What's going on with the bunch of you?"

"I'd love to tell you, Ma, but I have to talk to Maggie—"

"Maggie," Ma scoffed. "You just remind that girl that she's the one started me thinking. Asked me about my birth date not long ago. You tell her I'm old but not senile, and I know how to reason out when something's going on behind my back."

"You can tell them yourself if you come to Thanksgiving dinner at my house."

"Now, I might just do that."

But she wouldn't agree to it, kept avoiding the question whenever Paige tried to pin her down.

By the time Alec came to collect her, Paige was already bundled and waiting. Ma had nodded off in her chair; Paige kissed her papery cheek, received a sleepy mutter in return, and smiling, saw herself out.

* * *

The Horizon, like the rest of town, was pretty much deserted.

They'd found the restaurant door locked, so they'd gone in through the hotel lobby. Helen and AJ came out of the kitchen and met them at the door. Behind them, the empty dining room stood in darkness, but for the lights over the bar.

"You were closing for the night," Paige said, starting to rebutton the coat she'd half opened to the warm air.

"We've taken to closing a couple weeknights during the winter," AJ said. "Mondays and Thursdays were slow anyway."

"We'll go home. To your house, Paige," Alec amended, and braced himself when Helen's eyes lit.

But she surprised him by saying, "Nonsense. AJ was just about to whip us up some dinner. He can cook for four as easy as two."

"We'd be fools to pass up an offer like that," Paige said. "I'm as tired of my own cooking as you must be, Alec."

"Don't take the bait, son," AJ said.

Alec spread his hands. "When a man's a fool either way, it's best to keep his mouth shut."

"Now what fun would that be?" Helen hooked his arm and drew him in.

Alec glanced over his shoulder and saw Paige following. She shot him a deadpan look, one brow lifted, and had him laughing.

By the time Helen looked back at her, she was busy unbuttoning her coat, a study in innocence.

"I'm no fool, either," Helen felt a need to point out.

"Who said you were?"

Helen shot Paige another glance, this one complete with drawn eyebrows, before depositing Alec at the bar.

She left Paige to her own devices, scooting around to stand opposite Alec.

"What can I get you to drink?"

Alec gave his order, and without asking, Helen plunked a second beer in front of Paige, knowing full well she detested it.

Paige picked it up and took a long swig, never breaking eye contact with Helen. "You're right, Alec," Paige said when she set the beer down, "that really hit the spot."

Helen let out her braying laugh, swept the beer bottle off the bar, and plunked another down instead, one of the fizzy waters they'd have little cause to stock this time of year, Alec figured, but AJ would have on hand specifically for Paige. AJ was thoughtful like that.

Helen leaned an elbow on the bar in front of Alec and said conspiratorially, "This girl always was a ballsy thing."

Alec smiled slightly. "I'd call it stubborn and stand-offish."

"Well, stubborn and standoffish are a part of the ballsy package."

"This is really entertaining," Paige put in. "Can I play, too? Because I have some adjectives for the pair of you."

"Honey, I've been called everything you can imagine and some things you can't."

"Oh, I have a pretty good imagination. And I'll bet we both know a few...adjectives Society Boy here hasn't heard."

Helen laughed again, but Alec caught the considering look she sent him. "You're likely right, Paige," she said. "Blue blood and blue collar don't have a lot of common ground—including the kind of language we use."

"You'd be surprised," Alec said. Even he heard the heat in his tone.

Helen only laughed over it.

Paige said pointedly, "Don't like people making assumptions about you?"

"You could get to know me a little..." His eyes shifted and held hers long enough to see the edge of satisfaction.

"Eureka," she said softly, and when she smiled, Alec couldn't help but smile back.

He'd felt a lot of things with Paige, exasperation, irritation, discomfort, embarrassment, guilt, regret, and God knew there'd been heat. Now he felt warmth, and it surprised him to realize how much he liked it, and how much he wanted it to continue.

He'd been a judgmental ass, and Paige had every right to make him suffer for it. To never forgive him. Instead, she was giving him another chance. He felt like a starving man who'd been offered food and drink, like a dying man handed a cure.

"Why do I get the feeling I'm missing something," Helen said.

"Oh, it's nothing important," Paige replied, but the look she sent him made him feel like her friendship was everything.

AJ backed through the swinging door between the kitchen and bar, and when he turned Alec saw the tray in his bear-paw hands. He slipped his big body sideways through the pass-through, stopping by a table and sending the three of them an expectant look.

Alec jumped to his feet and started pulling down the chairs that had been upended on the table.

"No reason we can't eat like the civilized," AJ said. He unloaded steaming bowls of hearty chicken noodle soup and dinner-plate-sized grilled chicken sandwiches while Helen brought over cutlery, napkins, and salt and pepper shakers. "So what brings you out on a day like this?" AJ said as he passed out bowls and plates.

"Thanksgiving," Alec began.

"Did you change your mind about having dinner with us?"

"Ma's house won't hold everyone," Paige said. "Can you imagine what would happen if I uninvited Maggie?"

"Yes," Helen said, "and I'd pay to see it."

"That's because you wouldn't be on the receiving end of her verbal smackdown." Paige slipped a spoonful of soup between her lips and closed her eyes. A little half smile curved her mouth before she said, "This soup is amazing, AJ."

Alec took a bite, and had to agree, not only about the burst of flavors, but the feelings of home, of family, those flavors evoked—as the best food did. "It's as good as any five-star Boston restaurant."

"Make that the world," Paige said. "I did stop by Ma's today. She's as feisty as ever. I asked her to Thanksgiving dinner and she pretended to consider it, but I couldn't pin her down."

AJ slurped up some soup, took a huge bite of his sandwich, and talked around it. "She likes to stay at home these days."

"She was sleeping when I left her, just sort of dozed off in the middle of our conversation."

"She does that."

Paige set a hand on AJ's arm. "She's okay, right?"

"Sure, just getting up there in years."

"I took her lunch around midday and she was fine," Helen put in.

"She ought to turn over her island duties to someone else."

"To you, AJ."

"No, I'm not right for it. I think that's why she's held on this long. Waiting to find someone suited to the unique needs of Windfall Island." AJ chewed contemplatively for a moment. "Meeker's the only one who's shown any interest."

"Pissant" was Helen's opinion.

"Ma wouldn't put him on as dogcatcher," AJ said.

"Doesn't stop him from hoping. Meeker has been in here almost every night for dinner the last few weeks," Helen said. "Strikes me odd, seeing as he'd rather bed down with a skunk than rub elbows with the rest of the Windfallers. Lord it over us? Yes. Socialize? No."

"I don't want to rub elbows, or anything else, with him," Paige said. "I've met some seriously creepy men in my line of work, but Meeker is the absolute creepiest. Have you been in that store of his lately? The place is like some kind of...weird nest."

"I know," Helen said, "and Meeker pops out when you least expect it. Scared the stuffing out of me last time I was in there."

Both women shuddered.

"He's harmless," AJ said. "Folks like that usually are. All bark and no bite."

Maybe, Alec thought, but someone on the island might be in Clayton Stanhope's pocket, poised to cause trouble. Meeker was the obvious choice. Maybe too obvious.

"He may be harmless," Paige said, "but that place of his is a hazard." And she proceeded to recount the story of the chain reaction furniture disaster.

"It was bound to happen sooner or later," AJ said with a laugh, "the way he piles things up to the rafters in that place. One of those piles was off balance enough, all it would've taken was a gust of wind when you opened the door. Just you passing by did the rest."

"Should have known better than to go in there," Helen said.

Paige rubbed the wrist Meeker had grabbed, and Alec had to put down his sandwich before his hands fisted and gave him away. "It'll be awkward standing at the kitchen counter while we eat Thanksgiving dinner."

AJ waved that off. "There're some folding tables and chairs in the back."

"We were hoping you'd say that," Paige said.

And with the problem of seating solved, they passed the rest of the meal in pleasant small talk. It was the most relaxed Alec had been in days, so much so that by the time they headed home he'd begun to wonder how far he could push the peace that seemed to have settled between them.

The clouds that had socked in over the island for the past week sailed across the waning moon in tatters now, promising a clearer sky on the following day, and probably, Alec decided, a drop in temperature.

"The storm is finally blowing itself out," Paige said as they got out of the car at her house. "Look at all those stars. It's like someone sprinkled diamond dust across a length of blue velvet." She tipped up her face and sighed. "I don't get a sky like this in most of the places I find myself."

"It's not the sky that interests me." Another kind of storm had eased, he thought, one that had darkened his days more completely than nature had ever managed to do. He moved in, took her gorgeous and slightly parted mouth, and found himself surprised when she relaxed against him with a little sigh. When she kissed him back.

Heat moved through him, tempered with caution. "Tell me to stop," he said against her mouth.

"You kiss me like this and it's hard to think."

"Then don't."

She placed a hand, very lightly, on his cheek, eased back a whisper. "One of us has to."

"Why?" he breathed, sinking into her mouth again.

The hand slipped down to his chest; the distance she established was wider. "It can't go anywhere."

"Because you don't think I respect you."

She met his eyes. "That's for you to answer."

"Paige, I—" But damn it, he just wasn't sure. He turned to unlock the door and push it open.

She stepped through, turned to lock eyes with him. "You're angry."

He blew out a breath. "At myself mostly." For the moral streak that kept him from telling her what she wanted to hear. The rest was for Paige, for neither confirming nor denying. The lawyer in him understood her decision to guard her guilt or innocence; the man didn't like twisting in the wind.

"Mostly?"

"Mostly," he echoed with what he hoped was a smile and not a grimace. "I pushed you for more than you're ready to give." But with the need roaring through him, it was hard to be put off yet again. "Just one question. How long are you going to let that tape stand between us?"

Chapter Ten

It's not the tape standing between us." Paige slipped out of her coat and hung it on the stand beside the door. "I could go up those stairs with you, Alec. I could let you take me to bed. Then what would you think of me?"

She turned into the living room, heard Alec swear under his breath as she reached for one of the decanters that were usually locked away in deference to the children who might be among the summer renters. They could both use a drink, she thought, as she poured whiskey into a couple of short, heavy glasses.

"I'm not..." She stopped, drew in a breath, and let it out slowly while she settled her nerves and gathered her thoughts. "I didn't mean to lead you on, Alec. It's just..." She spread her hands, at a loss for words for the first time in her life. How could she tell him she no longer trusted her own feelings, her ability to resist the attraction she felt for him? She handed him one of the glasses, then moved away again, to a safe distance. "I'll apologize for losing control, for being thoughtless, and for kissing you back when I had no intention of letting it get to that point. What I'm not, what I won't be, is who you think I am, at the most basic level."

"And what is that?"

She shot him a glance, feeling a bit of the heat in his voice. "Don't play dumb, Counselor."

He started to answer. She held up a hand, then rubbed the heel of it between her breasts, barely giving the pain there a second thought.

She owed Alec an explanation now, if only because she needed him to understand why they couldn't ever take this...whatever it was between them any further.

"I campaigned hard for the part. Jackson Howard may be a total loss as a human being, but he's a hell of a director. It was no secret how badly I wanted that role." And when she'd been told she hadn't gotten it, she'd accepted the decision. Until she'd learned who was cast. "When I found out who got the role, well, I didn't handle it particularly well."

"You're used to getting what you want."

"That wasn't it." She smiled a little. "Or not all of it. I'm right for that part. The actress who got it is too green, too..." She spread her hands, swallowing back the accusations she wanted to let fly. Alec wasn't likely to repeat what she said to anyone who mattered in her world, but her mouth had already gotten her into enough trouble. "Well, I planted a word in ears that I knew were attached to indiscriminate mouths and that did the trick." And Jackson Howard, and his leading lady—on film and in bed—had gotten their revenge on her.

"You haven't said whether or not the tape is authentic," Alec said.

She tossed back the whiskey in her glass, wondering why she'd thought it would settle a stomach already churning. "You want to hear me deny it, Counselor, but you won't believe me."

"Yes, I will."

"Until the morning after?" She didn't regret the implication in those words, even when she saw anger leap into his dark eyes. "When you wake up in my bed, will you still believe my denial? A man like you doesn't live with that kind of self-delusion for long."

"A man like me?"

She heard the dangerous calmness in his voice, and only hoped honesty would serve them both best. "You're a man of quick judgment, and your judgments are rarely wrong, so you've learned to trust them. Only incontrovertible proof would change your mind, and I've none to give you.

"You're a man of high morals, of black and white, although I consider that a failing on your part. Life is never black and white. Trying to make it so will always lead to unhappiness. Still, you'd overlook right and wrong where I'm concerned, because you want me. At some point you'll begin to wonder about that tape again, no matter what claims of innocence I make.

"You'll hate yourself for being weak, and you'll hate me for tempting you."

"So you're a fortune-teller as well as a psychiatrist?"

"I'm neither. I'm a flawed, uneducated woman who's learned to read people very well because it's necessary to being a good actor. And I am a good actor, Alec, a very good one. I have the awards to prove it."

"You're doing a hell of a job now."

She absorbed that, let the pain run its course until she could talk around it. "I'm sorry you feel that way."

Alec scrubbed his hands back through his hair. "I didn't mean that. I can see I've hurt you."

She met his eyes, held them. "I'm responsible for my own feelings."

"Now who's lying to herself?"

"You see, that's one thing I learned very early in Hollywood. Actors who lie to themselves, or believe others' lies, are only headed for trouble. The Paige Walker you think you know is just my armor. She's what the world expects to see, she's who they understand. Underneath it, I'm just a simple woman with an extraordinary job."

And if his words cut her to the bone, she wouldn't let him see it. She'd kissed Alec back. She'd let him through her guard, and when she wanted to be sure they both understood why she wanted to take it slow, he'd hurt her. Now all she had left was her pride.

She set her glass down and walked out of the room, pausing to look back at him from the doorway. "I know exactly who I am, Alec, and I don't believe my own press. It's unfortunate that others do, but I can't control that. Now, if you don't mind, I'll say good night."

She managed to take the stairs at a deliberate pace when she wanted to run up them, to lock herself behind her bedroom door, to be alone.

Alec followed her.

She confronted him at the door. "I can leave or you can."

"That won't solve anything."

"There's no mystery to solve here, Alec. Except why you choose to see me the way you do. What are you afraid of? You have everything, a loving family, a fulfill-ing career, friends who'd do anything for you, and yet you're alone. Why is that?"

He opened his mouth, then apparently thought better of whatever he'd been about to say. What mattered to Paige was that he backed off, physically if not verbally.

"What are you looking for, Paige?"

She smiled sadly. "It's not a what, Alec, it's a who—and I'm almost positive he doesn't exist. Like you, I'm expecting entirely too much from a mere mortal."

She closed the door before she broke down. More than a brood now, she decided, she deserved a nice long, cleansing pity party and when she was out of tears, Alec Barclay would be nothing more than a houseguest again, just another man who couldn't separate the woman she was from the roles she played.

* * *

Alec stood on the other side of the door, listening to Paige cry. It wasn't a storm of sobbing, and he found himself to be mildly disappointed that nothing was heaved to shatter against a wall. She cried quietly for a couple of minutes, sniffled a time or two and blew her nose heroically.

Still, even as the room went silent he moved away. Coatless, he stalked out to the car, jammed himself into the driver's seat, and shot backward into the road, tearing off to the airport.

He felt like he would explode from the storm of emo-tions raging inside him. Frustration, regret, desire. Guilt.

I'm responsible for my own feelings. Paige's words

came back to him; so did the look on her face and the pain in her eyes. He dropped his head to the steering wheel and took a couple of cleansing breaths. And couldn't banish her face.

I'm responsible for my own feelings, she'd said, and so was he. And what he felt was small, small and pig-headed and foolish. Instead of confident, he felt stupidly rigid, instead of assured, uncertain, and where he'd always been supremely at peace with himself, he was questioning...everything. How he viewed the world, who he deemed untrustworthy, why he considered his own opinion so fucking absolute. Who the hell did he think he was? And what was he afraid of?

That last question snuck in, and while he wanted to blame Paige for planting that kind of doubt in him, he couldn't. Because she was right. And even if she hadn't called him an arrogant ass, what other description was there for a man who walked—no, strutted, he amended, there was no better word for the way he moved through the world like he owned it. Like he was perfect. He was anything but perfect.

"Where's Paige?" Hold asked when he opened the door.

"At home."

"What did you do wrong?" Jessi looked up at Hold. "He did something wrong." Then back at Alec. "Is Paige crying? I'll bet she's crying," she muttered as she disappeared into Maggie's house.

Alec let his chin drop to his chest. He already felt raw and sick enough without Jessi dumping another load of guilt on top of it.

"I could use a beer," he said to Hold, and the quiet

support of men who, even though they were both in love, were still just as confused by the moods and behavior of women as he was. "Where's Maggie?"

"Gone to bed, has an early flight."

"Be grateful I don't wake her up," Jessi said as she reappeared and made Alec swallow his relief.

She opened the closet in Maggie's front entryway, but Hold reached past her, which wasn't hard seeing as he had a good foot on her.

"Where are you off to?" Hold wanted to know as he helped her into her puffy yellow coat.

"I'm going to Paige's, of course. What is it with men that they're all morons where women are concerned? Is it ingrained from the womb or do they take you aside in middle school and teach you the best way to break a girl's heart?"

The look she shot him told Alec the question was aimed at him. Wisely, he chose not to answer.

"Jessi," Hold said quietly.

"What?" She swung around, locked eyes with her fiancé, then turned back to Alec. "I know, you can't help it."

"You're going to trash men," Dex said as he wandered out to join them, beer in hand.

"Bet your bottom dollar," Jessi said, "because that's what Paige will need first. And don't tell me you won't be doing the same—to women, I mean."

"Mostly, we just drink beer and scratch our heads," Hold said, "because we have no idea what went wrong."

"I know exactly what went wrong," Alec said. "What I don't know is how to fix it."

"You're on your own there, but my advice is just to

give her time right now. She won't want to see you yet."
Always kind, Jessi stepped up to Alec and gave him a
hug, then kissed Hold. "Keep an eye on Benji."

"He's sleeping."

"Then it won't be difficult, will it? At least not until
tomorrow morning."

"Tomorrow morning?"

"I'll spend the night at Paige's. She shouldn't be
alone."

"Aw, sugar."

Jessi kissed him again, a little longer, a little deeper.
"Have your male bonding time, and I'll see you tomorrow."

Hold sighed as she headed out the door.

"Do you think they'll be safe?" Alec asked.

"I wouldn't want to take them on," Hold said, "but by
all means, feel free to go back to Paige's and do your
manly duty."

Alec's response was to flop down on the sofa and
heave a sigh.

Dex handed him the beer he held. "I think you need
this more than I do."

"Keep 'em coming," Alec said, and took a long pull.

"I'm not your waitress."

"You have the legs for it," Alec insisted, pushing himself up to trail into the kitchen after the other two men.

Dex chuckled, but Hold still looked morose.

"Your legs aren't bad, either," Alec said.

"Don't try to cheer me up; this is not the way I intended to spend the night." He reached into a cupboard
and pulled out a bottle of bourbon. "But since I'm stuck
with the two of you, might as well make the best of it."

* * *

"I have to concentrate on this, Paige." Maggie held up her checklist, then went back to prepping her new plane.

The sun was just rising, a pale wash of light far off to the east in an otherwise clear sky. The plane still sat in the hangar, and although the huge door stood open, at least they were sheltered from the worst of the wind off the ocean. The last dregs of the storm were blowing inland, and the temperature had crept up above bone-chilling. Still, the wool slacks and fur-trimmed coat Paige wore didn't keep her very warm. She looked good, though, not in the least hurt or angry, and if fashion helped with the illusion, then it was worth a little pain.

And peace was worth losing a little sleep—not that she'd slept all that well. Still, she'd dragged herself out of bed before Jessi, made sure she was dressed and ready so she could hitch a ride to the airport. She already knew Jessi's opinion on Alec, had known it even before Jessi showed up at her house the night before. Now she wanted to hear from Maggie, if only she could get her attention for five minutes.

"If I want tomorrow off, I have to fly today," Maggie said, gritting her teeth over the words as she tightened a bolt.

"Sounds like that mainland charter company you paired up with is keeping you busy."

Maggie made a sound Paige chose to take as agreement. Because of the increase in her business, Maggie had been flying as often as FAA rules allowed. Paige knew she shouldn't distract her, but she needed to talk to someone, and Maggie would tell her straight, even if it hurt. Especially if it hurt, Paige thought with a half smile. Maggie believed in pulling the Band-Aid off fast.

"This is important, Maggie."

"So is this. If I don't get in the air in the next thirty minutes, I'm going to be late. People with the where-withal to charter a plane generally get cranky if they don't receive prompt service."

"Maybe I could go with you."

"And talk my ear off the whole way?" Maggie shook her head. "Talk to Jessi. She's better at this stuff anyway."

"Alec is in there, pretending to help Hold with the genealogy. And Jessi is probably busy doing paperwork."

Maggie stopped and looked over at her, amused. "Jessi is always doing paperwork. It baffles me, too, but it keeps Solomon Charters running so I don't interfere."

Paige smiled, relaxing a little. "You're right. Someone has to handle the business end, and Jessi is so good at it."

"Jessi is good at everything. And she knows it, so if you repeat that I'll hunt you down."

"If I do repeat it, I won't tell her it came from you."

"You do like working from a script."

Paige shrugged. Alec had accused her of the same thing, but coming from Maggie it didn't bother her. "Other people's words are usually so much better than my own."

"You don't believe that."

"Easier, then."

Maggie spared her a glance, and a smile. "There've been a few times in my life I could have used a writer."

Silence fell, but for the clink of tools—and Maggie's sigh when she accepted that Paige wasn't going away.

"So tell me what's wrong with you and Alec," she said, adding, when Paige didn't answer immediately, "you don't want to talk in front of him, so he must be the reason you're driving me to distraction."

Paige took a deep breath, then let it out slowly. "I'm not sure how to begin."

"Why don't you sleep with him and take it from there?"

"I meant begin talking."

"I know what you meant, Paige, but there's too much talking a lot of the time, too much thinking." Maggie consulted her checklist, then buried her face in the plane's engine compartment so that her voice, when she spoke again, was muffled. "You're attracted to him, he's attracted to you. You have the house all to yourselves, what's there to talk about?"

"How about when it ends?"

"You go your separate ways. Unless you're in love with him." Now Maggie turned, pinning Paige with a stare from her intense blue eyes. "Are you in love with him?"

"No." Paige huffed out a laugh, clamping her mouth shut when she heard the edge of hysteria in her own voice. "No."

"There you go, then. Have a fling. You've had them before, right?"

"Yes, of course, but..."

"But what?"

It was such a risk, she thought, and that saddened her. She'd left everything and everyone she knew behind at sixteen, moved all the way across the country with no contacts, no safety net. No thought to what would happen if she failed, or how much she had to lose.

What she'd lost, she realized, was that sixteen-year-old girl. The girl who'd been so courageous she'd captivated the world. She'd realized the dream, Paige thought, except for the part where she looked around to discover she had no one to share it with.

It might explain why she felt so drawn to Alec. Her dream hadn't been all about fame and fortune, she remembered. Maybe marriage and family had been secondary, but there had always been a Prince Charming in the picture she'd painted in her imagination.

Alec certainly fit the bill: attractive, personable when he wasn't digging at her, successful, everything she'd dreamed about as a girl stuck on a tiny island. The kind of prince who'd whisk her away to a big house in a bustling, important city, who'd lay the world at her feet and love her without reservation. Someone she could love in return and grow old with.

The happily ever after to go with her Hollywood star.

She whisked away the single tear on her cheek, told herself to cancel the pity party. She'd gotten the big house all by herself, even if she spent so little time there. The world would be at her feet again, once the scandal was only a fading memory. She had friends. Maggie and Jessi, Dex and Hold. And there was always Harvey Astor, agent, mentor, honorary brother, guide. She wasn't alone, even if she hadn't found someone to love.

"What's this?" Maggie demanded. "First talking, now crying?"

"The crying part of the program is already over."

"Good, because I really don't have time to mop up your tears." Maggie worked for a minute, then swore as she slammed her wrench down and turned around. "Is he still being an ass?"

"No—notwithstanding last night." And for that she'd already forgiven him. He'd been frustrated...keyed up. She'd been a little keyed up herself, and no matter what he believed, it hadn't been easy for her to turn away from him. So, yes, she understood his anger, and she'd already let it go.

His attempt to befriend her, now, that was so much more difficult to ignore. Because she wanted to be his friend. And more. She wanted everything, even if she knew it was wrong—he was wrong for her. Even knowing it would end painfully. "He's being nice to me."

"Let's kill him."

Paige laughed, and if it was a little watery, it still felt good.

"It's easier to keep them at arm's length when they're being jerks," Maggie said.

"Yes. Yes, it is."

"It's easier because you're afraid if you let go even a little, you'll let go all the way. And then how will you pull back?"

"Jessi isn't the only one who's good at this."

"I've had some experience lately."

"I know I'm afraid," Paige admitted. And since Maggie was the strongest person she knew, it gave Paige a slight, bolstering sense of pride to have faced that already. Still..."Fear isn't always bad, Mags."

"Unless you let it stand in the way of living your life. You came here to avoid—"

"I came here to hide," Paige corrected her. Alec was right about that. "I don't want to talk to the press right now. For very good reasons."

"Whatever those reasons, Paige, you're lonely."

"I've been lonely a long time, but here…it's different." It was a good kind of lonely, she realized, an opportunity to live in her own body rather than inhabit the skin imagined by some author or screenwriter, superimposed with the director's vision and her own interpretation of what the creator had intended. That got confusing, and while she'd been careful to carve out a few weeks to herself between every project, looking back now she could see she'd always been focused on her next role, studying, preparing. Those days she'd believed brought her back to herself were only transitions from one pretense to another. "However it came about, I needed this break."

"So take it. Stop thinking about yesterday and tomorrow. Live in today."

"You don't think Alec and I can be a long-term couple, either."

"Does my opinion matter to you?"

"Yes."

Maggie grinned, but she didn't get all mushy. Neither of them would be comfortable with that. "If my opinion matters enough for you to make decisions based on it, you're as big a fool as I used to believe you were."

"I think there's a compliment in there somewhere."

"What I'm trying to say is, you've always had a goal in sight, even when we were kids. Everything you did was in pursuit of that goal. I doubt that's changed over the last ten years."

"Fat lot of good it did me."

Maggie waved that off, nearly clocking Paige with the wrench in her hand. "This scandal will blow over. Pun intended."

"Ha. Ha."

"Your reputation will survive. Hell, some of those Hollywood idiots release sex tapes to *get* famous. You're already there. Anyone who's ever worked with you has to know you wouldn't sleep with anyone to get a part. Your pride wouldn't allow it. And when the truth comes out, the press will be falling all over themselves saying they knew it wasn't true."

"Yes, well, when they start falling I hope there are some convenient cliffs around."

"As for Alec, I'm sure he's sorry he was an ass."

"So he says."

"He probably means it."

"Because he wants to get in my...never mind."

"He's a guy, of course he wants to get in your never mind."

"At the moment he's pretending he wants to be my friend."

"So he's a guy with manners. Enough not to push you until you're ready."

"And you think I should be ready?"

Maggie sighed in frustration. "Why am I talking if you're not going to listen?"

"I'm listening." She'd heard every word Maggie had said. She just wasn't sure it changed anything.

Chapter Eleven

Paige drove this time, parking the Jeep on the shoulder of the road by the tall iron gates with their curved arch of letters spelling out *Cemetery*. The place needed no other name on an island barely ten square miles.

It was Thanksgiving morning. She'd gotten up early to put the turkey in the oven; then, with hours before dinner, she'd become restless. Truth was, she could see now that she'd been restless for a long time. Even before the scandal struck and she'd left Hollywood, she'd been... searching.

She poured herself into the characters she played, and once upon a time the few short weeks she'd taken for herself between roles had been enough to rejuvenate her. But that had been in the early years, when the energy and adoration of her fans and the occasional fling was enough to refill her emotional well.

She'd stopped enjoying the fame the first time one of her lovers sold the story of their romance to the tabloids, and she realized there were only two types of men who pursued her: those who wanted her for her money and those who craved fame.

Trust, once destroyed, wasn't easily mended, and the trust she'd lost was in herself—at least where her private life was concerned.

She chose her roles with the same confidence and certainty she always had, and if the critics trashed her performance, at least it was something she'd put out for public consumption.

The few times she'd met someone who'd tempted her, she'd found herself considering the risk, and inevitably deciding that the cons outweighed the pros. She knew it was fear holding her back, but she hadn't met the man she'd wanted enough to overcome that fear.

Alec Barclay might be that man. True, he'd judged her without having all the facts, and he hadn't made much of an effort to hide his opinion. But he'd been honest. She found honesty nearly irresistible. Add in the amazing body, the incredible face, and she could have been a goner. If not for the fear.

She made her way over the frozen ground with its slippery coating of ice and snow, placing one of the bouquets she'd brought at the foot of an ornately carved headstone. She spent a silent moment there, trying to find the right words. The trouble was, she'd lost her mother at too young an age, before they'd formed the kind of relationship where Paige would have gone to her for advice.

Instead, she moved past Suzie Walker's grave. "Hey, Daddy," she said as lay the small bouquet of fresh flowers she'd brought at the base of the simple headstone she'd commissioned for him.

The flowers wouldn't last long, but plastic wouldn't have done; Matt Morris had always preferred natural to man-made. He'd been a quiet man with a forgiving nature and an open heart, even after it had been broken.

He'd loved her mother, Paige knew, accepted what she was willing to give, and ignored the gossips who'd chosen to look down on him for turning a blind eye to her affairs. They'd labeled him pathetic, but Paige had seen how strong her father was, how unshakable in his love.

"Alec thinks I made that tape and released it for publicity," she said out loud. "I could tell him I didn't, but why would he believe me?" And what did it matter? "I'm not looking for marriage and happy ever after—even if Alec was the kind of man who could be happy with a wife who lived the kind of life I live.

"The important thing is that I don't believe he would betray me in the press. And I think we could be friends at the end of it all, Daddy." And sure, maybe she was justifying, but she'd already made up her mind.

Paige smiled because she could all but hear those words in her father's deep, comforting voice. She'd made her decisions and lived by them, and every single one of them had been made with her eyes wide open. Matt Morris would have been the first to tell her those truths. And guilt, he'd been known to say, was a waste of time. But she voiced hers anyway. "I'm sorry I wasn't here when you needed me," she said, and felt the weight of it lift off her heart, because she knew her father would wave it off with his wide, working man's hands. He'd have smiled his slow, beautiful smile, and told her he loved her no matter what.

"Thanks, Daddy." She touched her fingertips to her lips and sent a kiss flying heavenward.

She turned around and saw Alec waiting at the iron gates—out of earshot, thankfully.

"I can't protect you if I don't know where you are," he said, once she'd joined him. "I walked into the village."

"I'm sorry, I hadn't intended to be gone for so long," Paige said as he fell into step with her.

"You could have gotten me up."

Interesting choice of words, she thought as she turned, stopped in front of him, and kissed him. She tasted his surprise, let her lips curve a little before she deepened the kiss, let it go steamy, filled it with promise.

His hands were fisted in the back of her coat before she was done with him, but he let her go when she eased away. She didn't miss the confusion in his eyes when she continued walking to the Jeep.

"How did you know where to find me?"

And it made her smile when he had to shake himself a little before he could form words, or make his feet move. "I, uh, figured you needed something from the market."

"And Mr. McDonald told you I bought flowers for my father's grave."

"I get that you didn't want company," Alec said, "but you scared a year off my life, on top of leaving me with a kitchen full of baking ovens and simmering pots."

"One oven and one pot. And I left you a note clearly telling you not to touch anything."

"You're not supposed to go haring off without me."

"I guess we're neither one of us very good at taking orders."

"Yeah, well, I shut everything off before I left the house."

"What?" Paige stepped up her pace and nearly lost her footing. Alec took her arm, and warmth spread through her. "If you want to eat Thanksgiving dinner today, we'd better get home and turn them back on."

And best, she reminded herself as she casually put some distance between them, to keep some boundaries. Tempting as it might be to take his hand and let him steady her, it would be so much smarter to keep relying only on herself.

* * *

Hold pushed back from the table, groaning a little. "You should have stopped me after my second helping," he said to Jessi.

She leaned into him and rubbed his stomach. "I was afraid I'd get stabbed with your fork if I got between you and that turkey. Everything was wonderful, Paige."

"Damn fine job," Hold added, with the others echoing his sentiment.

Everyone else had finished fifteen minutes before. Benji had asked to be excused to watch television and had promptly fallen asleep on the sofa. Chewie, all four legs in the air, his little tummy bulging with tidbits sneaked to him under the table, was snuggled up next to the boy, fast asleep.

Before she did the same, Paige rose and began to clear. Jessi and Hold helped her. Once all the plates and glasses, platters and serving bowls, were ferried into the kitchen, Maggie and Dex broke down the tables borrowed from AJ and leaned them in the entryway. In deference to the still-sleeping boy and dog, they left the living room furniture as it was, still pushed into the far corner of the room.

"There's pie," Paige said. "Lemon meringue and cherry. Jessi made them."

"Sign me up," Hold said. "Some of each."

Jessi only sighed. "You know," she said to the room in general, "he insisted I make two of each and leave the extras at home."

"You're going to get fat," Dex observed.

Hold slipped his arm around Jessi and pulled her against him. "Trust me, I get enough exercise."

"*Hold*." Cheeks bright red, Jessi shoved away from him.

Laughing, he took the pie Paige handed him and began eating as if he hadn't seen food in a month.

Jessi rolled her eyes. "And they say *women* let themselves go after they get engaged."

"You know that gravy is going to be a solid instead of a liquid by tomorrow," Paige told Maggie, watching as she poured the leftover gravy into a plastic container.

"And your point would be?" Maggie said.

Paige just sighed and continued to strip down the turkey and portion it into Ziploc bags.

"Do you want some of these rolls?" Jessi asked Maggie.

"Are you kidding? I'm going to live on these leftovers as long as humanly possible."

"You can take my share," Paige offered.

"Then what will I eat tomorrow?" Alec said. He'd barely spoken during dinner, so just hearing his voice was enough to catch Paige's attention.

She looked over at him, their gazes collided, and something she saw in his eyes made her wonder. "You're awfully quiet," she said to him.

"There's news. Hold heard from the lab."

"I got the call yesterday," Hold said around a mouthful of pie. "I thought, since it concerned all of us—Paige mostly, but all of us—I'd report it today when we were all together. I told Alec they called, but not what they said."

Paige looked up from the sink, where she was washing turkey off her hands. "And?"

"They lost the sample."

There was a beat of silence, then Alec spoke. "What did they say, exactly?"

Hold put his empty plate down and turned to Alec. "That they couldn't locate the anonymous sample."

"As simple as that?"

"I don't think we should read anything into it," Dex said. "We've never had cause to question the integrity of the lab. If someone working there was being bribed, they'd just say Paige wasn't a match, like Maggie and Jessi."

"Maybe it's because I'm the last possibility," Paige said.

"Go on," Dex said.

"Well," she began, working it out as she spoke, "we have evidence that Eugenia made it to Windfall. The letters from the maid who took her from the nursery that night. Emmett Finley's firsthand account of finding a baby in the boat his father and the other men took to the *Perdition* to buy illegal liquor, and the blanket Jessi found in her attic."

"But we haven't found any proof that she survived to have children," Hold put in.

"Are you sure?" Paige waited until she had everyone's attention. "What if Maggie or Jessi is a descendant, and someone at the lab was paid to report otherwise?" *What if I am?* "Are you really going to give up the search if the report comes back and rules me out as well? Dex?"

"You're asking me because you already know the answer."

"I don't think any of us would give up," Maggie said, "but yeah, this has been your quest from the start, Dex."

"And Paige is right, even if she's not a match, I'd always have to wonder."

"So where do we go from here?" Paige asked the question that had to be on each of their minds.

"Investigate the lab," Maggie answered, her eyes still on the man she loved. She had to know it would take him away from her, at least for a time, but she didn't hesitate.

Neither did Dex, although his fingers linked with hers. "I'll be talking to a friend in Boston who's in the business," he said. "He'll do most of the legwork. For the rest, I'll be commuting, Maggie. If Paige is right, it puts all three of you back in play."

"Although," Alec said, "I think Maggie and Jessi are pretty safe as long as Clayton doesn't think we're taking a look at the lab and its employees."

"Which means we have to resubmit your sample, Paige," Dex said.

And although Paige had known that was coming, she closed her eyes for a second and simply accepted that there'd be more waiting and uncertainty, more worry.

More time with Alec.

Every cloud had a silver lining.

She took a bite of lemon meringue pie, let the tart, sweet combination of flavors explode on her tongue. "My God, Jessi, this is fabulous. Better than anything I've had in the best five-star restaurants in the world. You really should write a cookbook."

"Like I have time. But I'll let AJ know. It's his recipe, which he says came from Ma."

"Oh, that reminds me," Paige said. "I stopped in to see Ma the other day. It slipped my mind with all the holiday preparation, we had a very interesting conversation. She mentioned you specifically, Maggie."

"Well, she likes me."

"Even though you're keeping secrets from her. Not very subtle, asking her when she was born."

"Subtlety is not one of Maggie's charms," Dex said.

"It's Ma," Maggie said simply. "She's the oldest woman on the island, so we needed to rule her out. There was no way to get that information out of her without making her wonder what I wanted it for. She was curious, but she never really pushed me for a reason."

"That was before Hold and Alec came to Windfall."

"Run us through your conversation with her," Dex said.

Paige shrugged. "There wasn't much more than that." She flashed Alec a look, and knew from his faint smile that he'd already deduced they'd discussed him, and that she wasn't going into detail there. "Ma knows something is going on," she said instead. She closed her eyes, and recited that part of the conversation, almost word for word.

"That's it?" Dex asked her.

"Dialogue is my business. It's not a hundred percent verbatim, but it's pretty close."

"Ma doesn't believe I'm a lawyer," Dex said, boiling Paige's report down to the high points. "She's wondering why Hold, and now Alec, came to Windfall, and why Alec quit working for the Stanhopes. And she doesn't buy that you and Rose were secretly engaged and had a falling out, Alec."

"And she's been Googling," Paige reminded them. "She already connected the Stanhope name with Alec."

"And she's not the only one on this island with access to the Internet," Maggie added grimly.

"I shouldn't be here," Alec said.

"Too late now," Maggie observed, "and probably lucky for us that you're shacked up with Paige."

Dex held up a hand. "What Maggie is implying so elegantly, is that if the rest of the Windfallers think the pair of you are having an affair, it can only be good for us."

"We'll need to talk to Ma," Maggie said. "All of us. I'm flying every day this week, until the annual holiday bash, but I kept the day after clear, for obvious reasons."

"So we'll talk to her then," Hold said. Paige braced herself when he turned to her. "I brought along a DNA kit."

"What's the rush?"

"I can drop it off tomorrow, since I'm taking Alec to Boston," Maggie said, her eyes shifting from Paige's shocked face to Alec's closed one. "And you didn't know," she finished. "Damn it, Alec, you were supposed to tell her."

Paige lifted her gaze to Alec's, refusing to acknowledge the apology she saw in his eyes. Go or stay, it was his business. That didn't mean she ignored the little sting she felt over not being told.

"I'll only be gone for the day—it's my mother's birthday," he said.

"It's fine," she said, and meant it. She had no hold on Alec Barclay, and he had no responsibility to her. They'd been thrown together by circumstance, nothing more. "So, who's babysitting me while Alec is gone?"

"That would be me," Jessi said, "only instead of babysitting I'm going to call it *Paige and Jessi do something fun*. I'll forward Solomon Charters' phones to my cell, and we can get our nails done or something."

"I could use a manicure," Paige said, studying her nails, the worse for all the cooking and cleaning she'd been doing. She turned to Dex. "What's the news from Rose?"

"Nothing," he said. "According to George, Rose says Clayton's keeping to himself."

"Maybe he's taking the holidays off," Maggie quipped. But her eyes were shadowed.

Paige could understand why. Dex was pacing, clearly restless. There wasn't much for him to do now. They knew who the mastermind was, but Clayton Stanhope hadn't made a move since the charity ball in Boston, where Jessi had been kidnapped and nearly killed. Jessi's ex-fiancé was still in a coma, so he wasn't talking, and Mort, well, he'd put himself beyond questions.

All they could do was wait.

"I've been checking on the villagers, quietly," Dex

said. "Nothing. No intriguing gossip, no odd visits to the mainland. Business as usual."

Which meant, Paige interpreted, that everyone was hibernating for the winter. It was typical for Windfallers to keep to themselves when the temperatures dipped below zero and the weather had two moods: bad and worse. "Most everyone will make an appearance at the holiday party next weekend," she said.

Dex stopped, blew out a breath. "No offense, but I don't understand why Clayton hasn't made a move on you, Paige."

"He must not have a hit man on the island yet," Hold said. "If he'd hired someone to do his dirty work, he'd know Paige is here and something would have happened."

"Is it okay with the pair of you if I'm glad he hasn't heard my name in connection with Eugenia yet?"

"For my money, it would be better if he'd made an attempt," Maggie said. "The longer we sit around waiting, the more relaxed we're going to get. Sooner or later our guard drops and boom"—Maggie sliced a hand across her neck—"game over."

Paige lifted a hand to her own throat.

Then Maggie, damn her, turned to Alec and said, "Be at the airport at seven if you want to get an early start."

Paige held Alec's gaze for a few humming seconds before she turned away. "Anyone want coffee? Tea?"

She could have saved her breath. Hold and Jessi already wore their coats, and were busy trying to rouse Benji enough to get him into his. Dex, too, had his coat on, and was holding Maggie's.

"Have a good flight tomorrow," she said to Maggie, moving past her and back into the kitchen.

They were all clearing the field of battle, Paige thought, but she'd be damned if she gave Alec the fight he expected.

Chapter Twelve

Paige packed leftovers into bags and saw the others off, returning to the kitchen to put the pies away and finish the little bit of cleanup left.

"You should go to bed," Alec said from behind her. "You must be exhausted."

"I am." But it was a good kind of exhaustion, cooking for friends, talking and laughing with people she trusted not to betray her. She couldn't remember when she'd been able to relax so completely.

"I'm going early because I have a lot to do," Alec said, "and I don't want to be gone overnight."

"Okay."

"Paige—"

She held up a hand. "There's no need for you to explain yourself, Alec. You have no obligation to me."

"I said I'd protect you."

"If you would all just stop hovering..." She hissed out a breath, not caring if he mocked her for it. "I'm not upset you're going home. You don't need to race through your business in one day. Take all the time you need."

"So if I wanted to spend two days in Boston?"

"Spend two days."

"How about the entire weekend?"

She stretched plastic wrap over the cherry pie, grateful her hands weren't trembling. "Whatever."

"Or if I decided not to come back?"

She put the coffee filters into the cupboard, closing the door a little harder than she'd intended. "Like I said, I'm not your responsibility."

"I'd like you to be more than a responsibility."

Paige went still. "Why?" she asked as she turned to face him. She needed to see his face, and what she saw gave her hope.

"I don't know." He gave her a half smile.

The confusion in his eyes, the bafflement, told her he felt more than desire for her. Even if he couldn't put it into words.

"Can we just agree there's more than heat between us?"

Hope swelled inside her. He couldn't have chosen more perfect words if he'd read her mind. She wasn't ready to explore what she felt for Alec, either. Or maybe she was afraid to put a name to her feelings. Either way, she'd simply live in the moment.

His hands settled on her shoulders. She closed her eyes and let herself float on the lovely warmth that spread through her. Warmth built into heat as she turned, and she stopped denying the attraction she'd felt for Alec since the moment they'd met. It felt wonderful to be held, just held, and it took so little effort to let herself believe the arms around her belonged to someone who truly cared.

"Paige," he began.

She opened her eyes and met his, the gray darkened by desire. He eased back, but she said, "People talk too much."

He opened his mouth again. She stopped him by slipping her arms around him, rising to her toes, and nipping his earlobe, then soothing it with her tongue.

His hands slid into her hair, sending pins flying so the messy updo fell. The feel of her own hair, cool against her heated skin, was almost unbearably erotic.

She kissed him, laid her body against his, and took the kiss to a place where the taste of him made her burn, where the beat of her own blood drove her to the edge. It had been a while since she'd indulged this particular appetite, she thought breathlessly, but she'd never risen so fast, wanted so desperately.

She breathed his name, just his name, and felt his hands tighten on her, felt his body, already rock hard, quiver against hers, like a stallion ready to mate.

And still he held back, and the leashed strength beneath her hands made the need inside her rise another impossible notch. She wanted his hands on her, wanted to feel his skin hot against hers, didn't realize she was begging until he growled, "Upstairs."

"Here," she groaned. "Now." And stumbled when she tried to walk on legs gone to jelly.

Alec swept her up and by the time he'd carried her the few short steps to the living room sofa, she'd found her strength again. Still, her hands shook so much she fumbled with the buttons of his shirt. In the end, he undid them himself, then removed her clothes, slowly, until she wore only her bra and panties.

He skimmed his fingers over each inch of skin uncovered, although she noticed he wasn't wasting any time now. He slipped her bra strap down and ran his mouth from her neck to her shoulder, not touching her but so close she could feel the heat of his skin and feel the wash of his breath.

She slipped her hands into his hair, tried to draw his mouth to hers, but he said, "I've been imagining this for so long."

Paige drew back a little, trying to put a finger on why that comment bothered her.

Alec pulled her close again. "Just...let me."

So she let him, her head dropping back as her drew her bra away, as he took her breast into his mouth, as need flared into desperation. He scraped his teeth over her nipple, ever so lightly, before his tongue laved and his mouth tugged. She felt the pull all the way to her center, was going over the edge even before his fingers slipped beneath the elastic and speared into her.

She exploded, a rush of pleasure verging on pain, that stayed locked inside her for a few glorious seconds, tightening, intensifying, before it pulsed into waves that spread, built, spread, weaker and weaker until she felt only an ache the best orgasms leave behind.

And a little awkward to be standing all but naked in her living room while Alec watched her through slitted eyes.

He didn't allow her the time to work her way up to embarrassment. He kissed her, his hands almost bruising as he hauled her against him. His mouth demanded, took. She tasted his desire, his frustration, and braced herself.

He wasn't gentle. She didn't want him to be. She relished the roughness of his hands moving over her. Pleasure grew, spearing through her like an arrow and stealing her strength so that she sank to the sofa.

Alec was there, tearing her panties away, kneeling between her thighs and driving into her with one fast, deep thrust that tore a cry from her. He lifted her knees and began to move, dropped his mouth to her breast and suckled. Left her nothing to do but meet him, thrust for thrust, as her hands raced over his body. She felt the bunch and slide of muscles under his heated skin as he took her, slipped her hands around to cup his backside and pull him tighter each time their bodies met. And cried out when the second orgasm ripped through her.

Alec locked himself deep inside her, so deep she felt the pulsing of his body as a counterpoint to her own. When he collapsed on top of her with a breathless groan, when she felt his heart racing and heard him gasping for breath, she smiled in utter satisfaction.

* * *

A half hour later, Paige came back into the living room wearing a silk robe in deep blue that matched her eyes. She'd taken the time to comb her hair and touch up her lipstick, but that wasn't the reason she'd gone upstairs, Alec knew.

He'd been shattered by the strength of what had happened between them, at the overpowering way he'd wanted her, and the almost brutal way he'd taken what he'd wanted.

It had caught her by surprise, too. He could see it in her eyes, though they didn't quite meet his, and read it in her body, the hesitation in her step.

He was determined not to let it get awkward between them. It was why he'd pulled on his pants and shirt, but left both unbuttoned. He'd fought hard for even this level of intimacy; he wouldn't give up ground now.

Still, there were issues yet to be addressed before they could move forward.

"I think I owe you an explanation," he said, "and an apology."

"If you're about to tell me you're sorry for being a little rough"—her eyes lifted, met his almost in challenge—"I'll admit I enjoyed it."

Alec grinned, he couldn't help himself, especially when she smiled back. He wanted to drop a kiss on those beautiful curved lips, as lovers might do. If felt too intimate, though, which was an odd interpretation, considering what they'd just done to each other. But they hadn't reached a place where they could share such thoughtlessly affectionate gestures.

"I'm sorry I'm a little...out of practice," Paige said.

"Could have fooled me."

She gave him a faint smile. "I wasn't fishing for compliments, Alec. It's been a while since..." Her eyes shifted to the sofa, and when they met his, he saw the vulnerability she didn't trouble to hide. "I know it's not my reputation, but the rumors are rarely true."

He acknowledged her point with a nod. It was the closest she'd come to a defense. Not that she owed him one. "I'll hold the apology then, and say thank you instead."

She smiled, this time warmly. "And the explanation?"

"Why don't we sit down?"

"Maybe you should pour me a glass of that wine first."

Alec looked down, surprised to find he was holding a bottle of wine. He'd completely forgotten taking it out of the refrigerator while she was upstairs, and now it didn't seem quite the right thing. "I think I'll have a whiskey."

"Make it two."

He returned the wine to the refrigerator, then went straight to a glass-fronted cabinet in the living room. "My grandfather is Garrett Barclay. Have you heard of him?"

"Who hasn't?" Paige turned on a lamp, took the glass he handed her, and curled her feet under her as she settled into a generous wingback chair nearby.

Not too close, he noticed, and wondered if he should take it as a compliment—that she didn't trust herself enough to sit next to him. Either way, he had no choice but to respect the distance she put between them.

"So," she said, taking a careful sip from her glass, "tell me about your grandfather."

Alec smiled a little. "He's one of a kind, opinionated, confident to the point of pigheaded, overbearing."

"You love him."

"He raised me," Alec said simply. "My father left before I was born."

"I'm sorry," Paige said. "I can't imagine growing up without my dad."

"I'm fairly certain mine did me a favor." Alec sat forward, seeing he'd shocked her. "That's what I'm getting at Paige. My grandfather is a man of uncompromising opinions. He makes up his mind fast, and once it's made up, he doesn't change it."

"And he taught you to do the same."

Alec smiled faintly. "By example, if nothing else. Paige, when I made that comment about you…It was only…I didn't really know you. And when I met you…" He let it go with a sigh. "I have no excuse for treating you the way I did, Paige."

"Except you're human."

He lifted his head, locked eyes with her.

"Millions of people around the world reacted the same way, Alec."

And wasn't that a lowering thought? "Which brings me to the second part of the evening's entertainment. I'm sorry."

"You already apologized days ago. Before you threatened me with your friendship."

He smiled over the word *threat*, although, in hindsight, telling her he wanted to be friends had been another skirmish in their war of wills. "I'm still sorry."

"So am I," she said, surprising him. "I would have liked to know how we'd get on with a different first meeting." She tossed the whiskey back, grimaced a little. "I guess we'll never know."

"I hope you can forgive me." Even if it was impossible to ask her to forget.

"I already forgave you. I don't believe in grudges, they only hurt the person silly enough to harbor them." She put her glass down on the table next to her chair and got to her feet.

Alec caught her hand. "Paige...I just want you to know I don't believe you made that tape."

Her hand tightened on his, just for a second, and he could see he'd taken her completely off guard.

"Being here, getting to know you—the real you. You'd never use your body to get a part. And then there's logic. After going to so much trouble to create publicity, why would you run away from it?"

"Why, Counselor, I'm surprised."

He grinned. "I'm usually faster on the uptake."

"But?"

"I don't understand how you can let someone control you like this," he said. "The best way to handle it is to either deny it or admit it and get it behind you."

"Oh, so now you're a publicist?"

"Any lawyer worth his retainer is aware of the impact public opinion can have."

"And knows how to manipulate it?"

"This isn't about spinning a story, Paige, it's about the truth."

"You think I'm not angry because I don't throw tantrums for the whole world to see?" She crossed her arms, turned away.

"Why don't you give an interview, tell them it's not you?"

She whirled back to face him. "A denial will only make me look more guilty. No, I'll handle this when the time is right for me, not you or anyone else."

It was exactly what he'd have asked any client who came to him for help. *Are you ready to fight?* The odds of victory were low if the heart wasn't in the fight. He understood that very well.

It didn't mean her attitude didn't frustrate him. "I don't want to control your destiny, Paige, or make you do something you're not ready to do."

A smile bloomed slowly across her face, lifting the shadows from her eyes. She bent, kissed him lightly on the lips, and said, simply, "Thank you, that means a lot."

"And?"

"I have a lot to think about." She straightened, but made no attempt to pull free of his hand still curled loosely around her wrist. "You mentioned courage, Alec. It takes courage for a man, any man, to admit he was wrong. At least in my experience."

He slipped his hand from her wrist, twined his fingers with hers. "I'd like to think I'm not just any man."

"No, you're not just any man." She smiled softly, squeezed his hand once. "It's been a long day and I'm exhausted. Coming?"

"Are you sure?"

"I just had sex with you on the living room sofa."

"Yeah, I'm thinking of having it bronzed."

Chapter Thirteen

They made love again, every bit as urgently as the first time, all heat and hunger, hearts pounding, bodies straining toward a completion that, for Paige, was more than physical.

As their pulses calmed and their bodies cooled, Alec pulled the covers over them and gathered her against him.

Paige indulged herself with the feel of his arms around her, his body curved so perfectly to hers, his breath brushing the side of her face as he fell asleep.

No, she wasn't ready to put a name to what she felt, she thought hazily as the long hours of cooking and the emotional upheaval of the last few days finally caught up to her, but her last thought as she drifted off to sleep was that she might be in trouble.

She awoke, floating warm and safe, in a lovely fantasy world, where there was no stress or hurt or conflict. Just the feel of a man's hands on her body, a man's mouth at her breast.

Alec.

Reality washed over her even as he whispered her name against her lips. As he rose over her and slipped inside her. As he began to move. There was none of the desperation of the first time, or the urgency of the other times they'd come together during the night. This was quiet sighs, soft caresses, deep, drugging kisses. It was a slow, lovely, gentle rise to peak that was all the more shattering with her defenses down.

Even with her body humming, all she wanted to do was feel Alec spooned around her like they'd been during the night. Instead, he eased out of bed, tucking her in and dropping a light kiss on her lips.

She tried to stay awake, to savor the wonder of a man in her bed, of feeling cherished. Alec would never understand how much he had given her in one night. But even as she heard the shower, she was drifting back to sleep.

When she woke later it was to the kind of hazy light that told her it was snowing. It had been a long time since she'd lounged in bed like this, but it was irresistible to burrow under the covers again, to be cozy and warm while fat white flakes fell lazily past the windowpane.

To revel.

She could tell herself it had been a long time between men, but sex had never been like this before, not for her anyway. She'd lost herself completely, become...not a part of Alec, but of the whole they'd made together. And after, well, how could she resist spending the night in his arms?

She threw the covers back, energized suddenly, and too happy to waste the morning in bed. She wanted to walk in the snow, feel the soft, cool caress of the flakes brushing her face. She showered, smiling as each ache and pain reminded her of Alec. When she came downstairs and smelled coffee, she remembered there were perks to living with someone. Not that she and Alec were living together—

"It's about time you surfaced."

—or that he'd made her coffee.

She turned to the living room and saw Jessi sitting on the couch, paging through a script.

"Why didn't you wake me?"

"Alec said to let you sleep. I got the impression there wasn't much of that going on last night."

"I got plenty of sleep." But she could feel the smug expression on her face, which only made her smile wider.

"I want details."

Paige's gaze shifted to the couch where Jessi sat.

"Really?" Jessi said. "Couldn't wait for the bedroom? Nice." But she got up and moved to the wingback chair. "I still want details."

Paige found she didn't want to talk about it. "I'll just say it was lovely, and it felt wonderful to wake with a man wrapped around me." And to be loved before she was quite awake. "You have a man of your own, you don't need to know about my love life."

"I really do, but I understand it's private." Even if the disappointment on her face said otherwise.

"It's so hard to keep anything private, Jess. I know you won't talk about it—"

"No, I get it. There are some things you just want to have for your own. Important memories. Someday you and Alec can look back—"

"That's not what this is about." Although coffee would only make her pitching stomach even more upset, Paige opened the cupboard and took down a mug. "I'm not thinking about the future, or having these memories as a milestone in our relationship. I only want to enjoy it for a little while."

Jessi nodded and smiled. "Well, you certainly look rested for the first time since you came back."

"Oh, better. I'm all...loose and limber." And happy. She'd been satisfied with her life and her work before, but she hadn't felt this buoyant since her early days in Hollywood, when every role she landed had felt like a major accomplishment.

As she'd told Jessi, she wouldn't overthink or build up expectations. She'd just enjoy Alec, and not shadow their time together with what *if*s and *what then*s. "Let's go for a walk."

"What?" Jessi looked toward the wide window overlooking Secret Harbor. Snow still fell lazily, in big, white clumps with the temperature hovering around the freezing point. "In this?"

"Why not?"

"Because it's cold."

"Not that cold. The snow is melting as soon as it hits the ground."

"Yeah, well, that snow is pretty from in here, but out there?" She shook her head. "Not so much."

Paige laughed. She put down her empty mug, descended the two steps from the kitchen to the living room, and took Jessi by the hand, tugging her to her feet. "I don't feel alive until I've had a walk. And maybe I'll let you in on a detail or two of my last twelve hours."

"You have no intention of telling me anything good."

"Alec's hands are magic, and he does this one thing—" She broke off, shuddered delicately. "Maybe a nice, invigorating walk will help me find the words."

"Now, that's just mean."

Paige grinned. "We won't stay out long, Jess, and then we'll go and get our nails done."

* * *

"And she kept saying, only a little farther, Jessi, and then she'd walk for another mile," Jessi said, extracting every bit of revenge—and enjoyment—out of the retelling.

As promised, Paige had accompanied Jessi to the Clipper Snip, Windfall Island's one and only salon. The small space had changed little since Paige had left the island. It was still owned by Sandy Rogers, who'd been Jessi's mother's best friend. It was still a small, rather dim and cramped space, ripe with the aromas of hairspray, perm solution, and cigarette smoke.

Paige had been pampered at the best spas in the world, been made up by the foremost artists in the business, but the Clipper Snip held a special place in her heart. It had been here she'd learned the magic that could be found in a few swipes of mascara and some cleverly applied eye color. She'd haunted the place with Jessi, observing the mannerisms and mysteries of women and making them her own.

Today it was filled with women, not all of them indulging in a haircut or mani-pedi. Many of them wandered in to keep cabin fever at bay, and to hear the latest gossip. Along with its other functions, the Clipper

Snip was Windfall Island's equivalent of a newsletter—or maybe the *National Enquirer*.

"I swear she would have walked around the entire island if I hadn't turned back," Jessi was saying.

Paige laughed. "I thought we could walk around the entire island after lunch."

"I plan on eating a whole lot of leftover turkey and napping on the couch."

"I'd be happy to walk with you," Shelley Meeker put in. Josiah Meeker's only child, Shelley was pretty and petite, with as smarmy a personality as her father. The Meekers believed they were a cut above every other Windfaller—except, apparently, the one who'd gone away and made herself rich and famous.

"Stop sucking up to the movie star, Shelley," Sandy said to her.

Shelley had been doing just that from the moment she'd arrived—when she wasn't asking pointed questions about what Paige found to do on Windfall Island after the excitement of Hollywood.

Paige had done a pretty good job of ignoring her, but clearly hers weren't the only nerves Shelley had stretched to the breaking point.

"It's not a crime to be curious," Shelley said sullenly. "I only want to know what it's like to be a world-famous movie star, and rub elbows with all those rich, famous people I read about in the magazines."

"I hope you took notes," Jessi observed sarcastically. "You've asked Paige enough questions to fill a library."

"She's probably going to sell a story to the tabloids," Sandy said.

"I'm just interested," Shelley muttered. "There's nothing to do around here."

"She's got a point," Maisie Cutshaw put in. "If I had movie star money, I'd be in Cannes." Maisie pronounced the name of the city like something you'd find on a grocery store shelf with mushy, overcooked green beans inside. "And I'd be wrapped around George Clooney. How about it Paige, ever been wrapped around George Clooney?"

Paige looked over at Maisie and smiled. "I'm saving it for my memoirs."

"That's a yes if I ever heard one," Maisie hooted. She was tall and apple-shaped, with a plain face that was always wreathed in a smile. She was the kind of woman who became a friend instantly, to tourist and Windfaller alike. No one could resist her infectious happiness for long.

She owned a gift shop she opened only for the tourist season. The rest of the time she did odd jobs to make ends meet, including managing rental properties like Paige's house.

"That's a *none of our business*," Shelley said sourly.

Jessi looked up from her manicure. "Suppose you tell us all your private business, Shelley."

"Yeah," Maisie added, "who have you slept with lately?"

Shelley's face went an interesting shade of red. She was fuming, but she was silent.

"Exactly," Jessi said. "It's not so much fun when it's your life people are poking their noses into."

"I'd be happy to share," Maisie said. "Feel free to sleep through the story. You won't miss anything."

"I hear Alec Barclay is staying at your house, Paige," Shelley ventured, undeterred.

"He is," Paige said shortly.

"Now if I remember correctly," Maisie said, "there isn't a whole lot of sleeping space in that house, even after the renovation."

And since Maisie was her caretaker, Paige thought, she'd know. She caught Jessi frowning at her, and simply looked away.

"There are three bedrooms," Jessi pointed out when Paige stayed mum.

Maisie snorted. "There's a tiny room with a single bed downstairs, and the second bedroom upstairs is little more than a closet."

"Don't forget the sofa in the living room," Paige said, ignoring the urge to wink when Jessi gaped at her.

Maisie snorted again. "You wouldn't make that prime hunk of man sleep on the sofa."

"Alec is an adult; I don't make him do anything."

"Well," Shelley huffed, "if you don't care where he sleeps, maybe I should go over there and give him some other options."

"Oh, he went to Boston with Maggie this morning."

They all swung around to stare at Maisie.

"Gert Hazlett's grandson, Dougie, is part-timing it out at the airport," Maisie said by way of explanation.

Jessi rolled her eyes, then sent Paige a look: *So much for keeping secrets.* "Alec will be back tonight."

Shelley bolted out of her chair so quickly it fell over. "I have, uh, I forgot, I have an appointment," she said, and all but ran out of the place before anyone had a chance to ask her the particulars.

Everyone stared after her, and they all had to be thinking the same thing, Paige decided, although Maisie was the one who put it into words.

"Appointment, my very ample ass," Maisie said. "I'd bet real money she's going to turn up at the airport right about the time Maggie gets in with the very handsome Mr. Barclay."

And take on Maggie? Paige didn't think so. But there was no doubt Shelley Meeker was up to something.

Chapter Fourteen

Alec's house sat toward the end of a row of houses on a steep street in Beacon Hill. It rose three stories, narrow and deep, with lead-glass windows and a beautifully faded and perfectly maintained rose brick exterior that belied the truly dismal state of the rooms behind the blue door.

He'd bought the house for exactly that reason. He might have started out a complete waste when it came to anything involving tools, but he liked to pride himself that he'd come a long way. He'd all but driven the workmen crazy, asking questions and hanging over shoulders, but he'd wanted to see firsthand how tile was laid, how floors were refinished. How to repair a toilet.

It made him think of Paige, and thinking of Paige made him smile. They'd loved each other in just about every way possible, and still he hadn't had enough. He wondered if he ever would.

He could still hear her sighs, feel the way her heart

raced under his lips, smell her soft, subtly sexy scent. He knew every inch of her body, from the delicate skin at the nape of her neck to the sexy pink polish on her toes.

And he'd be back there tonight, he reminded himself as the doorbell rang. He opened it to find caterers on the slanted front walk, and stepped back to let them in. Home repairs he could handle; cooking was still beyond his skills.

Before he'd closed the door, he spied his mother's car and crossed the street to open her door. Janet Barclay stepped out, a willowy woman with elegant features and a lovely smile. She was, as always, tastefully dressed in a trim pantsuit under a fur-lined leather coat. Her makeup was understated, her hair was carefully colored an ashy blond, and her eyes, the same gray as her son's, sparkled.

"Happy birthday, Mother."

"Ugh." She took both of his cheeks in her gloved hands and kissed him square on the mouth, then rubbed the lipstick away with her thumb. "Let me look at you," she said, and he had to stifle the urge to shuffle his feet and lower his eyes.

His mother might be a soft-spoken woman, but she had a way of looking right through him, with eyes that were so disconcertingly like his own, he felt like he was staring into a mirror, with nowhere to hide.

"You're unsettled," she said. "A woman?"

"You're the only woman in my life."

"Well, that's going to have to change. I want grand-children while I'm still young enough to get on the floor and play with them." She gave him a smile that took the sting out of her no-nonsense comment, then tucked her hand into the crook of his elbow and let him lead her across the street and inside the house. "And spare me the flattery. I can't really object to being another year older, considering the alternative, but aging is hell. I never know what's going to ache when I get up in the morning."

"I don't buy it. You could be my sister." Although the birthday they were gathering to celebrate put her firmly into the middle of her sixth decade, she could have passed for forty. Her meticulous antiaging regimen didn't just extend to her appearance, either, Alec knew. She exercised religiously.

"Well, there's nothing quite like a birthday to make you feel the passage of time. But this is lovely," she added as they moved through the foyer.

He'd replaced the old, badly damaged parquet floor with wide cherry planks bordered by intricately woven ribbons of pine, oak, and walnut, all stained to show their true natural grains and colors. As of yet there was no furniture, and only a worklight—a bare bulb in a metal cage—hanging from the wires in the ceiling.

Janet looked up at it, laughing a little. "I really don't understand why you haven't invited me over before this."

Alec took the coat she handed him and hung it in the closet. "I wanted you to see the house at its best, which is at least a year away. So don't blame me if you fall through the floor."

"I'm sure the floors are perfectly fine. You would never buy a house with structural problems."

"No, but I haven't renovated much beyond the entryway." The kitchen was still under construction, and the dining room had been stripped of its dreary, faded wallpaper, leaving the plaster walls patched and ready for paint. He'd done all he could to make the place presentable, though, clearing away the clutter of renovation and bringing in a cleaning service to make the best of the shabby rooms.

"Anyone can see the potential," Janet added, both of them turning as the front door opened and Garrett Barclay strode in like a whirlwind.

Tall and lean, with a full head of silver hair and the piercing gray eyes Alec had inherited from him, being nearly eighty hadn't diminished his strength, of body or character, one bit.

"Potential," he boomed, having apparently only caught the last word. "Are you talking about the house, or my grandson?"

"The house, of course." Janet went to her father immediately and gave him a kiss and hug, and another kiss when he wished her a happy birthday.

Like everyone else in the world, she deferred instantly to the force of nature that was Garrett Barclay. There'd been a time when Alec had wished she'd sheltered him a little more, or that his father had stuck around, so that visitation would give him an escape from his grandfather's heavy-handed discipline and impossibly high expectations.

Now he realized his mother had sheltered him just enough, exposed him just enough, so he understood at an early age that he had to find his own method of handling Garrett Barclay's steamroller personality. And with Garrett in his life, Alec had never missed having a father.

And while Alec never questioned that Garrett loved him—in his own irascible way—his grandfather de-

tested weakness. It was all about respect, Alec understood, and realized that he'd learned a lot about respect
recently. Not just earning it, but giving it as well. "You're
late," Alec said.

"Don't be impertinent, boy."

"You're never late. What are you up to?"

"Who might be the more appropriate question," Janet
observed.

Alec simply stared at his grandfather, one eyebrow
raised. Even when there was a knock on the door, he
stood his ground.

"If you want an answer," Garrett finally grumbled,
"open the damn door."

Shaking her head at both of them, Janet went to the
door and pulled it open. A woman stood on the stoop,
young, pretty, and very elegantly dressed in a dove gray
pantsuit that was exactly right for a luncheon at the club.

"You're Victoria Bowman's daughter, aren't you?"
Alec heard his mother say to her.

"That's right. April."

Janet took the hand April offered, ushering her inside.

"It's lovely to meet you," April said. "I ran into your
father last week, and he invited me to lunch. I know it's
a bit forward of me to crash your birthday party, but he
was so insistent..." Her gaze shifted slowly.

Alec met her eyes, remained silent while she flushed
a delicate and fetching pink. No doubt she came from
the right kind of family, and she'd make the perfect wife.
For someone else.

In the meantime, she didn't deserve rudeness from
him. Alec shook her hand and gave her a slight smile.
"I'm Alec. Welcome to my home, such as it is."

"It's wonderful," April said, a dimple winking to life when she smiled up at him. "Good bones. And you get to make it yours from the ground up instead of living with the last owner's paisley wallpaper and hot pink powder room."

"The wallpaper was flocked, and the powder room is a shade of green that defies description. But there's a hot pink room upstairs."

"Why don't you show her around a bit?" Garrett suggested.

"I think you and I need to have a conversation, Grandfather."

"Come along, April." Janet took her by the hand. "I'll give you a tour of the house."

"Start upstairs," Alec suggested, without taking his eyes from his grandfather's. "This may take a while. You should have told me you were bringing a date," he said to his grandfather as soon as they were out of earshot.

"Don't be an ass, boy," Garrett said in his gravel-chewing voice. "She's a third my age. You know I invited her here for you."

"I can get my own women."

"I'm aware," Garrett said dryly, "but it's time to stop sowing wild oats and settle down."

Wild oats? Alec didn't trouble to tell his grandfather that he'd left that phase of his life behind years ago. By the time he'd finished law school, he'd been so accustomed to spending every spare moment studying and interning, that he'd gotten past the need to notch his bedpost.

Instead, he'd found himself thinking about family, about settling down, in part because his grandfather hounded him constantly about doing just that—with the woman of Garrett's choice, beautiful, well-mannered, and of a certain social standing. It was the one thing Alec defied his grandfather on; he had no objection to those things, but he wanted to choose his own future.

When Paige Walker's face popped into his head, Alec was grateful he had his grandfather to concentrate on.

"You're settling into bachelorhood, and I don't like it," Garrett said. "Or this house."

"It seemed a little strange to still be living at home in my thirties."

"A man ought to wait until he takes a wife before he buys a house." He looked around. "And renovates it. Take my word, boy, get a woman before you pick out throw pillows. It'll save you time in the long run."

"I want to pick out my own throw pillows," Alec said, his tongue firmly tucked into his cheek. "I particularly like paisley. In lavender." He grinned. "Watch your blood pressure, Grandfather."

"You should be concerned with my blood pressure," Garrett snapped. "I'm not going to be around forever." That, too, was a recurring theme, and although Alec knew it was a ploy, it still gave him a pang.

"By your age I was married, had lost a son, and had your mother. What are you waiting for?" Garrett asked him.

Alec led the way into the dining room, with its half-finished walls and hastily bought table and chairs. "Why did you get married?"

"I fell in love, more's the pity." Garrett accepted the coffee, fortified with a shot of Irish whiskey, that Alec offered him, then took a chair—at the head of the table, naturally. "Your grandmother, bless her soul, led me around by the nose most of the time."

Amanda Barclay had been all of five feet tall, with a pretty face and a gentle smile. And she'd been an absolute tyrant, until her sudden death when Alec had been a boy.

For all his big talk, Garrett had changed after the death of his wife. He'd grown gruffer, more ruthless. Because he'd been lonely, Alec realized for the first time, and wondered how he'd managed to miss that all these years.

Paige? he wondered. Was it the fact that, for all their friction, he hadn't been able to get her off his mind all day? He couldn't wait to get back—and yes, the night in her bed had been incredible, but it wasn't her body he kept thinking about, it was her smile.

"You'd be far smarter to find a woman you can respect and be friends with," his grandfather said.

"Would you change it?"

Garrett lifted a brow and took a moment to consider that question. "We fought like cats and dogs sometimes," he finally said, "but we never went to bed angry." A grin lit his eyes and softened the severe lines of his face. "No, I don't suppose I'd change a thing."

"But you want me to accept less."

"*No*," he roared, slamming his cup down on the table. "I bring those women around because they're the ones I know. If you found a woman of your own, I'd back off."

"You mean if I found a woman you can approve of."

"Of course I want to approve. Why in hell would I enjoy seeing you with a bimbo?"

His grandfather's wording should have made him

laugh, Alec thought, but he couldn't. "And you get to decide who's a bimbo."

"Society decides, Alec. I just want you to be settled and happy."

"And a couple of great grandkids wouldn't hurt."

Garrett chuckled. "Let's have lunch. You might like that girl out there. You never know."

But Alec did know. Society decided, just like his grandfather had said. And society had already passed judgment on Paige Walker.

Because of that damned sex tape. Paige hadn't made it; he knew that now. What bothered him was that she wouldn't explain the circumstances, and she seemed to have no need to make the truth known, to him or the world. Since she had nothing to hide she must be protecting someone. And yeah, he acknowledged the sting he felt as jealousy.

So where, Alec wondered, did that leave him?

* * *

Once cleanup was done, he had less than an hour before he had to meet Maggie at the airport. It would take him all of that to get from one end of Boston to the other, Alec knew, even if it hadn't been rush hour.

Still, he pulled out his laptop and settled at the dining room table. It took him only seconds to find the tape. Truth was, he spent more time convincing himself to watch it—not that he was a stranger to the genre. But seeing the occasional smoker at a bachelor party was a far cry from watching a woman he had such complicated feelings for romp around naked with another man.

It didn't fit with what he'd learned about Paige Walker. None of her movies had ever included a nude scene. Alec had always thought it was a hell of a lot sexier to leave something to the imagination, and Paige was unsurpassed in her ability to make a man desperate to have her without giving more than a hint of what she had to offer.

The dim, grainy quality of the recording left a lot to the imagination. Chief among those mysteries was the identity of the woman.

Because, he confirmed, it wasn't Paige.

And yes, he'd already known that, in his mind and his heart. But he could see why everyone else in the world was convinced it was her. The woman on the screen was similar to Paige in build and coloring. He never saw her face, yet that, in itself, made a sick kind of sense.

Assuming it was Paige, and she was ignorant of the camera, the man involved would have wanted her face to show. What kind of triumph would it be otherwise?

If it wasn't Paige, whoever had filmed the tape would keep her face hidden in order to support the wrong assumption. When Alec added in that the man responsible for the tape was an experienced director, well, that said it all.

Something rose inside him, so fast and so overwhelming he barely heard the shout that ripped from his own throat. He picked up the phone, then put it down again, paced from one end of the room to the other trying to contain his excitement. Believing it wasn't her had been one thing; proving it another. But he didn't have to prove it—not when he could get others to do it for him.

He sat back down in front of the computer and opened

a search window. The blogs had condemned her; they'd prove her innocent now. Riding the wave of exhilaration, he responded to a gleefully nasty comment in the blog that accompanied that incarnation of the tape, inventing a username for himself.

DonQ.

Chapter Fifteen

By the time he made it to the airport, barely a half hour late, Alec had started to come to his senses. Looking at the sex tape was one thing; it could be marked down to simple curiosity. Responding to blogs—not one but several—how did he justify that?

Paige would be furious, and rightly so. She'd made it clear that she would deal with the tape when she was ready. She'd let him know, in no uncertain terms, that she didn't need a defender.

He'd just been so angry at whoever had claimed it was Paige, and so damned helpless. He was a man who saw a problem and immediately found a way to deal with it.

And that's all he'd done, he reminded himself. No one could possibly trace those blog comments back to him. And what harm had been done? The truth would have come out anyway; all he'd done was give it a little push.

He walked through Paige's front door, she came hurrying down the stairs, and he completely forgot about the tape and his reaction to it. She stopped halfway. Alec stayed where he was, just inside the door. They grinned foolishly at each other.

"I wasn't waiting for you," Paige said.

Alec dropped his laptop case and stripped off his coat. "I'm aware."

"I would have been perfectly all right if you'd spent the night in Boston."

"I'm supposed to protect you."

"Then why are you so far away?" She began to climb the steps slowly, her hand trailing ever so lightly along the banister. He could all but feel the touch of her fingers on his skin. "There could be a murderer hiding in my closet."

"Consider me your knight in shining armor." He made it to the foot of the stairs before his knees tried to give out.

When she reached the top, she turned. Her eyes met his, and his brain simply emptied out. As his heart filled.

"I'm not going to fall in love with you," she warned.

And what could he say to that? Alec wondered, as he took the stairs as deliberately as she had. She was stubborn, opinionated, maddening, and more beautiful than ever. And he loved her. He knew it without a doubt.

His blood was surging like the surf, the storm inside him raging like the Atlantic at its worst. Love was the eye, the calm that let him sweep her up into his arms, then set her carefully on the floor, when what he really wanted was to drop her on the bed and devour her in one greedy gulp.

As soon as her feet hit the floor, she dived at him. Her mouth was hot and insatiable, her hands seemed to touch him everywhere at once, and when she pressed her body to his, the heat pumping off her nearly burned through what little control he had.

He shoved the robe she was wearing off her shoulders, groaning when he saw the short nightie she wore beneath, hot red silk molded to truly mouthwatering curves. He slipped the thin straps from her shoulders, the nightie slithered to the floor, and the body beneath took his breath away.

He ran his hands slowly from her shoulders, down the slopes of her breasts, and across nipples gone hard. Her moan sliced into him like a hot knife, stripped him bare. She quivered, and he felt strong, elemental, almost primitive as he cuffed her hands over her head and feasted.

"Please," she begged. "*Alec.*"

He dropped to his knees and used his mouth on her, plunging his fingers inside her and driving her to a peak so powerful he had to catch her when she crumpled.

He bore her to the bed, fumbling as he stripped his clothes off. And then he was next to her, and it was hot, drugging kisses, caresses that pushed him to the edge of control. He linked his hands with hers and staked them to the bed as he rose over her, as he entered her in one long, slow thrust.

She closed around him hot and tight, and the pleasure was so intense he had to stop and simply absorb it for a second. Paige pleaded again and he felt her body squeeze around him. Knowing she was close pushed him nearly over the edge, but he waited, waited until he could find some control.

And then he began to move, long, slow strokes. He used his mouth again, nibbling at her lips, suckling her

breasts. He brought them both to the brink, slowly, torturously, letting the pleasure build and grow by tiny
degrees.

"Paige," he groaned as they balanced on that razor-
sharp blade of pleasure, "open your eyes."

"Please," she whispered.

"Look at me."

Her eyes fluttered open and locked on his, the blue so
deep it was almost black.

Her mouth curved as she twisted beneath him. Even
the small movement she managed was too much, taking
him past reason so that all he could do was hammer himself into her.

She cried out, a sound of pure joy, and met him thrust
for thrust. He went blind and deaf but for the waves of
pleasure that swamped his senses and stole his strength.

He caught himself, barely, before he collapsed on top
of her. He slipped to the side and gathered her against
him, felt her tremble as she settled into his arms. They
stayed like that as their pulses calmed and their breath
slowed to normal. He couldn't seem to stop touching her,
rubbing small circles on her back with his fingertips.

Paige shifted, looking up at him.

He met her eyes in the dim lighting filtering up the
stairs. "What?"

She shook her head. "What I said to you before, about
not falling in love with you. I meant that."

She looked away, but he tipped her chin up until she
met his gaze again. "Why?"

"I don't know. We live such different lives, you and
me, Alec. I'm gone for months at a time on some location or other, and your life is in Boston."

"I will have to get a job at some point. And if my grandfather has his way, it'll be in the family business. Probably in the mail room." He chuckled. "Garrett Barclay believes in learning from the ground floor up, even for his only grandson."

"You wouldn't be happy sorting letters, any more than you would be trailing me around the world."

"Why don't you let me be the judge of what makes me happy?"

She sighed, snuggling against him. "You might as well know now, I've been burned a time or two. Money and fame are powerful incentives."

Only to the greedy, Alec thought. Still, those men who'd been so focused on the money and the fame had done him a favor. They'd seen Paige as nothing more than a tool, and so she was here, free to be his. Even if her heart wasn't.

But he could work his way through those walls and win her over. Failure wasn't an option. Neither, in light of the obstacles already in his path, was the truth about what he'd just done. Not yet. The time would come for full disclosure, once he had the confidence she wouldn't use it as an excuse to shut him out.

"I don't need money, and I don't want fame" was all he said.

"What do you want?"

"You," he said without thinking. And when he felt her flinch, his heart lurched painfully in his chest.

He cupped her breast and ran his thumb over her nipple. "I want you in every way I can have you," he said, deliberately putting the interchange back on the physical by replacing his hand with his mouth.

She moaned, cupping his head and holding it to her. But when his hands started to roam, she rose over him, straddled him. Took him in. "You had me the first time," she said, and began to move, as slowly and torturously as he had when he'd been in control. "It's my turn to have you."

* * *

Alec woke alone. His searching hand found the sheets and pillows next to him cold and empty. He shot out of bed and into the bathroom, then stood there, feeling foolish when just her scent aroused him.

Especially after the night they'd just spent together.

He'd had her every way he could, just as he'd told her. And she'd had him. He wouldn't have to worry about a future with her, he thought with a wide grin, because they'd kill each other before the first haze of lust burned away. He stepped to the window, knowing he'd find her walking the cliffs. She was the damnedest woman for braving any weather for the sake of a little exercise. The sky was clear, which meant it was probably frigid out there; her only danger was likely frostbite, but he wasn't about to take chances with her.

He would have loved a shower, but he settled for brushing his teeth and splashing some water in his face to battle back the exhaustion. He threw on clothes and his coat, and headed out. Paige was nowhere in sight, and he felt a lick of panic until he spied her on the beach below, stretching against one of the huge boulders that littered the narrow fringe of shore.

He made his way to the steps cut into the rock, and lost his footing on the fourth or fifth step in his rush to get down to Paige. "Railings," he muttered, taking the rest of the stairs more carefully, watching for icy patches.

Paige looked up as he came around the outcropping of rock that sheltered the stairs. She wore no makeup, and her skin was rosy with the color brought out by the cold air. She looked impossibly beautiful, even dressed in baggy sweats, an ancient pair of running shoes, and a slicker that was big as a tent. After the nights they'd shared, he could have sculpted her body from memory, but only a true artist would have been able to capture the genuine beauty that shone from within.

She watched him, eyes as blue and deep as the ocean behind her. She didn't smile, not even teasingly, and he saw, clearly, the vulnerability she usually hid from the world. He could hurt her—they could hurt each other. If they weren't careful.

"Why didn't you wake me?"

She gave him a bright, unshadowed smile. "I thought I'd let you sleep for a while. You were exhausted."

He stepped forward and kissed her, sweetly, slowly, before he pulled back and rested his cheek against hers. "We could go back in where it's warm, and get some rest."

Paige cupped his cheek and pulled back, far enough for him to see the teasing sparkle in her eyes. "Oddly enough, I feel extremely energized this morning."

"I can work with that."

She laughed as she stepped back. Alec took her hand, pleased when she didn't pull away. They walked in a companionable silence for a little while, concentrating on navigating the rocky beach.

"Why do they call it Secret Harbor?" Alec asked after a little while.

"My mother said it was because the harbor is difficult to navigate. You have to know where the channels are or you run aground, which made it a perfect place for men involved in illegal activities to use as a hiding place, including during Prohibition."

She spoke matter-of-factly, but Alec remembered her fondness, shadowed by grief, when she talked about her father. What he heard in her voice when she mentioned her mother was different.

"You've never mentioned your mother before."

"She died when I was little."

"It's more than that."

Paige shook her head. "I didn't really know her. What daughter ever really does, especially one so young? I found out after she died... Well, I don't think this was the right life for her. She wanted more. She went to the mainland to find it."

"Jessi told me," Alec said. "She thought it might help me understand you a little better."

Paige looked over and met his eyes. "I look so much like my mother, Alec. If I put pictures out, you'd see that."

"And you wonder if you take after her in other ways."

"I wanted more than Windfall could offer."

"And you got it, through hard work and sacrifice. It sounds to me like your mother took the easy way."

Paige smiled a little, sadly. "I should be insulted, but I've had that same thought myself. Still..." She let her breath out to cloud the air. "If the last little while has taught me anything, it's to avoid making judgments about a woman I barely knew."

They reached the farthest point of land and turned back.

"But there's heredity, Alec. I've made room in my life for no one. It was all about me. Just like my mother."

"Did you intentionally hurt anyone along the way?"

"Not that I know of. But I'm in this...predicament because I went after something I wanted, and when I didn't get it, I wasn't exactly shy about letting the world know I was unhappy." She laughed a little. "I threw a tantrum. It seems to me that's what my mother did. She was unhappy, so she went looking for love and excitement. She didn't care who was hurt by it."

Suzie Walker had thought of no one but herself, her wants, her needs. Her happiness. Paige had done the same, and for the first time in her life, she began to understand how unhappy her mother must have been. It broke Paige's heart.

"She must have been so miserable, Alec," Paige said, her throat thick with tears. "Maybe her dreams weren't as big as mine, but we're not all that different."

"You think you deserve this?" Alec took her by the shoulders and shook her a little. "Your reputation is being destroyed and you're going to stand there and blame yourself because of something your mother did twenty years ago?"

She shoved his hands off, anger joining the complicated mix of her emotions. "That's not what I'm doing. I'm just, I don't know, hurt. I guess when you climb so high there's always someone wanting to shove you off your perch. It just...everyone turned so fast."

"Then why aren't they turning on that damn director?

If he'd cheat on his wife, why don't people suspect him of lying about who it was with?"

Paige shrugged, an irritated move of one shoulder. "I guess they expect men like him to be unfaithful, so they just accept it."

"But you're supposed to be perfect."

"I knew the game when I signed up for it."

"Bullshit," he ground out. "Fight back."

"Is that the lawyer talking?"

He wanted to shake her again, make her see she was only hurting herself by hiding from reality. Instead, he took her in his arms, waited until she relaxed against him. "It's someone who doesn't care to see you hurting yourself."

"Alec—"

"Did you second-guess yourself when you left everything and everyone you knew to go after your dreams?"

"No. I was too naïve."

He held her at arm's length and searched her face. "Did you second-guess yourself when you took on the role in *December Sunshine* and gave the kind of performance that won you an Academy Award?"

"I was only doing what felt right."

"You went with your instincts, both times, and I'd imagine every time since. So why are you letting some half-bald director with a Napoleon complex make you doubt yourself now?"

She tipped her head to one side, her brow furrowed. Alec realized he'd come dangerously close to letting her know he'd already taken steps to exonerate her. "I've seen pictures of Jackson."

She smiled slightly. "He seems bigger in person. But

you're right, I am letting him make me doubt myself. That stops now."

He blew out a breath. "So you'll get the truth out?"

"No, not yet." When he tried to interrupt, she took him by the hand and pulled him to the foot of the stairs. "I have my reasons," she said as they started up.

"You keep saying that. Are you ever going to tell me what those reasons are?"

"At the moment I just want to get somewhere warm."

Alec started up behind her. "It was icy near the top. Watch your step."

"I've been walking up and down these stairs all my life."

All the same, it was a good excuse to keep his hands on her. He set them on the sides of her waist, just as she shrieked and fell backward. Her weight dropped on him. His feet began to slip on the wet steps, and he scrabbled frantically for a grip anywhere. He teetered on the edge, Paige's weight overbalancing him, his fingers sliding along the rock wall. And into a crack.

It was too narrow for his gloved fingers, but he dug in, muscles straining to hold them both while Paige found her footing again. It seemed like forever while his fingers slipped and cold sweat ran down his back. And then her weight was gone. She grabbed him by the arms and pulled him upright.

"What—" she began, but he shoved her to the top.

He just wanted to feel firm ground beneath his feet again. But he was only too happy when she barreled into him—now that he wasn't worried about breaking his neck.

"That was close," she said, her voice muffled with her face buried in his shoulder.

"Do me a favor and walk up here from now on." Alec looked over the edge of the cliff, pulled her another six feet away. "At least this far from the edge."

Paige glanced back to where they'd been standing. "I can do that." She took his hand and pulled him toward the house. "Now you really are my knight in shining armor." She looked over her shoulder. "I don't want to think about what a tumble down those stone steps would have meant."

Neither did he, but he couldn't seem to shake the mental image of Paige, lying broken and bleeding, on the beach below.

"The least I can do is make you breakfast."

"That would be great." And first thing he was going to shake her loose and take a look at those steps. It was probably just ice, but he wasn't taking anything for granted.

* * *

"I don't see any obvious signs of tampering." Dex rose from his study and returned to the top.

Hold, huddled in the heaviest coat he could find, nodded.

Alec took Dex's place, gingerly making his way down the steps. "There's a pretty big fissure in the stone here," he said, studying the rock wall, then the step where Paige had lost her footing. It was half-gone, chunks of rock littering the steps below. "It runs from the sidewall right through the step. It could have given way on its own."

"It's possible," Dex said as Alec straightened and climbed to the top of the cliff. "I don't see anything that looks like chisel marks, but it's too much of a coincidence for my liking."

"The temperature has dropped below freezing the last couple of nights, but the days have been warm enough to melt the snow we've had. Water runs down the stairs, and into the crack. Every time it freezes, the crack is opened up a little more, like the potholes on the roads. The top layer of rock gets loose, so when Paige went down it, and I went down it, we loosened it more. When she came back up, it gave way."

"It wouldn't have taken much to help Mother Nature along," Dex said grimly. "Pound a wedge in the right place and give that stone a helping hand. And there are things that wouldn't leave a trace, wood, plastic."

"So what do we tell the women?" Alec wondered.

"The truth."

"Can we tell them inside?" Hold wanted to know. "My thin Southern blood is about frozen in my veins."

"Wuss," Dex said.

"Lightweight," Alec added.

Hold just grinned. "Y'all want to come down to my neck of the woods, I'll introduce you to crocs the size of cars and mosquitoes that can suck you dry in under a minute. We'll see who's a wuss."

They were laughing when they walked through Paige's back door, into air that was blessedly warm and redolent with something that made Alec's mouth water.

Hold scented the air like a hound. "That's Jessi's potpie," he said, shucking his coat, gloves, and scarf in record time. He all but ran them over getting into the kitchen.

When Alec joined him, Jessi was just taking a casserole dish out of the oven. It was filled to the brim and covered with golden-brown pastry, with holes in the top that piped steam.

"Real food," Dex said, and earned a poke from Maggie, which didn't stop him from adding, "Bless you."

"You should be thanking Paige," Jessi said. "She wanted the recipe, but since I don't measure I had to show her instead."

"What's different?" Hold asked.

"Leftover turkey instead of chicken," Jessi said as she began to fill bowls. "I swear you have a nose like a hound."

"Don't be so stingy." Hold peered into the bowl she'd handed him, then into the casserole dish.

"I'm saving some for Benji."

"The boy chose the sleepover," Hold groused.

Jessi just laughed and shook her head. "Stop complaining. I made enough for an army."

"That's a great description," Dex put in.

Jessi stopped, exchanged a look with Maggie and Paige, then passed Dex the bowl in her hand.

"We can't say for sure the step was tampered with, but I don't believe in coincidences," he said, and told the women what they'd found.

"So you're leaning toward sabotage," Paige said. "By someone who knows I walk there almost every day."

"A Windfaller," Maggie added grimly. "There are no outsiders on the island right now. It has to be one of us."

Jessi sighed heavily. "I hate that."

"My money is on Meeker," Maggie said.

"Because?" Paige asked.

"He's a slimy, scheming, underhanded, greedy bastard."

"You're predisposed to think badly of him," Jessi

pointed out. "For good reason," she added, knowing, as they all did, that Meeker had tried to take advantage of Maggie when she was sixteen.

Maggie had fought Meeker off, and told only George. They'd kept it to themselves until Maggie had used the secret to blackmail Meeker into loaning them journals authored by past Windfall residents, to aid in the search for Eugenia's descendants.

"We need more proof than his disgusting personality," Jessi finished.

Maggie snorted softly. "You never want to think badly of anyone."

"I'm thinking badly of someone right now," Jessi said. "I just don't know who."

There was a beat of silence as they all digested the truth of that. It couldn't be easy for the women to wonder which of their friends or neighbors might have tried to orchestrate Paige's death.

Alec just wanted to get his hands on whoever it was. "Next steps?" he said. "Besides the fact that you're never alone, Paige," he qualified, turning to her. "I'll see to that myself, but it would be helpful if you didn't put yourself in potentially dangerous situations."

"I won't use the harbor stairs again, but I'm going to walk."

"Buy a treadmill," Maggie advised.

"It's not the same. And I'm not letting anyone maneuver me into changing my lifestyle."

No, Alec thought, she wasn't one to compromise. "At least let me know before you leave the house."

Paige met his eyes. "I'm not comfortable with you being a human shield."

"You can't have it both ways, Paige," Jessi said kindly. "If you're not going to make some changes to preserve your safety, you have to accept that you're putting Alec in jeopardy, too."

"That's playing dirty, Jess."

"Maybe. It's also the truth."

"And it's a hell of a lot nicer than I'd put it," Maggie said.

"Meaning if something happens to Alec," Paige said, "it'll be my fault."

"Not your fault," Maggie corrected her, "but you'll have to live with knowing you could have prevented it by not making yourself a target."

"You're right, I like Jessi's way of putting it better." She sighed, and when she shot him a glance, Alec simply lifted an eyebrow.

What could he say when Jessi and Maggie were right?

"I'll make a nuisance of myself with the lab," Hold put in. "If we can get your DNA results, and you're ruled out, this will all be over."

And if she was a match, Alec thought, she'd be in even more danger. But none of them chose to voice that fear. "All we can do is try to figure out who tampered with the steps."

"Everyone will make an appearance at the holiday party," Maggie said. "Whoever it is will either give Paige a wide berth or they'll be asking her a lot of nosy questions."

"So," Dex concluded, "we're in a holding pattern until Saturday."

And they'd see what they could see, Alec thought. He couldn't wait.

Chapter Sixteen

Every year, a party was held in the village to celebrate the holiday season. The big old white pine in the vacant lot across from the Horizon was decorated to within an inch of its life. The bins beneath were filled with presents—small, inexpensive ones for the children, and gag gifts for those who chose to participate in the exchange. Copious amounts of eggnog helped add to the humor.

The party spilled over from business to business, but centered around the Horizon, being the biggest public space in town, and equipped for it as well.

When Paige and Alec arrived, the Horizon was already packed and overflowing onto the street. Barrels had been set at intervals, filled with wood and burning cheerfully.

"We should work our way up and down the street, and end in the Horizon," Paige suggested. She lifted a hand in greeting, and smiled at the knot of men, mostly twenties and younger, huddled around one of the barrels.

The response ranged from open-mouthed appreciation to the one young man who clutched his heart and fell dramatically to the snow-covered street.

Paige laughed.

"I don't think that's the reaction we're interested in," Alec said.

"I kind of enjoyed it." Including, Paige decided, the part where Alec seemed to be a little jealous.

He only slanted her a look, one that was so wonderfully deadpan it made her laugh again as he steered her into the market.

Mr. McDonald, dressed up as Santa Claus, was surrounded by awestruck children and camera-wielding parents. None of them spared her more than a glance, Paige noted, as she and Alec made a quick circuit before exiting again.

They continued from storefront to storefront, stopping to chat now and again, but making steady progress through the village. The mild turn in the weather had held. Still, by the time they wandered into the Horizon, Paige's feet were all but frozen.

"Now I know how a Popsicle feels," she said, shivering a little when the warm air hit her cold skin.

"Warm spell, my ample ass," Maisie Cutshaw agreed as she came out of the Horizon's big dining room. "Heard the bell," she said, meaning the bell over the door that alerted AJ and Helen that someone had used the lobby door. "Wanted to see who it was, and here you are, looking fresh as a daisy, and with a handsome man on your arm. And look at the pretty pin on your coat."

"It was my mother's," Paige said when Maisie stopped to draw breath. Paige ran a finger over the brooch she'd forgotten she'd pinned to her lapel. On a whim, she removed it, slipped her coat off into Alec's waiting hands, and pinned the brooch to her dress.

"Oh," Maisie said, "that's a pretty dress." She stepped back to take a long, admiring look.

Smiling, Paige did a red carpet pose, one hand on her hip to show off the seemingly simple black dress with its demure scoop neckline and form-fitting bodice and long sleeves. The skirt was full and flirty, ending a couple of inches above her knee. But the back dipped low, making Maisie hum in appreciation when Paige turned.

"Where'd it come from?" Maisie asked. "France? One of them big-name designers, right? Not that it matters. A gunny sack would look amazing on that pretty figure of yours." She let out her big, infectious laugh. "You ought to stay out here, give the rest of us women a fighting chance."

"Your men are safe from me," Paige said.

"It's not you who's gonna give 'em hell for staring," Maisie hooted again. "It's their wives they're gonna have to look out for. And maybe Lawyer Barclay here, if any of the Windfallers trespass on his territory."

Paige laughed, and neatly sidestepped Alec when he tried to take her arm. Keeping her distance from him would speak louder than any denial she could make.

Maisie just hooted again, and with a parting wink, went back into the dining room.

Alec hung their coats in the little room off the lobby. When he came out, he didn't touch her. "Sending a message?" he asked instead.

"Protecting my privacy. Our privacy." Paige lifted a

hand in greeting for Ma Appelman, but her smile felt strained. "If I hurt your feelings—"

"What feelings?"

"Oh. Well." She smiled up at him, patted his arm. And hid the sting, surprisingly strong, that she felt. "No apology necessary then."

When he turned toward the bar, she deliberately chose the opposite direction. She could have used something to ease her tight, dry throat, but the sooner she put herself on display for everyone in the room, the sooner she could go home. And be alone with Alec, she reminded herself.

If he wanted to take offense just because she was being cautious, logical, it was fine with her. He ought to be thanking her, she thought, fuming a little that he couldn't understand why she wanted to keep their relationship between the two of them. He'd made it clear from the beginning that all he ultimately wanted was friendship. He might say now that he believed the best of her, but first impressions usually held true, and his first impression of her had been dismal.

And she had a purpose in coming here tonight, she reminded herself. Having Alec at her side would only inhibit Windfallers from speaking freely.

Not that anyone was going out of their way to talk to her, she admitted dryly. It was nothing new. Some would be jealous, some intimidated, some simply giving her privacy. She hadn't spent much time in the village since she'd been back, and most of the island's residents would take it as a broad hint that she wanted to keep to herself. Windfallers might consider gossip a kind of religion, but they'd respect her desire to be left alone.

She spied AJ and Helen talking to Maggie and Dex, and Maggie's great-uncle Emmett Finley.

Emmett had been just a boy the night Eugenia was kidnapped; it had been he who'd discovered her bundled away on the rumrunners' boat. Only weeks before, Emmett had confirmed that to Maggie and Dex. Emmett hadn't known what happened to Eugenia, if she'd succumbed to the chill she'd taken that night, or if she'd replaced a child who'd lost the battle with the measles epidemic. Still, it had been a turning point in the case, the first moment it became possible that Eugenia had lived to marry and produce descendants.

Paige didn't join the little group, but she got near enough to hear the end of a story Emmett was telling about AJ's father. She should have moved on, but she got sucked in and had to hear the ending.

"—who was a mean bastard by all accounts," Emmett was saying.

Far from being insulted, AJ laughed and wrapped his arm around Helen's shoulders.

"Always figured that Melly," Emmett continued, using Ma's given name, Melinda, "married him to spite herself. Lord knows she was the only one could control him, and that not all of the time, being as he came from a long line of mean bastards, and all of them named John. When he came along"—Emmett hooked a thumb in AJ's direction—"we all figured she'd name him after his father and he'd turn out to be another John."

"Whoa." Maggie swung around to confront AJ, hands on her hips. "Another John?"

AJ grinned from ear to ear.

"I'll be damned," she said.

"You didn't figure it out," AJ told her.

"I had little chance of that. Who names their kid Another?"

"I do." Ma joined them, leaning heavily on her cane. "I wanted to call him after my family name, which was Jackson."

"That's not so far from John," Maggie observed, still staring at AJ out of narrowed eyes.

"You'd think not," Ma said. "John insisted his son was going to be another John. Couldn't talk him around, so by hell, that's what I named him."

They all laughed. AJ kissed his mother's cheek and steered her to a table so she could sit. Maggie helped Emmett to the same table.

"How about I fix you both a plate," AJ offered.

"Jessi, Hold, and Benji just came in," Maggie said. "I'll bet she brought shepherd's pie. She always does, and I'm going to get some before the scavengers descend."

"That girl pays an awful lot of attention to her stomach," Ma said. "Good thing she burns those calories off."

"True," Paige said, "but she doesn't have my bone structure."

Ma threw back her head and brayed out a laugh. Paige bent and kissed her cheek before she moved on.

She'd only begun to weave her way through the crowd when Alec fell into step with her.

"Truce?" he said.

She took the glass of white wine he held out and sipped, grateful for the moment it gave her to catch her breath. "Are we fighting again?" she said, slanting him a glance that hid, she hoped, the way her heart was racing.

"I'd rather not."

"Then we won't." And she'd try not to feel the awkward tension between them. "I think we're about to have a close encounter."

Shelley Meeker was making her way casually, but very deliberately, in their direction.

"Hello, Shelley," Paige said, smiling brightly as she'd done dozens of times to invite conversation. "Happy holidays."

"Same to you," Shelley said. "Both of you."

"Have you met Alec Barclay?"

"No," Shelley breathed. "You're from Boston, aren't you? I just love Boston. Daddy took me there last year. He had business, but I just wandered the city all day long." She sighed. "I especially liked all those pretty houses in Beacon Hill. Is that where you live?"

"I live at my family's place outside the city."

"Like the Kennedy compound? I mean, your family has been here longer, like from the *Mayflower*, right?"

"You've done some research, Shelley," Paige murmured, somewhat amused by Alec's discomfiture.

"Daddy always says you have to make your own opportunity."

"He probably meant you should go to college."

"Oh, I'm not smart enough for college. Daddy always says so."

"That's despicable," Paige said. Her father had been so encouraging, so confident in her abilities. She had no idea what it must be like to have a father who tried to hold her back.

Paige felt Alec give her a little nudge, but Shelley didn't seem to take offense. Or maybe she had no idea what *despicable* meant.

"That's a beautiful pin," Shelley said. "Is that part of the set you wore at the Oscars last year? You know, you wore that deep green mermaid dress and all that ruby jewelry."

"Those jewels were on loan, but they were real. This is just costume."

"Oh," Shelley said, sounding disappointed. "Don't you ever get to keep all those pretty things?"

"For the most part, they're borrowed so the designer can get publicity." Not that she didn't have her share of diamonds and precious stones, stored away in a bank vault. "The real thing is more trouble than it's worth most of the time, Shelley."

"But they're so pretty," Shelley said.

"Pretty isn't everything."

Shelley snorted. "Yes, it is."

* * *

"Except for Shelley," Paige said to Alec an hour later, "no one has shown any more interest in me than I'd expect. And she was really interested in you." There'd been questions and pride about her life in Hollywood, winks over her relationship with Alec, sly references and sincere sympathy regarding the sex tape. In short, it had been so endearingly Windfall Island she wondered how she could ever have forgotten how much she loved it.

"I don't imagine anyone will be interested in you or that brooch now," Alec said.

She looked, as he was, toward the door, and the commotion going on there. For a moment, all she could see was George Boatwright, head and shoulders taller than most of the others in the room. The crowd parted finally, and Paige's mouth dropped open.

"Rose Stanhope. On George's arm." She squeezed Alec's wrist. "Oh, boy," she said, mentally rubbing her hands together. "I'll bet Rose gets something going. Besides the fact that she's here with George. Half the women on the island will be nursing broken hearts, and everyone will want to know who she is."

"What I want to know is why George chose to bring her here, in this very public setting."

"That's a great question." Dex and Maggie joined them, Maggie with a plate in her hand. "If they're trying to smoke out Clayton's hireling, they picked a better way than we did."

"You aren't having any luck, either?" Alec asked him.

Dex shook his head.

"They're headed this way," Maggie said around a mouthful of cake, "but it'll be a while before they get here."

They were stopped repeatedly, interrupted, surrounded time and again. It was only due to George's ability to work his way around the Windfallers that they made any headway at all.

"At the rate they're going," Maggie said, "it will take them all night."

"Well, then," Paige said, watching George and Rose get stopped yet again, "you'll have time for more cake."

"Jealous?" Maggie asked sweetly.

"Intensely."

Maggie handed her the plate, with a wedge of double chocolate cake still on it. "Stop worrying about the size of your ass, and just enjoy yourself."

"I wouldn't worry about the size of my ass if the rest of the world didn't feel a need to comment on it every time I gain or lose five pounds."

"I would think they're all too busy commenting on the sex tape these days." Maggie grinned at Jessi and Hold as they joined their little group. "Where the size of your ass is right out there for everyone to see."

Paige laughed. Alec didn't, she noticed.

"You don't believe she made that tape, any more than I do, Maggie," Jessi said.

"True, but the rest of the world will continue to believe it until she stands up for herself."

Paige glanced at Alec. "I think we should concentrate on our collective problem, and let me worry about what the world thinks of me."

"Okay." Maggie popped up to her toes, then scooted off into the crowd. She came back with George and Rose in tow.

"How did you manage that?" Paige wondered.

"She was completely rude," George said.

"It was wonderful," Rose added with a laugh. "The Morgensterns weren't even offended."

"They're used to her," George said mildly. "Rose, this is—"

"Oh, no introduction is necessary," Rose said, "at least on my side." She kissed Alec's cheek and said, "Wonderful to see you looking so well," before turning to Paige. Rose held out her hand, enclosing Paige's in both of hers. "Rose Stanhope. I've seen every movie you've ever made, and I've loved them all."

Paige couldn't help but smile. It might have been gushing from someone else, but Rose's words were so sincere, and her smile was open and warm, reaching all the way to her sparkling eyes that were the same bright blue as Maggie's.

Paige had been prepared to distrust her, but she found it impossible.

"I know exactly how you feel," Rose said. "I wasn't sure—" She gasped and reached out, not quite touching the brooch Paige wore pinned to her dress. "Where—where did you get that?"

Paige looked around, saw they'd caught the interest of the people nearest them, including Maisie Cutshaw and Shelley Meeker. "It was my mother's," she said, keeping her voice down. Concerned over how pale Rose had gone, Paige took her hand. "Tell me what's wrong."

"That—" Rose broke off again and made a visible effort to collect herself. "There was a suite of jewelry in my family, rubies and diamonds," she said, sounding a little steadier. "The necklace went missing when Eugenia was taken."

Now Dex stepped forward and took Rose's arm, steering her away from the crowd. The others followed. "It's not in any of the histories."

"No, it was never released to the public. Great-Grandfather held it back, even from the police."

"But this is just a brooch," Paige pointed out.

"Perhaps now." Again Rose took a second, letting out her breath. "The necklace was made up of rubies smaller than that one, each set off with a circlet of diamonds, with a larger ruby and diamonds suspended from the very center. The piece you're wearing as a pin was once that center pendant."

"You're sure?" Dex asked her.

"As sure as I can be—although I have no way to prove it at this moment."

"I never dreamed...I thought it was fake." Paige un-pinned the brooch and held it out. "A very good fake."

Rose refused to take it. "It's yours," she said simply. "I only want to know how you came by it."

"I don't know." Paige didn't pin it back on. It felt wrong somehow, like she'd stolen it herself then had the nerve to wear it in public, and in front of the true owner. "My mother died when I was just a girl. I don't even remember her wearing it, and my father never mentioned it."

"Ma will know," Maggie said, looking to where Ma sat with Emmett Finley. "But we can't all go over there."

"We'll go," Alec said. "The rest of you can distract everyone else."

"Rose is distracting enough, all by herself," Jessi said. "As long as she and George stay on the other side of the room, no one will give a hoot what Paige and Alec are doing."

Jessi was right, but still, Paige held back a moment, the brooch fisted so tightly in her hand it cut into her palm.

"It's better to know the truth," Alec whispered.

"Not always," Paige answered, but when Alec took her by the arm, she let him steer her to Ma's table.

"It's about time," Ma said. "Emmett and I have run out of things to talk about."

Alec pulled a chair out for Paige.

She didn't take it. "Emmett—"

"Was there that night, remember?" Alec said close to her ear.

She sat, pinning the brooch back on her dress as she

did. If she handed it to Ma, everyone in proximity would know they were talking about it.

Before Paige could ask, Emmett sat forward. His eyes were on the brooch, his face draining to white. "Where did you come by that pin?"

"I found it with my mother's jewelry," Paige said. "I thought Ma might know something about it."

"It was handed down through your father's family," Ma said. "Your mother wore it a time or two that I recall, but she never got along well with your grandmother, Paige. Your father's mother never thought, well, no mother thinks a woman is good enough for her son." Ma's eyes sharpened on Paige's face, then lifted to Alec. "What's going on?"

Paige looked to Alec, too.

Instead of addressing either of them, Alec sat next to Emmett. "You know something," he said gently.

"No." Emmett lifted a hand that shook badly. Han, his grandson, broke away from the group of people he'd been talking to not far away. "I want to go home," Emmett said.

"Okay, Pops." Han helped him up, and with a parting smile, helped his grandfather toward the lobby.

"Han is living with him now," Ma said. "Emmett's memory has been getting worse lately."

Paige was no expert on the kind of illness Emmett Finley was facing, but she would have sworn it was a good memory that had made him dig his heels in and refuse to answer Alec's question.

"We need to talk," Ma continued, "but not here. Tomorrow at my house—all of you, and bring that woman George Boatwright has sprung on us."

"Won't it look strange, all of us gathering there?" Paige said.

"It's not unusual for me to invite friends to lunch," Ma said, "especially when there are new people to get to know. And if you all bring me presents, it will look like a Christmas celebration."

Chapter Seventeen

So Emmett was there that night," Ma said the next day, once they'd all gathered at her house. "He held the child, and it was clear he recognized that brooch."

They'd told Ma the story of their search for Eugenia and her descendants, start to finish, leaving nothing out. She'd listened without interruption, her dark, intelligent eyes moving from face to face as each of them contributed to the tale of Eugenia's kidnapping, how she'd come to Windfall Island, what they'd uncovered so far. And the dangers they'd faced.

It had taken some maneuvering, but they'd all managed to crowd into Ma's overstuffed, overcrowded parlor. Hold and Jessi occupied a love seat by the large front window. George had brought a pair of ladderback chairs in from the kitchen for himself and Rose. Paige sat in one of a pair of wingback chairs, with Alec perched on the ottoman in front of her.

Maggie sat in the matching chair. Dex stood next

to her, but he would have been pacing if there'd been room for it, Paige thought. He was all nerves—understandable, since he'd started the search for Eugenia, and it was all coming to a head now.

"Emmett admitted he found Eugenia that night," Dex said. "He must have seen the necklace."

"So let me get this straight," Ma said. "Maggie has the Stanhope eyes, Jessi has the blanket the babe was wrapped in, and now Paige has part of the necklace that went missing the same night."

"That about sums it up," Maggie said.

"There are no other possibilities?"

"Only Shelley Meeker is the right age," Hold put in, "but she only had male relatives in that generation."

"Since Jessi and I have been ruled out through DNA," Maggie concluded, "Paige is the last potential descendant."

"And someone tried to kill you," Ma said to Paige, her eyes glinting dangerously. She'd had the same reaction with Maggie and Jessi—but they were out of danger now.

"We don't know that for a fact," Alec said. "One of the steps down to the harbor gave way. It could have happened naturally."

"But you don't think so. None of you believe this was just an unfortunate coincidence. And you think this girl's uncle is the culprit."

"I can't say for sure," Rose said miserably when no one else answered. "It appears that way."

"Buck up, girl," Ma said with no sympathy. "You aren't responsible for your relatives."

"Thank you for that." Rose sighed. "Clayton has been

very busy lately, and very secretive. Paige is the last possible match, as Maggie said, and now she has a jewel that points directly to Eugenia. I'm afraid I didn't hide my reaction very well last night."

"It's understandable," Alec said. "You were shocked to see it."

"Yes, well, if Clayton has someone on Windfall, and that someone was present and paying attention, Clayton will already know about it."

"What about Paige's DNA test?" Alec asked Hold.

"I'm still waiting to hear back, but I'll turn up the heat tomorrow, when the lab is open for business."

"Well." Ma pointed a finger at Alec. "How much do you charge?"

"For?"

"Your legal services, what else?" She rolled her eyes and shook her head. "What'll it take to put you on retainer?"

"Oh, I think five." Alec let it hang. Like everyone else, Paige expected him to say five thousand, but he said, "Dollars," and left them all staring.

"You patronizing me, boy?" Ma said.

"No, ma'am. Although I am curious as to why you'd want to hire me."

"For the good of Windfall Island. Does that change your mind?"

"The price has been quoted."

Grinning, Ma thumped her fist on the arm of her chair. "Five dollars it is." She held out her hand, and Dex stepped forward to help her up.

She disappeared into the depths of her house, and when she came back she carried a small wooden chest tucked against her hip. The chest was obviously old, inlaid with ivory and beautifully hand carved. She set it on the table next to her chair, settling back with a sigh.

"Let's get something straight first," she said, laying her hand on top of the chest. "None of you have seen this. It doesn't exist."

"If you didn't trust us," Paige said, "you wouldn't have brought that out here."

Ma narrowed her eyes, but she nodded briskly. She lifted the chest onto her lap and opened the top. Inside were leather-bound books in neat rows. "These are the island ledgers, kept by those who've managed Windfall near back to its beginnings. Meeker never got his hands on these, though I think they're why he wants so badly for me to step down in favor of him. He knows records were kept, starting with the salvaging times, a way to keep track so those who felt slighted later on could see proof of how things were divvied up.

"Each successive Elder has kept up with it," Ma concluded. "For my part, it's only major issues, seeing as the sheriff's office keeps records of births and deaths and such."

"And you think, if Eugenia came to the island, it will be in there," Alec said.

"I can't say, as I've never had cause to read them. I'd wager it's worth a look, though." She dropped a wad of change and dollar bills on the coffee table, and waited while Alec gathered it up. "You're bound not to reveal what you learn of island business."

"I am," he acknowledged, "with this retainer."

"Best you count it."

He did, smiling as he uncrumpled three dollar bills

and counted out the change, down to the penny. "There's five dollars here. Do you want a receipt?"

"Damn straight," Ma said. "This is business."

"To us, maybe," Dex put in. "To Clayton Stanhope, it's life-and-death."

Alec reached for the chest, but Ma slid it aside. "Not so fast, I have a condition."

"And that would be?"

"I need someone to take over the running of Windfall Island."

And as she was staring straight at Maggie, Maggie jumped out of her chair. "No. No way."

"Then you don't get your hands on these books."

"We only need one, maybe two," Maggie said, "the year Eugenia disappeared and the year after."

"None of them," Ma said with the kind of finality that told them she meant exactly what she said.

"We could take them," Maggie grumbled.

"But you won't." Ma sat back. "Try to see it from my side, girl. You're strong—stubborn most say. When you make a decision, it's not based on sentiment."

"But—"

"You run a very successful business. It's not that different from running this island. I'm not going to live forever, you know. I want to see this place properly helmed before I go."

"Maybe it's time for a mayor and town council."

"They're politicians," Ma scoffed, "I'm tradition. Place like this, it's easy to get swallowed up and lose our voice. Politicians are ambitious by nature. They'd trade Windfall Island's welfare for a handful of coattail."

Maggie hung her head. "You can't be serious."

"Just say yes, Maggie," Paige said.

"You think I should give in to this blackmail?" Maggie demanded, swinging around to glare at Paige.

"It's not as dramatic as all that."

"Then you do it. In fact"—she jammed her hands on her hips—"I think that's a great idea." Maggie turned back to Ma. "I'll do it, on the condition that Jessi and Paige run this place with me."

"Wait a minute," Jessi said, "how did I get dragged into this?"

"Oh no you don't," Paige said at the same time.

Maggie just waited them out. "Jessi's the one who really runs Solomon Charters. She has the business knowledge. Paige, you understand publicity. You can put a good face on the island, make it even more popular than it is."

"There, you see?" Ma crowed. "Already she's thinking of ways to make Windfall Island prosper."

"That leaves you to make the hard decisions," Jessi said. "Are you sure—"

"We'll make them together."

"But you'll be the one who takes the heat, Maggie."

"I can handle it."

"Then it's settled." Ma removed the journals for 1931 and 1932 from the chest, and held them out to Maggie.

"No," Maggie said, "you're right. Alec should read them, as Windfall Island's legal representative."

When Alec stepped forward to take the journals, the smile on Ma's face said it all. "Now, where are my presents?"

* * *

Since Paige's house wasn't much bigger than Ma's—if a lot more uncluttered—they met up again at Maggie's house after they left Ma's. Benji was upstairs, playing video games; he wouldn't make an appearance until he was dragged, kicking and screaming, downstairs. Or until his stomach was empty, Paige figured.

As they had at Ma's, they'd ranged themselves around the small living room. The journals Ma had loaned them sat on the coffee table and, even with her life in jeopardy, Paige felt more contentment than she could ever remember. Hold sat on the floor, his back against the chair where Jessi sat looking adoringly into his upturned face. George, smiling slightly, sat at one end of the leather sofa with Rose snuggled tightly against his side. Maggie sat at the other end of the sofa with Dex, still radiating nervous energy, perched on the arm where he could take to his feet when he needed to pace.

Alec came in from the kitchen. Paige scooted over to the side of the double-wide chair, then took the cup of coffee Alec handed her so he could sit beside her. It was a tight fit; he had to put his arm around her shoulders so she could lean against him. She wasn't complaining.

She belonged to these people; she loved each and every one of them, and they loved her, she thought, as warmth spread through her. In days to come, wherever in the world she found herself, she'd remember this moment, the laughter and teasing, the smiles and the caring, and her heart would be full because she'd know she had a real family.

"You look good together," Paige said to Rose and George.

"We do, don't we?" Rose smiled up at George, her

face glowing with love. "I just have to convince him I'm serious, and then we can get married and start a family."

George's face turned red, all the way to the tips of his ears. "You won't come to live here," he said.

"Why not? Hold and I aren't that different. If he can find a way to work from Windfall, why can't I?"

"But what about shopping and"—George gestured vaguely to her head—"your hair and manicures and stuff."

"I should be more concerned that you think that's all I'm about."

"You know what I mean. You're used to a big city, where you can get whatever you want at the snap of your fingers."

"It will be a change," Rose agreed, "and you're right, there aren't as many amenities here. And there's no way we're living in an apartment the size of a thimble," she added, referring to the quarters George occupied over the Windfall Island sheriff station. "My bathroom at home is larger than the entire building."

"Exactly my point," George said.

"Stop being a snob, George. And don't forget, any time I want to go to the city, there's a private charter company just down the road."

"It sounds like Rose has thought this through," Jessi said.

George folded his arms across his chest. Paige could all but see him digging his heels in. That didn't mean Rose wouldn't wear him down.

"Suppose we talk about Eugenia? Or rather," George qualified, "whoever tried to harm you, Paige. Been nos-

Anna Sullivan

ing around the village a bit. Sorry to say I don't have anything to show for it."

"I still say it's Meeker." Maggie held up a hand when they all turned to her. "Hear me out. I've been giving this some thought since Jessi pointed out that I need proof. Although I think his *disgusting*"—she made air quotes—"personality is enough.

"First"—Maggie ticked off on her finger—"the journals he loaned me when Dex first came to Windfall. He was awfully quick to hand them over."

"You blackmailed him," Jessi reminded her.

"Yes, but he barely objected. It didn't occur to me at the time, but he didn't put up much of a fuss. He never asked any questions about why I wanted them, and he never mentioned it to anyone else."

"Wait," Paige said, "how would he know you were looking for Eugenia?"

"Any number of ways," Dex said. "Someone might have talked back then. We always assumed it was kept quiet because no one knew which family Eugenia ended up with. But it's possible somebody had a few too many and let something slip."

"To Floyd Meeker?" Paige snorted softly. "Not likely. He was as sour as his grandson, by all accounts."

Maggie spread her hands. "Floyd could have been there that night, for all we know. He wasn't part of the usual crew, but there was so much illness, one or more of the men might have elected to stay close to home that night. They would have called in a replacement who wasn't part of the core team."

"Emmett didn't say anything about it," Dex reminded her, pacing now. Only weeks before, they'd questioned

Emmett about that night. He'd admitted to finding the baby; it had been their first confirmation that Dex wasn't on a wild-goose chase.

"He's in his nineties, his memory is spotty." Maggie looked to Dex. "We'll talk to him in the morning, when he's rested."

Dex rubbed a hand along her shoulder.

"You know, Meeker has been collecting those journals for years," George put in. He spoke slowly, and the others waited, knowing him to be a deliberate man who liked to work his way through a thought in his own time. "Seems to me he'd've read them all through, likely more than once, seeing as how he tried to make something of them once or twice."

"Yes," Dex murmured, taking to his feet. "When I first arrived, Meeker accused me of being from a college or university, trying to get my hands on the journals. I didn't think anything of it until now."

"So he'd know there was nothing to find when he handed them over to you," Alec concluded.

"Nothing definitive."

"It all makes sense," Alec said, "even if it's circumstantial."

"It's not just the journals, though," Jessi said. "Meeker provided Lance an alibi for the day my house was broken into, remember? When did any of us know him to put his neck on the line for anyone, let alone someone who's been gone from the island for a decade? And why did Lance choose to come back now?"

"Mort could have told Clayton you were working on the genealogy with Hold," Dex said to Jessi.

"Yes," Hold said, "and Clayton could have checked

Maggie out and decided Mort was the best way to get to her. But it just doesn't track that he did all that from off island, with no knowledge of any of the players. He must've had someone here all along, someone who knew Mort's mother was sick and Mort needed money badly enough to betray a woman he—sorry, Maggie—loved?"

"It's Mort I'm sorry for," Maggie said. "But I think we're on the right track. Clayton could have figured the best way to get to you, Jessi, is through Benji, but how would he have tracked Lance down?"

"The only person who knew how to find Lance was his mother," Jessi put in. "I wouldn't say she and Josiah Meeker were bosom friends, but they were two of a kind. I don't doubt Meeker would have known how to get around her. And Shelley was asking you a lot of questions in the Clipper Snip the other day, Paige."

"True," Paige said. "She wanted to know about my daily activities. But do you really think Meeker would use his own daughter?"

"In a heartbeat," Maggie said immediately.

"I agree," Alec said. "He tried to kill you, Paige, twice."

"Both could have been accidents."

"Which would be exactly what Clayton would want," Rose put in. "You're beyond famous, Paige. Can you imagine the kind of interest there would be if you were seriously hurt or worse? Every law enforcement agency in the country, including the FBI, would descend on Windfall Island."

"Then we'd better find out if Meeker is our villain," Paige said. "Before he arranges another accident for me."

Chapter Eighteen

Hold's cell phone rang, seeming so loud in the tense quiet of the little office that his hand jerked and he drew a line clear across the genealogy he was transcribing into a form that could be gifted to the people of Windfall Island—once Eugenia's fate was known.

He heard Jessi's chair fall over as she jumped to her feet in the outer office, appearing in the doorway before the phone chimed again.

It had been three days since they'd met at Maggie's and gone their separate ways, each with their own assignments. Dex and Maggie were going to speak to Emmett. Paige and Alec were going to read the journals Ma had lent them. Rose had gone back to Boston, but George had intended to speak to Josiah Meeker.

Hold had put a call in to the lab first thing Monday morning, and he'd been on pins and needles ever since. Jessi joined him at the desk and took the hand he held out, though she was too nervous to sit.

"Is it—"

He held a finger to his lips, and put the phone on speaker so she could listen in.

"It's not a match" were the words that seemed to echo into the silence, once the niceties had been exchanged.

"Hello?"

"We're here, Dr. Finster."

"I take it this is not the result you expected," Dr. Finster said.

"It's not that, exactly." It just puzzled Hold that, after they'd found so much proof that Eugenia had arrived on Windfall Island, there'd been no genetic match. But there was another explanation none of them had considered.

"Could either of the earlier samples have been tampered with?"

"Results can be entered but not deleted without approval." Hold could all but hear Finster drawing himself up in affront. "And I can assure you there has been no inappropriate handling of samples here. Every worker in this lab is held to the highest of ethical and scientific principles."

Hold grinned at Jessi. "So how did you come to lose the first comparative sample?"

The silence that greeted that question was thick enough to cut with a knife.

"Let me guess, a client of a certain status called and asked you to postpone the results." And seeing as he'd traded on the Abbot name in order to get Paige's results fast-tracked, Hold allowed he had little cause to complain. "You don't have to answer that, Dr. Finster."

That earned Hold a sigh of relief. "Thank you, Mr. Abbot."

"Not at all," Hold said, and disconnected.

"Why—"

Hold put a finger to his lips again.

"That's getting annoying," Jessi said in a tone of voice that told him he was pushing his luck—which he already knew. "Just hold your horses, sugar," he said, "and I think you'll see where I'm going."

He dialed the phone, then curled an arm around Jessi's waist and snuggled her close.

"Hello?"

"Rose," Hold said, only to have her cut him off.

"Just a minute," she said, and the line went quiet.

"You're right," Hold said, grinning at Jessi, "that is annoying."

"I had to get somewhere I could talk," Rose said when she came back on a half minute later.

"Am I right in thinking Clayton supplied the DNA sample that was used to compare with Maggie, Jessi, and now Paige?" Hold asked her.

"Yes. I was right here when Dr. Finster swabbed Uncle Clayton's mouth. Why do you want to know?"

"Just a theory I'm working on."

* * *

"You go on and have a couple hours to yourself," Maggie said to her cousin, Han Finley.

Han threw a glance over his shoulder, into the gloomy depths of his grandfather's house. "Are you sure, Maggie? He's been awful cranky the last couple of days."

"I'm used to Uncle Emmett's moods," she said, as she

saw Han out the door to have a well-deserved hour to himself.

"Where's that boy?" Emmett said the moment she and Dex joined him in the main room, where he was parked in his easy chair in front of the television.

"Han went to have a beer," Maggie said. "It's nice that he's staying with you."

"Boy needed some help," Emmett said shortly.

They all knew it was the other way around, and Han was only letting Emmett keep his dignity.

"I'm tired," Emmett said. "I'm going to take a nap."

"Okay." Maggie crossed her arms. "We'll make ourselves comfortable, and when you wake up, we can all have a nice chat."

Maggie might not have noticed that the expression on her face was so much like her uncle's, Dex thought, but Emmett seemed to.

He heaved a mighty sigh. "You're a cold, hard girl."

"I learned from the best. I love you, Uncle Emmett," she began.

"Then leave me in peace."

Dex met Maggie's eyes. He could see it broke her heart to upset a man she loved like a father. But they both knew the pain on his face meant his mind was clear enough to understand what they wanted from him. There might not be a better time for days or weeks to come. They had to act now.

Maggie knelt down by his chair and took his hand in hers. "Burying your head in the sand only leaves your ass sticking up like a nice, big target for me to kick."

It took a second or two, but Emmett couldn't hold

back a grin. "Like I kicked yours a time or two. For your good, of course."

"This is for your good, Uncle. Wouldn't you like to get it off your chest?"

Emmett reached out and flicked her nose.

Maggie smiled. "You used to do that when I was a girl."

"Old habits die hard," Emmett said. "I dearly loved my da, and he told me never to speak of it. But I think he'd want you to know the truth, Maggie, or as much of it as I have to give."

Maggie rose to take the chair Dex brought over and placed close to Emmett's. "Can you tell us about that night on the beach? We're especially interested in who all was there."

Emmett's brow knit, his mouth thinning in frustration. For a minute, Dex thought they'd pushed too hard. Then Emmett closed his eyes and lifted his arms, as if he held a baby. And laughed.

"Me and my da were there," he said, eyes still closed and arms still folded. "You knew that already. Da brought me along for the extra hands, in part, and to get me out of the house in case—" He broke off, swallowed, shook his head a little.

His sister had been deathly ill with the measles, Dex knew, and rubbed Maggie's shoulder when he saw the sorrow of it in her eyes as well.

"Fiske and Norris were there. They were part of the normal crew who made the weekly run. And old Meeker was there—Floyd Meeker, and a sourer individual you never knew."

"That apple hasn't fallen far," Maggie muttered. "Are you sure it was that night, and not another?"

"Ayah," Emmett answered, his New England accent broadening with the memories. "Da usually made the trip out in the boat, but he stayed back, wanting to be close to home. Didn't know if my sister would make it through the night. Meeker didn't usually go along, but they needed the extra hand to get the cases off the big boat."

"You didn't say anything about it before," Dex said.

"You didn't ask me," Emmett grumbled. He dropped his arms and opened his eyes. "All you cared about was the babe. So did old Meeker, which is why I was laughing. Floyd Meeker didn't have a kindly bone in his body, but he offered to take the child. He couldn't have had any good reason, so my da and the others refused him. Warned him not to talk. None of us spoke of it again to anyone, friend or foe."

"And the necklace?" Maggie asked, but gently.

Emmett shook his head. "A king's ransom in rubies and diamonds, though I was too young to know it at the time. Sparkled like fire and ice in the moonlight."

Maggie and Dex shared a look, and a smile.

"I don't know why, but I hid it from the others," Emmett continued. "Except my da, o'course. Don't know whatever became of it. Must've been broken up and pieced out when necessary for the good of the island. That was the way back then. Shame," Emmett added, rambling a bit now. "It belonged to the babe. I understood why she had to be a secret, but she should've had something of her own heritage."

When Maggie turned to him, Dex held her gaze. "Maybe she did."

* * *

Paige held her hand over her shoulder. Alec passed her the magnifying glass. They'd been able to find only one in the village market, so they were sharing. Not that Alec was complaining.

He sat at the end of the sofa, half turned toward the big picture window in Paige's living room. The sky over the Atlantic was a mass of clouds in every shade of gray, like a painting that would have been titled *Brewing*.

With the room cast in gloom, the only floor lamp had been moved to stand directly behind Alec's end of the sofa—which meant Paige had snuggled against him, her back to his front, so she could share the light. She'd stretched her legs out on the sofa and covered them with a crocheted throw, and she felt warm and soft—and distracting—cozied up against him.

She'd bundled her hair up on top of her head and wore her black-rimmed reading glasses. It made him think of libraries with their dark, remote stacks, of prim, apparently repressed women and the secret fires they held within.

The nape of her neck was right there, begging to be nipped, and all he had to do was tip her chin back to kiss her. He drew her in with every breath, and wanted her with every beat of his heart.

Yeah, Alec thought, distracting was a mild way to put it. But he was content to stay there, in their own little oasis of light and warmth, and simply enjoy being with her.

"Here." Paige handed him her journal, twisting against him as she did and making him reassess his last thought. There was being with her, and being *with* her.

"Can you make it out?" she prompted, reminding

him that sometimes it was good to let an appetite build slowly.

He stared at the page, stopped briefly to rub his aching eyes, then squinted at it again. "Something about ballast stones. I think."

Paige sighed, "Oh," and took the journal when he handed it back to her.

They'd had so many moments like that, when the pulse raced and hope exploded that they'd found a mention of Eugenia or the necklace. Only to be disappointed.

They were each reading one of the journals Ma had loaned them, for the years 1931 and 1932. The writing was tiny and cramped, all but illegible in places what with the damage time and water had wrought; Ma hadn't kept them in a heat- and humidity-controlled environment, like Meeker had.

They'd been at it for three days now—three days that felt like forever, considering what hung in the balance.

"Everyone will be here this afternoon," Paige said. "I'd really love to tell them we found something."

"If there's anything to find," Alec qualified. "There's no guarantee we'll find the answer in here."

"Yes, well, I may be blind before…we…" She twisted around and grabbed Alec's wrist.

He could feel the excitement pumping off her, and it sent goose bumps chasing over his skin. "What?"

Paige only gripped tighter and continued to read.

"What?"

She swung her legs down from the couch, started to stand, then sank back down beside him. "God, Alec, my knees are shaking." So was her voice. She handed him the journal. "Read that," she said, placing a sheet of clean paper under the sentence she meant.

Alec read it, then read it again, blowing out a breath. "Jesus."

Paige jumped to her feet, doing a little dance before she pulled him up and threw her arms around him. "I want to celebrate. Let's celebrate."

"Okay." Alec kissed her, sinking in, enjoying the way the heat rose when she kissed him back.

She pulled away a little, just far enough to meet his eyes. "The others are due here in less than an hour."

"I'd say that gives us plenty of time for some good old-fashioned necking."

She smiled as she stepped back. "How about lunch instead."

"I'm not feeling that kind of hunger."

"Maybe not, but you're going to need your energy later." She took him by the hand and pulled him toward the kitchen. The look she shot him over her shoulder was sizzling. And full of promise.

* * *

When Maggie and Dex showed up early, followed closely by Hold and Jessi, Paige could tell, just seeing them through the front window, that they had news, too. Excitement rose inside her, humming along her nerve endings. One look at Alec's face had her laughing.

"You look like the cat that ate the canary," she said to him.

"I don't have your poker face," he said. "You answer that," he said when her phone rang, "I'll get the door."

Paige pulled her phone from her pocket, smiling when she saw the name on the readout. But she let the call go to voice mail.

Harvey Astor, her agent, had been calling since Monday, but she'd been too focused on Eugenia's mystery to talk scripts or be badgered—even good-naturedly—about when she was coming back. And now she was bursting with excitement. Hollywood could wait.

"Floyd Meeker was there that night," Maggie announced before she'd even gotten her coat off.

"Hey," Jessi said from right outside the door. "Wait for us."

She and Hold crowded into the entryway, coats were removed and hung up, and everyone trooped into Paige's small living room.

"Okay," Jessi said from her perch on the arm of Hold's chair. "Talk fast, we have to pick Benji up in an hour."

"It's not a very long story." Dex stood in front of the window; Maggie perched on the wide sill next to him. "Emmett remembers Meeker's grandfather Floyd being there the night they went out to the *Perdition* to buy booze and came back with Eugenia Stanhope."

"He's sure?" Alec asked Dex.

"Sure enough that I believe him," Dex said.

"Uncle Emmett said Floyd Meeker offered to take Eugenia, but they wouldn't let him," Maggie added.

"Good call," Jessi said.

"Old Meeker couldn't take advantage of his knowledge, either," Hold reasoned. "It would have brought the authorities down on Windfall Island. No one would have benefited from that kind of attention."

"He must have handed the story down," Paige said from the wide kitchen doorway. Alec stood not far away. Both of them were too nerved up to sit, but his nearness gave her comfort. "It's probably what sparked Meeker's interest in the island journals."

"Josiah's father wasn't one to go out of his way for anyone or anything," Maggie said, "but Josiah has been chasing money his whole life. I'll bet he heard the story from Floyd, and he combed every journal he could lay his hands on for some inkling of her whereabouts."

"It's still circumstantial," Alec said, "but I'm willing to take a leap of faith. We already know Eugenia's location isn't in any of the journals Meeker loaned you, Maggie, which makes sense. If she survived, the family that took her in would not have wanted it known."

"What about the brooch?" Hold asked.

Maggie rubbed her hands together. "This is where it gets really good. Emmett recognized the ruby brooch."

There was a beat of silence before Paige said, "Did he know how it came to be in my family?"

"No," Dex said. "He never saw the necklace again, and he has no idea if Eugenia survived, or where she ultimately wound up."

"Which brings us to our news," Jessi said. She looked to Hold, who gestured for her to go on. "Paige's DNA doesn't match."

Every eye in the room tracked to her, but Paige kept her expression carefully blank.

"Wait, how did you get it back so fast?" Alec asked when she remained silent as well.

"I may have implied there could be a donation involved."

Jessi snorted. "He all but said it outright." She nudged Hold. "What are you going to do when no donation is made?"

"Who says I won't make one?"

Jessi just shook her head, but her gaze shifted to Dex, Paige noted, as did everyone else's.

"It doesn't make sense," he muttered, pacing as far as the small room allowed. "We found so much evidence that she survived."

"Exactly," Hold said, "so I called Rose and asked her who gave the baseline sample."

"It was Clayton," Dex said. He stopped moving to frown across the room at Hold. "We knew that before. But he could have sent some completely unrelated DNA."

"It was his," Hold said. "Rose was there when he gave the sample, and the owner of the lab collected and ran it himself." He related what Finster had told him about the security protocol at the lab, and about the request Finster had received to delay Paige's test results. By the end of it, both men were grinning.

"So...no one's a match?" Maggie stood, shoved her hands back through her pixie-cut hair. "It's over? Dex?"

It was Hold who answered. "You've all been eliminated as a match. But only to Clayton. What if Clayton isn't a Stanhope?"

Maggie sat again, so abruptly her backside slipped off the narrow windowsill and she dropped to the floor. It might have been humorous, Paige thought, if they weren't all just as shocked and trying to reason out the ramifications.

"It means you'll all need to be retested," Hold said, "using Rose as a baseline this time."

"It means any one of us could be a match?" Jessi rose unsteadily to her feet, her face pale. For her, Paige knew, one of those ramifications was Benji. "That puts us all in danger again."

"That would be true," Alec said, "except Paige and I have some news, too."

Which made them the center of attention, Paige saw, with Jessi clearly hoping for a miracle.

"As far as Clayton knows," Alec continued, "we're accepting the test results. To his mind, that would mean it's over."

"We need to retest," Dex said immediately.

Paige shook her head. "No." She retrieved the journal from the island counter and handed it to Maggie.

Maggie took one look and said, "Jeez, no wonder it took you so long to read this. I'm amazed you made out anything at all." She brought the book close to her face then held it out at arm's length, like she was working the slide on a trombone.

"For heaven's sake," Paige said, "it's right here." She pointed to the line, then read it out loud herself: " 'There is great sorrow for the Finleys this day, but also great happiness. One child cannot replace another, and yet may ease a broken heart.' "

"No." Maggie took a step back, immediately looking to Dex. "It doesn't say for certain."

He stopped his pacing to wrap his arm around her shoulders. "I think it's pretty clear," he said quietly.

"I don't want it."

"I'm sorry," Dex said. "I never imagined...I can't believe it was right there, under my nose, all this time. If I hadn't kept it a secret, Ma would have given us the island journals, and Paige and Jessi would never have been in danger."

"And we'd never have met," Jessi said, cuddling closer to Hold.

Nor would she and Alec, Paige thought, and wished Alec would comfort her, like Dex was comforting Maggie. But a glance at him told her he was ignoring Jessi's comment as studiously as she was. Even with her heart aching.

"Don't second-guess yourself, Dex," Paige said into the silence. "Everything turned out for the best."

"Speak for yourself," Maggie said glumly. "You got to earn your money fair and square."

Jessi laughed. "You're the only person I know in the world who'd turn her back on an opportunity like this, Maggie."

Maggie sighed and rested her head on Dex's shoulder. "It's like winning the lottery, Jess. It sounds great in theory, but then you read about all those people whose lives have been ruined by money."

"You should at least sleep on it," Paige said.

"I won't want it tomorrow, either."

Paige couldn't understand how Maggie felt—not entirely, but she knew how it was to have her life turned upside down.

"Think of the improvements you could make to Solomon Charters," Jessi said. "All the plans you have."

"Where would be the satisfaction in that?" Maggie wondered. "Part of the fun is in the planning, and the rest of it is in working, and seeing that hard work get you what you want." Still looking a little shell-shocked, she straightened. "Where's George? He was supposed to be here."

"What do you want George for?" Dex said.

"I don't want him." Maggie shoved away, scrubbed her hands over her face. "I'm relieved he's not here. I don't think he should tell Rose. Not yet, anyway."

"No," Dex said, "not until you decide what you want to do."

"It's not that." Looking a bit more settled, Maggie took his hand, twining her fingers with his. "We have to think about the best way to handle this."

"We should let Clayton believe he's off the hook," Alec said. "You'll all be safe that way."

Paige heard a knock at the door and moved to the kitchen window that looked out to the front of the house. "Here's George," she said, and went to let him in. "Where's Rose?"

"In Boston," George said, slipping off his heavy coat, then hitching up his cop tool belt. "What did I miss?"

"Come into the living room," Paige said. "I'll get you some coffee."

"I'd be grateful," George said.

Considering how much had changed, the others had brought George up to date in the few minutes it took Paige to pour his coffee and carry it out to him.

"Thank you," George said, taking a sip and closing his eyes as the heat and caffeine hit his system.

"George," Maggie prompted.

"Yeah." His eyes popped open, and he took another hit of coffee before he spoke again. "So, Eugenia didn't leave any descendants behind."

"My DNA was not a match," Paige said when the others hesitated. It wasn't a lie, she reasoned, just not the entire truth. And really, they had no way of knowing if Maggie actually was a Stanhope, not without DNA proof.

"What kept you?" Maggie asked George.

"I went to talk to Meeker on Monday," he said. "Shelley was minding the antiques store. She told me he'd gone to the mainland on a buying trip, and he'd be back today. When I went by the store this morning, it was closed."

"It's never closed," Maggie said.

"No, so I tried to track him down," George continued. "He wasn't at home, either, so I took a turn through the village. I finally ran into Shelley, reading magazines and contributing to the gossip down at the Clipper Snip. Meeker called her this morning, told her he was extending his trip, and didn't know when he'd be back."

"That doesn't make any sense," Paige said. "Why wouldn't he just come back?"

"Maybe he really is on a buying trip," Jessi said.

"Right," Maggie said, "and maybe hell froze over."

"The mystery might be solved," Dex said, "but it looks like the case is far from over." He exchanged a look with George, who nodded.

"Until Meeker turns up," George said, "let's all keep our eyes open and our guard up."

Chapter Nineteen

Josiah Meeker sat in a booth in a small Irish pub on the south side of Boston. A heavy glass sat on the table in front of him, filled with ice cubes and a few inches of pale gold whiskey. He'd have preferred a draft, but he had to think about his image. A man with a seven-figure bank balance didn't slurp beer.

Millionaires didn't frequent a place like this, either, Josiah thought distastefully. The place smelled like beer, grease, and the dusty spice of the peanut shells that crunched underfoot. The jukebox wailed some maudlin Irish tune, and the patrons—men dressed in hooded sweatshirts and baggy jeans, and women dressed in hooded sweatshirts and skin-tight jeans—raised their voices as they called clear across the room to one another.

The decor reminded him of the Horizon, with its mirrored bar and well-used tables and booths, not to mention it was clearly family owned. The ruddy-faced men pulling the taps were obviously father and son, and the waitresses were pretty and red-haired, and bore the same family resemblance. They smiled, a flash of even white teeth in pretty faces, shot suggestive glances over their shoulders, and twitched their backsides.

The tips likely flowed like rain.

"Quite the place, isn't it?" Clayton Stanhope III slid onto the worn bench seat opposite him, smiling broadly as he looked around the big room. There was a fondness in his muddy green eyes that told Josiah he'd been here before. "The burgers are amazing, and they treat everyone like, well, family."

"Clay!" one of the waitresses called out, swiveling her way between tables with her tray held high. "The usual?"

"I've had dinner, Patty, one of those rubber chicken charity gatherings. But I could use a drink."

"You got it, handsome."

She swung away without giving him another glance, Josiah noticed. She returned only a minute later to set a large beer mug in front of Stanhope, filled with dark brown liquid with a foamy head.

"Guinness," the waitress called Patty announced. "Dad started building it when he saw you come in."

Clayton took a sip and sighed in pleasure. "Thank Mickey for me," Clayton said. "You, darling, have my undying gratitude."

"Say it with your tip." Her grin flashed, and she was gone into the crowd.

"She's attending Boston University," Clayton said. "Premed."

"And you're helping her with tuition," Josiah smirked.

"Don't be disgusting," Clayton said heatedly, "she's a family friend." Clayton's gaze streaked to meet his, hardening. "And kindness costs nothing."

Like the kindness Clayton had shown Maggie Solomon, Jessi Randal, and Paige Walker? Josiah thought. Although this time he kept his opinion to himself.

"You insisted on this meeting, Meeker. Threatened to go to Alec Barclay and the others, and tell them a nice little story."

"George Boatwright wants to talk to me."

"And has you running scared, which makes you look like you have something to hide."

Not from where Josiah was sitting. "I was on a buying trip when my girl told me Boatwright came by looking for me. I just extended my trip."

"Why do I have a feeling I'll be doing the buying?"

Josiah leaned across the table. "Rubies and diamonds," he said, smiling smugly when Clayton's eyes cut to him, and his face went pale. "That's the same reaction your niece had. But you aren't interested, are you?" He leaned back.

And oh, how satisfying it was for him to see Clayton lean across the table this time, even if he was spouting orders. "Tell me," he demanded. "I'll make it worth your while."

Josiah told him about the brooch Paige Walker had worn to the Windfall Island holiday party, and Rose's reaction to it. "It's the necklace that went missing when Eugenia was abducted," Josiah felt a need to point out.

Clayton's gaze sharpened. "How do you know about it?"

"The same way I knew about Eugenia. My grandfather was there that night."

"So you came to Boston to tell me about it, where any one of a million people might see you?" Clayton shook his head. "Not that I'm surprised at your failure to understand the danger. You've never managed to accomplish any task I set for you."

Josiah found himself fidgeting. "I made poor judgments, hiring those first two losers. That's why I'm handling this one myself."

"With as little success."

"You want it to look like an accident."

"She's famous," Clayton said through his teeth. "Murder will bring too much scrutiny. We can't have the FBI poking around because a celebrity of Paige Walker's stature died under suspicious circumstances."

"Why don't you wait to see if her DNA matches?"

"I'm running this show," Clayton snapped. "Just do what I tell you. And get it right the next time. And if you can't get Walker, get one of the others."

"Wait. What?"

"Walker is well protected right now, but the other two have let their guard down."

"But you already know they aren't related. I don't think—"

"I'm not paying you to think."

"So…"

"Christ, Meeker, you have to think a little."

"You want one of them dead, or all of them. And it has to look like an accident." And while he'd already committed himself to that end, now it puzzled Josiah. Why would Stanhope want to kill two women who'd already proven they were no threat to him?

"There, that wasn't too hard, was it?" Clayton drained

his glass and set it down with a thunk, then reached into his inside jacket pocket. He pulled out an envelope and laid it on the table. "For your troubles," he said as he calmly stood, removed two twenties, and dropped them on the table. "Don't call me again until you have a success to report."

Chapter Twenty

The meeting turned into an impromptu dinner featuring Carelli's pizza and breadsticks, and the salad Paige threw together. Once the leftovers were divided—which Hold and his bottomless pit of a stomach monitored carefully—everyone took their leave. Bedtime came early for Benji, who had school in the morning, and Maggie, who had a charter flight in Boston.

Since Harvey, her agent, had been trying to call her all day, Paige settled in the living room with her piles of scripts. She'd intended to spend a couple of hours culling the most obvious rejections. She couldn't keep her mind on the task at hand, though; it kept wandering to Alec.

He'd gone upstairs after everyone left. She'd heard him moving around overhead. She'd nearly gone after him to see what he was doing, but part of her was afraid she knew.

When he came down and went into the kitchen, she'd made a decision. Rising, she went to join him. She barely noticed the bottle of wine he took from the fridge and set on the counter, next to two stemless wineglasses.

"It's okay if you want to leave," she said.

He stopped, turned to her, met her eyes. "Are you kicking me out?"

"No."

"Then I'll stay. I'd like to know how this turns out."

She deplored her own neediness, but she had to ask. "Is Eugenia the only reason?"

He smiled. "Not even near the top of the list." He cradled the wine bottle in the crook of his elbow, held both glasses in his cupped palm and fingers, and with his free hand, took hers.

She went with him, up the stairs, but she paused in the bedroom doorway, surprised, dazzled, and impossibly touched.

She'd heard the music as she came up the stairs, something low and smooth, but she hadn't understood until she saw the room glowing with the light of the dozen candles set around. The bed was turned down and strewn with rose petals.

He let go of her hand to cross the room, setting the glasses and bottle on the bedside table. "You're not going shy on me all of a sudden..."

She shook her head. "It's just..."—she spread her hands—"unexpected, beautiful."

She crossed the room and picked up a handful of rose petals, bringing them to her face so she could feel their cool silkiness and smell their delicate scent. "Where did you get the flowers?"

"Why do you think I went into town with Hold to get the pizza?"

"I didn't—think about it, that is."

Alec poured wine, but although Paige's throat was hot and aching she didn't take a glass, not with her stomach pitching along with her jangling nerves. He must have seen it on her face, the puzzlement. The hope.

"It occurred to me that I've never given you this. Given you romance," he said with a kind of quiet solemnity that told her it meant something to him. She meant something to him.

Her heart stuttered, lifted. "I don't need—"

"You'd never ask," he corrected her. "Every woman needs romance, Paige."

"I..." Words failed her. "Thank you. It's lovely."

He brushed the backs of his fingers across her cheek, and simple delight moved through her. "You're lovely," he said, and swayed her into a slow dance that was so sweetly relaxing and invigorating at the same time.

She tipped her head onto his shoulder and closed her eyes. It felt wonderful to rest in his arms, to feel warm and wanted and cherished.

Alec's thigh slipped between hers as they circled. Heat licked along her skin, and she shuddered delicately. He nibbled at the lobe of her ear, and the heat began to build. He brushed his open mouth down her neck to the place where it joined her shoulder, and bit lightly. Her knees went weak.

Alec steadied her. He always steadied her. The thought encompassed more than that moment, but she couldn't reason it out just then, not with her nerves humming. She reached for the hem of her cashmere sweater.

"Let me," Alec said. He slipped the sweater over her head, then stepped back.

She wore nothing but a lace camisole beneath. When he touched her, just the skim of his fingertips along the lace covering her breasts, need speared through her, need so intense she reached out.

Alec was there. He wrapped his hands around her waist, slipped them up her rib cage, feathered his thumbs over her nipples.

Her breath slipped out on a moan. Alec swept her up. Even when he laid her on the bed, the world continued to spin. She felt his hands sweep over her skin as he removed her clothes. Before she could notice the chill, he was next to her. A sense of...*rightness* seemed to settle over her, another layer of emotion swamping her.

Then there was only heat, building, blinding heat. His lips were a brand on the slope of her breast, nibbling, licking, then biting gently before he drew her flesh into the heated depths of his mouth. She felt the pull all the way to her toes.

She reached for him, wanting to feel him under her hands, her lips.

"What's your hurry?" he whispered, his breath hot in her ear.

She would have laughed if she'd had the breath. What was her hurry? Her blood pumped hot through her veins, and her skin burned. She was a mass of strained nerves and aching emptiness. The need to belong to him was so strong and deep it felt as if her very bones yearned.

She lay back, though, lay back and let him set the pace. Lay back and forced herself to take it as his lips moved to her breasts again, licked and nibbled and suckled until her breath panted and her hands fisted in the sheets. Then his lips moved down, over her ribs, her belly. The sensitive skin of her inner thighs.

His mouth closed over her. She bucked, cried out, and when he gripped her hips all she could do was writhe as his tongue and teeth drove her to an orgasm that shattered her, and left her entire body trembling with pleasure.

"Look at me," he said, "Paige."

She opened her eyes, and reached for him.

He slid up until his body covered hers, slipped inside her slowly, sipping the moan from her lips. When he moved, he moved just as slowly, long, languid strokes. She rocked beneath him, growing wilder as the blood beat hot under her skin. Instead of slaking her need, the feel of him over her, in her, only increased the hunger. It grew and spread until she was caught in it. In him.

"Look at me," he demanded, and her eyes opened, fixed on his.

In the gray depths she saw more than desire. She saw tenderness, and it rushed through her, twined in and around the need. Words trembled on her lips now, three little words she would have uttered, if she'd had the breath.

Before she could fill her lungs, he was kissing her, as slowly and deeply as his body stroked hers. She opened herself, took more of him, and yet more, joining him in a slow, sinuous rhythm until, in the space of a heartbeat, he went from controlled to feral.

With a groan, he gathered her up, pounded himself into her, hard, deep thrusts that rocked her. Drove her.

"More," she gasped, glorying in his desperation and her own, wanting the violence.

As her climax rolled and raged, wave after wave of pleasure, Alec threw his head back and roared, locking himself deep. She could feel his orgasm shudder through him, felt his arms tremble, though he tried to spare her when they finally gave out.

Her arms flopped to the mattress, as damp and boneless as the rest of her. They stayed that way, until Alec drummed up enough energy to move.

"Where are you going?"

"If I don't get something to drink, I'm going to die of thirst." But he only sat on the edge of the bed.

Paige ran a hand over his back. "Change your mind?"

He grinned over his shoulder at her. "I'm not sure my legs will hold me."

She scooted over and put her mouth where her hand had been.

Alec hissed out a breath. "Suddenly I'm feeling rejuvenated."

"Good," she said when he turned to her. "But maybe you should fetch the wine anyway. I have a feeling it's going to be a long night."

The end was coming, she feared as she drank the tart red wine. Eugenia's mystery was nearly solved, and then he'd go back to his life just as she'd go back to hers. They'd made no declarations, no plans, no promises to each other. There wouldn't be many more nights like this, she knew, so she'd make each one last.

* * *

When the phone rang the next morning, Paige hissed out a breath and covered her eyes until it stopped.

Barely a minute later, "That's Entertainment" sang out into the room again. Alec groaned and slapped a pillow over his head.

Paige opened one eye enough to read the clock face, sighing when she saw it was nearly noon. "It's my agent. I should answer it," she said, and while her voice was scratchy, her body felt wonderfully sore.

She reached for the phone, but Alec grabbed her around the waist and pulled her back, maneuvering her until she was beneath him. "I'll call him back later," she said just before Alec's mouth cruised over hers.

Later turned out to be a lot later, after a shower and a meal she ate as ravenously as she'd loved Alec that morning.

Love.

She looked over at Alec, sitting at the kitchen island with her, engrossed in his newspaper. He hadn't shaved, so he was a little scruffy. Beautiful, she thought with a sigh, tall and lean and perfect. Like an ad out of a glossy magazine, for coffee or...whatever. It didn't matter; if he was selling something, women would buy it.

His gaze lifted. Paige met his gray eyes and smiled because it felt so right to be there with him, after a night of marathon lovemaking. It should have scared her to death; it only made her sad because she loved him. She'd admitted that sometime during the night; he'd torn down all her barriers, left her no choice but to face the truth of it. She was in love, and while a part of her wanted to run, she'd also decided to live in the moment. What else could she do with her heart so full of joy?

In her experience love never lasted, but that only

meant she should wring every ounce of happiness from
the time she would be given.

"What?" Alec said, smiling quizzically at her over the
top of his paper.

"I..." *Love you* trembled on her lips, but saying those
two simple words would change everything. She only
wanted to share her happiness, and to have the truth between them. He'd take it as an expectation on her part,
and when he didn't say it back, the ease between them
would be destroyed. "I'm glad you stayed."

He took her hand to toy with her fingers. "You made
that pretty clear last night."

"I'm glad you're here now. Right now."

He frowned a little. "Me, too," he said, as if he was
puzzled to feel that way. He folded the paper, looked
around the room. "What do you want to do today?"

"I have to call Harvey back. He's been trying to get
me since Monday. Remember the phone rang and woke
us up?"

"Remind me to thank him." But his smile faded. "Is
he trying to get you to go back to work?"

"Maybe." It didn't feel that way, though. "He called
pretty early—for California time."

"It's the start of the business day."

Alec's observation made her laugh a little. "Harvey's
business day starts at lunch and ends with whatever party
he's attending."

"Should I be jealous? He sounds like more than an
agent."

Paige squeezed his hand. "Harvey would rather date
you than me. But you're right about him being more than
an agent. He's my best friend. I'd do anything for him

and he'd do anything for me." She picked up her cell phone. "This will only take a couple of minutes, then I'm all yours."

"Is that a promise?"

She stopped dialing to look at him. She could tell he wanted to say something, but he only shook his head.

"Call your agent." Alec picked up his coffee and wandered to the big window overlooking the harbor.

But Paige could tell he was listening.

"Harvey," she said when he picked up on the first ring. She forgot everything in the joy of hearing a friendly voice—even when that voice was cranky.

"Where have you been?" Harvey demanded.

"Right here."

"Not answering your phone—which, by the way, it took me two days to remember you had."

"It was your idea for me to leave my phone behind and use this untraceable one instead," Paige reminded him.

"Yes, well, the least you could do was *answer* it when I called."

"I was busy."

"Doing who?"

Paige looked over at Alec, and chose to change the subject. "Which script are you calling about, and why is it so important?"

"Who cares about scripts? Have you been on the Internet lately?"

"Me? On the Internet?"

She heard Harvey sigh impatiently, could almost see him pacing his office, his tall, elegantly slim body encased in something right off the menswear runway. His hair would be on end, she imagined fondly, because he'd been dragging his fingers through it. And he'd only get more annoyed with her if he realized she wasn't paying attention.

"Hell, who am I talking to," he was saying, "You never read reviews or blogs."

"What's the point?" Paige said, and then something he'd mentioned got through. "Wait, what about the blogs?"

"The tide has turned, darling. It's out there, all over the 'net that it's not you on that nasty tape."

Paige had to sit down. "What are you talking about? Start at the beginning."

"It's not a long story, kid. Someone is out there on the World Wide Web, tilting at windmills. Goes by the user name DonQ."

"Don Quixote. Cute."

"There are comments on several of the blogs, suggesting it's not really you on that tape. It was very cleverly done, too."

"Clever how?"

"A causal mention of the fact that it might look like you, but it doesn't seem like something you'd do. You know, why would an A-list actor with your kind of fame stoop to that kind of tasteless publicity ploy?

"It's posed as a question, which is very shrewd. A question makes people wonder, where an opinion would only have them arguing their own point of view. Oh," he continued, sounding gleeful, "my favorite is the one that comments on Jackson Howard, the director. If he's slimy enough to cheat on his wife, why doesn't anyone think he's cagey enough to lie about who he's cheating with, and use it as an opportunity to pay you back for the cutting comments you made about him?"

If she hadn't already been sitting Paige would have fallen down. Her stomach began to pitch, too, because it was almost exactly what Alec had said only days before, when he'd been trying to get her to fight back against the rumors.

"And then there's this one," Harvey continued, "about how interesting it is that your face is never shown, and has anyone checked to see if there's a way to prove it's you? But the really interesting thing—are you listening?"

"Yes," Paige strangled out. Her eyes went to Alec, still silhouetted against the window, with his back to her.

"All the comments were made on the same day, roughly at the same time," Harvey finished.

"When would that be?" Paige asked. As Harvey named the day Alec had spent in Boston, she closed her eyes.

"You've been holding out on me, love."

Her throat had gone hot and tight, so she said nothing.

"Not about the tape," Harvey said into the silence. "You're seeing Alec Barclay, one of the most eligible bachelors in the country."

"I—"

"Don't tell me nothing is going on, those clever questions have already been traced back to him. Paige, darling, when did it start? How did you meet him?"

"I have to go," she said, and disconnected. When the phone began to shrill again, she ignored it, even knowing Harvey would be angry and hurt.

Nothing else seemed to matter, now that she'd discovered she was in love with a man who didn't love her back. If Alec loved her, he'd have respected her wishes. He'd have trusted her to handle her own problem. If Alec loved her, he'd understand why his actions were wrong. But then, if he'd understood why responding to the blogs was wrong, he'd never have done it in the first place.

Chapter Twenty-One

When the room went silent, Alec turned away from the window to find Paige sitting at the kitchen island. Her head was down, and the elegant line of her profile that he'd admired when he'd been sitting next to her now seemed pale and set.

Clouds had swept in while she'd been talking, turning the house gloomy. Alec didn't switch on any lights. He didn't need them to see that her eyes, when she lifted her gaze to his, were deep blue wells of hurt and sadness.

It sent a chill down his spine. "What was that all about?" he asked.

"I think you know," she said softly.

Thinking furiously, Alec took a deep breath. But in the end, he knew there was only one way to proceed. "The blogs."

"It was you."

"It was stupid," he said. "A moment of anger. I saw that tape and—"

"You saw that tape?" Those big, blue, wounded eyes closed, but it didn't relieve him of the guilt.

"It wasn't you, Paige, why does it matter?"

"They've already traced the blog comments, Alec."

Now the chill that chased over his skin became a ball of ice in the pit of his stomach. "Why would anyone bother?"

"There are people who live for this kind of thing, or rather who make their living off of it," she said, her voice stronger as anger began to burn through the hurt. "Don't you understand what it's worth for the entertainment media or the tabloids to be the first to report that the tape is a hoax?"

"Aren't you being overly dramatic?"

"No," she said, sounding weary. "You're being naïve, Alec. You've only traded one salacious story—a story that had almost outlived its mileage—for another. The first photo of us together will sell for upward of a million dollars. Do you have any idea what that's going to mean when they find out where we are?"

"I thought it was anonymous."

Paige shot to her feet, began to pace. "Nothing is anonymous in this day and age. Everything can be traced." She seemed almost to be talking to herself now, working it out in her mind as she turned to him. "But you knew that."

"I didn't see why anyone would bother."

"And you never meant for me to know."

Alec scrubbed a hand over his face. It did little to curb his frustration. "If you had dealt with it before, it wouldn't be an issue now."

She whipped around. "You're blaming me for this?"

She laughed a little, an incredulous puff of air. "You're right, Alec, it's all my fault. I've made poor decisions right down the line. When I went after that part, even though I knew Howard wasn't inclined to hire me. When I commented publicly on how difficult he was to work with, and how we'd never clicked on the movie we did together before." She lifted her eyes. "And then when I got involved with a man who doesn't trust me to manage my own life."

Alec held her gaze. "You left out running and hiding."

"I didn't run, and I'm not hiding. Defending myself would only have made me look guiltier, and with the press in a feeding frenzy my only course of action was to leave Hollywood. I came here because it's home, and I knew the Windfallers would protect me."

"Meanwhile your reputation is in shreds."

She threw her hands up. "You're a lawyer. You should understand that silence is a viable defense. Sometimes it's the only defense."

"The truth works, too."

"Whose truth? All you've done by getting the truth out there is give them what they want."

"The press—"

"I'm not talking about the press this time," Paige snapped, all but crackling with fury. "Why do think the tape was leaked in the first place? That bimbo was trying to break up Howard's marriage."

"So the wife should be in the dark?" Alec asked. "There are children involved."

"That didn't seem to matter to you when I was the bimbo. Was it easier to forgive him for cheating with a legend?"

"Paige—"

"Now that he cheated with a nobody, Lucy Howard will have to face the truth that her husband wasn't seduced by my fame and glamour. She'll have to take a stand. And as you pointed out, there are children involved. She isn't the only one who'll be hurt. They could have handled it quietly, but now it's going to play out in public."

"And that's my fault, too."

"And you know who's going to win?" Paige continued as if he hadn't spoken. "The bimbo. She gets what she wants because Howard can't dump his family if it's not for love."

"He was wrong," Alec said.

"So were you, and you know what they say about two wrongs."

Alec shoved his hands in his pockets, pulled them back out. "I just wanted everyone to stop believing you slept with him."

She shook her head. "You did it for you, Alec."

"That's not true."

"And if you'd discovered it was me on that tape? Could you have accepted that I'd made a mistake?"

"Yes."

She braced her hands on the back of a chair, as if it was too much effort to hold herself upright. "You don't believe that any more than I do."

A defense sprang to Alec's lips. He didn't utter it. Sometimes, he admitted dryly, a defense only made you look guiltier. He'd started off on the wrong foot with Paige, a judgmental, opinionated foot. She remembered it, and so did he. "So what do we do now?"

"I think you know."

Panic washed through him, made his heart pound and his breath stall in his lungs. "I wish you wouldn't make more out of this than it is."

"You have no idea how big this is going to get. I wish you believed in me enough to accept my word on it."

"Believe in you?" Alec huffed out a laugh. "I love you."

Paige hunched her shoulders a little and half turned away from him, as if she'd taken a blow. "I know you believe that," she said so softly he could tell she was holding back tears, "but you can't love without trust, and you don't trust me."

"Paige," Alec began, only to be stopped by a knock at the front door.

"I don't think there's anything left to say, Alec."

* * *

Paige headed for the door, as thankful her eyes were dry as she was for the interruption. Though she'd spent the last ten minutes trying to make Alec understand the ingenuity of the press, it didn't occur to her to wonder if they'd already found her—until she opened the door and found a stranger on her doorstep.

He stood tall against the cold and wind, though he had to be in his seventies, tall and lean, with silver hair and a lined face that was still handsome.

"Garrett Barclay," he said, but she'd already marked the resemblance, the cool gray eyes. Alec's eyes.

"Grandfather," Alec said from behind her. "How did you get here?"

"That girl brought me," Garrett Barclay said in a booming voice as he stepped inside without an invitation and shut the door behind himself. "Damn fine pilot, not much of a socializer. Didn't even get out of the car and take the trouble to introduce me," he complained. "Said she needed to check on her fuel shipment, and a man who ran half the country could probably manage to knock on your door without her help."

"You were throwing your weight around again."

"I only wanted her to take a little shortcut to save time," Garrett said to his grandson. "She refused, something about flight paths and fiery crashes. Bah, girl pilots."

"Brace yourself," Paige said. "We may be about to have a girl president."

"Democrats." Garrett snorted. "I'll have to move to a more sensible country."

"I don't think they'll have you anywhere else," Alec said.

Paige looked over at him, brows raised. "I see where you get it from."

Alec gave her a ghost of a smile. "I'll take you to lunch, Grandfather."

"I didn't come to talk to you," Garrett snapped. "Not yet anyway."

Alec turned to look at her, but Paige held Garrett Barclay's gaze. It was very important, she suspected, not to flinch now. "Paige Walker," she said, offering her hand. "Welcome to my home, Mr. Barclay."

He shook her hand gingerly. "You say my name like you have a mouthful of something unpleasant."

"I imagine I'm going to feel like I have."

Garett stood back and studied her, his expression un-revealing.

Again, Paige held his gaze. Although she'd already given away her feelings about the situation, she wasn't going to let him browbeat her.

"I'll go warm up the car," Alec said in resignation.

That got Paige's attention. "I assumed the two of you would gang up on me."

"You don't need any help," Alec said without meeting her eyes. "You can join me when you're done, Grand-father. If there's anything left of you."

"I haven't met my match yet."

"You're about to," Alec said on his way out.

The door shutting behind him sounded so final, the thunk seemed to resonate in her bones. Already achingly lonely, Paige turned away, offsetting her rudeness by saying, "I'll get you some coffee." She poured him a cup, then stepped down into the family room to retrieve the whiskey decanter. She held it up and sent him a ques-tioning look.

When Garrett Barclay only stared at her, she poured in a healthy shot. He took a drink, exhaling loudly in ap-preciation. "You might want some of that yourself," he said.

"I don't need liquid courage."

His eyes narrowed, but he let her implication go. "My grandson has faith in you," he said instead.

"That's a matter of opinion."

"If he didn't he'd be standing here right now."

"You didn't come here to find out what he thinks of me," Paige said bluntly. "You're here to find out what I want from him."

"That's part of it."

"I don't want anything from him." But it wasn't true, she thought immediately. She wanted his love; she wanted his trust. She'd been foolish enough to hope he might give those things to her, even after he'd made it clear from the moment they met that he never would.

She wasn't, however, going to discuss such private and painful topics with Garrett Barclay, the lion guarding the gate.

"I've worked hard for what I've accomplished," she said, "and I didn't use my body."

"All indications to the contrary."

Paige had known that blow was coming, and she absorbed it without flinching, without dropping her gaze.

Garrett watched her, hands steepled, waiting for her to crack.

Instead of intimidating her, it shot steel into her spine. "It's too bad," she said. "From what I've read about you, I wouldn't expect you to be so gullible. It's never a good idea to believe something just because it's in the paper or on the evening news."

"Or on film?"

"I'm quite sure you know the difference between truth and fiction," Paige said, "just as I'd expect a man of your stature to understand the value of reputation."

"And that there are those who seek to tear it down for any number of reasons."

"Or simply because they enjoy the destruction."

"I doubt that's the case here," Garrett said, his eyes taking on a crafty gleam. "You know, I've had a few phone calls from the press."

"You think I leaked my whereabouts. Or Alec's."

His gaze narrowed on her face. "No, I can see it was a surprise to you."

"Not as big a surprise as it should be," she murmured, adding for his benefit, "I'd suggest you go home and let the press beat their heads against the walls of your estate, Mr. Barclay. They'll get frustrated eventually, and go away. Or there will be a new scandal to distract them. There's always a new scandal."

He got to his feet. "You'll come to Boston with Alec and me," he said in a tone that brooked no argument.

Paige, however, wasn't one of his lackeys. "No."

"Alec will want—"

"Alec has already made his choice."

He tugged on his bottom lip. "Interesting. You don't strike me as a woman who gives up so easily."

"You don't know me very well. I learned at a young age to pick my battles."

"And you don't think you can win this one?"

She didn't have the heart to fight it and lose. "Alec has a deep loyalty to his family."

"And you believe I would try to keep the two of you apart? That I would make him choose between you and me?"

Paige drew in a breath and let it out slowly, desperate to hold in the tears burning behind her eyes. "I'm aware of what you must think of me, but I would never try to separate Alec from the people who are important to him."

"You underestimate me, Ms. Walker, you underestimate Alec, and you even underestimate yourself. And you have no idea what I think of you."

"You didn't rush to Windfall Island because you thought Alec was in over his head?"

"Alec is never in over his head," Garrett said in his booming voice. "That being said, I did come here to reassure myself that he's aware of the press's interest in him." He picked up his cup and drained it. "As for my opinion of you, well, I may have come here with a particular frame of mind where you're concerned, but I'm not so inflexible that my mind can't be changed."

Paige didn't ask the obvious; his frame of mind didn't matter now that Alec was out of her life. "I'm sorry it turned out this way. I think we might have been friends under other circumstances."

She followed him to the door and opened it. She kept her gaze away from the Jeep, where Alec stood waiting beside the passenger door. "It was...interesting to meet you," she said to Garrett.

"I'll say the same, and hope it's not the last time our paths cross." Garrett stared at her for a second or two, and if his eyes had softened since she'd first met him, she decided it would be best not to acknowledge it.

She already had enough to regret.

* * *

By the time they parked in front of the Horizon, Alec had related the bare bones of Eugenia's story to his grandfather. No names were mentioned, especially Maggie's. That information was hers to share, if she chose.

Garrett had listened in silence, taking it all in and, Alec knew, working it around in his formidable brain. "So the girl was in danger? You were only here to protect her?"

"At first."

"Ah." Garrett climbed out of the Jeep, as limber as a man half his age. "And now?"

Alec looked at him over the roof of the car. "I'm going to marry Paige."

"Damn right you are," Garrett boomed.

"What? What about all those society women you've been parading around me?"

"I told you, boy, those are the women I know," Garrett grumbled. "I'm not such a snob as you think. There's nothing wrong with an infusion of fresh blood."

"Well, that widens the gene pool considerably. Maybe I should hit the strolls down by the docks next time I'm looking for a date."

Garrett sent him a sidelong look, not amused. "Don't be a smart-ass."

Alec opened the door and ushered his grandfather inside. He waved to AJ, in his usual position behind the bar. Otherwise, the place was empty.

"My grandfather, Garrett Barclay," Alec said to AJ. "Grandfather, this is AJ Appelman. He owns the Horizon."

"Pleasure," AJ said. "What'll you have?"

"Coffee," Alec said, "and whatever the special is."

AJ's smile bloomed, and he waved them off. "I'll have it right out."

Alec continued on to a booth, taking the side that let him keep an eye on the room.

AJ wasn't far behind, setting coffee cups on the table along with a carafe. He slid a basket of bread in the middle of the table, then placed a wide bowl in front of each of them, filled with a thick, steaming broth teeming with chunks of chicken and vegetables.

Garrett sampled a bite. His closed eyes and low moan

were commentary enough, even before he said, "Absolutely delicious. That's the second time I've questioned your judgment needlessly," he added after AJ, beaming, took himself back behind the bar. Then, unfortunately, he returned to his favorite subject. "You'll have amazing babies, you and Ms. Walker. Not only attractive, as befits a Barclay, but strong."

"I don't think she's going to let me back into her house, let alone in baby-making range." Alec shoved his bowl aside and picked up his cup, wishing it held a nice, stiff shot of whiskey rather than coffee. "I made a mess of things," he said miserably.

Garrett broke a fluffy roll open and spread it with butter. "There's not a man alive who hasn't been in your shoes, boy. Groveling will do the trick."

"You don't know how stubborn Paige is." Alec could see his life stretching out, long and lonely, seeing Paige everywhere and not being able to touch her, to hold her. He didn't know how he'd stand it. He couldn't stand it now, with his heart like ice in his chest.

"You'll find a way," Garrett said, his voice tempered a little, both in volume and roughness, before it firmed again. "You're a Barclay. We don't stop until we get what we want."

And Alec would get what he wanted, he decided. He'd get through to Paige no matter how long it took him. He couldn't imagine his life without her in it. "How—" He stopped, cleared his throat. "How did you find me?"

"Had one of the techs in my R&D division track your cell phone. My assistant chartered your friend to come and get me."

"Of course," Alec said. No sweat for a man of Garrett's resources.

"It wasn't that difficult," Garrett continued, "which is part of why I came. The press has been calling and coming around. Only a matter of time before they find you, too."

"My cell phone number is unlisted, but that won't stop them." They'd find Paige as well, despite her throwaway phone. Now that he'd created a new, and even more salacious, angle to the story, the press had a powerful motivation to locate her. Finally, he began to understand what she'd been trying to tell him. "I'll get you a room," he said to his grandfather.

"Can't that girl fly me out tonight?"

"What did Maggie say when you asked her?"

"She said no," Garrett rumbled in disgust. "Something to do with FAA regulations about flying hours."

"Then you'll need a room."

Garrett scooped up the rest of his stew, sighing and patting his stomach in satisfaction. "Ought to get yourself one, too."

"I don't plan on sleeping here tonight," Alec said.

"Then you'd better do a lot of fast talking, boy."

Alec made a noncommittal sound of agreement, but he knew talking wasn't going to get Paige back. Words would never gain him her trust. It would take a lifetime of actions to convince her his love was real. So a lifetime was what he'd give her.

* * *

It took another hour before Alec's grandfather finished nursing his coffee, delivered compliments to AJ, and curled his lip over the Horizon's best room. It was warm and clean, if not exactly the five-star accommodation Garrett Barclay was used to.

When he got back to Paige's house, Alec was surprised to find the door unlocked. He let himself in and, feeling like an intruder, made his way back to the kitchen. He found Paige there, looking pale but composed.

Scripts were piled on just about every flat surface and, while Alec watched, she picked one up from the island chair, studied its title, and added it to one of the stacks on the island.

"I really have to finish sorting through these," she said evenly, as if she were making polite conversation with a stranger.

Alec bit back on the urge to take her by the shoulders and shake her until she listened to him. Until she *heard* him. He loved her, not as a man who admired a perfect princess in an ivory tower. He loved her for who she was, stubborn, opinionated, frustrating, beautiful, and maddeningly independent.

But she was wounded now. He'd hurt her deeply, broken her trust. Nothing he could say would change that today.

And there was reality to be faced. "I have to go back to Boston, to deal with the press."

She glanced over at him, her expression placid, although her eyes were shuttered. "Now who's running away?"

Had he thought she was calm? "Do you want me to hold the press conference on Windfall?"

"I don't want you to hold a press conference at all. You'll only feed the frenzy."

"It's my fault we're in this predicament. I have to do something to fix it."

She turned to face him. "You could start by apologizing to me."

He could have done it—*should* have done it. But he couldn't bring himself to. "I may have gone about it the wrong way, Paige, and it may have come before you wanted it to, but that tape needed to be dealt with."

"And I wasn't getting to it quickly enough to suit you? It's my choice how I deal with this, Alec."

He said nothing.

"And if I told you I put it off because I wanted to spend a little more time with you? Eugenia's mystery has been solved. I should have left days ago."

He had to look away from the stark emotion in her eyes, but he couldn't stop himself from remembering her words, God, was it only a few days ago? *I'm glad you're here now,* she'd said, *Right now.* Worse, he now had a word for the look he'd seen in her eyes then. *Love.*

He'd admitted his feelings for her, but hadn't wanted to acknowledge what she felt for him. Acknowledging it would have meant thinking about the next steps, and he hadn't been ready for that, not until he felt her slipping away. Then he'd made up his mind in a hurry. Now he could only pray he wasn't too late.

"Come with me, Paige."

"No." It was flat, unemotional. Final. What he saw in her eyes now was determination.

"I'll worry—"

"I'm not in danger anymore."

"We don't know where Meeker is."

"He has no reason to harm me. I have no blood connection to the Stanhopes."

"Clayton has no blood connection to the Stanhopes. If he thinks we're suspicious—"

"Why would he?" She chose another script, flipped it open to the title page. "We haven't questioned the DNA tests, as far as he knows."

Alec blew out a breath, shoved his hands in his pockets, then pulled them out again. "You're not going to make this easy on me, are you?"

Paige slapped the script down on one of the piles, then rounded on him. "Oh, by all means, let's make this easy on you."

"Paige..." He sighed heavily. "This isn't like you."

"Isn't it? We only met a few weeks ago. You don't know me very well, Alec, and I clearly don't know you as well as I thought I did."

"Then come to Boston with me, let's spend some time together without any outside distractions, get to know each other."

"Right, you and I in Boston together, at the Barclay family compound. I thought you wanted to get rid of the sharks, not chum the water."

"Stop," he said, not sure if he aimed it at her or himself. The more she pushed him away, the shakier his hold on his temper became. "Why do you care what the press thinks?"

"I have to, Alec. I love my work. It's my life, and the press is part of that life, whether I prefer it that way or not. If I stopped making movies today, they'd still hound me. If you can't understand that, then you shouldn't be with me."

"I understand. It doesn't mean I like it."

"No, but you'd have to be able to live with it."

"I'm not a stranger to this, Paige. My family may not have your level of celebrity, but we've dealt with our share of attention from the press."

She closed her eyes, turned away. "I can't do this anymore."

Alec could see she was on the edge of a breakdown, but instead of convincing him to walk away, it gave him hope. He took her by the shoulders, spun her around. And when she wouldn't meet his eyes, he tipped her chin up until she had to. "Tell me you're not in love with me."

"Why?" She knocked his hand away, then dashed her fingers across her damp cheeks. "Because love conquers all?"

"Yes, if you want to put it that way."

"Experience has taught me otherwise, Alec."

"General experience, or with me, specifically?"

She smiled, and if it was a little wobbly, at least it was better than tears. "Take your pick."

"You don't trust me now."

"In hindsight you did exactly what I should have expected you to do, if I'd been seeing you clearly. It's me I don't trust, Alec."

"It's love you don't trust."

"That, too."

She turned back to her scripts, but not before he saw the flash of pain in her eyes. He wanted to win her back, but he was only hurting her. He'd known she wasn't ready to hear him, but he'd had to try.

"I can see there's no changing your mind, Paige," he

said. "I have to go to Boston, but I'll be back and we'll finish this."

"I won't be here."

"Then I'll find you."

She set down the script she was holding, and kissed him on the cheek. "Good-bye," she said, then made her way through the kitchen and into the back hallway.

A moment later, when Alec looked out the wide window that framed Secret Harbor, he saw Paige walking her cliffs.

Alone.

* * *

Alec couldn't leave Windfall until morning, and Paige didn't have the strength to ask him to leave. Asking him to leave would have meant talking to him, and talking to him meant opening the door to another attempt by Alec to convince her he was sorry.

She knew he was sorry. She'd heard his promises to never do it again. What she wanted was for him to take it back, and that he couldn't do.

Paige hadn't bothered to make a meal she knew neither of them would eat. Instead, she'd gone upstairs and closed herself in her bedroom with a pile of scripts that needed to be read.

After a while, she heard the unmistakable sounds of Alec packing through her bedroom door. If her heart hadn't already been broken, that would have done it.

She opened one of the scripts, even if her mind wasn't nearly clear enough to focus on the words she read. The pretense helped to steady her, the clear symbol of the life she had waiting for her when all this was over. It was a good life, she reminded herself, and if she spent the rest of it alone, well then, that would be her choice.

When her vision went blurry, she shut her eyes and fell into a fitful sleep. She woke sometime during the night, with tears leaking out of her eyes and Alec, fully clothed, on the bed with her. His arms were snugged around her, and she had her head pillowed on his shoulder. His chin rested on the top of her head. His breathing was slow and even.

Had she thought her heart was broken before? Paige wondered as her tears flowed stronger and hotter. She didn't know how she contained so much pain. Alec was only trying to soothe them both, she knew that, but it was like being shown a snapshot of what her life might have been like if things were different between them.

She wanted it more than she could ever have imagined. But how did she trust a man who could so completely ignore her wishes? How could she spend a life with Alec, when he refused to see what he'd done wrong?

She ought to move away from him, but she only turned so that her back was to him. Alec stirred, mumbled, and spooned himself around her, all without waking. It was torture, but Paige couldn't deny herself these last moments with him. She let her tears fall, and admitted that she'd already forgiven him.

The question was, could she trust him again? She wasn't going to give up acting, which meant she'd still be a target of the paparazzi, of critics, of other small minds who made up stories about her. If she didn't take a stand now, how would Alec handle the next situation?

She fell asleep without answering those questions. When she awoke, Alec was gone, and she faced the possibility that those questions would remain unanswered.

Chapter Twenty-Two

Within twenty-four hours of Alec's departure, the press descended on Windfall Island like a plague of locusts. Maggie brought most of them, and while she'd agonized over facilitating the insanity, in the end, free enterprise got the better of her.

Paige didn't blame her for it; they'd have found a way to get to the island anyway. Maggie might as well profit from it.

The day after Alec left the crowd of reporters and photographers were so thick around her house, she almost worried they'd push it off the cliff and into the ocean. Not that she'd have cared, with heartbreak dragging at her like a lead weight.

George arrived before noon and, after a brief statement regarding the merits of free speech versus the jail cell an arrest for trespassing would earn, he'd not only evicted them from her house, he'd also limited them to the main street of town. And if they blocked the roads, he'd told her, they'd be kicked off the island altogether. Paige had heard he'd made good on the threat—and that the rest of the press corps was toeing the line as a result.

Three days later she could actually smile over it. Paige Walker had never been one to wallow. She'd cried buckets of tears, she still wasn't sleeping well, and she knew her heart would ache for a long time. She hadn't put Alec behind her, not by a long shot. There'd be times in the days and weeks to come when the pain would overwhelm her again. But she'd find a way to live with it, to live her life. No other course was acceptable.

Still, when her locked front door opened, her heart nearly stopped dead. Maggie and Jessi walked in, squabbling good-naturedly, and Paige reached behind her, fumbling backward until she felt the counter at her back.

"See, I told you we should have knocked," Jessi said, rushing over.

Paige waved her off, although her heart ached so fiercely she still couldn't draw a full breath. "I'm fine," she said, but they all knew she'd thought it was Alec.

"I'm sorry we upset you," Maggie said, "but you haven't been answering your phone so it's your own fault."

"I told you what happened, what else is there to discuss?" Paige shot back, and when Maggie grinned she knew Maggie was poking at her on purpose—and it had done the trick. The trembling that had racked her was already easing, and if she still hurt with every beat of her heart, at least she could breathe again.

"We're taking you to the Horizon for dinner," Jessi said as she headed into the back hallway. She returned with Paige's coat. "You need to get out of this house."

And away from all its memories, Paige thought. "I don't think it's a good idea for me to go into the village."

"I'm in the mood for one of AJ's burgers," Maggie said. "I'm not letting a bunch of curious cats dictate my choices. Besides"—she grinned—"George has been arresting anyone wandering the residential areas, which limits the press to the two-mile business section of the village.

"Every single shop is wide open. Even the ones that normally close in the winter are decked out for Christmas, and the owners are shamelessly scalping every reporter who needs toothpaste or clean underwear. I figure they've whittled the crowd down by at least half, just by pricing them out of basic subsistence."

"In case that doesn't encourage them to go away," Jessi added, bundling Paige into her coat as she spoke, "George hired Han Finley and Sam Norris as temporary deputies. You know Han and Sam, so you can imagine what it means to give authority to those two boneheads—no offense, Maggie," she put in, as Han was Maggie's cousin.

Maggie laughed. "Giving those two badges is like handing crayons to a two-year-old and leaving the room."

Paige just shook her head, but a half hour later she laughed outright when she walked into the Horizon—through the back door—and saw a roped-off section with a hand-lettered sign: VIP.

Every reporter in the place jumped to their feet. Questions were shouted, flashes went off in her face.

AJ came out from behind the bar and stood in front of her. "Sit," he boomed so loudly the nearest reporters dropped into their chairs with a thud. "The next camera I see is mine," he continued, and equipment was hastily stowed in bags or pockets. "And you'll remember this is a peaceful establishment. Keep your voices down."

"Peaceful?" Maggie teased.

"Outsiders," AJ scoffed, "don't know any different."

"I'm sorry," Paige said. "Maybe I should go."

"Nonsense." He escorted them to the far corner booth. "But you might want to keep your back to the vultures."

She slid into the seat that faced the wall; Jessi sat beside her.

Maggie took the other side. She looked out over the room, her brows drawn in annoyance. "This is ridiculous."

Paige snorted softly. "It's nothing compared to what happens when I try to go to a restaurant in LA." Which was why she'd stopped going out almost entirely. But when she got home, that was going to change. She'd been hiding herself away, she realized, protecting herself behind walls—whether of concrete and steel or aloofness. Alec had made her see that. It might be risky and painful to put herself out into the world, but she wasn't really living if she stayed behind those walls.

"So," Maggie asked, "what are you going to do now?"

"I'll stay here a few more days, go through the rest of the scripts my agent sent me." Venturing into the world was all well and good, but not while the sharks were circling. "I'll have my publicist set up an interview or two. Once I've told my story on television, the feeding frenzy will die down."

"I hope you tear that…that director to shreds," Jessi said.

Paige smiled fully this time, and knew there was a spiteful edge to it. "You see, this is where the press is actually helpful. Now that the story is out there, Jackson Howard's wife can't ignore it anymore. She'll divorce him, and she'll take him to the cleaners. Word is there's no prenup."

"Good." Jessi rubbed her hands together. "I hope he marries that bimbo he cheated with. Those two deserve each other."

Paige's thoughts exactly, and she gave them two years before Howard realized he'd been used by someone who only wanted a shortcut to fame and fortune. It would be called karma or poetic justice by the entertainment venues, seeing as Howard had used Paige to hide his affair. But she'd already let that go, Paige reminded herself.

"I'd appreciate it if you could fly me down to DC at the end of the week, Maggie. Friday or Saturday, whatever you have open."

"You're not going to Boston?" Jessi asked.

Paige ignored her. "I'll charter a jet from there back to California."

"What about Alec?"

"What about him?" Paige asked, smiling at Missy Perkins, who sometimes worked at the Horizon during the tourist season. AJ and Helen must have called her in to help with the crowd. Missy delivered water and took their drink orders, then hurried away, too busy to worry about gathering gossip.

"Alec is where he needs to be," Paige said. "I will be, too."

"You know he didn't mean to hurt you," Jessi said.

"So he told me."

"But you don't believe him."

"I don't believe he was thinking of me at all." Paige took a second while she reined in her frustration—and admitted that maybe she wasn't entirely past her anger. "It was about him, his ego, his male pride."

"But—"

She reached over and squeezed Jessi's hand. "I don't want to talk about it." She'd been over it in her head so many times she was sick to death of it.

All she'd ever wanted was to be an actor. She hadn't understood in the beginning what it would mean to her privacy, but she'd accomplished her dream. The price had been paid; there was no going back now, even if she'd wanted to give up everything she'd worked for. Fame had ruined any chance at personal happiness, and fame couldn't be turned off.

"But you're in love with him," Jessi insisted.

Yes, Paige thought, fighting to take in air with her chest feeling like it was riddled with knives.

Maggie sighed into the silence. "You know," she said reluctantly, as emotional turmoil always made her uncomfortable, "he's a man. They tend to act first and think about the consequences later. Especially where the women in their lives are concerned."

"He wouldn't apologize," Paige murmured.

"So he didn't trust you."

"And he doesn't understand what he did wrong," Jessi added.

"No," Paige said, deeply grateful they understood, and she didn't have to rehash it all. "It's done. It's all done. I'm not—" She broke off, hissing out a breath as she bit back on her relief at being out of the Stanhope mess. "I'm sorry, Maggie. Have you decided what you're going to do?"

"I think so," Maggie said, so matter-of-factly it surprised Paige. "I'm going to tell Rose the truth, but the money is going to Windfall Island."

"Maggie!" Jessi smiled, but there were tears in her eyes. "That's wonderful, but are you sure?"

"This island took Eu—" She stopped, blew out a breath. "...took my grandmother in. This island should benefit."

"Even though they could have done what was right at the time?" Paige asked gently.

"They did what they felt was right *for* the time. I can't fault them for that. And I'm holding you and Jessi to your part of our agreement with Ma. We all took responsibility for the future of Windfall."

"I think I've done my share," Paige said wryly.

Jessi looked over her shoulder. "This will die down."

"Not soon enough," Paige said and, on a deep breath, determined to put it aside. "Publicity for Windfall Island...Maybe I can start a film festival here."

Maggie snorted. "And have the island overrun by your people every year?"

"Oh, they're not so bad. But maybe you're right, a film festival might be too much for the island. I know"— Paige laughed softly—"we'll do a reality show: George Boatwright versus the Fifth Estate."

"I think George already won that contest," Maggie said.

"Then maybe I can film a movie here. Windfall Island is very picturesque. And I could hire everyone on as extras. I'm sure I can find a script that will fit the location.

Or maybe"—she drew it out—"I'll buy the rights to Eugenia's story."

"Over my dead body—and yours if you open your big mouth."

"You wanted publicity, Maggie," Paige said on a laugh that felt rusty but wonderful. "We all have to do our part."

"It's nice to see you smile."

Paige looked up and saw Hold standing at the edge of the booth, Dex behind him.

"Especially at Maggie's expense," Dex said as he slid into the booth next to his fiancée.

Maggie poked him with her elbow. "You're supposed to be on my side."

He leaned over and kissed her. "I am."

"Couldn't prove it by me." But Maggie was holding back a smile.

Hold pulled up a chair next to Jessi and dropped a kiss on her lips, and Paige found herself battling back tears. She was so glad that Maggie had found someone who loved her. After the neglect of her childhood, Maggie deserved happiness. And Jessi had been through the romantic ringer at such an early age, who could begrudge her the joy Hold had brought into her life?

Still, it put Paige's future into stark relief by comparison. She could see the lonely years stretching out before her, endlessly.

"I think I'll go home," she said.

"Paige..."

The sympathy in Jessi's eyes was too much to bear. "Fifth wheel isn't my thing," she said with a slight smile. "You know how I like to be the center of attention."

Hold pulled Jessi out of the booth, but before Paige could slide out after her, he slid in. "You've had a rough time lately," he said, "and hunkering down in your house all by your lonesome might seem the right thing to do." He wrapped an arm around her shoulders. "But what kind of friends would we be if we left you alone when you needed us?"

Paige felt the tears slipping hot down her cheeks, crying even harder when Dex reached across the table and laid a hand on her wrist.

Someone stuffed a napkin into her hand. She dabbed at her cheeks, wiped carefully beneath her eyes. Jessi was crying openly, and even Maggie was blinking furiously. Which made Paige smile through her own tears.

"Not a word," Maggie said.

"I was just going to say, now I have brothers as well as sisters."

She'd realized her dreams, Paige thought, but she'd never imagined the cost. Looking back now, she could see so clearly how, when the loneliness swamped her, she'd thrown herself into work so she could pretend, at least for a little while, to be someone else who wasn't alone.

She'd come back to Windfall Island to get away from the tape—or so she'd told herself. She'd really been searching, though, for a place to belong and friends who cared about her, not her money or fame.

She'd found both.

"Cheer up, darling," Hold drawled when she started to water up again. "You're going to have Dex crying in a minute."

"I'm crying on the inside," Dex said, and had them all laughing.

Even AJ's wide, homely face was wreathed in a smile when he joined them, juggling a huge tray crowded with dishes. "The press was getting awfully interested in what's going on over here."

"The fun is over, Another."

AJ sent Maggie a look—raised eyebrows, mouth a flat line.

Maggie just grinned. She hadn't let up since she'd found out AJ's given name was Another John.

AJ unloaded steaming potpie casseroles for each of them. "Keep it up and I'll stop cooking for you."

Maggie pulled one of the dishes in front of her and hunched protectively over it. "Don't even joke like that."

"So," Dex said, after a hail from the bar took AJ away, "we need to talk about the case. I spoke with Rose, and she's providing a DNA sample herself. The three of you," he added, referring to Maggie, Jessi, and Paige, "can do the same. Hold will send them to a different lab. Rose won't know where it is, so Clayton can't get wind of it.

"I told her we found evidence of a living descendant," he continued, his eyes meeting Maggie's, "but I kept your name to myself."

"We don't really have proof anyway," Maggie said.

"The ledger Ma lent us is pretty clear, and your eye color cements if for me," Hold put in. "Stanhope blue. The new DNA test will provide confirmation. About you, Maggie, and about Clayton."

"We don't have any proof there, either," Paige pointed out. "All we have is conjecture that Clayton isn't a Stanhope by blood."

"Meeker will have to come back at some point, and

then we'll get the truth out of him." There was blood in Jessi's eyes. "The whole truth."

"We'll need to tread lightly," Dex said. "Paige is right that all we have to go on right now is circumstantial evidence. And Meeker won't exactly be eager to admit to his involvement. We'll have to find some leverage."

"How about good old-fashioned torture," Maggie suggested.

Paige wasn't sure she was joking, but she figured the others would keep her in line. "You'll have to let me know how it turns out," she said. "I'm leaving in two days."

"I know you have your reasons," Jessi said.

"One of them is this island being overrun by vultures from the press," Paige said.

"Are you kidding? Everyone is getting a kick out of torturing the outsiders," Maggie said. "Not to mention the bump to the economy."

Paige smiled. Trust the Windfallers to, well, make a windfall out of the situation. "I need to go back," she said. "I have a couple of appearances set up. I gave Howard and his bimbo enough rope to hang themselves, and now that they have"—thanks to Alec, she thought grudgingly—"now that everyone knows I'm the injured party, it's time for me to tell my side of the story."

"You shouldn't pander," Maggie said.

"Once I've had my say, the attention will die down to its normal level of stupidity." She took a deep breath and let it out slowly. Just because she knew she was closing a door didn't make it easy to do. "And it's time to get back to work. There are a couple of projects I'm interested in, and the offers have a shelf life."

Jessi reached around Hold and took Paige's hand. "As long as you know you'll always belong here."

Paige nodded. "This is home." And she'd be back. Just as soon as enough time had passed so she didn't see Alec around every corner.

* * *

A little more than a hundred miles away, at the same time, Alec sat in his office, at the Barclay family compound outside of Boston. Files were stacked in neat piles on the desk, each tab precisely lettered. One of the folders lay, open and empty, on the blotter.

His grandfather received dozens of proposals he didn't have time to consider. Garrett was always looking for a gem among the pebbles, so he'd asked Alec to review the offers Garrett's secretary collected and meticulously filed.

Alec held the single sheet of paper the open folder had contained, but he didn't see it. He stared out the window instead. The shadows were long, the sun had nearly set, but he wasn't seeing the well-manicured grounds covered in the previous night's snowfall.

He saw the sky, stretching from the placid surface of Secret Harbor to the far horizon. Under that huge expanse, the waters of the Atlantic were as deep a blue as Paige's eyes as he'd seen them last, filled with hurt and sorrow.

"Did you find anything worthwhile?"

Alec swiveled around in his chair to find his mother poised in the doorway. He felt the stab of twin emotions, relief that she'd saved him from wallowing any more than he already had, and resignation—because he knew she wouldn't let him wallow anymore.

"There are some interesting ideas in here," he said with a faint smile. "I may have to fight Grandfather for one or two of them."

"Not the battle I'd expect you to be considering," Janet Barclay said.

He'd told her a bare-bones version of the truth, one that didn't spare him responsibility for the idiotic thing he'd done, while skimming the surface of his relationship with Paige Walker.

He should have known his mother was too discerning, and knew him too well, to be fooled.

"She isn't going to wait for you forever."

"I know that," Alec said. "How do you?"

"Because of the way she handled this scandal." Janet walked into the room and perched on the corner of his desk.

"She could have circumvented all the drama by just making a statement earlier."

"And denial would have accomplished what, exactly?"

Alec sighed heavily. He'd already acknowledged that Paige had been right about the way she'd handled the scandal. Much as he hated to admit he'd been wrong. Worse, he'd had to face the fact that he'd bungled it from the start, that he'd only made matters worse by interfering where he wasn't wanted or needed. And that he'd been too stubborn and too childish to apologize when she'd called him on it.

"She won't listen to me now," he said. Another truth he needed to face—along with the knowledge that he procrastinated, at least in part, because he was afraid of being turned away. He rubbed a hand over his chest. Not that the pain of being apart from her was any easier to bear.

"Make her listen."

He sat forward, slapped the paper on the desk with the flat of his hand. "How?"

"I don't know, Alec. Go back to that island and make her listen to you. Whatever it takes."

He sat back, almost amused. "Grovel, Mother? I'm surprised at you."

"Surprised that a woman whose husband left thirty years ago might have handled it differently?"

"*He* left," Alec said coldly. "He could have come back."

"It's never just one person, you know that. I have my share of regrets." She stood and paced to the window. Alec knew she was no more seeing the view than he had. "I let my pride get in the way. I didn't go after him, and when he didn't come back, well, I let it close me off." She turned, came back, and laid a hand on his shoulder. "I don't want to see that happen to you. She stung your pride by asking you to go, Alec, but don't let that hold you back."

Alec stood and hugged her. For the first time in his life, he realized that she'd been alone for a long time. Not that there weren't people in her life, friends and family, but there had never been someone special. Maybe because he'd just come to understand what it meant to find the one person he wanted to spend the rest of his life with, he could finally understand how it must have felt for his mother to live her life without that.

"Why don't you ever go out?" he asked her. She was beautiful, slim and graceful, and if there were a few lines around her eyes, well, she was old enough to have a son his age. "Don't tell me it's too late," he said, seeing that very expression on her face. "There are enough men who ask you to dance at the club, and at those charity balls."

She laughed softly. "You want a new daddy?"

"I think I'm past that, but I wouldn't mind knowing you're not alone."

"Well, I might just think about that. It would be nice to have someone to go to the movies with, to travel with." She kissed his cheek lightly. "But I won't be alone if you bring that girl back here and the two of you give me a couple of grandchildren to spoil."

"I'll go back as soon as I finish this for Grandfather."

Janet took the paper and put the phone into his hand instead. "You'll go back now," she said with a smile.

Chapter Twenty-Three

The same evening, Josiah Meeker set foot on Windfall Island for the first time in days.

With the area crawling with reporters and photographers, the camera slung around his neck was the only disguise he'd needed to convince a mainlander to ferry him over and drop him at a well-hidden spot on the shore outside the village.

He'd been charged the exorbitant price of two hundred of the five hundred dollars Stanhope had given him, but Josiah understood the law of supply and demand. And he understood greed. If positions had been reversed, he'd have done exactly the same.

The sky was a bright blue, the air so cold and crisp it seemed to slice exposed skin. His face felt stiff and frozen from the open-air boat ride, but the walk to his house didn't take long.

He slipped in through the back door, only to be met by his daughter, Shelley, a fireplace poker raised in her hands. He nipped back just in time. The poker whooshed by his face and took a divot out of the wide-planked oak floor between his feet.

"Good lord, girl." Josiah grabbed the poker and wrenched it out of her hands before she could raise it again.

"Daddy!"

Josiah didn't have much use for people in general and women in particular. Shelley was the one person in the world he trusted. Still, he kept her on a short leash. For her own good.

"Go put this away," he said, handing her the iron.

"I'm sorry, Daddy," she said, rubbing her wrist. "It's just there are so many strangers in town, and with you sneaking in like you did..."

"It was necessary," Josiah said. And he didn't have time to waste on explanations, even if he'd been inclined to offer one. He took a slip of paper from his jacket pocket and handed it to her. "I need you to go to the store and bring these things here."

Most of the antiques and precious items he owned were already in his home. What he stocked at the store were reproductions, nostalgia items, and outright junk. But he salted the place with a few authentic pieces to lure in tourist traffic. Once he got them into the store, he could usually get them to spend some of their vacation mad money.

Josiah had made a good living that way, but he'd never made a killing. He was about to.

"There's not much on the list," he said, "just some precious jewelry and a piece of furniture or two."

Shelley looked at the paper. "What about the journals?"

"Useless," he said shortly. "Just do what I tell you. Now."

"Now? But...it's nearly six. Won't it look strange for me to open the store now?"

"You're not opening the store."

"What?" She took her coat off the peg by the back door and pulled it on. "*I'm* not opening the store? You're not coming with me?"

"I can't go into the village."

Shelley crossed her arms, tapped her foot. "What's going on, Daddy?"

"I can't tell you, but it's going to make me rich."

More tapping. "You have an interesting way of choosing your pronouns."

"You'll have to trust me."

She kissed his cheek. "Of course I trust you. How rich?"

"Just do what I asked, and let me worry about that."

"Okay, but I'm going to need help to move some of these things."

"Then get some help," Josiah snapped.

With a sigh, Shelley took the keys he handed her and headed out the back door.

Meeker went into the front room and took a seat at the antique desk, moving the chair so that he had a view of his end of the village.

Clayton wanted one of the three women killed; there was no way to get to Maggie or Jessi with their men hanging around them. But he had an idea of how he could take out Paige Walker, and not only make her death look like an accident, but capitalize on it, as well.

Like all good Windfallers, Josiah kept up with the

gossip. So when Shelley had told him that Paige and
Alec Barclay had had some sort of falling out, and that
Barclay had gone home to Boston, Josiah had known
he wouldn't be away long. Paige was rich, and any fool
could see she'd become as attached to Barclay as Barclay was to her.

It hadn't taken much effort to discover when Barclay
would be returning; nothing was ever secret for long on
Windfall Island. Josiah had to act before he arrived. It
was a narrow window of opportunity, but it might be the
only one Josiah would get. And if things went the way
he hoped, he'd make a killing—no pun intended—even
before Clayton's gratitude, or fear, came into play.

An hour after he sat down, Josiah had composed a
note in a passable imitation of Maggie Solomon's hand.
She wrote in bold, slashing strokes that were easily em-
ulated, Josiah thought with a sneer. In any case, the note
was good enough to fool a woman who wanted to believe the words Josiah had put into Maggie's mouth.

He heard Junior Semple's rusted-out pickup truck
rumbling and farting. Josiah looked out the window in
time to see it pull up in front of the house, an armoire and
a couple of tables loaded into the back. Shelley stepped
out of the passenger side, just as George Boatwright, the
sheriff, strolled around the corner.

George must have called out, because Shelley hesitated, turned, and walked toward him. But George was
looking at the house.

Josiah knew he couldn't be seen, but he scuttled back
from the window, watching as Shelley and George chat-
ted a minute or two. Then, after another long stare at the
house, George retraced his steps back into the village.

Josiah stayed out of sight while Shelley and Junior maneuvered the armoire inside, then the tables and a leather case that Shelley must have used to pack the small items.

Once Junior's truck had rumbled away, Josiah came out of hiding. "What did Boatwright want?" he asked Shelley. "You didn't tell him I was back."

"Of course not," Shelley said. "I told him we always keep some of the stock at home, and I was bored with what was here so I decided to rotate it."

"Well." Josiah smiled and patted her shoulder, surprised but gratified. "Now, I have another errand for you to run, and this time make sure no one sees you. Especially Boatwright."

* * *

The morning dawned overcast. The wind that had blown strong all night had died by the time Paige took her walk along the cliffs. The air felt heavy, calm and still, as if the world held its breath, waiting. She didn't venture far. A storm had been forecast, a bad one, she reminded herself. That was why she felt so... unsettled.

She shook off the feeling of dread, reminded herself how much she loved wild weather, loved hunkering down—as Hold put it—in her house, all snug and warm in bed with a book and a cup of tea. Or maybe she'd try her hand at writing, she mused as she made the walk back toward home. She'd put Eugenia's story down on paper—in a fictionalized version, of course. Names and places had been changed to protect the innocent, she thought with a smile.

She was a storyteller, and if she'd discovered one thing in the past decade of reading script after script, it was that there weren't enough good stories being told. The kind of stories that didn't rely on CG or explosions and car crashes.

Paige rounded the final curve, and hurried, anxious to be back where she could relax and feel safe. If she hadn't been concerned about turning her ankle, she wouldn't have dropped her eyes to watch her footing. She wouldn't have seen the parchment-colored patch among the snow- and lichen-covered rocks—an envelope, she discovered when she detoured to pick it up. An envelope with her name on it in water-smeared ink. In Maggie's handwriting.

The wind must have blown it off the back door, she realized when she saw the strip of tape there, matching the one still stuck to the envelope. She frowned, wondering why Maggie hadn't called her.

She let herself in the back door, already ripping into the envelope. Water had soaked through, thinned the writing on the single sheet of paper—but not so badly that Paige couldn't read Maggie's words.

Before she was done, she almost wished it had blown away altogether. Having read it, though, she couldn't ignore it.

"Can I talk to Maggie?" she asked when Jessi answered the Solomon Charters phone.

"Paige." The hesitation, that note of surprise in Jessi's voice, said it all. "Maggie is prepping the helicopter."

"To pick up Alec."

"How do you know that?"

"I got Maggie's note."

More surprise from Jessi. "Note?"

"The one she taped to my back door. To tell me she was going to pick up Alec in Boston."

"But... I'm sorry we didn't tell you. We—I thought it might be a good idea for you to see him, Paige."

"And Maggie doesn't want to get caught up in my emotional drama," Paige said, and let it go. Both her friends had acted according to their nature. Jessi looked for the happily ever after, Maggie chose to keep her distance. "Is it wise to fly with the storm coming?"

"It's not expected to hit until late afternoon. They'll be back by then."

"Still, shouldn't she wait until it's past? This storm is supposed to drop a foot of snow or more, and you know how unreliable the weather forecasts are."

"You just want another day before you have to face him," Jessi said, and this time Paige heard the humor in her voice.

"Maybe. Or I want her—both of them—to be safe."

"Maggie doesn't take chances with her equipment or with her life," Jessi said. "Besides, I can watch the storm develop on radar. If anything changes..."

But Paige wasn't listening. "Maggie said Alec wants me to meet him at the Horizon," she blurted out.

"Boy he works fast. But then he's coming back to see you, isn't he?"

Paige put her hand to her hot cheek. Her heart was racing as fast as her mind. "Is he?" she said faintly.

"Of course. The case is over," Jessi reminded her needlessly. "Why else would he be coming here if not to see you?"

"I don't want to think about it."

"I know," Jessi said, her voice so warm and understanding Paige felt like she'd been hugged. "Anything you want Maggie to pick up while she's in Boston?"

"I'm leaving in two days myself. There's no point in buying things I'll only have to give away or throw away."

"Okay, then I'll talk to you later. Eat something."

Paige smiled. "I will, Mommy."

She opted for cold cereal. It settled her stomach as well as filled it, and she would need the strength. And since she couldn't think about seeing Alec without making herself sick again, she continued with her preparations for leaving Windfall.

She'd already cleaned upstairs, so she started downstairs, packing away the mementos in the family room.

She picked up a framed photo and ran her fingertips over her father's face. Missing him was still a bone-deep ache, even after all the years that had passed. But she was at peace because her father was still with her, in every decision she made, every joy she felt, and every sorrow.

Matt Morris had been as unlucky in love as she, and it had only made him stronger. He'd never let it color his relationship with Paige, never shown her anything but true faith and love, and both had been unshakable. She couldn't let him down by allowing what had happened between her and Alec to shadow her life.

She put the photo aside to take back to her house in Los Angeles, along with her mother's jewelry box. Then she finished packing the rest of her personal family things. She could have left the boxes for Maisie, but it felt more final, more settled, to put them away herself.

The wind had begun to blow when she took the first

box out to the storage room built into the foundation of the house. She went in and out several times. By the time she made the last trip, she had to fight to keep her balance. The wind that buffeted her smelled of salt and snow, and the clouds had begun to gather in a dark, boiling mass as far as the eye could see.

It made her think of Maggie and Alec; she couldn't help herself anymore.

Maybe Alec's time in Boston had proved to him that he could live without her.

Then she rolled the eyes that had begun to tear up, almost amused by her own melodrama. Of course Alec could live without her, just as she could live without him. A broken heart could be survived. It just had to be faced first.

A few moments before noon, Paige pulled into the alley behind the Horizon. She'd taken a long, hot shower, creamed her skin, and applied her makeup in subdued shades. She wore black wool slacks and a snow-white stretchy tee under a gray tweed jacket. Nothing wrong with a little sex appeal; it made her feel more confident, she decided.

She needed confidence, needed to feel as strong as she would for any other performance. That's what this would be, she thought as she parked behind the Horizon, the performance of her life. The emotions were real. The stakes were impossibly high. And although she knew she shouldn't get her hopes up, she couldn't help herself. If she left the Horizon alone, she'd be alone the rest of her life.

The alley, when she eased down it in the Jeep Maggie had loaned her, made her shiver. It was narrow, barely wider than the Jeep, and gloomy from the steel-gray clouds overhead and the houses that had been built close together two hundred years ago, before building codes were established.

A rusted old pickup truck was parked a little way ahead; Paige pulled up behind it, stepped out of the Jeep, and then everything happened at once.

Her hands were dragged roughly behind her, and before she could scream or call out, something was shoved over her head. The world went black, then spun as she was lifted then dropped, jarring her shoulder and hip.

She fought for breath, clawing at whatever covered her face and trying to shove herself up when she felt a needle prick her thigh, through the wool of her slacks.

And darkness closed in.

Chapter Twenty-Four

As soon as Maggie set the 'copter down, Alec had his harness off. Once he felt the bird steady, he jumped out and strode across the tarmac, heading straight for the parking lot.

"Hold up, slugger," Maggie called after him. "Unless you're going to hotwire vehicles, you might want to ask me for the keys."

He stopped, turned. "Can I have the keys?"

"No."

"No?" He threw his hands up, turned in a circle as the urgency in him demanded action. Maggie had talked to him, at him, the entire way back from Boston. She'd lectured, cajoled, reasoned—and hadn't changed his mind. "What now?"

"I think you should take a couple of deep breaths, because if you go over there with that head of steam, you're going to scare her away."

"If I don't go over there now, she'll think I don't care."

"Come into the office for a minute."

"Maggie—"

"Just long enough to calm down and think through what you're going to say." Maggie crossed to him, took him by the elbow, and tugged. "C'mon, I bet Jessi talked to Paige today. Maybe we can find out what Paige is thinking."

"And you're not going to give me the keys until I do."

"The keys are inside."

Alec let his head drop forward, just for a second, while he found some patience, then tagged along after Maggie. And maybe she was right, he mused; maybe he needed a few minutes to swallow down this sense of urgency that had dogged him since his mother had forced his hand the night before. She'd been right, he saw that now.

"I really want to get going," he said.

Maggie studied him, then turned. But before he could begin to hope she was going to fetch some car keys, she said to Jessi, "Call Dex. Get him over here."

"I'm surprised he's not here already," Jessi said as she picked up the receiver and dialed. "He must've heard you land. He's not picking up, either."

"He's researching a new case," Maggie said. "Let it ring. He'll pick up when he realizes you aren't going away."

"You should," Jessi said, to Alec. "Get going, I mean. You're going to be late for lunch with Paige."

Alec shifted around. "What lunch with Paige?"

Jessi held up a finger. "Alec is here, Dex," she said into the phone. "Maggie wants you to come over to the office." She replaced the receiver on the ancient desk phone.

"What lunch?" Alec demanded.

"You know, the note you had Maggie write for you, asking Paige to meet you at the Horizon for lunch."

"I didn't write any note," Maggie said.

"Wait a minute." Alec tunneled his hands into his hair, fisted them there, hoping the pain would help him think. "Start at the beginning."

"No," Maggie said. "Wait for Dex, only tell it once."

Alec spun, clamped his hands around Jessi's upper arms, and lifted her from her chair. *Tell me what's going on.*

"You should probably let Jessi go," Maggie said in the calm tone of someone talking to the criminally insane.

"He's not hurting me." Jessi put her hands on his cheeks, her touch warm and soothing. "Panicking won't help Paige," she said.

* * *

Alec bore down, managed to find a tiny nugget of calm. "What did the note say?" he asked Jessi. Maybe it was all a misunderstanding, he thought desperately.

But he didn't really believe that.

"I don't know exactly," Jessi answered him, squeezing his hand. "Paige never read it to me. She said you asked her to meet you at the Horizon for lunch."

"Why would I ask her to meet me in public with all those reporters in the village?"

"I doubt she thought of that," Maggie said with infuriating calmness. But she was already pulling keys off the board next to Jessi's desk.

Alec caught the set she flipped him and headed for the

door, vaguely aware that Dex, Maggie, and Jessi were hot on his heels. Maggie and Jessi detoured to Maggie's house, Jessi on her cell phone, talking to Hold. Alec heard Benji's name, knew she was making arrangements for her son to be looked after. He knew, too, that Hold would find someone to watch Benji so he could join them, but all that mattered to Alec was finding Paige.

She wasn't home.

Alec knew it as soon as he got to her front door. The house had an empty feel to it, the windows dark and almost sinister in the prestorm gloom. He ran around to the back, to her cliffs. He didn't see her. She wasn't on the stingy curve of beach below, either. He saw a light in the wide window overlooking Secret Harbor, and didn't remember racing around to burst through her front door.

Paige wasn't there.

Maggie, Dex, and Jessi stood at the kitchen island, a slip of paper on the counter in front of them.

"It's very short and to the point," Dex said quietly. "And Maggie didn't write it."

Alec reached between them and picked up the note. " '*Bringing Alec back from Boston tomorrow*,'" it read. "'*He wants you to meet him at the Horizon. Noon. That's all I know. Maggie.*'"

"Paige said she found it this morning by her back door when she returned from her walk," Jessi said.

"Clever."

"I'd guess it was left sometime last night," Dex said, "probably after Paige was asleep. She wouldn't have found it until this morning when she walked, so it was someone who knows her routine. And that person was aware that Maggie would be in the air and Paige couldn't call her."

Alec didn't need to reason it out. "Meeker." He crumpled the note in his hand and stalked out the door, again with the other three behind him.

There was a chance she hadn't gone, he thought, praying she was still angry enough to thumb her nose at what she'd see as a summons. She could be somewhere else. At Ma's maybe.

He went to the Horizon first.

"Haven't seen her all day," AJ said. "Hey Missy," he called to his temporary waitress. "Have you seen Paige Walker today?"

Missy shook her head and, hefting a loaded tray, started on her way to deliver its contents, only to turn back. "There was something I wanted to tell you, AJ," she said. Her eyes rolled back into her head as if she could read the thought off her brain cells.

Alec leaned forward, on the verge of violence when her eyes rolled forward again.

"You said you were expecting a delivery today, and there's a car blocking the alley."

"What kind?" Alec demanded.

Missy shrugged. "One of those boxy ones."

"Jeep," Maggie breathed.

They raced out back, half a dozen reporters on their tail, to find the Jeep Maggie had loaned Paige, parked, as Missy had said, blocking the back door of the Horizon.

Someone shoved a microphone in Alec's face, and a couple of flashbulbs went off. "You're Alec Barclay," a voice shouted at him. "Are you and Paige Walker having an affair?"

"Where is she?" someone else shouted. "Why are you looking for her? Is she avoiding you? Are you a stalker?"

Alec grabbed the nearest reporter by his lapels and pulled him up to his toes. "Did you see who was driving this Jeep?"

"N-no. We're not allowed back here."

"Maybe you should go back in before you get arrested," Dex said. "George might not be around, but I'm here, and AJ is right inside."

Alec let the reporter go with the others, scrubbing his trembling hands over his face, trying to reason his way past the urge to panic.

"In this weather, everyone will be indoors," Dex said. "And even if someone did happen to notice Paige driving into the alley, nobody would be back here to see what happened."

Except whoever had been waiting for her. "Meeker," he said to Dex. "His store and his house."

"You and Dex pick up Hold and do that," Maggie said. "I have another idea."

"Wait." Dex grabbed Alec's arm and hauled him to a stop. "Don't do anything stupid," he said to Maggie.

"Like breaking and entering?" she countered with a grim smile.

"We just don't want to lose you two as well."

"Jessi and I will stay together," Maggie said. "Don't worry about us."

* * *

"At least the reporters are following the guys," Maggie said to Jessi as they started off in the opposite direction from Meeker's antiques store. They'd let Dex threaten them with pain for as long as he was stationary, then they'd set off to follow—at a safe distance, of course.

"What I'd like to know is where we're going?"

"After Shelley," Maggie said.

Jessi drew in a breath, her eyes going wide and bright. "That's brilliant. Shelley is the only one Meeker has any use for."

"That doesn't mean he told her anything," Maggie said.

"But if he told anyone, it would be her."

Maggie paused at the door to the Clipper Snip, met Jessi's eyes. "If he told her, I'll get it out of her."

"We'll get it out of her."

That brought a smile to Maggie's face. The thought of gentle, sweet Jessi Randal sweating Shelley was absurd. Then again, sympathy had its uses, too. "We'll get it out of her," she agreed, and pushed through the door.

A cloud of warm air, heavy with the scents of chemicals and perfumes, hit her in the face, and a half dozen pairs of eyes swiveled in their direction.

"We, uh..."

"Let me handle this," Jessi said, and brushed by her.

Maggie watched her pull Sandy Rogers, owner of the Clipper Snip and Jessi's mother's best friend, once upon a time, aside. They spoke briefly, then Sandy came over, the rattail comb she'd been using to tease Martha Stockton's hair still in her hand.

"I haven't seen Shelley today," Sandy said, "which is odd since she spends half her time in here, steeping herself in gossip and annoying the hell out of me. You should talk to Junior Semple. The two of them have been thick as thieves lately."

"Interesting phrase," Maggie said. "Thanks." She waited in the tiny lobby while Jessi hugged Sandy, then joined her.

They went to Junior Semple's house, on one of the narrow back streets in the village. They were met at the door by his aunt, a bear of a woman with the attitude to match. "Junior ain't here," she said, leaning her ample frame on the doorjamb as if it were too much for her to hold her bulk upright. "And before you ask I don't know where he is. Probably cozied up with that Shelley Meeker on his old scow of a boat, doing the unspeakable." And she slammed the door in their faces.

"Rude," Jessi announced.

"I was done talking to her anyway," Maggie said as she clattered down the wood slat steps. "And anyway, she told us everything we needed to know."

"Except where Junior's boat is docked."

"I already know that." Maggie set off for the Horizon, where she'd left her Mustang. "Junior bought it thinking he'd get into the ferry business. When he found out how much money it takes to renovate a boat he decided I should go into business with him."

"We have enough boats, Maggie. We don't even run them all during the week."

"That's what I told him," Maggie said as they reached the main street and turned the corner toward the Horizon.

"I can't imagine he's holding a grudge, Maggie. Junior isn't vindictive, and he isn't, well, he isn't that bright."

"Neither is Shelley." Maggie hit the unlock button on her fob and angled herself into the driver's seat. She already had the car running when Jessi opened the passenger door, barely waiting for Jessi to plant herself in the seat before she put the car in reverse and gunned it.

"It's a good thing no one was coming," Jessi observed.

"Paige's life is on the line," Maggie reminded her.

"We can't help her if we're T-boned backing out of a parking spot."

Maggie glanced over at her, and was met with the placid expression that always made her squirm. "We're still in one piece." But she slowed down, and since nothing was very far on Windfall Island, it was only minutes before she pulled the Mustang into a short dirt path that ended at the shore. A rickety old dock stretched thirty feet into the water. The pilings were ragged, eaten away by time and weather, and there were boards missing from the decking. She barely gave it a second thought as she climbed out of the car and stepped onto the dock. She didn't like the way it swayed and groaned when it took her weight, but Paige's safety might be at the other end of it.

She felt Jessi grab the hem of her short coat and felt the dock give some more as Jessi's weight was added. She chose her steps carefully, as much for stealth as safety, but she wasn't about to let the risk of a dunk in the cold ocean stop her—any more than she allowed the locked door to keep her from her goal. She put her shoulder against it and her weight into it, sneering a little when the old molding splintered and gave way.

"Hey!" Junior Semple shot to his feet when she

stepped into the main cabin, playing cards in his hand. He sat at one side of a built-in table and Shelley sat on the opposite bench seat, gaping at her. "You could have knocked."

"I could have," Maggie agreed equably, "but I don't think kidnappers deserve any courtesy."

Maggie crossed the short expanse of worn teak flooring and hauled Shelley up by the front of her sweater. "Where is Paige?"

Junior stepped out, but Jessi planted herself in front of him. "You'll sit back down, if you know what's good for you."

Junior plopped down onto the seat and cringed a little. "Nice, Jess."

"He's just conditioned," Jessi said, then turned to Junior again. "Now, no one is going to hurt you, Junior. We just want to know where Paige is."

"We don't know."

"Wrong answer." Maggie let Shelley go, but she stayed close, giving her nowhere to run. "Where's your father?"

"I don't know."

"But he's back on the island, isn't he?"

Shelley crossed her arms and shot her chin up. "I don't have to talk to you."

Maggie took another step forward and pasted the coldest, meanest expression she could manage on her face. "Want to bet?"

Shelley shrank back. "Junior," she whimpered.

"Now, Maggie—"

She rounded on Junior. "Paige is missing. Shelley's worthless pervert of a father is behind it."

"You don't know that," Shelley said, and while it was interesting that she didn't object to the words *worthless* and *pervert*, Maggie was busy watching the blood drain out of Junior's face. "You know something," she accused him.

Junior lifted his eyes to hers. "He told me we were filming a movie."

"Who told you?"

"I'm sorry," Junior said to Shelley, then turned back to Maggie. "I didn't hurt her."

"You'd better hope she's still okay," Maggie said. "If she's not, there won't be anywhere for you to hide."

"I told you I don't know anything." Shelley wilted onto the bench seat. "My father told me to stay out of the house and out of the village today."

Maggie took her by the arm. "We're going to talk to George. Get Dex on the phone," she added to Jessi. "Tell him to meet us there."

"But—"

"Your father wanted you out of the way," Maggie cut Shelley off. "A jail cell is as good a place for it as any. And while we're on the way there, Junior, you can finish telling us what Meeker had you do."

Chapter Twenty-Five

Paige swam through layers of darkness for hours, it seemed. She'd no sooner fight her way through one than she'd be swamped by another, then another. So when her eyes fluttered open, and all she saw was more darkness, she despaired.

Her eyes closed, then opened again. A bit of the confusion faded as the gloom lightened, marginally. She saw shapes, smelled the odors of wood and dust on air that was close and stuffy, although there was a feeling of space...

Meeker's.

Panic raced through her, chased over her skin with the scrabbling feet of spiders. She struggled, pulling and straining to get up, to run. She couldn't move her feet though, her hands, either, no matter how hard she fought, fought until she was exhausted.

Her ankles and wrists ached, but with the bonds secured around her gloves and over her boots, at least her skin wasn't torn and bloody. Her heart was racing, but her mind was almost painfully clear now. She remembered parking in the alley behind the Horizon, being grabbed and thrown into the back of a car—no, a truck. She hadn't heard a car door or a trunk lid slam. Or maybe she'd passed out. Her face had been covered, her breathing would have been hampered. No...

She'd been drugged.

She started to fight again, angry now rather than afraid, letting loose a tirade of cuss words and threats as she struggled against her bonds.

"You've got quite a mouth on you."

Paige went still, ears straining to hear over the pounding of her heart. "Who's there?" she asked. But she already knew. "Meeker."

He laughed. "Very good."

Now she tasted fear, had to bear down until she regained a little control. Struggling wouldn't do her any good, and she refused to provide entertainment.

"Why are you doing this?" she asked. "My DNA doesn't match. I'm no threat to Clayton's plans for the family fortune," she added when Meeker remained silent.

"Clearly you are," Meeker said.

And clearly, Clayton Stanhope was behind this. "The least you can do is explain why killing me is necessary."

"I'm being paid," he said simply.

"So after all your big talk, all your maneuvering to be someone important, you're content to be a blunt instrument." Paige snorted softly. "You were always a greedy, shortsighted little man."

"Careful."

Paige laughed outright. "You don't even know why you're doing this, do you?"

"It doesn't matter."

"No? You're going to blackmail Clayton, aren't you? But you're not smart enough to understand how much more money you could soak him for if you knew the whole story."

"I'm smart enough to be the one who's not tied up," Meeker snapped. "Smart enough to know you're stalling for time."

"Of course I'm stalling for time."

"No one's coming for you," Meeker said, laughing again. "Your boyfriend is back on Windfall. He's probably tearing the village apart by now, but he won't find you. They've already searched this place. Then, while Barclay and Keegan were searching my house, I brought you here. So predictable," he said scornfully. "They won't come back here looking for you. Until it's too late.

"You see," he continued, "there's going to be a tragic fire." He reached for a box of wooden matches sitting on a table near to hand, lit one, let it drop to the floor where it incinerated the wood dust around it then sputtered out, leave a small circle of black.

"People have been warning me about it for years." Meeker was watching her, sneering at her fear as he lit another match and held it close to her cheek, close enough for her to feel her skin start to burn. "I have all this stuff piled up, they'd point out, it's a maze in here. A fire trap." As the flame burned down to his fingers he dropped it. This time the tiny flame caught, began to spread unbelievably fast in the dust and dryness. Before Meeker stamped it out.

Everything inside Paige went still and cold. And afraid.

"It's a shame they'll be proved right," he said, "and that you happened to be in here when the place burned down." He lit another match and dropped it, closer to her feet this time. Again it caught. Again he stamped it out.

"You don't think anyone will believe I just wandered in here," she said, battling the panic back, "or that this place spontaneously caught on fire."

"What does it matter?"

Paige could see that he truly didn't care. There was a light in his eyes, a sort of crazy edge to his smile as he lit those matches and stared into the flames, that told her Meeker had either convinced himself that his plan was flawless, or he was beyond logic.

"They won't be able to prove otherwise, now, will they?" he was saying. "I'll get a tidy sum from the insurance company. You'll die tragically young, as befits a movie star of your beauty and talent, and you'll be famous forever, which is what you want. No growing old and seeing your star slip as your looks go.

"And once you're dead"—he lit another match, then dropped it closer again so that it licked at the hem of her slacks before he stamped it out—"I'll get my payoff, and Stanhope will continue to pay and pay and pay." He held the next match, breathing heavily as he watched her watch the flames.

Paige thought he might burn her this time, but he put it out.

"You're crazy," she said faintly, the roaring in her head and the rolling in her stomach threatening to swamp her. All she could think about was the flames, the agony, and the devastation of dying alone, before she'd told Alec she loved him.

What he'd done felt so unimportant now. Pride was a cold companion.

But Meeker had made a mistake when he told her Alec was searching for her. Meeker might believe he had the upper hand, but he had no idea what he was up against. Alec wouldn't give up. Neither would Maggie or Jessi, or the others. Faced with that, how could she give in to her fear?

"I have a lot of money," she said. "If you let me go you can name your price, Josiah. I'll top whatever Stanhope has offered you. And I won't turn you in."

"You're rich, no doubt about it, but you can't possibly pay me more than Clayton Stanhope. I can soak him for the rest of my life." Meeker shifted uncomfortably, though, and when he spoke again, it was almost to himself, as if he wanted to convince himself he was making the right decision. "I'm already committed," he said. "I can't turn back now. And I can't trust you not to talk."

Paige shook her head in disgust. "And you're not going to tell me why Clayton Stanhope wants me dead because you don't know." She met his eyes. "But I do."

"Dead is dead." Meeker lit another match. "And blackmail is blackmail."

Paige laughed softly, surprised that she wasn't just feigning calm now, she felt calm. "You don't really think you're going to get away with this. If the police don't get you, Stanhope will."

Meeker's self-satisfied smile faded away.

"Do you actually believe he'll let you ride him for the

rest of his life, Josiah? He's paid for murder once, how long do you think you'll live?"

"He'll have to find me first."

"He won't be the only one looking for you. Alec, Dex, Hold, Jessi, Maggie, George, not to mention the FBI. None of them will give up until you're caught." She stopped for effect before she twisted the knife she'd driven into his confidence. "Personally, I hope it's Maggie who finds you."

All the blood drained out of Meeker's face.

"She'll blame herself for letting you walk around free after what you did to her," Paige said. "And if you doubt her ability to track you down, she's marrying a man who makes it his living to find people. And you're just not that smart."

"I'll be rich." But all the bluster had gone out of him.

So Paige played her last card.

"Alec has the Barclay name and wealth behind him. Do you think Stanhope will pay you enough to offset that? How long will Stanhope's money last with someone breathing down your neck every time you hide?" She leaned forward to drive her final point home. "Every time you crawl out of the woodwork to tap Stanhope for your next payoff, you're going to be vulnerable."

Meeker didn't respond, but she could see him working it out. He was on his feet now, pacing. He kept lighting matches, but he wasn't dropping them anymore, just letting them burn down before he shook them out.

He turned, started back to where she sat. His eyes met hers, he opened his mouth. But what came out was a yelp as the last match he'd lit burned down, forgotten, to his fingers. He flung it away out of reflex. There was a whoosh, a slight boom as the dust covering the nearest stack of furniture ignited.

Paige felt the flames singe her skin and screamed.

* * *

Alec paced the confines of the Windfall Island Sheriff's Office, barely twenty feet from one end to the other. They'd searched Meeker's store and house, and found nothing. No scrap of fabric, no dropped earring. If this had been a movie, Paige would have found a way to let them know she'd at least been held in one of those locations. But this was reality.

"House to house," he said shortly. "She has to be on the island."

George came back inside. "Damn reporters," he said, closing the blinds on the two small windows. He couldn't do anything about the glass door, or the crowd milling around outside. "They'll keep to the sidewalk, thanks to the threats I made. Which didn't include jail, since I have no doubt one of them would get the hare-brained idea to push their luck so they could get thrown in the cell and have a front-row seat to the goings-on in here."

Alec couldn't have cared less if the entire population of Windfall was present. "House to house," he repeated.

"Let's wait for Maggie and Jessi," George said. But he got out a map of the island and spread it across his desk. "You've already covered Meeker's store and house, but it won't hurt to check them again. It'll take a good long while to go through every building on Windfall."

"We don't have to check every building. Just the ones until we find Paige."

George took a step back, lifted his gaze to Alec's, then met Dex's eyes. "If he didn't take her off the island."

"Somebody would have seen him," Alec said.

"Nobody saw her disappear from the alley behind the Horizon."

"It's an alley," Dex pointed out. "Block one end, lure the vic—" He glanced at Alec, then said, "Lure Paige there, grab her when she gets out of her vehicle. Takes all of thirty seconds. A little bad luck on our side means no one witnessed—"

There was a ruckus outside, a cacophony of noise from the reporters. Like everyone else, Alec turned to the door, almost smiling when the men in front jumped out of the way and Maggie appeared, shouting back at them at the top of her lungs.

Alec sobered quickly when he saw Shelley Meeker behind Maggie. Judging by the sulky look on Shelley's face—and the hand Maggie had clamped around her wrist—Shelley wasn't there willingly.

Dex beat him to the door, which left Alec free to rub his hands together. If he couldn't get to Josiah, he'd take Shelley.

"Guess who we found hiding out at her daddy's instructions," Maggie said without greeting.

Alec didn't need the niceties. "Who's the string bean?" he asked Shelley, tipping his head toward the tall, gawky man standing behind her. "Hired muscle?"

The string bean's face drained white, and he shrank back.

"Actually," Maggie said, "yes. Junior Semple, meet Alec Barclay. Alec, Josiah Meeker hired Junior to abduct Paige."

Alec lunged, so blinded by rage all he saw was red. His hands reached for Junior's throat, but he couldn't seem to move, no matter how hard he fought. It could have been seconds or hours before sound began to cut through the fury. Someone was shouting his name. He could barely hear it over the roaring in his ears. Roaring that came from his own mouth.

Reality came back in pieces, Dex and Hold at each arm, restraining him, George at the door, preventing Junior from leaving. Shelley stood to one side, her hands over her ears. Maggie stood beside her, hands on her hips. Jessi had sympathy in her eyes and tears rolling down her cheeks.

He pulled back, and the minute Dex and Hold relaxed, he lunged again. He almost got past them.

Jessi's voice stopped him. "Alec," she said sharply. "You're not helping Paige."

He capitulated so abruptly Hold and Dex had slammed him against the wall before they could let up.

"Sorry," Hold said.

Alec clasped him on the shoulder and nodded, mostly because he needed a minute to get his wind back.

"Sit," Maggie said, and when Junior only looked over at Alec, she took him by the arm and towed him one of the chairs in front of George's desk. "Sit."

Junior folded his six-foot-plus frame into the chair and hung his head, seeming to collapse into himself. Shelley didn't need any urging at all to take the other chair.

"You first," Maggie said to Junior. "Spill."

"I usually get to be the bad cop," George said under his breath as he passed Maggie and took his chair.

"Not today." Alec came over and sat on the front corner of the desk, so close he could have leaned over and been head-to-head with Junior.

It only took a look for the kid to start babbling.

"I thought it was a movie," he said. "That's what Mr. M—"

"Junior," Shelley snapped.

"That's what your old man told me," he said defiantly. "It was a movie, and I was supposed to pretend to kidnap Ms. Paige. But then he stuck her with a needle, and I thought it was only acting again, but she passed out. For real."

Alec held himself under control, even when the thought of Paige drugged and manhandled made his hands fists.

George was on his feet, though, and around the desk. He caught the back of Junior's chair in one of his big hands, swung it around, and put his face close to Junior's. "It looks like there aren't any good cops here today, kid. You have about five seconds to tell us everything you know. And then it's your turn," he said to Shelley.

She cringed away. "I didn't have anything to do with it."

"Bullshit," Jessi said, and when they all turned to stare at her, she added, "I don't want to be a good cop, either."

Alec almost smiled over the idea of Jessi hurting anyone, physically or verbally, but Junior demanded his attention.

"I swear I didn't know it was real," Junior squeaked. "I put her in the back of my truck and Mr. Meeker drove away. I don't know where."

"And it never occurred to you to come to me."

"I..." He looked helplessly at Shelley.

"Never mind," George said with a heavy sigh. "Your truck wasn't at the antiques store, and it wasn't at Meeker's house."

"That's all I know," Junior insisted.

"We'll see." George turned to Shelley. "What do you have to say for yourself?"

"I told you, I don't know anything."

"First, lose the attitude," George warned her. "You have no business being snotty. Second, how did Paige get the note? Because I don't believe Josiah taped it to her back door."

Shelley went sullen.

"Wrong attitude again," George said.

Alec, out of patience, leaned over her chair. "Talk, goddammit, or I will see you charged as an accessory, and if anything happens to Paige, I'll make damn sure you go to jail for the rest of your life."

"Can he threaten me like that?"

"I didn't hear him threaten you with anything but the law," George said equably, "and I have to say the law is not your friend at the moment.

"You may be thinking of Paige as the girl you grew up with, Shelley, but the world knows her as Paige Walker the movie star. If anything happens to her, there isn't a prosecutor in the country who won't be out for blood, or a jury that won't give it to him. Do you want it to be your blood?"

"It wouldn't hurt my feelings," Maggie muttered.

"He's my father," Shelley said.

"He's a kidnapper," George shot back. "Maybe you can stop him from being a murderer."

Alec met George's gaze, knew he was doing what he had to do. It still stopped his heart to hear the possibility put into words.

"He...He wouldn't actually hurt her."

"He would if someone paid him enough money," Maggie said.

Shelley sat back, her defiance draining away into uncertainty.

"What?" George asked her.

"He said he was going to be rich." Her hands twisted in her lap, and she looked at each of them in turn, beseechingly. "He wouldn't explain. I didn't even know he...he took Paige until Junior said so."

Alec turned away, and when pacing didn't help, slammed his fist into the wall.

Shelley cringed. "If I knew anything, I'd tell you."

"You haven't answered George's second question," Dex pointed out. "How did that note get taped to Paige's back door?"

"I did that," Shelley admitted, "but it was sealed. I didn't know what was in it."

"That means you talked to him when he got back to the island," George said.

Shelley nodded. "He got back last night and sent me to the store to bring some things back to the house. You remember," she said to George, "you saw Junior and me unloading them at the house."

George exchanged a look with Dex.

Alec knew what they were thinking, and it made his blood run cold.

"What did you remove from the store?" George was asking.

But Alec was already on his way to the door. Meeker would have retrieved anything of real value, and there was only one reason—

"Fire!"

The first shout lanced straight through Alec, stealing his breath, stopping his heart. The rest of him kept moving, though, through the door and out into the street with what seemed like the entire population of Windfall Island.

And they were all looking toward the end of town, staring in silence at the yellow stain against the gunmetal gray sky.

"Meeker's," Alec said on a horrified breath of air already sparking with embers and stinging with the acrid stench of smoke.

Chapter Twenty-Six

As the flames shot higher, Paige strained futilely against the bonds around her hands and feet. Panic drove her, and with adrenaline flooding her system she barely felt her muscles straining to the breaking point. She couldn't—wouldn't—die like this.

"Meeker, you son of a—"

Meeker dragged her, chair and all, away from the fire. He stopped to untie her, but the flames were moving too fast, devouring the crowded stacks of wooden furniture piled to the roof of the onetime warehouse and igniting the wooden beams high overhead.

"The knots are too tight," he panted, and took off.

Paige was pretty sure he wasn't coming back. She looked toward the huge windows fronting the street, already partly obscured by billows of smoke. She had no idea what time it was, but it had to be late afternoon at best, judging by the amount of light and the cloud cover. There'd be people around.

People who thought Meeker's store was unoccupied.

They'd already searched the place, Meeker had told her. So it was up to her to let them know otherwise.

She drew in breath to scream, but her lungs filled with smoke instead of air. She coughed, hard, but every breath she drew was filled with smoke until she began to feel woozy—but not so much she couldn't see the flames all around her now.

Best, she thought as the world spun, as darkness closed in, best she pass out. But there was a sudden gust of fresh air that blew the smoke away from her face and fanned the flames.

And denied her even the blessing of unconsciousness.

But at least now she could scream.

* * *

Alec ran the half mile between the Sheriff's Office and Meeker's store flat-out. He didn't feel the cold, didn't hesitate to shove his way through the crowd gathered in the street. He saw only Paige's face and heard her screaming as the flames that had already eaten through the roof danced gleefully on the frigid wind.

He picked up a loose cobble from the street and heaved it through the big front window. Shaking off the hands that dragged at him, he hurled himself through the remaining glass and the smoke that poured out, shouting Paige's name.

"Alec," he heard her say faintly.

"Keep shouting," he yelled, hoping to orient himself by the sound of her voice.

She called out, but even though her voice had grown weaker, Alec felt like he was getting closer.

The smoke was choking him, so he stopped long enough to tear off his jacket, draping it over his head and shoulders to cut off some of the smoke and protect him from the embers flying everywhere. Then he headed straight into the fire again.

Flames crackled and leaped around him, smoke swirled, driven by the wind from the open roof and the window he'd broken. His eyes stung, his throat burned. His heart pumped so hard from the combination of fear, oxygen deprivation, and exertion, he thought it might beat its way out of his chest.

And he was losing hope—before it started to rain.

"Paige!" he roared, turning down another of the twisting pathways through Meeker's merchandise.

The wrong pathway, he realized when it took him in a huge circle back to where he'd started. He stopped there, but the despair sneaking through the cracks of his resolve never had a chance to take hold. A whisper of sound reached him, sent him diving through an opening in the stack of furniture to his left, barely big enough for him to fit through.

He fell onto something soft, something that whimpered.

"Paige."

"Alec," she choked out before giving in to racking coughs that left her wheezing for air.

He swung his coat over her shoulders.

She looked up, her tearing eyes widening as they focused on something behind him. Alec looked back in time to see the stack he'd pushed himself through begin to topple. He hunched over Paige, pulling her, chair and all, out of the way. Something hit him hard on the back, but he kept going until they were in the clear by the front windows.

"Alec!"

"Over here."

Dex climbed inside, already pulling a knife from his pocket.

"I'm carrying one of those from now on," Alec said as he watched Dex cut the plastic ties around Paige's wrists and ankles.

She tried to stand, but her feet, starved of blood, wouldn't hold her. Alec scooped her up before she fell—and nearly dropped her again. He managed to keep hold of her, but pain shot through his left arm and ribs.

Paige tried to push away. "You're hurt."

"I think a chair fell on my back." And the pain had really just begun to register, but she felt so good in his arms he couldn't let her go.

"Your arm is bleeding," Dex pointed out.

Alec looked down and saw a shallow gash along his right arm, dripping blood. "I must have cut it when I went through the window."

Paige tipped her head to his shoulder, tears carving tracks in the soot on her face.

Alec rested his cheek on the top of her head and closed his eyes, simply taking her in. Even with her soaking wet and her face streaked with soot, she was the most beautiful sight he'd ever seen. "Paige" was all he could choke out before emotion swamped him.

"This is touching and all," Hold said from the other

side of the broken window, "but you should get out of there before the roof falls on your heads."

"Help!" a voice shrieked from the smoke-filled depths.

"Meeker," Paige said, and looked back, into the fire.

Alec merely carried her through the door Dex had opened.

"We can't leave him in there."

"Why not?"

"Because we're not the bad guys."

"It won't bother my conscience," Alec rasped, still working the smoke out of his lungs.

"Sounds like he's coming this way," Hold said.

Sure enough, the shrieking was louder, and by the time Alec had pulled Paige through the door, Meeker raced out of the smoke and into the waiting custody of George Boatwright. George handcuffed and perp-walked Meeker through the crowd, to the accompaniment of camera flashes and cheering.

What Alec had taken for rain must have been the water pumped by the volunteer firemen, because it was snowing, big fat flakes that slashed on the gusting wind.

The volunteers had moved to either side of Meeker's now, and were wetting down the buildings to keep the fire from spreading. Every able-bodied man in town had come out to help. With the town being almost entirely built of wood, a fire could level the village if it wasn't checked quickly.

"Even the reporters are helping," Paige murmured.

"George put them to work," Maggie said as she and Jessi joined them, bundling Paige and Alec into blankets from the volunteer fire brigade.

Jessi put a hand on Alec's arm. "My house is closest. Bring Paige there."

"No. I want to go home."

"Well, we're going with you," Jessi said firmly. "Alec is bleeding and you—"

"I'm fine," Paige insisted, and to prove it she pushed out of Alec's arms.

He hissed out a breath and let her feet fall to the boardwalk.

"See? He's the one who's really hurt."

"You were drugged and kidnapped," Jessi reminded her.

"What about Benji?"

"Benji is fine. I already told him he could sleep over at Bobby Cassidy's tonight. They're taking the puppy, too, bless their hearts."

All Alec wanted was to be alone with Paige, but he could see it was hopeless, at least for the moment. Even understanding that her friends wanted to be sure she was safe and cosseted, he could have cheerfully wished them to perdition.

Maggie pulled up in the Jeep.

Alec bundled Paige into the backseat, meeting her eyes. He wasn't sure what he saw in the deep blue depths. He wasn't even allowed to sit with her. Jessi climbed in beside Paige and pulled the door shut after her, leaving the front passenger seat for Alec.

So, he thought, he was still in limbo. He'd saved Paige's life, but he had no idea if there would be a place in it for him.

* * *

Paige only let them take her home so she could shower and change. The stink of smoke kept taking her back to those helpless moments, tied to a chair with flames licking so close...

She was more shaken than she realized.

Though she drew the line at Jessi helping her shower, she didn't object when she was bundled into bed—once they promised not to question Meeker without her.

Jessi had patched up Alec's arm. It was just a shallow cut, but he was going to have a thin scar, because he'd refused to go to the mainland and have it looked at by a plastic surgeon.

Hold and Dex had stayed behind to help make sure the fire wouldn't spread. When the men returned, soot-covered and exhausted, they took Alec with them. He could shower at her house, Maggie said, and sleep in the guest room. Maggie and Jessi insisted on staying, in case Paige needed them.

Alec came to the door of her bedroom before he left, just stood there and stared at her. Paige lifted her chin and met his eyes, hoping. She wanted him to stay with her, so much she ached.

She couldn't bring herself to ask him, though. He'd saved her life. He made love to her. Both things were true. He'd also proved he couldn't live her kind of life. As much as she'd needed the comfort, she'd watched him turn and walk away.

Morning brought a new world. The storm had blown itself out during the night, leaving behind a blanket of snow at least a foot deep.

Symbolic, Paige decided, as she gathered her things and headed for the stairs, and Maggie waiting below.

She'd come home because of one scandal that had changed her life, Paige thought, only to find herself embroiled in a mystery that might have taken it. Now the scandal had turned in her favor, and the mystery was solved.

She'd be back in LA in a couple of days; neither the sex tape nor Eugenia's fate would leave more than a ripple in the big scheme of things. Alec Barclay, what might have been, would haunt her for the rest of her life.

"Ready to go?" Maggie asked her. "Jessi went on ahead with Hold. Dex is outside shoveling your front and back walks, but he'll be done in a couple minutes."

Paige rinsed the teacup she'd brought downstairs with her and set it in the sink. "Yes and no."

"I'd think you'd be anxious to get your hands around Meeker's throat. Or maybe you'd rather claw out his eyes."

"I'm just glad it's over."

"All of it?" When Paige didn't respond, Maggie sighed. "You're going to make me ask about your love life, aren't you?"

"No, I need to talk to Alec about that. He saved my life"—she smiled faintly—"the least he deserves is honesty."

"Well." Maggie shoved her hands in her pockets. The expression on her face was half relief, half disappointment. Curiosity turned the tide. "You're not even going to give me a hint?"

Paige laughed softly. She gathered her purse and went to retrieve her coat. How could she answer Maggie when she didn't know herself how her conversation with Alec would go?

"You have a charter later?" Paige asked, realizing Maggie was wearing her flight suit.

"I just got back from one," Maggie said. "I went to Boston—and don't look at me like that. I didn't take Alec there, I picked up Rose Stanhope. Dex and I dropped her off at George's before we came to get you."

That stopped Paige. "Why?"

"If you get moving you'll find out. And pouting won't help." But Maggie grinned.

So did Dex when Paige stepped outside. Then he came over and bundled her into a strong, hard hug that made tears spring to her eyes.

"You'll both have me bawling in a minute."

Dex ignored Maggie. "All right?" he asked Paige.

"Yes, thanks to all of you."

"Thanks to Alec. The minute he couldn't get to you he went crazy. I think he would have torn the island apart to find you. As it was, he hurled himself through a plate glass window and into an inferno to save you."

"I know." The trouble wasn't in believing Alec loved her, it was believing he could live with her.

She received a variation on the same greeting when she arrived at the Windfall Island Sheriff's Office. Hold gave her a long, hard hug. So did George; it was the first time he'd touched her since she'd come home, and it meant he'd forgiven her for using him to hurt Maggie all those years ago.

Even Rose Stanhope clasped both her hands, then said, "What the hell," and hugged her.

Alec kept his hands in his pockets, and kept his distance.

"Isn't this touching," Meeker sneered from his cell behind George's desk.

Paige looked at him and smiled. He still wore the clothes he'd had on the night before, holes singed in them and reeking of smoke. Soot streaked his face and stiffened his hair into wild tufts.

His eyes shifted away, then back to meet hers again, defiantly. "I tried to save you."

"I remember you running away."

"I went to get a knife to cut your bonds."

"Bonds you put on me. And you never came back. In fact, I seem to remember you shrieking like a ten-year-old girl who's seen a spider before you ran straight for the door. For all you knew, I was still in there, burning."

"I'm injured," he whined, sticking his hand through the bars. "Look at my fingers."

"Let's not forget who set the place on fire," Maggie said.

"It was an accident."

Paige snorted softly. "He got those burns playing with matches, lighting them and dropping them in order to frighten me."

Alec took a step forward. His hands were out of his pockets, and fisted.

Meeker held his ground, protected by iron bars. But he pulled his arm back into the cell.

Alec stepped up close to the bars. "You're just a bird in a cage," he said, his control so tight his voice was little more than a rumble of sound through clenched jaws. "Time to sing."

"I've got nothing to say."

George snatched a key ring off his desk and opened the cell. He dragged Meeker out and shoved him into a chair. "Talk."

Meeker looked from George to Dex, to Hold, and finally to Maggie. He swallowed hard.

"Let me get you started," George said. "How much insurance did you have on your place? It's public record," he reminded Meeker when no answer was immediately forthcoming.

"Two million dollars."

George smiled with contempt. "You won't be seeing a penny of that."

"But...All my precious things."

"It was mostly junk," George said. "Everyone knows that, especially you, since you had Shelley move anything worth money out the night before."

"Shelley had no idea—"

"If I thought she did, she'd be sitting next to you right now."

"Speaking of Shelley, where is she?" Paige asked.

"She and Junior are upstairs, for the moment," George said. "Right now I'd like to tell Josiah what he's looking at after he's convicted of the attempted murder of a thousand souls—every man, woman, and child on this island—and a fair number of reporters and photographers."

"You...you can't be serious."

"I am. Dead serious."

"I didn't mean to kill everyone," Josiah squeaked in outrage.

"Just Paige," George shot back. "But the fact is, you set a wooden building on fire in the middle of a town built of wood. If anyone was hurt, it would be your fault."

"It's called depraved indifference murder," Alec said.

"I want a lawyer."

"It's your right," George said, "and you can have your one call just as soon as you spill your guts."

"You're trampling my civil rights."

"You know"—George stepped back—"you've got a point."

"That's right, and you don't have any proof I did anything."

"I have an eyewitness."

"That would be me," Paige said. "And you were a lot more talkative when you figured I wouldn't be around to repeat what you said. Like the part where Clayton Stanhope hired you. Sorry, Rose."

Rose, from her seat behind George's desk, merely waved it away.

"Once you'd collected the insurance money for your store and the payoff for killing me," Paige continued, "you planned to blackmail Clayton for the rest of his life."

"Hearsay."

"Actually, it's not," Alec said. "It's called a Declaration of Intent. And it can be used against anyone conspiring with you. I wonder how Clayton is going to feel about you when he finds out you implicated him."

Meeker exhaled sharply, as if he'd taken another blow. But Paige could see he wasn't ready to give up yet. "Either charge me or let me go."

"Okay." George dragged him to his feet, then to the door, opening it.

Everyone on the street stopped, and since the station house wasn't far from what was left of Meeker's store, that was a lot of people. A crowd started to form, and

Meeker's name was on everyone's lips, whispered at first, then shouted.

Meeker cringed back against George.

George didn't give an inch. "You mentioned trampling?"

"You can't send me out there."

"Of course I can. I haven't charged you with anything, so I guess I have to let you go."

"I...I want to give a statement."

"Without your lawyer?" George shut the door because the crowd was beginning to get really ugly.

Unfortunately, once the threat was gone, Meeker began to reconsider his options.

"My lawyer will want me moved to the mainland," he said.

"Probably. But I imagine your lawyer will have a hard time getting to Windfall. I'm afraid our little jailhouse will get overrun before he can arrive."

"Those are my friends and neighbors out there."

"Neighbors, maybe, but friends?" George snorted. "They were almost your victims, so I think you're safe in calling them enemies now."

"I can give you Stanhope," Meeker said. "I want a deal."

"Fine, here's the deal. You tell me everything you know, and I won't let your *friends* and *neighbors* in here. And before we even get started, you're going to pay for the damage you did to your store and the surrounding buildings."

"I don't have any money," Meeker whined.

"You can use the proceeds from all the treasures you removed from your shop and secreted away before you burned it down."

Meeker slumped, shoulders down, head hanging.

George slapped a pad of paper onto the desk next to him. "Write while you talk."

Meeker glanced up at him. "What's going to happen to me?"

"Even without an attempted murder charge, you're still looking at insurance fraud and arson." George considered for a second or two. "Fifteen years in prison would be my guess—although the prosecutor and judge will have a say in your sentencing."

Meeker went bone white.

George turned to Paige. "How about it, Paige, am I charging him with attempted murder, too?"

"Three counts," Jessi chimed in before Paige had even an inkling how to respond. "He got Lance back here, and Benji and I were—" She broke off, still unable to speak about what might have happened.

"There's Mort, too," Maggie said.

"Mort committed suicide."

"Because of you," Maggie shot back, shaking Dex's hand off her arm when he tried to stop her from getting in Meeker's face. "He would never have tried to hurt me if you hadn't manipulated him into it." She swung around to face George. "I say you throw everything you've got at him."

"I'd be happy to," George said, turning to Paige. "But is that what's really best for everyone?"

"Why do I have the feeling you've already decided how you want to handle this?" Paige said to George, then turned to take in the rest of their little group. "It feels to me like there's already been a meeting of minds."

"We did talk it over a little last night."

Paige simply turned away, closing her eyes when George confirmed her suspicion. A part of her wanted vengeance, but while she knew it would feel satisfying, cleansing, to see Meeker on death row, suffering the same fear and despair he'd put them all through, she also knew it wouldn't really atone for anything, and in the long run it would cause only more pain.

"If you breathe a word about any of the rest of it," George was saying to Meeker, "I'll hit you with everything I have. Shelley, too."

"She doesn't know anything," Meeker insisted.

"She delivered the note that set Paige up to be abducted."

"And I'd bet she was asking Paige all those questions about her daily activities so you'd know to sabotage the stairs at her house," Jessi added. "She bolted out of the place pretty fast when she found out Alec was gone that day he went to Boston. You made her an accomplice."

"But she had no idea what the note said. And she had no idea about the steps."

"It won't matter," Alec said bluntly.

"And if I confess?"

"She and Junior can leave Windfall. Permanently."

"It's part of the deal," Dex said. "You hold up your end or your daughter will be wearing an orange jumpsuit by nightfall."

Meeker crossed his arms, his face sullen. "Doesn't Ma have the final say?"

"Not anymore." Maggie stepped up to him. "You see, she's turning the island over to me, well, to us, Jessi and Paige and me."

Meeker's breath leaked out and he hunched forward,

like a balloon deflating. Why that should rock him when the rest only pissed him off, well, that was Meeker, Paige decided.

"I'll take the deal," he said. He pulled the pad over to him, and after a last hesitation, began to write. "What choice do I have?"

"Absolutely none," George said as cheerfully as George ever was in the performance of his duty.

"What about Stanhope?"

George looked over at Rose. "That's not your problem."

"He's gonna walk?" Meeker leaped to his feet, his face going a mottled red. "Stanhope goes free because he's rich."

"He won't be going free," Rose said grimly. "You can trust me on that."

Chapter Twenty-Seven

Meeker slid around some points, but he hit the high ones. As far as his confession went," George said. "When I was reading what he'd written to make sure he got it all down," he added in disgust, "I could still hear the whining tone of his voice."

So could Paige. She wondered if she'd ever get it out of her mind. Even now, more than an hour later, she could still hear it. Meeker had alternated between pleas for leniency, and a sick sense of pride over the way he'd played on Mort's desperation, on Lance's greed, and ultimately relied on his own cunning to try to eliminate anyone possibly related to the Stanhope family. All for the sake of money.

While George, Dex, Hold, and Alec had reviewed Meeker's written statement, Maggie and Jessi had gone with Shelley to her house, to help her pack her personal belongings—and only those. The rest would be sold to repair the buildings Meeker's fire had damaged.

Paige had taken Rose to the Horizon to get her a room, chafing at being relegated, yet again, to the easy task. The rest of the group joined them there, in what the Horizon boasted as a suite. For privacy's sake.

"I felt kind of bad for Shelley," Jessi said, and when Maggie rolled her eyes, added, "So did you. You gave them a boat."

"I traded Junior," Maggie corrected. "I didn't realize how pretty that old tub of his was, all that teak and brass. I can renovate it for charters, fishing, whale watching, whatever. You can give me some advice," she finished, turning to George. "You come from a long line of boat builders, Boatwright. You rebuilt that old sailboat of Ma's. It was a showpiece once you finished with it."

George smiled a little. "It had beautiful lines going in, and being more than a hundred years old, was built from prime materials and made to last. It was a joy to turn it into what it was meant to be."

"You're hired," Maggie said.

"We'll see" was George's response. "Can't make a yacht out of a canoe. But if the foundation is good, it'll be a pleasure."

"They'll have a hard road, Shelley and Junior," Jessi said.

"It's not prison," George said simply. "You're okay with it, right Paige?"

"Interesting time to ask."

"We all agreed," Maggie said to her. "Majority rules."

"And if you'd been the one nearly incinerated?" Paige snapped at her.

"I was nearly drowned in a plane crash." But Maggie flushed. "And I wanted a say."

"I deserved to have one, too," Paige said, turning to the window so she could hide how much it hurt to be left out.

"You were…" Jessi began. "We didn't think you'd want to talk about it."

Talk about it? Just for a moment she relived it, those endless seconds of believing she was about to die in one of the most gruesome ways possible. She hadn't slept a wink, worried that in sleep she'd go back there…

It wouldn't be the last time she relived it, Paige knew. "I want him strung up from the nearest tree. Your uncle, too," she said to Rose. "I won't apologize for it."

"I don't expect you to," Rose said, and she was so clearly distressed, Paige couldn't hold on to her anger.

"I'm not saying I don't understand the punishment you settled on," Paige said grudgingly. "If the murder came out, so would Eugenia's story and all the sordid details." And it would have impacted everyone, not just those in the room, but everyone on Windfall Island. "I guess sending Meeker to jail for fifteen years will have to be enough."

"Then why are you giving us grief?" Maggie demanded to know.

"People have been underestimating me my entire life, but they don't really know me. You're my friends."

"And we should have known you're strong," Alec said.

It hurt just to hear his voice. Paige took a deep breath, then let it out. Let it go. What they'd done, they'd done for her, at least in part. Without the attempted murder charges, there'd be less publicity, less grief for her. "What about Clayton?"

"First," Rose began, "I have the results of the DNA testing. But we already know the outcome."

"So, I'm..."

"Yes, Maggie. You're a Stanhope."

Maggie closed her eyes for a second, absorbed the truth. "And Clayton?"

"His mother was discreet about her affairs, but apparently not careful. He's not a Stanhope, not by blood."

"He is under the law," Alec put in.

"I've had a couple of days to think about it," Rose said. "And I consulted with Alec, who knows Clayton's business inside out."

She took a breath, then let it out carefully. "We've already frozen all of Clayton's accounts. He probably has some funds squirreled away offshore, but I've decided to let him have that, and his personal possessions, as long as they aren't family heirlooms."

"If he goes away quietly?" Maggie said scornfully. "Special rules for the wealthy?"

"I know it appears that way," Rose said. "Money does buy happiness to some extent, which you'll find out for yourself now."

Maggie opened her mouth, then clamped it shut.

"Please bear in mind that Clayton has a son and a daughter, with a husband and a small child. Granted her life is in Europe, but it's a small world. What happens to their father reflects on them."

Maggie, Paige thought, knew that all too well.

"You're a Stanhope now," Rose continued, laying a hand lightly on Maggie's arm. "Whether you choose to let the world know, I won't make this decision unless you agree. It's a family matter."

"I know it doesn't seem like a fitting punishment," Alec said, "but he'll be an outcast, Maggie, and for Clayton Stanhope, that's worse than any jail sentence."

"Somehow that doesn't sound right."

"Because wealth and status are meaningless to you," Rose said kindly. "Those things mean a great deal to Clayton."

"He's lost everything," Alec said. "He was a board member of several Fortune 500 companies. No reputable firm will hire him now. He won't be welcome in his own social circle. He'll be stripped of everything that means anything to him."

"Clayton was willing to do anything to keep his secret," Paige said. "It seems appropriate that he succeeded and lost everything really important in the process."

"Yeah," Maggie said. "It's the definition of irony, all right." Dex, sitting beside her, covered her hand with his. Maggie turned hers palm to palm and twined her fingers with his, making them a unit.

"Clayton will leave the country," Rose predicted. "He would be wise to choose a country that doesn't have an extradition treaty with the United States. Do you know what those places are like, Maggie?"

"No, but I've heard stories."

"In addition," Rose concluded, "if I discover that he has traded on the Stanhope name in any way, the truth will be revealed about his heritage and his misconduct. I've already retained Dex to keep tabs on him."

"Believe me when I tell you it will get around very quickly that Clayton's own family has disowned him," Alec said. "It will be assumed that there was some kind of financial irregularity, and the family let him off because they want to keep the talk to a minimum."

"And money is so much more important than a life or two," Maggie said bitterly.

"In some circles, that's unfortunately true," Rose said evenly.

But she had to be hurting, Paige thought, as George crossed to Rose and laid a hand on her cheek. Rose placed her hand over his, the love all but glowing from her.

"I'm glad it's over," Paige said.

"It's just beginning," Jessi corrected her. She looked up at Hold, and he looped his arm around her waist and snugged her to his side.

With the rest of her friends coupled up, Paige was very careful not to look at Alec. "I still have the tape to clear up," she said, "and it will be necessary to do some damage control over this latest excitement. So"—she got to her feet—"I think I'll give a little press conference before I leave the island. The reporters and photographers are a nuisance, but they did pitch in to keep the entire village from burning to the ground."

"That's a nice gesture," Jessi said.

"Who knew I'd actually be glad they were around?" Paige shrugged into her coat, gathered her purse, and pressed a hand to her stomach when Alec said, "I'll drive you home."

Paige went over to Rose and gave her a hug. "I'll see you again, I hope."

Rose looked up at George. "I'm counting on it."

* * *

George lingered after the others had gone, though he knew it was a mistake. Now that Eugenia's fate was known, he should cut all ties with Rose Stanhope. No matter what she thought she felt, she was as far out of his reach as the stars.

"Would you like to talk about it?" she asked.

"About what?"

"Whatever has you prowling this room like a lion in a cage."

He turned, and the sight of her hit him, as it always did, an almost physical blow to the heart.

She sat at the small table, cool and regal in her somber suit. Her skin was pale and perfect, her sunny hair pulled back and secured by a pair of pins that were, Jesus, probably real diamonds. She watched him, her expression as placid as the ocean on the best of summer days. Her eyes, those Stanhope blue eyes, were on him, patient, implacable, and her lips were curved up, just a little, at the corners.

He felt dazzled, looking at her, and more than a bit uneasy. "When are you going back to Boston?" he asked her, already feeling hollowed out at the thought of never seeing her again.

"That depends on you, darling."

"Rose...At the risk of flattering myself, I think I know where this is going."

"And you're going to tell me—again—that we're all wrong for each other. You're just a small-town sheriff with small-town manners and modest ambitions."

"It's the truth."

"You don't know how to fit into my world, and I don't fit here."

"I think you'd fit anywhere you really wanted to."

"Except with you." The hands she'd folded in her lap were clasped tightly now. A pulse fluttered in the soft curve of her throat, and the certainty was gone from her face.

Foolishly, it calmed him to know she wasn't. "Can you see yourself living here?"

"Yes. But—" Rose stood. "Do you love me?"

George stepped back. His hands were shaking, so he stuffed them in his pockets. "What?"

"Do you love me? Come on, George, you're the black-and-white thinker, and that's a yes or no question. Pick one."

"Yes," he said on an outrush of air. Though he'd meant to say no, and that was the right answer for so many reasons, the lie just didn't sit well. "I love you. I love everything about you."

"And I love you. You're strong and gentle and trusting and honest right down to the core. You're the kind of man who cares for people, and who does what's best for everyone else first and yourself last."

She took a step toward him. He held his ground, unsure if he wanted to meet her halfway or run out of the room.

"And it's not a bad package, either," she said with a smile, and the heat in her eyes seemed to lick into him, setting off flames it was hard to quench. "You're the kind of man," she said softly, "who'd spend the rest of his life alone if you thought it was best for me."

"And you're the kind of woman who doesn't know what's good for you."

"Yes, I do." And she kissed him, pressed her long,

slim body to his, and took his mouth with so much fire and passion he forgot that he always thought of her as precious, breakable.

He groaned, fisting his hands in the back of her jacket and kissing her back with all the longing and desire he'd been holding back since the day he'd first heard her voice. He lifted her off her feet with one hand, cradled the back of her head, and plundered.

Her breathless moan drove his need even higher. His innate concern was stronger—just barely. It was the hardest thing he'd ever done to step back from her.

Rose refused to let him go. "No, hold me tight, George, so tight I can't breathe. You don't know how much I love having your arms around me, how safe you make me feel." She peppered his neck with soft little kisses, testing his resolve.

"I want you, Rose, more than is good for either of us."

"You can't want me too much." She framed his face with her hands. "Marry me, George."

When he pulled back, when the shock of those words jerked through him, she only wound her arms around his neck and kissed him again, until all he could think of was her. How she smelled, how she felt in his arms, how she was soft and sweet—with a will of iron.

"I won't take no for an answer," she whispered with her cheek pressed to his. She eased back, met his eyes. "I'm used to getting what I want."

"It won't be easy," he warned her. "Your friends will look at me and see a gold digger."

"No, they'll look at us and see two people in love. And whatever they think of you, you'll prove them wrong. You won't be satisfied until you do."

George smiled his slow smile, then laughed a little. "It's a bit intimidating to know you have so much faith in me. I don't want to let you down."

"That's what I'm counting on." Her smile was wide, and a little predatory. "Since you don't have a ring, how do you propose we make the engagement official?"

He swept her up.

She gave a little squeak of surprise as he carried her into the bedroom. "Did I mention strong when I was listing what I love about you?"

"Yeah, that was on your list."

"I'm really appreciating that particular quality right now."

George set her on her feet next to the bed. "You left slow and thorough off your list." He started to remove her clothes, enjoying every sliver of skin as it was revealed.

"Oh, by all means," Rose said, hissing in a breath as he ran his thumb lightly over her nipple, "please educate me."

Chapter Twenty-Eight

The press conference was short and sweet. Paige thanked the reporters and photographers for helping to save Windfall Village, at the risk of their own lives. She skirted any questions pertaining to her own involvement in the fire. All other questions, she ignored.

She couldn't, however, ignore Alec. He drove with both hands fisted around the wheel, silent, not so much as sending a glance her way. There might as well have been a brick wall between them for all that they sat less than a foot apart from each other.

So it surprised her when he asked if she was really okay with the outcome.

"There's no reason Rose should have to pay for Clayton's greed. Or his daughter, or Maggie, or any of the rest of us, for that matter."

That earned her more silence, lasting until Alec pulled the Jeep into her driveway, turned off the ignition, and climbed out. Paige opened her own door, and although Alec had come around and held out a hand, she didn't take it. She couldn't touch him, not with her heart aching at the distance between them.

He took her arm anyway.

She jerked it away. "I'm perfectly capable of walking by myself."

He simply took hold again.

"You're not listening. As usual." She took out her key, opened the door, and tried to close it in his face.

He wouldn't let her, calmly letting himself in once she gave up on her futile attempt to shut him out.

He took her coat, hung it on the coat tree, then put his over it.

Paige moved his coat to a separate hook. She could send messages, too.

"Do you want tea?" he asked with that same maddening calmness. "Something to eat? You didn't have much at lunch."

"No and no. Damn it," she erupted. "I'm not made of glass."

"I'm just trying to help."

"You saved my life, that doesn't make you responsible for it."

"Responsible?" He turned away, whirled back. "I should have been here, it's my fault—"

"Oh, sure, let's make it about you."

"Meeker used me to get to you."

And now she could see the pain behind the anger. She couldn't let it soften her. They were both hurting, and prolonging it wouldn't help either of them. "You were there when I needed you, and I'll always be thankful."

"But that's it. End of story. I made one mistake and now you don't trust me."

"Trust you? I love you, you idiot. You're the one who doesn't trust me to handle my own life." When he only stared at her, she fisted her hands in her hair out of sheer frustration. "I asked you to stay out of it, but you just had to interfere. And you didn't do it for my sake, either, you did it because you couldn't stand—"

"Wait a minute, back up. What did you say?"

"You don't trust me."

"Not that, before."

Paige knew what he was getting at. She'd tossed that declaration out mid-tirade because it had seemed easier to say it that way. Because she was scared to risk. Her heart had been broken before, most recently by Alec himself, and she was still hurting too much to take that kind of chance again.

"You saved my life?"

He locked his hands around her arms and shook her a little. "I'll end it if you don't repeat what you said."

She pushed away from him, and felt another little slice of pain when he let her go. "I don't think you understand how big a deal this is for me, Alec. What I do...I won't say it's a hard life. I love my work, and I'm able to lead a very privileged existence. The one thing I lack is privacy, and that's an awful big trade-off. One I'm willing to make. But this won't be the last time someone concocts a story, tells an outright lie, or just uses me to get press."

"And I didn't handle it very well."

"You completely messed up. I'm not sure you get that."

"Because I haven't apologized."

Paige threw her hands up. "What you did was wrong."

"What I felt wasn't. I love you, Paige, and I can't promise, under similar circumstances, that I wouldn't do the same, or worse. Thinking of you that way"—he closed his eyes—"it killed me."

Everything inside her went still. "You were jealous?"

"Jealous? I was pissed off. I wanted to kill that director for lying about you. And you're right, even though I knew it wasn't you on that tape, I couldn't stand the thought of everyone believing it was. And what I did, I did for me as much as for you. No one is allowed to treat you that way."

"If that's an apology, it's a pretty good one."

"I can't promise I won't step in if it happens again."

"I'm not asking you to change, Alec." She wouldn't want him any other way.

"But you want me to try to let you handle it."

"I want us to handle things together."

His smile spread, slow and easy, warming his gray eyes. "Because?"

"You're an idiot, but I love you."

He pondered that for a second. "Not exactly the same words, but I'll take them. And you." He kissed her, slow and deep and thorough.

Paige let the sweetness of it wind through her, stir her desire and haze her mind. But she wasn't completely befuddled. "You'll take me?"

Alec dropped to one knee, clapping a hand over his heart. "Paige Walker, marry me and make me the happiest man in the world."

"Hmmm, not a bad proposal, all in all, but not the best one I've ever received. There was this earl—"

He held up one finger, digging into his pocket with

the other hand. He came out with a beautiful antique ring, the large center diamond surrounded by smaller sapphires. "It was my grandmother's. My grandfather gave it to me because he said you'd be as much trouble to me as she was to him."

"It's perfect," she said as tears started to fall.

Alec climbed to his feet and handed her a handkerchief. "Grandfather loved every minute of the years they had together, even the ones when my grandmother gave him grief. Especially those moments, I think."

He tipped her chin up, until, through her swimming vision, she recognized the love in his eyes. "As long as we're together, there's no challenge we can't overcome. Will you marry me, Paige?"

"Yes." Suddenly it was so clear, the way their life would go—and that hers wouldn't be worth living without him in it.

He slipped the ring on her finger.

She threw her arms around his neck. "I love you, Alec. I'll love you forever."

"I'll hold you to that."

She held her hand up behind his back and studied the ring he'd given her. "I imagine I'll have to apologize to your grandfather. I gave him a pretty bad time when he was here." She pulled back a little, met Alec's eyes. "Maybe I should get him something. Does he like flowers?"

"He thinks flowers are for women."

"All right, so what do you give the man who has everything?"

Alec swept her up and carried her up the stairs. "A great-grandchild."

Epilogue

Maddie Finley stood in her tiny bedroom, in the little cottage she'd grown up in, dressed only in her slip. Her mother, Claire Finley, slipped a gown over her head, and Maddie drew in her breath sharply.

"Oh, Mama, it's absolutely beautiful." Long-sleeved and high-necked, it nevertheless showed her willowy figure off to perfection. The skirt was a mile of white silk that had to have come dear, but Claire had insisted Maddie have the finest.

From the doorway, Jamie Finley watched his wife struggle through her tears to pinch the loose bits together and pin them so she could make the final alterations.

When Claire looked over, Jamie met her eyes. She put the pin she held back into the cushion secured to her wrist by its elastic band, and stepped away from her daughter.

"What is it?" Maddie asked, turning to her father.

"We want to talk to you, child," Jamie said, "me and

your mother." He took Maddie's hand and drew her to the bed.

She sat, blushed. "Mama already talked to me."

Jamie's face heated. He didn't even want to think about his daughter...

His daughter. She was that, had been since the moment he laid eyes on her, he realized now. And she deserved to know the truth before she decided on the course of her life.

"Maddie." He stopped and shook his head. How did you tell a child you loved that she wasn't really yours, not by blood? How did you tell her that, but for your own selfishness, she might have lived an entirely different life, one of ease and comfort?

They'd had no more children after her, Jamie thought. God's punishment? He'd always wondered. But how could it be a punishment to have such a lovely daughter, inside and out?

Claire clasped his hand briefly, then sat on the bed beside her daughter. She smoothed Maddie's honey-blond hair away from her face, as she'd done countless times, then took her hand. "What would you do if you came into money?" Claire asked the daughter of her heart. "Not a few dollars, but the kind of money that meant you could have anything you want, go anywhere you want, live in real luxury."

Maddie studied her mother's face, then her father's. Her striking turquoise blue eyes filled with sympathy. "You mean like the Stanhopes?"

So, Jamie thought with a pang, she'd suspected. And why shouldn't she wonder? he asked himself. There was no family resemblance, and even now, eighteen years later, there was still talk, still speculation about what had happened to Eugenia Stanhope.

"Daddy." Maddie reached for his hand, pulled him over to sit on the narrow bed at her other side. She kept her hand in his and made tears spring to his eyes. "I love you both so much," she said softly. "I love my life. I always have, and I can't imagine anything more wonderful than marrying the man I love and having a family of my own."

Claire had begun to cry quietly. Jamie fought off his own tears, but it was a near thing. He'd never been a demonstrative man, but he felt a need to say something he'd only ever said to his wife, and that in the privacy of their bedroom. "I love you, Maddie."

"I know, Daddy."

Jamie slipped a hand into his pocket, removed the object there, and pressed it into her hand.

Maddie looked at the ruby and diamond pin, her eyes going wide.

"I want you to have this, child, to help you start your new life."

"But—"

"It's yours, Maddie. Keep it and hand it down, or use it as you see fit. It's little enough to give, and less than you deserve."

Maddie, tears streaming down her cheeks, leaned over and kissed him, then her mother. "I want a house, just a little one, of my own."

Jamie found himself smiling over her good sense and simple wants. "Go to Walker," he said. "He'll build you a good, solid home."

"I will, Daddy. Thank you." She jumped to her feet

and rushed to the door, turning back when she realized she couldn't leave while she wore her wedding dress. "Thank you," she said again, "for everything." Her gaze shifted from her father's tear-streaked face to her mother's. "I'm the richest girl in the world."

Charter pilot Maggie has never cared much for outsiders. But her latest passenger arouses the curiosity of Windfall Island...and something hot and irresistible in Maggie.

See the next page for an excerpt from

Temptation Bay.

Chapter One

"Portland Tower. This is N277HK requesting approach."

"N277HK hold your position. We have outgoing."

"Roger that, Portland Tower, holding," Maggie Solomon said from the cockpit of her AS355 Twinstar helicopter, hovering at a safe distance and altitude over the Maine coastline east of Portland International Jetport.

She didn't mind hovering. Things were so much more appealing from the air. Less…messy. A little distance was never a bad thing. A fitting rule of thumb, she thought, for life in general.

"You got a fare, Maggie, or just cargo?"

"It's a suit, so I guess it depends on your outlook."

The radio was quiet for a few seconds while the controller dealt with the outgoing traffic, which turned out to be a small commercial jet taking off. "Roger that, N277HK," the controller said once the plane was airborne and safely away. "By suit I take it you mean some sort of corporate stiff."

"Lawyer." Maggie patted her control panel lightly. "I'll have my baby fumigated later."

A slight laugh crackled through the radio static. "Come on in, one thousand."

"Roger that." Maggie brought the 'copter in for a landing, and saw her fare, standing at the edge of the tarmac like one of those Easter Island statues she'd seen in *National Geographic*. Inscrutable expression, oddly compelling, just a little scary.

Most people hunched automatically, instinctive fear of thirty-five feet of rotor blade edged with stainless steel spinning at approximately 400 rpm right about head level. Dexter Keegan just stood there, not moving, even though the wind was fierce enough to scour the paint from the buildings, not to mention mold his suit to his body—his long, lean, nicely muscled body. The kind of muscles that came from a gym, she told herself, and when she realized she was staring, she took a good long look at the suit again, because the suit, with its crisp white shirt and almost military cut, instantly put her back up.

Too bad, because she liked looking at him, in spite of the bland lawyer expression that said "trust me," and made her want to do exactly the opposite. His hair was dark and just a bit too long, his features a shade too handsome, and his attitude struck her as self-confident, with an edge of swagger. Swagger irritated the hell out of her.

His gaze found hers through the chopper's windows, dark eyes cool and shadowed. There were depths there,

Maggie thought, and despite her better instincts, she found herself intrigued. Maybe if he relaxed enough to get out of that suit he'd be worth a fling. She didn't have them often, and not with anyone she could get seriously involved with. But this man didn't strike her as being any more interested in entanglements than she was. Entanglements were a while off in her life plan.

She powered down the helicopter and put on her business face as she climbed out. "Dexter Keegan?" she said, holding out her hand.

He took it. "Call me Dex, Miss…"

"Solomon," Maggie said, taking her hand back and telling herself he hadn't held it a bit too long. And that she hadn't been flattered by it.

"You have a first name?"

"Yes." She stepped around him to retrieve his luggage.

"I'll get that."

"Part of the service," she said, shouldering the hanging bag and snagging the roller. She noted the quick flash of irritation that crossed his face and remembered her first rule of operation: *make the customer happy*. Word of mouth traveled a long way in the blogosphere, and he looked like a guy who knew his way around a cutting phrase.

And maybe the keyboard was mightier than the sword in the twenty-first century, but she'd be damned if she let the potential for bad press compromise—

He reached for the suitcase. She nipped it away. "Really," she said through her teeth, "it's no trouble."

"Something to prove?" he said equably.

Maggie shrugged, a lift and drop of one shoulder. She

always had something to prove. And if it rankled that Dexter Keegan had read her so easily, at least she looked away before he saw the little snap of peevishness in her eyes because she was attracted to him, and she didn't want to be.

But that wasn't his fault.

So she handed him the shoulder bag—compromising as much as she could manage—and waited until he stowed it, then lifted in the roller and secured the luggage net.

She opened the passenger door and stood back while he climbed in, and nearly took a right to the jaw when he reached for the door handle just as she leaned in to buckle his harness.

He lifted both hands, his expression missing only a pair of waggling brows.

"I need to make sure it's properly latched," she said, adding in a deadpan voice, "Wouldn't want you to fall out," cinching the straps tight before she stepped back. "I'd hate to have wasted the trip. Fuel is an ugly price these days," she said before she secured the door and headed around the front of the Twinstar.

He gave her a look through the glass, mostly amusement. At least the man could take a joke, she allowed, and by the time she'd boosted herself into the pilot's seat, she was almost optimistic about having to spend the next twenty minutes with him.

She completed her pre-flight checklist before slipping on her headphones, unhooking the ones hanging behind the passenger's seat and handing them to Keegan. "All set?" she asked him.

"You're driving."

She smiled, just a little, and put him out of her mind. Or rather labeled him, which amounted to the same thing. Instead of an attractive man he was simply a tourist. She knew how to handle tourists.

"Portland Tower, N277HK requesting clearance."

"N277HK, this is Portland Tower. You're cleared for liftoff. Keep it under a thousand, Maggie, I'll hold traffic until you're away."

"Roger that, Portland, and thanks."

"Maggie," her passenger said.

She ignored him, grasping the stick on her left that lifted the bird and the control lever in front of her that moved them forward. Her feet were already resting on the pedals that served as the rudder, determining the pitch of the tail rotor and turning the helicopter left or right. In a choreography that was as natural to her as breathing, she lifted the Twinstar off the tarmac and put it into a smooth turning climb that took them out over the Atlantic coastline, her spirit soaring along with the bird.

She loved this, loved that weightless moment when she hit altitude and leveled off, when her stomach dropped out and she went a little breathless and a lot awestruck. No matter how often she flew, plane or helicopter, it was never anything less than pure magic. Utter freedom. It was the only time in her life when she was truly at peace and absolutely her own woman because she'd built a thriving business around something she loved, something she never allowed to be just business. And even though she knew Mr. Dexter Keegan could see the childish delight on her face, she didn't care. She simply let herself *feel*.

When she reached the height and distance she

wanted, she checked in with the tower, reported her stats, and was given the all clear, meaning she was out of range to present any impediment to airport traffic.

"If you look to your right there's a wonderful view of the city of Portland, Mr. Keegan," she said.

"Dex."

"If you have some time on your way back through, the Old Port district is a great way to spend a day," she continued evenly, more at ease than she ever was on the ground.

"I doubt I'll have time for shopping and sightseeing."

Maggie glanced over at him, and saw a veteran flier, calm and relaxed. To all appearances. What she felt from him was different. What she felt was alertness, energy, focus. His eyes never stopped scanning the skyline, and yet she felt like she was being watched.

She didn't comment; those were personal observations, and personal observations invited personal questions. Instead, she swung the Twinstar wide in the usual flight pattern, and lost herself in what she loved.

"The extreme point of land below us is Cape Elizabeth," she said, filtering the radio chatter and keeping an eye out for birds from the other charter services that worked the Portland area. "As we move northeast, you'll see dozens of islands, large and small. In all there are nearly three thousand islands along the Maine coast. Only Louisiana and Florida have longer coastlines."

"Fascinating," he said, with a tinge of sarcasm Maggie told herself she'd imagined, as when she looked over she didn't see it on his face.

Then again, self-control was a vital tool in his line of work, and winning or losing might hinge on how good a show he put on. "I can lose the spiel, but I have to stick to the flight plan."

His eyes shot to hers, boredom sharpening into irritation that was quickly smoothed over. "Lot on my mind," he said, the practiced, chagrined smile making it an apology as well as an explanation.

Maggie had nothing to say to that, so she said nothing.

"For a tour guide you're not very talkative."

"I get the feeling you prefer it that way."

"I don't want the spiel," he corrected her. "I'm not against conversation in general though, and since I'm the customer, and it's your policy to make the customer happy..."

"It's not usually this difficult," she said, and she'd ferried some pretty wobbly fliers in her time as a pilot. Then again, an airsickness bag wouldn't solve this problem. Maybe a cold shower. Or a bullet. She glanced over at him. A silver bullet. And maybe some Holy Water. Dex Keegan had wolf written all over him, wolf with a veneer of civility, which was a devastating combination. What woman didn't want a gentleman in the dining room and a beast in the bedroom?

"What's going on between the headphones?" Dex wondered into the silence—silence being a relative term in a helicopter.

"Thwarting gravity."

"Nope, flying for you is like driving for most people. You do it without even thinking."

"How about landing, can I think about that?"

"Sure, but you weren't thinking about landing, either."

"I'm beginning to think about crashing."

Dex chuckled, and it was such a rich, infectious sound

she couldn't help but smile. At him. That wasn't good. Especially when she caught the glint in his eye. That glint told her he thought he'd won. Which meant she'd lost.

Maggie hated losing. "Mr. Keegan, why are you baiting me?"

He sat back in his seat, and just when she thought she'd gotten the last word, he said, "I'm a lawyer. It's what I do."

She slanted him a sideways glance. "You cross examine every stranger you encounter?"

"You're more likely to get truthful answers when you keep people a little off balance, don't give them time to think."

"So I'm not just a liar, I'm neither smart enough nor imaginative enough to lie on the spur of the moment."

"Everyone has an agenda," he said mildly.

"Including you, Mr. Keegan?"

"Including me. But you knew that already."

"Very cynical."

"It saves time."

Maggie huffed out a breath, as much humor as derision. "Suppose you ask your questions, and I'll do my best not to mislead you. Or at least confine my lies to the little white kind."

He laughed, full out this time, a contagious peal of sound that tugged at some part of her she had no intention of acknowledging. She didn't so much as smile, tempting as it was.

"Tell me about the island."

It surprised her enough to have her glancing over at him. Their eyes met, held. The air between them began to...sizzle, she admitted, before she turned away. And warned herself not to look at him again—or at least not to get so caught up it took her a moment to remember where she was in the conversation. She recovered admirably, she decided. "I figured you knew all about the island, seeing as you have business there."

"It would be helpful to get the impressions of a native."

"Isn't it a shame I left my grass skirt and coconut bra back at the hut."

"I've been to Hawaii," he said, although the once-over he gave her, complete with the kind of speculative edge that said he was imagining her in the bra, gave her a nice little ego bump. "I'm more interested in what Windfall Island has to offer."

"Windfall," Maggie echoed, and although she knew he had ulterior motives, suspicion couldn't drown out the surge of warmth she always felt. Windfall Island wasn't just a dot on the map; it was, simply, home.

Her father had meant it to be a prison when he'd banished her there. He'd never know the amazing gift he'd given her, could never understand what it meant to love unconditionally. Windfall was hers; it had been since the day she'd set foot there.

"You strike me as a man who does his homework," she said, "but if you want a firsthand account, I can give you the island's background, tell you how it got its name, that sort of thing."

"I'd rather talk about the present."

"Not big on history?"

He shifted a little in his seat, and she could feel his eyes on her. "Is there a reason you don't want to discuss the island?"

"Oh, I don't know, because I feel like I'm getting the third degree? I'm your pilot, not your witness."

It was his turn to use silence as a response. He settled back in his seat, eyes forward again, oozing nonchalance.

Maggie glanced over at him, not buying it.

"I'm really just trying to get a feel for the place," he finally offered.

Maggie smiled a little, fondly. Growing up, she'd never really felt she belonged anywhere. That just meant she got to choose her home, and she was lucky enough to have been welcomed with open arms to Windfall Island. The place might be peopled with the truly eccentric and the downright loopy, but there was no place on Earth she'd rather live. "Windfall has to be experienced."

"That's my intention."

"And I'm happy to provide transportation."

"It's a small community, a small, close-knit community. And I won't be around long enough to—"

"To what? To waste your time getting to know people?"

"Maybe you missed the part about my time crunch."

"No, I got that loud and clear," she said, shooting him a wry grin. "Just like I didn't miss your reason for coming to Windfall, because you didn't give me one."

"Can't," he corrected, "on the instruction of my client."

Maggie snorted. "That sounds like a line."

"It is a line. From the Bar Association."

"Have they met you? Because you do fine without a script."

"Be careful, I think you just complimented me."

"That wasn't a compliment; it was a commentary on your ability to prevaricate."

"Yeah, I'm taking that as a compliment, too."

"Well, prevarication is probably a required course in law school. I bet you got an A."

"You just can't help yourself, can you?" He sat back, crossed his feet at the ankles. "Keep the compliments coming; I can take it."

She grinned over at him, caught him grinning back, and when her pulse scrambled she turned forward again. Before he could see it, too. And comment on it. Not that she couldn't fend him off—once she got her nerve endings to stop throbbing so her brain could kick back in. She just had to stop thinking about how much she liked the shape of his mouth, not to mention the rest of him—including his brain, which she was finding delightfully agile. Probably like his body.

She closed her eyes, took a deep breath, dug for strength.

"Admit it," he said in his richly amused voice. "You're enjoying this."

Maybe, Maggie thought, but she didn't like being called on it, especially with Dex Keegan's brand of smug confidence. In fact, it pissed her off enough to want to put him in his place. "You want to know about Windfall? These aren't the families who came over on the *Mayflower* looking for religious freedom. You won't find any Brewsters or Bradfords or Aldens in the phone book. Windfall was settled by outcasts, by escaped slaves and shipwrecked sailors, some of them just one short step up from pirates. They took Native American women for wives, and they're proud of that heritage, proud enough to make *native* an insult."

"I didn't mean—"

"It was the way you tossed it off," she said, still riding

that defensive surge. "They didn't build stately mansions on huge tracts of land, and every man of every color was free, or as free as possible on an island run with an iron fist. It was a hard place inhabited by hard people."

"The apples haven't fallen far from the tree."

"Johnny Appleseed never made it to Windfall."

He shifted, and she could feel him watching her again. "Are you always this hostile to men you're attracted to?"

"Has your ego always been this big?" she shot back.

He considered that for a beat, then said, "Pretty much."

Maggie shook her head, amused despite herself. Amused and wary. Best to keep her guard up around Mr. Dexter Keegan, at least until she found out what he wanted with Windfall Island and its people.

"So you've lived on the island all your life?" he said at length.

"No."

Maggie heard a soft huff of air over the headphones before he said, "The look on your face can't be good."

"What look?"

"This isn't a contest."

"Everything's a contest. Life is a contest."

"Who raised you? Attila the Hun?"

Close enough. Admiral Phillip Ashworth Solomon had treated his only child with as little care as Attila had the men he sacrificed for conquest and glory. If she'd been a son…But she hadn't, and she'd stopped wishing otherwise a long time ago. She'd made the life she wanted, and if it couldn't be enough for the admiral, well, it was his loss.

"I thought you were curious about the island."

"I'm curious about everything," he said, sounding like he found it a blessing and a curse.

Maggie looked at the landscape laid out below her like a picture postcard. "Take a look out the window," she said.

"What direction?"

"Down." Hundreds of islands dotted the inlets and waterways of the coastline, some of them so small they were no more than a pile of moss-covered rocks, only a dozen or so large enough for year-round habitation. The sight always made her catch her breath, the blue, blue water with its mosaic of browns and greens like a huge fascinating jigsaw puzzle that changed mood and appearance from day to day. It never looked the same twice, but it was always familiar. Always hers.

"Islands everywhere," Dex observed, maddeningly underwhelmed. "I'm only interested in one."

"To understand Windfall you have to understand that," she said, pointing down, "and that," gesturing to the endless, blue-gray stretch of the Atlantic Ocean, eerily calm today.

Dex didn't say anything, just looked at her expectantly, waiting for her to fill the silence.

She obliged him, answering the initial question he'd asked her. "I wasn't born on the island. My mother and I moved there when I was a teenager."

"And your father?"

"Didn't. But you're interested in the island, and we'll be landing in about five minutes."

"So you'll be rid of me. Without finding out why I'm asking all these questions?"

"If Windfall Island was a country, gossip would be

our national pastime. It won't be long before everyone knows your business."

"Does that go for you, too?"

Maggie bumped up a shoulder. "I manage to keep to myself. No crime in that."

"So you're not the least bit curious about why I'm here?"

"In that suit it's probably bad news for someone."

* * *

Bad news for someone. Maggie Solomon left it at that. So did Dex. He couldn't tell her why he was there, but he could have assured her it had nothing to do with her. There was no way she could be descended from Eugenia Stanhope, taken more than eighty years before at eight months of age. Eugenia's kidnapping had come to be known as the crime of the century, considering the Stanhope family was not only insanely wealthy, but also boasted connections in all the highest circles of business and politics, including the White House.

Dex had good reason to believe Eugenia, if she'd lived, had ended up on Windfall Island. And if she'd not only lived, but married and given birth as well, her descendants would either still be living on the island, or he could at least pick up the trail there and follow where it led. Not having been born on the island, Maggie wouldn't be on that list...

Except there were her eyes, brilliant, almost turquoise blue. Not exactly the Stanhope eyes, but close enough that at first he'd thought his search had ended before it really began.

Still, while her eye color was rare, it certainly wasn't isolated to the Stanhope family. Maggie had no reason to lie to him about her origins, and questioning her any further would only raise her suspicions—and the whole island's, considering her huge and obvious loyalty to her adopted home.

If his reasons for coming to Windfall became public knowledge, it could pose serious problems for the investigation. There was money involved, big money, and even the most level-headed people went a little crazy over millions of dollars.

He had a reputation to build, and nothing could get in the way. Especially not a woman with all the warmth and welcome of a North Atlantic iceberg. And the strength. His eyes shifted sideways. He would have admired her for it if he wasn't so sure she was going to cause him trouble.

He reminded himself yet again that he should remain objective, but in his mind's eye he was seeing her stride from the helicopter as she had moments ago, that long, slim body encased in a dark blue flight suit no doubt intended to project skill and professionalism. He found it ridiculously sexy.

She wasn't classically beautiful, he thought. More like effortlessly arresting, with perfect, milky skin set off by a cap of sleek black hair, spiky choppy bangs on her forehead and just curling over her ears and the collar of her battered flight jacket. Dex saw character there, in the lift of her chin and in her eyes, those brilliant blue eyes that told him she liked nothing better than to laser through bullshit.

Then there was the way she moved, energy and confidence in every economical step. Her words were just as spare, and while she'd made her opinions of him and her home clear, she kept to herself. Not his usual type, and he figured there must be something perverse in him that he found the sulky set of her mouth appealing, something a little self-destructive that he looked forward to her next cutting comment. And he delighted in not knowing what that comment would be. He'd never enjoyed the predictable.

The woman definitely had dimensions, unexpected dimensions, to her. Take the way she flew, a symphony of movement and emotion so beautiful and raw that watching her made him feel like a voyeur. The fluid grace of her body and the striking, stirring, orgasmic— there was no better way to describe it—bliss on her face made him envy her for the amazing good fortune of making her living doing something she so obviously loved.

If he'd had to choose the one thing about her that intrigued him the most, though, it would be her kiss-my-ass, get-the-hell-out-of-my-way attitude. She was independent as all hell, Dex thought, and in his line of work—no, that wasn't true anymore. He'd left the military and his Special Ops unit behind a long time ago. Problem was, the I-could-die-tomorrow philosophy was hard to shake, especially when he'd chosen a profession that could be every bit as dangerous—and not just to the one in peril.

Hadn't he watched his own sister simply dissolve when she got the news that her cop husband had gone down in the line? Hadn't it broken his heart when she fell apart, killed him to stand by when his parents took her and her two small children in while he could do nothing? Even as he'd grieved, he'd promised himself he'd never do that to someone who loved him.

He glanced over at Maggie Solomon and relaxed. She didn't want anything to do with him, so as long as he resisted his baser urges he'd be fine. Hell, even if his urges got the better of him she'd send him packing, probably by putting him in the dirt—a mental picture he deep-sixed since the idea of a nice, sweaty bout of wrestling with her wasn't doing a whole lot for his self-control.

She glanced over and caught him staring. He looked away, feeling ridiculous that just a meeting of gazes had the heat rising to his face. He hadn't blushed since he was eight and Jenny McWhorter had leaned over and kissed him on the cheek in front of God and his entire third grade class. But he wasn't in third grade anymore. Any heat he allowed himself to feel on account of Maggie Solomon was going to be a hell of lot farther south than his face.

"You sure know your way around a silence," he said, and if keeping his voice even was a struggle, well, he'd managed it, hadn't he?

"You change your mind about the spiel?"

"No, I still don't want to be lectured like a fifth grader. Although"—he gave her a long, speculative look—"you wouldn't happen to have any horn-rimmed glasses around, would you?"

"Yeah, I keep them next to my snood, sensible shoes, and the wooden pointer I spank my naughty pupils with."

"Now you're talking."

"You don't set the bar very high, do you?"

"I'm a simple man."

Maggie snorted softly, derisively. "Every woman's fantasy."

"Including yours?"

She didn't dignify that with a verbal response, but the way she set her jaw spoke volumes.

Dex grinned at her. "Did I hit a nerve?"

The helicopter dropped suddenly. Dex grabbed the door handle.

"I'm sorry," she said as she leveled the Twinstar off, "did you say something about nerves?"

Dex considered and discarded a dozen different comebacks.

His silence was all the response she needed. "That's what I thought," she said, smiling one of the small, wry smiles he already knew represented a major display of emotion for her.

And she'd gone silent again. Dex swore under his breath, but he made sure his tone was light when he spoke for her benefit. "So you were wondering why I'm on my way to Windfall Island."

"Not really, but I gather you want to talk about yourself."

"Your lack of curiosity is unnatural."

She glanced over at him, still amused. "Okay, I'm positively dying. Why are you here?"

Dex smiled so it felt like she was laughing with him, not at him. "Business."

"Who's getting sued?"

And now his smile had some actual humor in it. He'd laid his back trail carefully, and he'd worn the suit for a reason. Nice to know it had paid off, especially with a woman who not only sliced her way through bullshit with the skill and finesse of a master chef breaking down a side of beef, but kept her opinions to herself. If he could fool Maggie Solomon, the rest of the island's population would be asking him for legal advice five minutes after they touched down.

"Why else would you be coming to Windfall with small bags and a big briefcase?"

"If I'd known you were here, I'd have left the briefcase behind."

"Flattery?"

"Not entirely."

She looked over at him, and Dex lost his breath. The heat in her eyes seemed to incinerate all the oxygen in the cockpit. He should have thought about the case, but he was caught, mesmerized. Hungry. And Maggie Solomon, he thought in amazement, was the only one who could satisfy him. She was testy, sarcastic, and way too smart to be fooled for long, and he wanted her beyond reason.

"Maggie—"

"N277HK, I have you on radar," crackled the voice from Windfall Island Airport.

Dex hissed out a breath in frustration. But he thought better of what he'd been about to say. He needed to stay far, far away from Maggie.

She radioed back, requesting final approach. She didn't look at him again, just sent the helicopter into a banking turn that redirected his attention. He watched the ground rushing up at his face with something approaching gratitude. Of all the dangers he faced on Windfall Island, Maggie crashing the helicopter wasn't the worst that could happen...

Fall in Love with Forever Romance

SOULBOUND
by Kristen Callihan

After centuries of searching, Adam finally found his soul mate, only to be rejected when she desires her freedom. But when Eliza discovers she's being hunted by someone far more dangerous, she turns to the one man who can keep her safe—even if he endangers her heart...

WHAT A DEVILISH DUKE DESIRES
by Vicky Dreiling

Fans of *New York Times* best-selling authors Julia Quinn, Sarah MacLean, and Madeline Hunter will love the third book in Vicky Dreiling's charming, sexy, and utterly irresistible Sinful Scoundrels trilogy about a highborn man who never wanted to inherit his uncle's title or settle down...until a beautiful, brilliant, delightfully tempting maid makes him rethink his position.

Fall in Love with Forever Romance

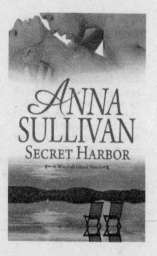

SECRET HARBOR
by Anna Sullivan

Fans of *New York Times* best-selling authors JoAnn Ross, Jill Shalvis, and Bella Andre will love the last book in Anna Sullivan's witty contemporary romance trilogy about a young woman who left her beloved home in Maine to become an actress in Hollywood. Now a star, and beset by scandal, she wants nothing more than to surround herself with old friends...until she meets an infuriating—and sexy—stranger.

MEET ME AT THE BEACH
by V. K. Sykes

Gorgeous Lily Doyle was the only thing Aiden Flynn missed after he escaped from Seashell Bay to play pro baseball. Now that he's back on the island, memories rush in about the night of passion they shared long ago, and everything else washes right out to sea—everything except the desire that still burns between them.

Fall in Love with Forever Romance

HOT
by Elizabeth Hoyt
writing as Julia Harper

For Turner Hastings, being held at gunpoint during a back robbery is an opportunity in disguise. After seeing her little heist on tape, FBI Special Agent John MacKinnon knows it's going to be an interesting case. But he doesn't expect to develop feelings for Turner, and when bullets start flying in her direction, John finds he'll do anything to save her.

FOR THE LOVE OF PETE
by Elizabeth Hoyt
writing as Julia Harper

Dodging bullets with a loopy redhead in the passenger seat is not how Special Agent Dante Torelli imagined his day going. But Zoey Addler is determined to get her baby niece back, and no one—not even a henpecked hit man, cooking-obsessed matrons, or a relentless killer—will stand in her way.

Fall in Love with Forever Romance

ONCE AND ALWAYS
by Elizabeth Hoyt writing as Julia Harper

The newest contemporary from *New York Times* bestselling author Elizabeth Hoyt writing as Julia Harper! Small-town cop Sam West certainly doesn't mind a routine traffic stop. But Maisa Bradley is like nothing he has ever seen, and she's about to take Sam on the ride of his life!